SAB

Peter O'Donnell

SABRE-TOOTH

A Modesty Blaise
Adventure

SOUVENIR PRESS

First published 1966 by
Souvenir Press Ltd,
29 Cloth Fair,
London EC1A 7JQ

This edition published in paperback 2003

ISBN 978 0 285 63676 7

Printed in Great Britain by Clays Ltd, Elcograf S.p.A.

For Jill and Janet

ONE

'UNFORTUNATE that it should be this one,' said Liebmann. 'His report-sheet shows that he was a good man.'

Sarrat shrugged and ran a hand over his heavy chin. 'He is still a good man. The Twins will not have an easy kill.'

'For entertainment, so much the better,' said Liebmann. He was fair, with a thin ascetic face and the voice of a fallen angel, perfectly shaped words dropping from his thin lips like pieces of ice.

English was not his mother-tongue, neither was it Sarrat's, nor that of more than one in five of the men who lived here in the four mile long valley which lay imprisoned amid the soaring ridges and peaks of the greatest mountain range in the world. But by rigid rule, English was the language which must at all times be spoken, and the American accent was favoured though not mandatory.

Behind the two men, set between towering spurs of rock which thrust out from the valley wall, rose the dull yellow façade of a palace built with sun-dried brick by men who had died when Islam was young.

It stood three storeys high and covered a full acre of ground. The walls and the plastered timbers of its rambling interior had held out well against the destroying hand of the centuries. Only the roof had crumbled, the flat areas between the four domes, and here the damage had been made good with light wooden frames and heavy plastic sheeting.

A man came out of a small arched doorway and walked towards Liebmann and Sarrat. Like them, he wore a coarsely-woven tunic of plain grey, buttoned to the neck, and dark denim trousers. An M-16 automatic rifle was slung on one shoulder and there were ammunition pouches on his chest.

'Hamid,' said Liebmann, and looked at the watch on his wrist. 'We were just going down.'

7

Hamid nodded. He had the lean pale face of a Berber Arab and cold black eyes.

Sarrat grinned, looking at the rifle. 'You will not need that, my friend. Leave it behind this one time. I will look after you.'

'It's part of him,' Liebmann said absently, staring down the valley. 'Don't make trouble, Sarrat.'

'One day,' said Hamid, looking at the big Frenchman, 'one day, Sarrat, when this matter is finished, we should go into the mountains. You with your big loud machine-guns, I with this alone.' His long fingers tapped the rakish seven-pound rifle. 'I would kill every team in your section and they would not see me.'

Sarrat grinned again. He was a bulky man but the bulk was all muscle. 'If ever I kill you, Hamid, my little cabbage, I will see that you fall facing Mecca.'

Hamid's eyes narrowed dangerously but it was Liebmann who spoke, lifting one hand in a signal towards the row of a dozen sand-coloured jeeps standing fifty yards away. 'You will stop this,' he said without emotion. 'Karz will not be pleased if I report stupid provocation between his commanders.'

'It is nothing—a joke,' Sarrat said quickly, and Hamid nodded. Both men stood in silence. A jeep pulled out from the line of transport and drew up beside them. The driver was a thin, wiry man with a long scar on one sunburned cheek. He wore the tropical uniform of the United States Army, or a fair replica of it. The shirt and trousers were rumpled and faded but scrubbed clean.

He waited, relaxed, while the three passengers climbed aboard, then let in the clutch.

'Down to the ring for the punch-up?' he said as the jeep moved on to the dusty track which led from the big square in front of the palace. His English was natural and held the adenoidal accent of Liverpool.

'Yes.' Liebmann looked at the driver. 'You're Carter, in one of the drop-sections, aren't you?'

'That's right.' The reply was casual. Here in the valley

8

there was no saluting or springing to attention, no orthodox discipline. To the extent that Liebmann recognised any personal feelings of his own he would have preferred the normal trappings of discipline, but he acknowledged that there was no need for them. No need at all. Karz used more direct and lasting methods to get the results he wanted.

'How long have you been with us, Carter?' Liebmann asked in his chill, passionless voice.

'Eight weeks.' Carter changed gear. 'I was one of the first.'

The jeep moved steadily along the track, following the deep curve of the narrow river which hugged the mountain wall in a cutting along one side of the valley and vanished underground somewhere to the south, beneath the snow-capped peaks and ridges towering twenty thousand feet above. To the left lay rows of grey barrack huts, built of lightweight metal framework and sheet asbestos. Beyond them, across the half-mile width of the valley, was the small-arms range.

A few men, all dressed in the same style of uniform as Carter, were moving away from the huts in loose order, heading for a point where the valley narrowed to a two-hundred yard bottleneck before opening out again.

'Stragglers,' said Hamid, watching them. 'Most of the men will be there already.' He leaned forward to speak to Carter. 'This thing, the entertainment, it is popular with the men?'

'Most of 'em like it. With them Twins it's a kick, like. Dead kinky. I can take it or leave it meself.'

A hint of curiosity touched Liebmann's thin, austere face. 'You don't find it interesting, Carter?'

'I'm just not bothered.' Carter's mouth stretched briefly in a reptilian grin. 'If I want kicks I save it up for the knock-shop.' He jerked his head back slightly, towards the palace they had left over a mile behind now. 'I'm on a short-time tonight, and I get an all-night with a free choice from the long list next Monday.' He spat over the side of the jeep. 'I've booked that little Malayan bit. They reckon she can just about turn you inside out.'

Sarrat gave a grunting laugh. Liebmann's nostrils twitched

9

with distaste. He gestured ahead towards the bottle-neck and said to Carter: 'But this is not your kick?'

'Ahh, it's awright. Better at first though, when you could 'ave a gamble. But you can't get a bet on The Twins now, not even at odds-on.'

'It does not perturb you that one of your . . .' for once Liebmann hesitated, feeling for the word, 'that one of your mates will be killed?'

Carter was slowing the jeep. He turned his rodent's face to stare at Liebmann. 'There's no *mates* 'ere,' he said contemptuously. 'Wouldn't do, would it? You know that as well as I do.'

'Yes,' Liebmann said briefly, and got out as the jeep halted. With Sarrat and Hamid following, he climbed a rocky incline which led to a flat, roughly circular area of ground. On one side there were stepped ridges rising in tiers to meet the mountain wall, like the tiers which surround a bull-ring. On the other side the arena ended in an abrupt drop to a cluster of crags and boulders twenty feet below.

The stage of this natural amphitheatre was clear, but the slopes were thick with men, several hundred of them, standing or squatting wherever they could find a good viewpoint. Late-comers were clambering higher up the rocky slopes to find a perch.

The blend of many voices echoed curiously from the curving mountain wall. Liebmann led the way towards a space left clear at the end of the lower tiers. His ears were alert for the sound of any language other than English, but he detected none—though some of the English was so accented that it was hard to recognise.

The other commanders were already here, close to the arena and a little apart from the mass of men. Sarrat, sweating under the hot sun, mopped the back of his neck with a khaki handkerchief and jerked his head towards the men on the slopes.

'They look pretty good,' he said.

Liebmann surveyed the blur of faces. More than sixty percent of the men were of Asiatic or Arab stock. The faces

10

ranged from the dark brown of Indian hillmen to the tanned but fresh complexions of Northern Europe. There were Guhayna Arabs from the Sudan, thickset Caucasian Mongols, and a heavy sprinkling of Sinkiang Chinese.

With clinical satisfaction Liebmann noted that there were no racial groupings. The French Algerians were scattered. The half-dozen Spaniards and the Latins were intermingled with the rest. So were the Germans, the British and the Americans. Even the two big rangy men from Australia, the country with the great cobber-complex, had not gravitated together.

With all the variety of race and background, this group of some four hundred men had a common denominator. Each man was a proven expert in his trade—the trade of killing. They were hard, cold, self-confident men, void of the faintest scruple.

This was not an army in which any man was ready to die for a flag or a cause. But every man was ready to take his chance for a solid fortune of twenty thousand pounds sterling. For this, each one had sold himself, body and soul, on a six-month lease.

The hint of a smile touched Liebmann's gaunt face as he wondered how many men existed in the world who could have assembled such an army. There might be several, he acknowledged to himself, but only one man could have dominated and controlled it.

He looked across the valley and saw the moving jeep, the heavy grey-clad figure with the massive head, seated beside the driver.

Karz.

Liebmann enjoyed the *frisson* of fear that touched his nerves. No other stimulus raised a flicker in his burnt-out emotions now. Nothing that man or woman could do, beast, god or devil, stirred the strings of Liebmann's gutted soul— only the presence of Karz. And for this reason he savoured it.

The hum of talking faded away as Karz walked up the slope and joined his little group of commanders. He surveyed

11

them with sloe-coloured eyes set in a broad Mongol face beneath a thick basin of short-cropped black hair. The face might have been hewn from brown granite, but it was wholly alive, a face from antiquity, brutal, sagacious and ageless. Behind such a face the mind of Genghis Khan had planned the battles which made him master of an empire stretching from the China Sea to the banks of the Dnieper.

Karz ran his gaze over the men gathered on the slopes, then turned to look at the flat bare platform of rock which formed the arena. Slowly he linked his hands behind his back, planted his booted feet firmly, and was completely still, like a living statue growing from the rock.

Once only, at another time and in another place, Liebmann had seen Karz move fast. Then he had struck a man with his fist, as if using a hammer—not a classic or well-placed blow, but it had crushed a four-inch segment of the skull.

Two men had alighted from the back of the jeep. A whispering murmur ran round the arena. Both heads were shaven to the skin and both faces were dull yellow. They stood an inch under six feet, with long arms hanging from broad shoulders. Their legs were thick and a little short for their bodies. Both wore the grey tunic and dark trousers of Karz's commanders. They walked with a smooth but curious rhythm, shoulder to shoulder, their outer arms swinging, their inner arms still, with thumbs hooked into belts.

As they drew nearer, Liebmann could make out the strange shoulder-harness linking them together. It was of heavy plaited leather, fashioned like two pauldrons from a suit of armour, each consisting of a short sleeve and shoulder-piece secured by a strap; the pauldrons were joined by a short bar at the points of the shoulders, a solid roll of leather enclosing a flexible steel-chain core.

Despite the six-inch bar thus linking them at the shoulders, the two men moved easily and without clumsiness.

Carter, squatting on a ridge of rock, watched them join the group with Karz and turn to face the arena. Beside Carter a man with a square brown face whistled softly.

'Those The Twins?' he said with the clipped twang of an Afrikaner.

'You wouldn't think so.' Carter glanced round at his companion. 'Got a fag to spare?'

'No.' The flat refusal held no rancour. 'You been here long, then?'

'Long enough. You?'

'Came in last week. I haven't seen those two till now though.'

'You wouldn't. They've had us out on a week's exercise. I'm in their section.'

'What do they call themselves?'

'One on the left's Lok. The other's Chu.'

'I heard about 'em. I heard three different stories why they walk around joined like that. Is it right they're queer?'

Carter's lips lifted. 'Not much of a way for a couple of queers to be hitched, is it? You've been listening to the new boys.'

The Afrikaner dug into his shirt pocket and slowly brought out a flat tin of cigarettes. He took one out and gave it to Carter, who nodded.

'They were Siamese twins,' Carter said. 'Joined at the shoulder. Grew up like it, see? Then sometime, I don't know when, some quack got busy with the old knife.'

'Separated them?'

'That's right. Big job, but it all goes fine . . . except that when it's all over they go screaming up the wall, see? Running round like chickens with their 'eads chopped off.' Carter drew in a hissing breath of impatience at the other's blank stare. 'They got to be *joined* or they go nuts.'

The Afrikaner said: 'Jesus!'

Carter shrugged. 'It's psychological, see?'

'Poor bastards.' There was no feeling in the Afrikaner's voice.

'You don't know the funny bit yet.' Carter looked across at The Twins and his stained teeth showed in a humourless grin. 'They hate each other's guts. Always did, always will. Only time they stop blinding an' swearing at each other is

13

when there's a job on—like the exercise last week.' He nodded towards the bare platform of rock. 'Or like now.'

Karz had not moved. The Twins stood to one side and a little behind him, their eyes on a small covered truck making its way down the valley. Slowly Chu took a packet of cigarettes from his tunic and lit one. Lok turned his head and stared with seething eyes. A spasm of hatred contorted his face. He lifted a hand and slapped the cigarette from Chu's lips.

'No' now, you bassar!' The words were a comic mockery of English, but the venom in them was so shocking to hear that only a sick mind could have been amused.

Chu made an animal noise in his throat. He lifted clawed hands, shook them in an inarticulate frenzy, and dropped them to his sides. For long seconds the two stood with heads turned, glaring at each other, then slowly their faces grew blank and their eyes once more sought the approaching truck.

It was interesting, thought Liebmann, that Karz ignored quarrels between The Twins. He regarded them as one.

Sarrat chuckled softly. 'Do not be impatient, my friends. The medicine you want is coming.'

The truck drew up at the foot of the slope. Two men climbed out of the back. A third followed awkwardly, his hands manacled behind his back. He was a tall man, a Moroccan Spaniard with a powerful body and quick eyes set in a swarthy face. There was a hint of defiance in his walk as he moved up the slope between his two guards.

When he was in the middle of the arena one of them unlocked the handcuffs. The two moved away and the Spaniard was left standing alone, slowly rubbing his wrists.

'Listen,' said Karz, and though he did not lift his voice it carried to every man in the amphitheatre. 'This man is called Vallmanya. He signed articles to serve under me. There were conditions on both sides. You all know these conditions.' The great Mongol head turned slowly, gathering the eyes of all the men who sat on the stepped tiers of stone. There was complete silence.

'This man,' said Karz, 'we find Unsound.' His tone gave

14

the last word a capital letter, a specific meaning. 'He is guilty of using *nasswar* ... the green tobacco. A drug. Such a matter is dealt with in Article 24 of our agreement. Vallmanya must die. As with all those who may die in action or otherwise, his full pay will go into the pool to be shared between you when our task is completed.'

Liebmann was watching faces, alert for any hint of uneasiness or resentment. He saw none. Some were tense, some eager, some curious. A few showed no more than casual interest. This did not trouble Liebmann; it simply marked the men who had seen everything, to whom the business of killing had ceased to have meaning. They were the hard core of this small army.

Karz said: 'What will you fight with, Vallmanya?'

Vallmanya stared with slitted eyes, not at Karz but at The Twins. 'I fight wit' bayonet,' he said slowly.

Karz turned his head to look at Liebmann. 'We have a sword bayonet?'

'Not on the inventory. There may be one somewhere in the camp——'

'I got one,' Sarrat broke in. 'Under the seat of the jeep. My section jeep. Is better than a knife.'

'Bring it,' said Karz, and Sarrat moved away down the short slope to where half-a-dozen jeeps were now parked.

'So he gets a choice,' the Afrikaner said to Carter.

'Sure. They got all sorts in the truck—knives, axe, sabre, a length of towing-chain.'

'What's the other fellow use? I mean The Twins.'

'Nothing much. Just a pair of gloves each.'

The Afrikaner shot a suspicious glance at Carter, who grinned and said: 'Straight up. You'll see.'

'You seen this before?'

'Six, seven times. I forget. The last bloke chose a machete.'

The Afrikaner ruminated for a while, watching the lonely man in the middle of the arena. At last he said: 'What happens if he wins?'

'Well ...' Carter studied his cigarette, elaborately casual.

15

'He's tough, Vallmanya. Want a little bet on 'im? I don't mind a long shot.'

'A long shot?' The Afrikaner grinned contemptuously. 'And you've seen this seven times. I'm not a bloody fool, man. But suppose the bloke did make it?'

Carter drew a finger across his throat and hawked.

The Afrikaner nodded, then frowned. 'How do they make him fight if he's going to be croaked anyway?'

'He needn't fight,' said Carter. 'If he jibs, they just put him on the next plane out.'

'Where to?'

Carter waved a vague arm in a half-circle to north and east. 'To where the backing is. Where the big wheels are. I wouldn't know about that—and it's a bad question, that is. I wouldn't ask it again.'

'Okay. Never mind where to. They put him on the next plane off the air-strip. What for?'

'Guinea-pig,' said Carter, and picked a shred of tobacco from his tongue. 'You know what these bloody doctors are. Same everywhere. Always got things they want to try out.'

'Like what?'

'Like anything. A bit of nerve-gas, maybe. Or see how long you stay alive when they've switched your liver for a dog's. Research, like. Only one bloke chose the guinea-pig plane. The word came round from Liebmann later that they'd taken the top of his head off and stuck electric needles in different bits of his brain.'

'What for?'

'Just to find out,' Carter said irritably. 'Something to do with ... you know, brain stuff. Like they give him a jolt through one needle and he's laughing, another and he's crying, or maybe hungry. Or raving for a bint, with a beat up to his chin.'

'Man, I don't need bloody needles for that.' The Afrikaner grinned. 'It's a good thing they've got the women laid on in that harem thing. What do they call it?'

'The *seraglio*.' Carter's eyes narrowed lustfully. 'Listen, I'll lay a green ticket to a white—an all-night to a short-

16

time. Against Vallmanya. You on?'

'Don't lean on me too hard, you crafty bastard,' the other said without heat. 'I don't bet without knowing the form.'

Sarrat came up the slope. He carried a bayonet in a sheath, an old French army sword-bayonet with a blade just under sixteen inches long. He tossed it to Vallmanya in passing. The Spaniard caught it deftly, drew out the bayonet and threw the sheath aside. He felt the edge and the point, gave a little nod of satisfaction, then took a careful grip on the hilt and stood waiting.

He had shed the slight air of bravado that hinted at concealed tension. Now he was a cold, nerveless fighter, survivor of a hundred brawls and a dozen battles, experienced and dangerous.

The murmur of talk among the spectators faded to silence. Karz looked at The Twins and nodded. Lok and Chu moved slowly, each taking a pair of black gloves from the pocket of his tunic. The gloves were of mail, interlaced chain of blued steel, so finely wrought that the gloves were limp as heavy velvet.

Liebmann watched The Twins. They moved as one now, with perfect co-ordination. This moment always fascinated him, the moment when Lok and Chu ceased to be separate, hate-filled enemies and became one creature of four arms and four legs, with one mind controlling the whole.

Lightly, walking in such precise unison that the strange artificial link joining them at the shoulder took no strain, The Twins moved into the arena. At four paces from Vallmanya they halted, their yellow faces calm and watchful, gloved hands open and held at chest height a little away from their bodies.

Bayonet poised, Vallmanya began to circle them, side-stepping with a quick, dancing movement. Lok moved with him, turning slowly and easily until he was back to back with his brother. Then he stood still. The steel-cored leather joint at the shoulder would allow no further movement. Chu did not turn his head.

Vallmanya took another long side-step, as if to come in on

the flank, then swerved back and lunged like a fencer for Lok's throat. A mailed hand clashed against the blade, sweeping it easily aside, and there came a rasp of steel on steel as Vallmanya wrenched the bayonet fiercely from the closing hand.

On the stepped slopes the Afrikaner murmured an awed oath. 'They're quick . . . quick as a bloody whip, man.'

'Pick flies out of the air, they can,' said Carter.

The Spaniard moved to the right and came in fast on the flank. The Twins stood with their heads turned to watch him. As he lunged, two gloved hands flickered dartingly like great black dragon-flies. Lok's hand deflected the thrust, Chu's hand caught the turned blade a fraction of a second later. This time Vallmanya lunged again with the held blade, twisting it, trying to drive the point into Chu's forearm.

Chu jerked as the lunge came in, and Lok's hand slashed down edgewise on Vallmanya's exposed wrist. There came a choking grunt of pain, then Vallmanya sprang back, empty-handed. Chu held the bayonet.

Lok turned, wheeling quickly so that The Twins stood shoulder to shoulder again, both facing Vallmanya. At once he circled rapidly so that his back was no longer to the brink of the rocky platform, and together The Twins wheeled smoothly to face him.

With a casual movement Chu tossed the bayonet up over his shoulder and Lok caught it as it dropped behind his back. The weapon passed across the front of The Twins, spinning from hand to hand in a bewildering juggle, as if a single mind controlled each nerve and sinew in both bodies. Abruptly Lok threw the bayonet hard, taking Vallmanya by surprise.

The heavy hilt thudded against his breastbone in a glancing blow as he twisted to dodge the throw. For a moment he staggered off-balance, then bent and snatched up the fallen bayonet, darting back out of distance. The Twins grinned.

'They're making the most of it,' Carter said with approval. He had given up hope of a bet with the Afrikaner now. The

18

other moved his shoulders. 'I wouldn't keep a fight going just for kicks. Not against a man with nothing to lose.'

'It's their medicine,' Carter said, and watched with appraising eyes as Vallmanya crouched in a defensive posture, forcing The Twins to take up the attack. They moved in, the four legs co-ordinated as surely as the legs of a cat, steel hands poised.

Vallmanya lunged low for Chu's groin, and again there came the clash of the blade against mail. At the same instant Lok rested a hand on his brother's shoulder and jumped, both feet lashing out. One boot took Vallmanya on the side of the head, the other thudded against his ribs. He went down, dazed, rolling over and over to escape the follow-up, empty-handed again.

Chu held the bayonet now. Together the linked brothers moved forward. As Vallmanya came to his feet they were upon him, three mailed hands chopping with controlled force.

'Softening him up,' said Carter, stubbing out his cigarette. 'They could break his neck with one chop if they fancied it that way.'

Vallmanya was reeling backwards round the arena like a punch-drunk boxer, trying blindly to duck or side-step the sharp, punishing blows which were methodically numbing his arms and shoulders, draining breath from his heaving lungs and strength from his powerful body.

Suddenly all was still and the three men stood frozen as if in a tableau, Vallmanya swaying a little as he faced The Twins. He might have fallen had he not been held. The outer hand of each twin gripped one of his wrists, twisting hard to lock the arm rigidly. The inner leg of each twin was advanced, so that the legs crossed at the shins, with the feet turned to lock behind Vallmanya's ankles. He stood utterly helpless now.

The inner hands of The Twins gripped the bayonet-hilt together. Slowly the blade came up until the point rested against Vallmanya's heart. A quavering scream issued from the dry cavern of his mouth. The Twins turned their heads, smiled at each other, looked back at Vallmanya, then thrust steadily.

For a moment the scream grew shrill, then it ceased abruptly. Vallmanya sank to his knees, sightless eyes staring down at the bayonet driven through his body. The hilt rasped harshly on rock as he toppled forward.

Slowly, contentedly, The Twins drew off their gloves. With an arm about each other's shoulders they moved towards Karz and his commanders. A long sigh rippled through the watching men, followed by a buzz of talk.

Karz looked at Liebmann and said: 'Normal training this afternoon. Sections on parade at fourteen-thirty hours. Commanders' meeting in H.Q. Control Room at fourteen hundred.'

He turned and moved down the rocky slope towards the jeeps, followed by his driver.

Under Liebmann as Chief of Staff there were two other commanders besides Sarrat, Hamid, and The Twins. One was a dark, stolid Georgian called Thamar. He was the only man, Liebmann believed, who felt no hint of fear in the presence of Karz. This was not a matter of courage but of chemistry. Somewhere in Thamar there was a malfunction of glands or nerves or brain-cells which made him immune to the emotion of fear. This created no problem, since he revered Karz as a dog reveres its master.

The other commander was Brett, a sleek-haired Englishman of medium height, seemingly made of whipcord, with bitter grey eyes and a caustic tongue.

Karz took the head of the table in the main H.Q. Control Room, which lay on the ground floor of the great palace. The others seated themselves, and Liebmann remained standing by the bank of filing cabinets.

'The question of commanders,' Karz said, his enormous hands resting on the table in front of him. 'As you know, we require two more. They must be established here within four weeks.' His eyes roved the faces of his commanders. 'Do you make any recommendations from the ranks?'

20

There was silence for a while. At last Sarrat said: 'Toksvig, in my section, is good. Excellent with all weapons. Reliable. Plenty of stomach and stamina——'

Karz's hand flapped the table once, and Sarrat was silent. 'These qualities mean nothing in themselves,' Karz said. 'Can he lead? Can he drive? Can he *command*, Sarrat? I would give fifty good followers for one good leader.'

Sarrat shook his head doubtfully. 'I say Toksvig is the best prospect. No more than that.'

'Not enough.' Karz looked at Liebmann. 'We have no more probable candidates on the files?'

'Not for commanders. And only a dozen possibles. The standard is too exacting. And those of the right quality are precluded by other factors.'

'Show me.'

Liebmann opened a steel cabinet and took out a dozen buff-coloured cards. He handed them to Karz, who began to look through them slowly, scanning the information given on each one. After a while he put aside all but two.

'These are cross-referenced,' he said. 'One is a woman—called Modesty Blaise. The other is a man, Garvin.' He looked round the table. 'Who knows them?'

'She ran *The Network*.' It was Brett who spoke. 'Willie Garvin is her strong-arm man.'

'Good?'

'Which one?'

'Both.'

'I don't know the woman. Only whispers about her. But I know a fair bit about Garvin, and I met him once.' Brett looked at Chu and Lok. 'I just might back him against The Twins.'

'Can he lead?' This was Thamar, stolidly holding to Karz's point.

Brett shrugged, and Sarrat answered the question. 'I knew Garvin in the Legion. He has what you want, Karz. It did not show then, but after Blaise took him over he changed. It was something very strong. He handled many large operations for her.'

21

'But the woman,' said Hamid, staring. 'Can we use a woman?'

'I will use an ape or a camel if it can give what I want,' said Karz coldly.

'*The Network* was big—really big,' said Sarrat. 'If she's good enough for Garvin to follow, then I back her.'

Karz looked at Liebmann again, a query in the sloe-coloured eyes beneath the thick brows.

'The quality is there,' Liebmann said. 'No question of it. I discussed these two with the Chief Recruiting Officer when we were at the planning stage. He has had close acquaintance with their activities in the past.' Liebmann shook his head. 'They would be ideal, but they are not for hire.'

'Why not?' Hamid asked sharply, and Karz silenced him with a curt gesture, nodding to Liebmann to go on.

'They have retired and they are rich,' said Liebmann. 'Very rich. Also, they are not hirelings.'

Thamar said: 'The rate for commanders is fifty thousand pounds sterling. Are they so rich?'

'Yes. And even if they could be bought, there is another factor against them. They would be Unsound.'

There was a long silence in the room. An electric fan, fed by the power-plant established in the broad ravine at the back of the palace, whirred softly as it turned from side to side.

Karz broke the silence. His deep voice was remote, like a voice issuing from a stone idol and pronouncing an unchallengeable doctrine. 'It is possible to use Unsound persons,' he said, 'providing complete control is secured. For those who cannot be bought with money, it may be possible to find a different coin . . . one that is more binding.'

'A lever,' said Liebmann. 'But there is no information on our cards to indicate that such a lever exists.'

Karz looked at him. 'An immediate message to the Chief Security Officer. He is to delegate the remainder of the selection and drafting to his four assistants. He is to concentrate only on the possibility of securing Blaise and Garvin in a way which establishes total control over them. Progress reports every seventy-two hours.'

Liebmann jotted on a pad and nodded. 'If the thing is possible, do you want a capability-test run on them, Karz?'

Karz got to his feet, looking at Liebmann with bleak eyes.

'I do not take any potential commander on hearsay alone, Liebmann,' he said, and walked slowly from the room.

TWO

SIR GERALD TARRANT crossed the foyer of the tall block of flats standing on the north side of the park. Behind the curving desk of polished mahogany the commissionaire looked up.

'Ah, good morning, sir. Miss Blaise said you'd be along. Will you go straight up, please?'

'Thank you.' Tarrant moved towards the small private lift which served the penthouse surmounting the building. As the doors slid to, he relaxed.

It had been a bad week, a week of minor failures and frustrations, culminating last night in the kind of news he dreaded most. With an effort made many times through the long years past, Tarrant relegated the week to history and thought of the day ahead.

It was Sunday. He wore a well-rubbed Lovat green sports jacket, corduroy trousers which he knew to be unfashionably wide, and stout golfing shoes. As the lift climbed smoothly a sense of glad anticipation grew within him. He was looking forward to this day with intense curiosity and the slightest touch of apprehension, for today he would see something he had often wondered about but had never before witnessed.

'Come along to the penthouse after breakfast next Sunday,' Modesty Blaise had said as they walked together from young Fareham's box at Ascot down to the paddock. 'Willie Garvin will be there and we're driving down to the Riverside Club for nine holes, then over to *The Treadmill* for lunch.'

The Treadmill was the pub Willie Garvin owned, bought to help him settle down, but as an anchor it had proved a frail fetter. To the best of Tarrant's knowledge Willie Garvin had spent the last three months flying photo-surveys for a wild-cat mineral prospecting firm in Canada.

The invitation had delighted Tarrant. And then, as he thanked her, Modesty Blaise added: 'Willie can set you up for fishing later in the afternoon. He's got a stretch of water there. Oh, and we'll be having a work-out in his place at the back, if you'd like to watch.'

She was wearing a suit of ice-blue wild silk with a deep pink chiffon hat, looking utterly feminine and at home amid the elegant Ascot throng. Watching her as she studied the horses moving round the paddock, Tarrant had answered with simple honesty: 'I'm not sure whether or not I shall like it, Modesty—but I wouldn't miss it.'

He knew Willie's place at the back of *The Treadmill*. It was a very long low building of brick, windowless and sound-proof. Tarrant had been privileged to enter that formidable building once, and knew that he was the only man to have done so.

Today he would see something still more formidable.

The lift slowed to a halt and the doors opened on to the wide foyer with its flooring of ceramic tiles. Beyond lay a slender wrought-iron balustrade broken by three steps down to the huge living-room with the floor-to-ceiling window at the far end.

Tarrant looked about him contentedly. It was always a joy to enter this room with its strangely satisfying blend of styles in décor and furnishing. As he descended the three steps, Modesty Blaise came through the plate glass door leading out on to the long L-shaped terrace.

Her black hair was drawn up into a chignon on the crown of her head. She wore a flared camel-hair skirt with a poplin shirt in fine yellow and white check. Her shoes were flat and of biscuit-coloured pigskin.

At sight of Tarrant her face was lit by a smile of pleasure, and she moved forward to greet him.

'Sir Gerald. I'm so glad you were able to come along.'

'I'm invariably selfish, my dear.' He took her hand and bent over it. She raised it a little for him to touch his lips to it, and he was absurdly pleased.

'Is it too early to offer you a drink?' She moved to the little bar in an alcove, her feet treading the glowing Persian rugs scattered on the ivory-coloured tiles of the floor.

'A very small whisky with soda, perhaps,' Tarrant said. He wanted to look at the rugs, for they were balm to his soul; he wanted to study the new picture which hung with the others on the cedar-strip walls—it was a Chagall; he wanted to browse over the casually arranged little antique pieces on the broad, curving corner-shelves, knowing he would find new pleasures there, for she was always discarding and re-placing these pieces. But though a dozen attractions tugged at his attention he looked at Modesty Blaise, watching the play of her hands and bare arms as she fixed his drink.

'You've arranged fine weather,' she said, and handed him the glass. 'I didn't realise the Foreign Office had such influence.'

'We sacrificed two Civil Service maidens under a full moon last night,' said Tarrant, and shrugged. 'It seems to have worked better than some of our other operations recently,' he added in a dry tone.

She looked at him quickly. 'You're tired. Are you sure you want to join us today?'

'My dear,' he said with profound sincerity, 'I can't remember when I've looked forward to a day so much.'

'I'm very glad.' She smiled again. 'Will you excuse me for five minutes? I was dressed up last night and I want to take this nail-varnish off.'

'Of course.' Tarrant looked round the room. 'You could leave me here for hours and still find me absorbed. Is Willie calling for us?'

'Willie's been staying here for two or three days. He ought to be ready any minute. His bedroom's along that passage and on the left if you want to roust him out.'

'I wouldn't want to hurry him——' Tarrant broke off and

25

stared. A child had appeared through the door which he knew led to Modesty's bedroom. She was eleven or twelve years old, Tarrant judged, a slender creature with a smooth olive complexion and big dark eyes. She wore a sleeveless blue dress of self-striped linen with a saddle-stitched yoke, white knee-socks and soft kid-sandals. Her hair was dark and straight, tied back with a broad white Alice-band. The oval face had the haunting innocence of a Raphaelite madonna.

'This is Lucille Brouet,' said Modesty. Then, to the child, 'Come in, darling. I want to introduce you to a friend of mine—and Willie's. This is Sir Gerald Tarrant.'

Lucille moved hesitantly forward and put out a thin hand.

'How do you do,' she said timidly. Her English held a slight accent. As Tarrant took her hand she bobbed in a little curtsey.

'Hallo, Lucille.' Tarrant felt awkward. He had no easy way with children, and knew it. He always found himself being either too hearty or too forbidding. Also, he was a little bewildered at this moment. Lucille was something new to him. He had no idea where she fitted into the background of Modesty Blaise or Willie Garvin.

'Lucille is at school in Tangier,' Modesty said. 'But she's been spending part of her holidays over here.' She took the child gently by the shoulders and turned her round. 'Who on earth's been at your hair?'

'It was long, Modesty.' The voice was soft and contrite. 'I asked Weng to cut some off, but he wouldn't, so then I asked Willie, and he did. Just now.'

'But we were letting it grow long so that we could *do* something with it.'

'Yes, I know, Modesty.'

Tarrant was comforted to see that the answer left Modesty Blaise as helpless as it left him. She shook her head and laughed. 'All right. If you want it short I'll get it done properly. Willie's not exactly a genius with the scissors, is he? Now you talk to Sir Gerald for a minute or two while I get ready.'

Tarrant sighed inwardly as he watched Modesty disappear

into her bedroom. Laboured conversation with Lucille held no attraction for him—not through any fault in the child but because of his own inadequacy.

'Well ... are you glad to be away from school for a while?' he said, trying to strike an easy, casual note.

'It's very nice here,' Lucille answered politely. 'But I like it at school, too.'

Tarrant started to speak again, then hesitated. Almost any question that presented itself to him seemed unpleasantly inquisitive. Modesty had not told him who the child was, or what connection lay between them. It would be unmannerly to ask.

'Lucille ...' he said, looking thoughtfully at the ceiling, 'I think that's a very nice name.'

'Thank you. Won't you sit down?' She made a stilted gesture with one thin arm.

'Ah, perhaps I will.' Tarrant moved to the chesterfield of black hide. 'And—er—how are you going to amuse yourself today?'

'Weng will take me to the Zoo, and we shall have lunch there,' she answered in her soft, precise voice.

'Ah ... the Zoo. My goodness, it's a long time since I've been there.' Tarrant realised with despair that he was starting every sentence with 'Ah', and that heartiness was creeping into his voice. Lucille brought a small, slender-legged occasional table with an inlaid top, and set it at Tarrant's elbow. He murmured his thanks and set down his drink.

'Excuse me.' She leaned across Tarrant as she spoke, and picked up a folded newspaper which lay on the chesterfield beside him. 'I'll take that out of your way.'

For a moment she lost her balance and leaned against him, then pulled herself upright and moved quickly back, holding the newspaper and looking nervously embarrassed. 'I beg your pardon. I was clumsy.'

'Well, we didn't knock the glass over,' said Tarrant with what he hoped was a reassuring smile. 'Tell me what you're going to do after you've had lunch at——'

' 'Old it!' Willie Garvin's voice was sharp. Tarrant turned

27

and saw him coming from the passage with long strides. He wore charcoal grey slacks and a light zip-up golfing jacket. Normally the tanned square face was amiable and the blue eyes beneath the coarse fair hair were ready to smile. But now Willie's expression was a blend of anger and frustration.

Lucille froze, clutching the paper. In amazement Tarrant saw her big eyes narrow defiantly for an instant. Then she turned and ran towards Modesty's bedroom. Willie took the three steps in one huge stride, flashed across the room, and caught Lucille by one skinny arm. She struggled to pull free for a moment, then gave up and burst into a torrent of French.

'*Je n'ai rien fait, Willie! Rien, je te dis* . . .' Tarrant could barely follow the rapid gabble.

Willie cut her short in the same language. '*Tais-toi, petite voleuse!*' He moved back across the room to where Tarrant sat staring.

'Sorry about this, Sir G.' There was acute embarrassment on Willie's face. He looked down at Lucille, still holding her by the arm. 'Go on, give it back. And say you're sorry.'

Defiance had vanished from Lucille's face now. Her eyes, brimming with tears, showed nothing but contrition. 'I am sorry,' she whispered, and held out the newspaper. It unfolded, and Tarrant saw his wallet lying there in the fold, the wallet that had been in his breast pocket.

'Good Lord,' he said blankly, and looked at Willie.

'Old habits,' Willie said with a helpless gesture. 'I'm sorry.'

'Well . . . don't make too much of it,' Tarrant said, embarrassed himself now. He took the wallet and slipped it into his pocket.

'She worries me sick,' Willie said fervently. He sat down on the chesterfield and took Lucille gently by the shoulders. 'Look, love—*I've* told you never to do it again, and Modesty's told you the same thing. You've been a good girl for the last couple of weeks—why d'you go and spoil it now?'

'I didn't mean to, Willie.' Her small fingers straightened

Willie's tie, and Tarrant marvelled at the woman in her. She sniffed and brushed a hand across her eyes. 'But he was the type . . . you know? The——' she groped for a moment, said a word or two in Arabic, and added: 'Like the English tourists, Willie.'

'Never say anyone's like an English tourist,' Willie said hastily with another glance of apology at Tarrant. 'It's an insult, see? Even if they *are* English tourists.'

'What was the Arabic bit?' Tarrant asked, fascinated.

'Oh, she was—um—just saying you looked an easy mark.' Willie returned his gaze to Lucille and said sternly: 'You know I ought to wallop you?'

'Yes.' Lucille's voice quavered.

'And you know bl—' Willie checked the rising exasperation in his voice, 'you know very well I never do. So you can stop squeezing those tears out. I'm Willie, remember? I've seen it all.'

The door of Modesty's bedroom slid open. She came out carrying a headscarf and a suede jacket. Tarrant saw her give no sign that she realised a situation existed.

'I'm ready,' she said. 'Where's Weng?' The young Indo-Chinese houseboy appeared from the kitchen. He had discarded the white jacket he usually wore about the house and put on a light grey suit.

'Here, Miss Blaise.'

'You'd better be off with Lucille now, Weng. You can use the Daimler Dart. And try to be by the sea-lion's pool at feeding-time when the keepers throw fish for them to catch. Lucille will enjoy that.'

'Right, Miss Blaise.' Weng grinned at Lucille. 'And will you say what she can do this afternoon—to save any arguments?'

Modesty looked a query at Willie. He ran a hand through his hair, then shrugged helplessly and said: 'You're better at it than I am, Princess.'

She smiled with wry amusement and looked at Lucille, who had moved to stand in front of her. 'All right, now listen, darling. When you get back from lunch at the Zoo,

Weng will take you downstairs to the pool for a swim. After that you can play making-up at my dressing-table, and watch Children's Television if you want to. Write a letter to Mother Bernard this evening, and then you can watch an hour's television. But into bed at nine-thirty, and no arguing about it with Weng. All right?'

'Yes, Modesty.'

'Oh, and listen. Look through your clothes some time and see if there's anything you want me to get before you go back to school. It's only four days now.'

'All right, I'll do that.'

Modesty bent down. Lucille kissed her cheek then moved to say goodbye to Willie in the same way. She turned to Tarrant and offered her hand politely. 'It was very nice to make your acquaintance, Sir Gerald.'

'Ah ... thank you,' Tarrant said with relief, not even caring that he had used 'Ah' again. 'Well, goodbye Lucille, and have a nice time.'

In the garage beneath the penthouse block, Tarrant transferred his John Letters clubs from the four-year-old Rover he drove to Modesty's open Rolls. She sat in the back with him. Willie slid behind the wheel and the car moved silently up the ramp.

As they joined the traffic along the Bayswater Road, Modesty opened a locker. She took out a box of Punch Punch claro cigars and offered it to Tarrant.

'My dear,' he said, taking one, 'you spoil me.'

'Just trying to wreck your wind so I can beat you this morning.' She broke open a packet of Gauloise, lit two, and passed one forward to Willie. 'Now—what was that all about with Lucille?'

'She nicked Sir G's wallet,' Willie said wearily. 'What the 'ell am I going to do with 'er, Princess?'

Modesty looked at Tarrant with apologetic amusement. 'Did she really?'

'I'm afraid so. Apparently she considered me an easy mark. And she was right, of course, though I must confess I

30

wasn't on my guard. There were no notices about to say beware of pickpockets.'

'Thank 'eaven for little girls,' Willie quoted bitterly. 'I once 'ad visions of Lucille fetching me slippers, and all she's done so far is flog me Parker Pen.'

'That was over two years ago,' Modesty said protestingly. 'You know she's never taken anything from either of us since.'

'Not from *us*, maybe. But after three years at a convent school you wouldn't reckon she'd still 'ave itchy fingers.'

Tarrant finished lighting his cigar and exhaled. 'May I ask who she is?' he said politely.

'She sort of belongs to Willie.' Modesty eased off her shoes and wriggled stockinged toes. 'He picked her up outside Algiers one day about three years ago. A coach had run into the family on the road—her father and mother and a donkey. Lucille had a broken leg. The others were dead.'

'Is she an Arab child?' Tarrant asked.

'A quarter French, or maybe an eighth. We never found out. The family had no home. Everything they owned was on the donkey.'

'I see. And this was back in the days when you were going about your various illegal occasions, running *The Network*?'

'Yes. When Lucille came out of hospital Willie was too soft to leave her with an orphanage or something of that sort, so now he's got problems.'

In the driving mirror Tarrant saw Willie grin as he said: 'It was you that fixed 'er up in a private ward, Princess—and had Soultier flown in from Paris to do a bit of plastic surgery where her face was scarred.'

'Oh, well . . .' Modesty made a little gesture, and Tarrant was amused to see her on the defensive for once. He said blandly: 'Isn't Weng a similar stray that *you* picked up, Modesty?'

'Stop ganging up against me,' she said. 'It's Willie's stray who's the problem.'

'Too true.' Willie's face was gloomy again. 'Trouble is, Sir G., she was brought up stealing and begging. Last year we were in Tangier, stopping at Modesty's place there while the kid was on 'oliday. Know what she did one day? Found some perishing old rags to dress in, rolled in the dirt, sneaked down to the Medina, borrowed a baby and hawked it around, begging from tourists. Blimey . . .' He rubbed the back of his neck despairingly.

'Unfortunately it was one of the nuns from the school who spotted her,' said Modesty.

'It would be.' Willie heaved a sigh. 'Mother Bernard carried on at me as if it was all *my* fault.'

'That was because you tried to jolly her along, Willie love.' Modesty looked at Tarrant. 'Lucille picked up three and a half dollars American, twelve-and-six English, and fifty-odd dirhem in local money. Willie told Mother Bernard he didn't think that was bad going.'

Tarrant leaned back and laughed whole-heartedly. Her dark eyes were pleased. She said: 'That's better. You were looking very tired when you first arrived.'

'I'm sorry I showed it.' He eased the ash from the end of his cigar. 'We've had a bad patch this week.'

'Serious?'

He shrugged. 'One can't always tell at the time. A lot of little things have gone wrong.' He hesitated. 'And I lost a man yesterday in Prague.'

'I'm sorry.' She rested a hand on his for a brief moment. 'A good one?'

'As it happens, the best man I had there. But one always feels the loss, regardless of value.'

'Of course.'

Tarrant's eyebrows lifted slightly. 'You found the same thing, running *The Network*?'

'To some extent.' She leaned back in the corner, her eyes a little distant, remembering. 'Controlling a crime network is rather different. Most of the people you hire are villains, so handling them is something like being a lion-tamer, I suppose. You have to make them perform the tricks you want in the way you want. But they're not all villains, and they're working for you, anyway. So sometimes when you lose a man or he gets hurt . . . well, you feel a little tired, perhaps.'

'Yes.' Tarrant nodded. 'And there's seldom anything you can do about it.'

'Only pay disability pensions,' said Willie. 'The Princess set up a trust——'

'Shut up, Willie.'

He grinned and was silent. When they stopped for the traffic lights he turned and looked at Tarrant.

'Prague, where you lost this bloke?'

'Yes.'

Willie's eyes moved inquiringly to Modesty for a moment, then back to Tarrant. 'Must be nearly four years since we last saw Wenceslaus Square I reckon, Princess.'

'No,' said Tarrant before she could answer. 'Forget it, Willie.'

'I had dealings with some of the people there before we retired,' Modesty said. 'I still have levers we could use.'

Tarrant shook his head. 'No. It's too late, Modesty, he's dead. And even if he were alive it would be a bad move—speculating too much for a return too small.'

Willie turned back to the wheel and the car moved smoothly away.

'He's getting restless again,' Modesty said, and flickered an eyelid at Tarrant. 'That usually means he's between girls.'

'I'm not, Princess, honest.' There was a touch of indignation in Willie's voice. 'I've fixed to take Melanie to Le Touquet tomorrow for a couple of days or so.'

'Which one's that?'

'Dark girl with the big mouth—sings at *The Pink Flamingo*.'

'Oh yes, I know the one. Well, make sure you're back in time to see Lucille off, Willie.'

'I'll be back.' Willie waved on an impatient Mini and sighed. 'It shook me today when she whizzed that wallet off Sir G. I dunno why she keeps at it. And the way she can turn on the old crocodile tears . . .' He shook his head with reluctant admiration. 'You'll 'ave a talk with her won't you, Princess? She listens to you more than she does me.'

'I suppose,' Tarrant said diffidently, 'she needs a home with parents.'

'Yes.' Modesty shrugged. 'I know we're not the right people—but it could be worse for her.'

Tarrant thought of the barely credible fragments he had gleaned of Modesty's past . . . the small lone child in the prison camp, far younger than Lucille was now; the animal fight for survival during the years when, still a child, she had found her way through Greece and Turkey to the Middle East; the refugee and D.P. camps and the wanderings between, during the time of her puberty. And then there was some impossible trek she had made on foot with a frail old man whose protector she had become, a trek ending in Tangier, where the first seeds had been sown of *The Network*—that widespread but curiously selective criminal organisation she had run for almost eight years.

Tarrant had an intense curiosity about her past, but she would rarely speak of it. Neither would Willie Garvin.

Willie was the man she had found and recreated during the very early days of *The Network*. He had remarkable talents and rare qualities of character, but throughout his life these had been smothered under the weight of all those things which shape a criminal outcast, the dark and egocentric passions of bitterness, envy and hatred.

It was Modesty Blaise who by some strange magic had stripped away the veneer and liberated Willie Garvin from the gnawing demons who rode on his back. For this liberation the new Willie Garvin had made himself—not her slave, for she would not allow that, but her eternally faithful follower. And though she had raised him up to become her right arm, he still sat at her feet.

There was no loss of masculinity in this. Tarrant smiled to himself at the thought. Willie Garvin was wholly convinced that sitting at Modesty's feet set him head and shoulders above any man alive . . . even those few who had known the gifts of her splendid body.

Willie was perhaps the happiest man Tarrant had ever known; he was probably among the half-dozen most interesting; and, when occasion demanded, he was certainly and by far the most dangerous.

To the extent that anybody could know the whole story of Modesty Blaise, Willie knew it. Tarrant envied him that. Sometimes Willie would make a casual reference to her past, opening a shutter briefly on some fascinating story but shrugging off any attempt to make him enlarge upon it.

Tarrant had tried to imagine Modesty in those early years, a small wild creature in a world at war, fighting her daily battle against hunger and fear and danger, comprehending little beyond her own tiny world in which she struggled alone.

Alone. That must have been the worst part, Tarrant thought. Some men could fight alone—for a limited time and if there was an end in sight. But for a child to fight a battle, seemingly without end, and without the sustenance of human affection of any kind, yet to emerge with her mind lucid and unwarped . . . that was something close to a miracle.

Tarrant thought about the other child he had seen half-an-hour ago, in the superb penthouse, well-fed, wearing the finest of clothes.

'Yes, my dear,' he said quietly. 'You're right, of course. It could be a lot worse for Lucille.'

When Modesty turned from the window he expected her face to be shadowed by memories, but her eyes were laughing at him. 'Don't be sentimental,' she said, and he knew she had read his thoughts. 'And don't make comparisons. The same thing is easier or harder for different people. Willie, that's a police car you're overtaking, at ten miles over the limit.'

Willie said in disgust: 'My aching back.'

With a touch on the brake he kept the Rolls hovering alongside the police car. Two grim faces were turned to look ominously at him. Leaning across the passenger seat a little, he jabbed a pointing finger several times towards the off-side rear wheel of the police car, mouthed meaninglessly, and wobbled his hand to and fro. Then with a polite smile he dropped back. Seconds later the police car driver drew into the kerb and waved him on. As the Rolls went past, the driver nodded and gave him a quick wave of acknowledgment.

Looking back, Tarrant saw the two policemen get out and walk to the rear of the car, crouching to examine the wheel.

'Sorry,' said Willie. 'I wasn't concentrating. Still got Lucille on my mind.'

'You made a good recovery,' Tarrant said with dry amusement. 'What happens if they come after you when they find nothing wrong?'

'I'll do me righteous bit. That wheel looked a bit wobbly to me, and I was only trying to 'elp. "*The righteous shall flourish like the palm-tree; he shall grow like a cedar in Lebanon.*" Psalm ninety-two, verse twelve.'

The quotation did not surprise Tarrant. He knew that Willie, in his early days, had once spent a year in a Calcutta gaol with only a psalter to read.

Modesty leaned forward and patted Willie's shoulder. 'Don't fret about Lucille. These things take time.'

'I suppose so ... but I wish we could get through to the kid, Princess. She'll be in trouble sooner or later if she keeps on pinching things.'

'You worry too much, Willie love. She's far better than she used to be. Give her time and she'll grow out of it.' Modesty sat back, and her face was lit by a sudden mischievous smile as she added: 'After all, *I* did.'

Tarrant laughed aloud, feeling the muscles of his mind relax. The anxieties of the past week were laid aside now, and there was only one small shadow of tension hovering in his mind. It annoyed him, and he grew silent, looking out of the window.

Stupid to let this thing worry him, he told himself. The hunch was probably wrong. If there was anything in it at all, it was hardly likely that Modesty would be interested. And assuming she showed interest, the chance of danger was remote. This job wouldn't be a bad one, a big hazard.

Another part of his mind said: '*That's what you thought last time.*'

Tarrant sighed inwardly. Somebody had to send people

36

out to play the dirty games that went on in this difficult world, and he had been doing it for over twenty years in one way or another.

The fact that he was basically a man of old-fashioned principles, who disliked using women in general and Modesty Blaise in particular, made no difference to his tentative plans. A Frenchman had once told him that there was nobody more cunning and cold-blooded than an English gentleman of the old school doing what he conceived to be his duty.

Tarrant thought it was probably true. He had never allowed his personal views to interfere with the ruthless objectivity required in his work. And he knew, with melancholy reluctance, that whether this job looked like being a bad one or not he was going to use Modesty Blaise if he could.

THREE

A SMELL of cordite hung in the long room. From somewhere behind where Tarrant sat came the steady hum of the air-conditioning plant.

Modesty Blaise stood at one end of the hundred-and-twenty foot pistol range. She wore slim black denim trousers, a black shirt buttoned to the neck, and plimsolls. Her hair was bound in a short club at the nape of her neck. About her waist was a leather belt with a modified Gun Hawk holster bearing a Colt .32 revolver.

The pistol range lay along one side of the soundproof and windowless building. On the other side was the archery range, and between the two ranges lay the twenty-foot square *dojo*. A large part of one wall was almost hidden by the collection of small-arms and hand weapons hung there. Some were new, some very old. As Tarrant knew, few of the modern western weapons in the collection were used for business; and not all the old and mainly oriental weapons were mere curios.

37

He sat on the bench-seat near the shower cubicles, a little behind and to one side of Modesty. A man-shaped target had been set up at the far end of the pistol range, in front of the sandbagged wall.

Modesty said: 'Right, Willie. When you're ready.' She stood relaxed, eyes closed, hands hanging at her sides.

Willie was similarly dressed in black slacks and shirt. He walked thoughtfully round Modesty, and Tarrant wondered what he would do this time. On the last shot, half a minute ago, he had suddenly hit Modesty flat-handed on the back of one shoulder to send her stumbling forward.

Tarrant tensed, watching. But when the action came it was so fast that he was only able to follow it by reconstructing it in his mind later, in slow-motion. Standing alongside Modesty, Willie suddenly crouched and swung his leg like a scythe. It took her behind the calves, knocking her feet from under her. She spun as she went down, twisting to fall sideways rather than back. The gun was in her right hand as her left arm hit the floor in a breakfall, and the shot coincided with the slap of her arm.

The target shivered. Willie walked towards it as Modesty got to her feet.

'Four inches off the 'eart at two-o'clock,' he said with satisfaction.

'A little faster than the other draw, I thought,' Tarrant ventured. 'And no less accurate.'

Modesty nodded, her eyes crinkling in thought. 'Yes ... the high cavalry draw has its points, especially for a single action gun. But the Colt's a double action. I've tried the draw for six months now but I still like the hip-draw best.'

Tarrant said: 'I had the impression that the *position* of the gun troubled you in the high cavalry draw.'

'It's quite comfortable.' She sat beside him and flicked open the cylinder to reload. 'But you're right. It makes me uneasy having a holster strapped sideways across the small of my back, with the gun turned butt-down. All right for target shooting but bad for real business. If you fell on your back in a rumpus it wouldn't do your spine much good.'

'Yet you've tried it for six months, all the same?'

'It's necessary. A new way always seems awkward at first, but it might be better in the end. You have to give it a chance, just in case. Anything that might save a tenth of a second is worth six months' trial.'

She spoke simply, as if expressing a natural law. This was an aspect of her which never ceased to fascinate Tarrant—her total professionalism. During the past hour since they entered the building through the two heavy doors, the first of solid wood, the second of steel, he had been watching Modesty Blaise and Willie Garvin at practice.

He had seen Willie at work with his knives—the two knives with hafts of black dimpled bone and five-and-a-half inch blades, fashioned like miniature Bowie-knife blades with thin brass fillets on one edge near the haft, for knife-fighting.

They were carried in a simple harness which laid the sheaths in echelon across the left breast, or in twin sheaths stitched to the inside breast of a light wind-cheater. When Willie handled them they seemed to take on a cold and potent life of their own.

In the practice, Tarrant had seen Willie throw back-handed, flicking the knife across the small of his back by the power of the wrist alone and hitting a target fifteen feet away, dead centre. He had seen Willie make an over-arm throw at a hundred feet, the knife thudding home within four inches of its mark.

What had intrigued Tarrant most was to see how Willie made his draw when the sterner practice began, when he stood with eyes closed and Modesty sent him staggering at any angle so that he had to draw and throw off-balance, in the way Modesty had just fired the Colt.

At first Tarrant could not see how it was done, could not see how the knife appeared in Willie's flickering hand with the blade held between his fingers. It was only when Willie slowed down, by request, that Tarrant saw the method. The knife was drawn with two fingers and thumb at the lowest point of the haft, and in the instant of drawing it was tossed fractionally to transfer the grip to the blade, near the point.

'He's a natural,' Modesty explained, smiling a little at Tarrant's incredulous stare. 'When Willie was concocted he stole the fastest set of reactions in the store—otherwise he'd have lost his fingertips long ago with that double-shuffle.'

'It's just clean living,' Willie demurred.

'Righteous,' agreed Tarrant. 'Are your own reactions as fast, Modesty?'

'Perhaps. Now. But I had to develop them. Willie got them free with the packet.'

Willie shook his head. 'It varies. The Princess is faster when it's for real. That's what counts.'

It was after Willie's session with the knives that Modesty moved to the archery range. For twenty minutes she practised, first with a fibreglass centre-shot bow, then with one of laminated wood and plastic, and finally with the astonishing tubular steel bow which could be collapsed to an eight-inch tube and which shot thin steel shafts made from short screw-in sections.

Now she was at work with a variety of handguns. After another session with the Colt she took a .41 Magnum and tackled moving targets—clay-pigeon discs which sprang out in a smooth curve across the butts, shot from a trap Willie had rigged to work from an electrical control at the firing-point.

When the handgun practice was over, Willie took the guns into his workroom at the far end of the building, behind the butts, and left them there for cleaning later.

'All most interesting,' Tarrant said. 'I've genuinely enjoyed every moment, my dear.' He looked at the *dojo*, the padded mat spread in the centre of the long combat room, and felt a strange blend of excitement and unease. 'Is that all for today?'

'No. This is the part you may not like. We limber up and then we have a serious work-out. Against each other.'

She moved to a set of stepped parallel bars, jumped to catch the higher bar, then began to swing up and around

40

between the two with all the rhythmic skill of a trained gymnast.

It was an aesthetic pleasure to watch the swiftly circling body, the quick change of grip, the smooth transfer from one bar to the other. Willie returned from the workroom and stood watching. There was nothing of affection or admiration in his gaze now; it was the alert, critical gaze of the perfectionist.

When she dropped from the bar at last, Willie took over. He lacked the inherent grace of her slighter, feminine body, but he moved with the immaculate precision of a high-speed machine. She watched with the same sharp concentration as he had watched her earlier.

Tarrant was aware of a new and very sober element in the atmosphere now, something quite different from the light and casual atmosphere of the morning.

He thought of the Riverside Club, and of the moment when he and Modesty waited for Willie just outside the club house. A foursome of men moved past in leisurely fashion towards the first tee. They were all well beyond middle age, with the flesh of rich living upon them and the authoritative air of long-time members.

They paused, and one of them looked at Modesty with a hint of disapproval. 'New member?' he grunted tersely.

Tarrant expected a reaction of cold annoyance from her, but there was only a glimmer of amusement as she answered: 'A guest.'

'Hey?'

'A guest of Mr. Garvin,' she amplified.

'H'mph. Don't know the feller.'

The foursome moved on. Tarrant felt anger himself and was about to speak, but she touched his arm, smiling. 'Never mind. They're quite funny really—almost caricatures.'

Looking past her, Tarrant saw Willie Garvin standing in the doorway, and wondered if he had heard the exchange. There was an odd look on his face, and he was watching the foursome. After a moment he turned back into the club house again.

Tarrant looked at Modesty. 'They hardly seem the types to be Willie's cup of tea.'

'We've only played here once or twice, because it's handy for *The Treadmill*, but most of the people are pleasant enough. I suppose you're bound to run into a few blimps.' She glanced round. 'I don't know what's keeping Willie, but let's move on to the tee, anyway.'

It was two minutes later when Willie emerged from the club house. He had discarded his jacket to reveal a short-sleeved battledress style of shirt in navy blue. Above the pocket was a four-inch row of medal ribbons, and he was wearing a hairy ginger cap a little too small for him. His eyes were hooded and his mouth drawn down a little, creasing his face so that he looked ten years older.

'Oh, my God,' said Modesty, and made a sound that was as near to a giggle as Tarrant had ever heard from her. 'He's in one of his moods.'

'Where in heaven's name did he get that cap? And those *ribbons*!' Tarrant whispered in alarm.

'It's better not to know.'

The foursome were making a few practice swings as Willie arrived. They stared at him, first with amazement and then with suspicious unease.

' 'Morning, ma'am,' Willie greeted Modesty, touching the peak of his cap and speaking in a gruff military bark.

' 'Morning, Major.' Her own voice had become deep and horsey. 'How's the little woman?'

'Damn difficult.' Willie scowled at the foursome as if they were eavesdroppers. 'She's got this obsession, y'know. About swimming the channel.' He paused, waiting for the first man to address his ball and drive off. It was not a good drive.

'Ah,' said Modesty. 'Heard about that. Fruity told me.'

'Damn young puppy,' Willie growled. 'All his fault. He encourages her.'

'Actually training her, isn't he? I ran into him the other day with a big tin of that grease they spread all over them.'

Silence, while the second man sliced his ball into the rough.

42

'Over who, ma'am?' Willie said, frowning.

'Channel swimmers. Keeps them warm.'

'Oh.' A ruminative pause. The third man hooked his ball horribly.

'Can't say I've noticed any grease on her,' Willie grunted. 'Don't think she's been in the water yet.'

'Not in the water?'

'No. Fruity's still got her on dry-land training or some such rot. Up in the bedroom every afternoon.'

'He must be trying to get her breathing right, eh?'

Tarrant moved away and pretended to practise his swing. The conversation on the borderline of lunacy continued until the fourth man addressed his ball. Twice he stepped back, drew a deep breath, and started again. His drive carried for sixty yards, and a sizeable divot carried for three feet.

The foursome trudged away in silence.

Tarrant wiped his brow and said: 'I'm sorry, but I'm not up to this. I don't disapprove. I simply lack the courage even to be a witness.'

Willie frowned at him. 'Courage? My God, man, if you'd ever stood in a thin red line and——'

Modesty said: 'Willie, be quiet,' and tossed her ball at him. He caught it and set it down on a plastic tee for her.

As they played the first hole Tarrant discovered that these two had taken up the game only twelve months ago. With their natural co-ordination of hand, muscle and eye, they were already very good—and might have been far better if their approach to the game had not been irreverent and experimental.

At the second hole, which was straight, it was disconcerting to see Willie waste his first drive by making a dog-leg of it. This involved lofting the ball over a towering stand of trees; and even if the almost impossible drive succeeded, the ball would land in the rough.

'Five to one in pounds you don't make it,' Modesty said.

'You're on, Princess.' Willie took a number seven iron, addressed the ball briefly, and swung. It was an astonishing effort, and only just failed.

43

'You're five up,' said Willie, and put down another ball.

The side-bets continued. Modesty was exceptionally good on the green. At the third she had to sink a four-foot putt for a bogie three.

'Five to two you can't sink it with your eyes closed,' Willie said with interest. She nodded, addressed the ball carefully, closed her eyes, and putted. The ball trickled round the rim of the cup.

'Two to me. Leaves you four quid up so far,' said Willie.

Tarrant's conventional golfing soul had been shocked at first, but by the fourth hole he was not only inured to their lack of reverence for the sacred game, but was also somewhat infected by it. Despite the experiments of his opponents Tarrant was two strokes behind them both at the fifth; but then, driving and putting with fine insouciance, he came up from behind over the last four holes in a way that astonished and delighted him.

Later they had lunched together on the small private terrace by the river at the rear of *The Treadmill*. A narrow creek branched at right-angles from the river nearby, and in the angle so formed, screened from the pub by a row of evergreens, was the long low building where Tarrant sat now.

And now the mood was very different. He realised that for the last ten minutes, while Modesty and Willie limbered up on the stepped parallel bars, nobody had spoken. He felt a sense of exclusion and knew that these two had almost ceased to be aware of his presence. They were alone in their own strange world of intense mental and physical concentration.

Willie dropped from the bar and moved to one corner of the *dojo*. Modesty walked to the other corner, diagonally opposite.

There was a pause, then with quick light steps they moved towards each other. Modesty swerved, swung back, and the two figures were briefly one. Willie's body spun over her thigh. His feet hit the *dojo* and he twisted. Tarrant saw that his hands were clamped on her arm and wrist. As Willie came up Modesty somersaulted, anticipating the throw.

Tarrant let out a little sigh of relaxed tension. This, he

44

realised, was a free exercise, a series of throws and falls and counter-throws, but with no attempt to follow through. It was like a jam-session between musicians, with a motif explored for a while then discarded for something new.

It was an arabesque, speeded up to a fantastic degree, with the two bodies whirling and falling and rising, separating for an instant, then uniting again.

For five minutes he watched entranced. Then Modesty stepped back, breathing a little quickly, and said: 'All right, Willie.'

She turned away to pick up a small object lying on a shelf near the bench where Tarrant sat. This was the kongo, or yawara stick, her favourite weapon. Derived from the old Orient, it was a miniature black dumbell made of sandalwood. The shaft fitted into her fist with the two knobs protruding, one at each end of her clenched hand.

Tarrant knew its virtues, for on one occasion he had drawn her into talking about it. The kongo was used mainly as a striking weapon against nerve-centres. It could paralyse a limb, or stun, or kill.

For a moment as she stood there, fitting her hand about the black shaft, her gaze rested distantly on Tarrant.

'Willie takes a handicap on the next bit,' she said. 'It makes up for the weight advantage.'

Tarrant nodded, not speaking. His throat felt dry. She turned back to the *dojo*. Willie crouched slightly. His big powerful hands came up, open and rigid, like spades. One was poised palm-down a few inches in front of his throat, the other was held vertically beneath, like an axe ready to chop.

Modesty held her left forearm horizontally before her, looking over it at Willie. Her right hand held the kongo, poised just in front of her right hip.

Circling warily, they drew slowly closer to each other. And now, for Tarrant, the sense of exclusion was total. He was a man who had done many things in his time. He had known battle and danger himself, and he had sent both men and women into danger many times; some he had sent to their death. He was more than thirty years older than this girl, and

45

a quarter-century older than Willie Garvin, but suddenly he felt like a child looking upon some dark adult mystery.

This was how some men had seen Modesty Blaise just before they died under her hand. This was how some men had seen Willie Garvin in their last moments. One or two of these men Tarrant had known; others he knew of. All were killers, evil men and dangerous. He had seen, among others, the body of Canalejas in the monastery on Kalithos, where Modesty Blaise and Willie Garvin had fought a long and vicious battle against frightening odds. He had looked down at the body of Canalejas, knowing she had killed this creature, and he had been glad. He was still glad.

But now, for the first time, he was seeing that aspect of her nature which made such things physically possible—the dynamic of the will, the totality of her concentration.

For a moment he tried to call back into his mind the Modesty Blaise who had sent Lucille off to the Zoo; who had played up to Willie's lunatic Major, and tried to sink a putt with her eyes closed; who had walked with him at Ascot, and whose sudden smile made the heart grow warm. But that picture would not take shape.

Willie Garvin was watching her like a lynx. The blue eyes in his impassive, leathery face held no emotion at all. Tarrant knew what strength lay in that body; and one of his least impressionable men had told him that Garvin in action was the fastest thing he had ever seen.

There came a sudden flurry of movement. A feint, a swerve, a lashing side-kick from Modesty's plimsolled foot— a kick pulled back at the last instant because the counter-move was already headreaching on it.

For a full two minutes there was no actual contact. A dozen moves were begun but never completed. With awe Tarrant realised that this was combat brought to the deadly pitch of fencing or knife-fighting, where when you committed yourself it was once and for all. The preliminary engagements of the foils, the preliminary footwork and feints of the knife-fighters, these were approach-patterns only. There came a moment of decision, a true attack, and then either the thrust went home or the riposte came back against whatever part of body or limb had been exposed.

Tarrant's eyes were aching with the effort of trying not to blink. He saw Willie sway sideways, change direction abruptly—and this was the moment. The left hand had swept her kongo-hand aside and his right was chopping towards her shoulder.

She turned in a blur of speed, moving towards him, flank forward. Tarrant heard the smack of flesh on flesh, and saw that her left forearm had blocked the chop—not against the dangerous edge of the hand but against the inner side of Willie's wrist.

Her right arm coiled and straightened, flicking out like a whip. Tarrant neither heard nor saw the blow. It had not been a heavy one. She had told him once that the kongo, properly used, was as good as a lead fist.

Willie jumped back, cat-footed. But now his right arm hung limp, the fingers working slowly as he tried to bring life back into the nerves.

Modesty went in very fast. Willie, backing, turned to keep his good arm towards her—and, to Tarrant's stunned amazement, kept turning to present his back to her. But with the turn he gave suddenly at the knees so that she was behind and slightly above and a little too close as she struck with the kongo. The blow missed by a fraction, her wrist grazing his face and striking his shoulder. Then his left arm, bent at the elbow, the hand still hanging limply in partial paralysis, jerked back. The point of the elbow hit her solidly, high on the side of the neck, a little below the ear.

She was flung sideways, partly by the impact and partly by her own effort to ride the blow. For one brief instant as she hit the mat her crumpled body seemed boneless. Then she was rolling fast, away from him, coming to her feet.

Tarrant found his lungs were aching, and dimly realised that he had stopped breathing. With an effort he forced his numbed diaphragm to work, and a shaky exhalation escaped his lips.

They were facing each other again, both slightly crouched

47

in the ready position as before—except that Willie's left arm hung low and there was a new, almost anxious watchfulness in the way he peered at her now.

He dropped his hands and stepped back.

'All right, Princess,' he said gently. She seemed not to have heard. She was still circling slowly, poised on the balls of her feet, edging closer. Then Tarrant saw that her eyes, though focused, were curiously blank.

Willie backed from her, lifting his hands to a defensive position again. 'S'all right, Princess,' he repeated patiently, as if to a child. 'It's only me. Only Willie.'

She stopped, blank eyes regarding him doubtfully, and said: 'Willie . . . ?'

'That's right, Princess. It's me—Willie. All over now.'

Her arms fell limply, and he moved towards her. She swayed, legs buckling. He caught her round the waist and held her for a moment, shaking his right arm to get further strength back into it, then bent and picked her up. Her head fell back as he carried her to the masseur's table beside the shower cubicles.

Tarrant was beside him as he laid her down.

'She was out on 'er feet,' Willie said, gently prising the kongo from her rigid grip. 'I 'ad to go careful then, or she might have really done me, not knowing who it was.'

'I bloody well wish she had.' Tarrant's voice was taut with fury. 'For God's sake, did you have to hit her that hard?'

'I pulled it,' Willie said. 'We always do.' He looked at Tarrant with a faintly puzzled air. 'She wouldn't thank me for playing pat-a-cake with 'er, you know.'

He began to massage with sure, powerful hands, working from the solar plexus to the heart. 'You should've been 'ere for last month's work-out,' he said with a sudden grin. 'She knocked me cold and I was out for five minutes.'

'You mean you always let it go this far?' Tarrant said, appalled. His anger had passed but he felt a little queasy now from reaction.

'Not always. Just depends 'ow it works out. If she'd got in one good strike to me other arm, I'd 've had to quit. That's

48

why I took a chance and offered 'er a better target.'

He lifted one soft eyelid with his thumb. 'She's coming round now.' Gently he turned her face-down, head sideways on the hard low pillow, and began to knead the shoulder and neck muscles.

Tarrant watched anxiously. After a few seconds her eyelids flickered. Slowly the eyes opened. They were sleepy but no longer blank. After a little while a small smile tugged at her lips.

'Nice trick, Willie.' Her voice was a whisper. 'Risky . . . but good. I won't fall for it another time.' Her eyes moved slightly to rest on Tarrant as he bent beside her. 'Was it interesting for you?'

'It was terrifying,' he said simply. 'I'm glad to have seen it, but I never want to see it again. Do you have to take these work-outs to the point where someone gets hurt?'

'Getting hurt a little is important.' Her voice was stronger now, but still relaxed. 'If you just play at it, you're in trouble when the real thing comes along. You'll hesitate, lose just a fifth of a second maybe. And then you're dead. If I worried about getting hurt a little, Willie could just come at me like a tank.'

'But I don't,' Willie said with emphasis. 'She'd take me with the kongo like a bazooka takes a tank. She might go down under me, but I'd be out cold.'

Tarrant took a cigar from his case, hesitated, started to put it away, then looked at Modesty. 'Will it trouble you if I smoke?'

'Much better than seeing you stand there jittering.' Her eyes sparkled with laughter. As Tarrant lit the cigar and inhaled gratefully she said: 'All right, Willie. Thanks for the magic fingers.'

'How's it feel, Princess?'

'Pretty good.' She sat up on the masseur's table, rotating her head and neck. 'Better than I deserve for letting myself be conned like that.'

'I dunno . . . lucky with the timing, wasn't I?'

She considered, re-running the sequence of moves in her

49

mind. 'A bit lucky, maybe,' she acknowledged, and slid down off the table. Tarrant noticed that she was quite steady on her feet.

'There's a bag of crushed ice and some embrocation in the shower, Princess,' Willie said. 'That'll 'elp stop any bruising.'

'Fine.' She looked at Tarrant. 'Loser always gets first use of the shower. You go with Willie and see if he's got anything new in his workshop.'

Tarrant nodded vaguely. After all that had happened here under the daylight fluorescence of the combat room, he had lost contact with reality for a while. The cigar was helping to restore that contact, but his mind was still in mild chaos.

'Thank you,' was all he could think of to say.

'You stick it in your ear,' said Willie Garvin.

'And then what?' Tarrant asked. He was feeling more himself again now, and was very thankful for it.

'Well, you just listen like a bat,' said Willie. ' 'Old on a tick while I fix it up, then I'll show you.'

He busied himself with a watchmaker's screwdriver on the small black plastic object held in the felt-jawed vice. The two men were in the workshop which extended across the full thirty-foot width of the building and lay behind the pistol and archery butts, separated from them by a nine-inch brick wall.

The workshop was twelve feet deep, fitted with gleaming benches and racks of tools ranging from the delicate instruments of the micro-engineer to the heavier equipment of the skilled metal-worker.

Tarrant got down from the high stool on which he was seated, near the miniature forge. Moving to one end of the room he looked at a blue-print lying on a draughtsman's table beside a bench bearing an Emerson micro-manipulator.

After studying the blue-print for a full minute he gave up trying to make anything of it. Willie was working with deft, patient hands, his face absorbed.

'Now I understand why you two play golf like the Marx

Brothers,' Tarrant said irrelevantly, and waved his cigar towards the open door leading to the combat room. 'Nothing's serious compared with that.'

'I 'ad a girl once who was mad serious about golf,' Willie said reminiscently, not looking up from his task. ' 'Bout six months ago. Aileen, her name was. She came from Scotland. Tallish, lovely body, marvellous complexion. Only two things interested 'er. Playing golf and going to bed. Real obsessions they were. Only trouble was, she couldn't keep 'em separate.'

He picked up a tiny screw with tweezers and eased the tip gently into a threaded hole in the plastic.

Tarrant fought a brief inward battle with himself, but curiosity won. 'How do you mean, she couldn't keep them separate, Willie?'

'Just that. You'd be on the fairway, squaring up for a drive, an' suddenly you could really feel it. She'd be looking at you like she was just about ready to drag you off into the deep rough and eat you.' He screwed a jeweller's glass in his eye, found the slot of the tiny screw with the blade of the screwdriver, and began to twist it gently home.

'So all right,' he went on. 'She's geared up to eat you, so you've got something good lined up. A bit later you're in bed, clambering about a bit, and then you feel it again. She's looking at the ceiling, and she's about a light-year away, thinking about that drive she sliced at the fourth 'ole.'

'Aileen?' Modesty stood in the doorway. She was fresh from the shower and without make-up. Her hair hung loose and was clipped back at the nape of the neck. Her bare feet protruded beneath an ornate Chinese robe of Willie's, wrapped almost twice about her and belted by a scarlet sash. The shoulders drooped halfway down her upper arms, and her hands hung invisible within the sleeves. She looked absurdly young, like a child dressed in her father's robe.

Tarrant looked in vain for a hint of the woman who had faced Willie Garvin on the *dojo*, but she was gone. The steel and the fire and the diamond-hard will—all were at rest in some secret place within her. Now, when he looked at her,

51

Tarrant thought vaguely of fresh meadows, quiet blue skies, and clear spring water rippling over sunwarmed stones.

Willie lifted his head and nodded. 'That's right, Princess. Aileen. You met 'er once, didn't you? Reddish sort of hair.'

'*Reddish?* Willie, you've got no soul. She had the most marvellous auburn hair.'

'Did she?'

'Yes. And it was natural.'

'M'mm. I know that. But I'd 've done better on dyed hair and no obsessions.'

Modesty laughed and came into the room, her bare feet making faint damp marks on the cork-tiled floor. Tarrant moved the high stool forward for her and she sat with her feet on the rail, hands hidden in the long sleeves and resting on her lap.

'What's Willie been showing you, Sir Gerald?'

'I'm not quite sure. Something that helps you to listen like a bat, whatever that might mean.'

'Ready now,' said Willie, and held up the small flat oval of plastic. Half-a-dozen very fine short steel wires projected from one surface, a cone-shaped plug of hollow rubber protruded from the other, and there was a spring clip on the edge. A length of very thin flex led to a small power-pack containing a nickel cadmium cell. Willie slipped the power-pack into his shirt pocket.

'You clip it on with the earplug bit stuck in your ear,' he said. 'Like a deaf-aid.'

'What does it do, Willie love?'

'Works like radar. Or like a bat in the dark. The bat sends out short-wave squeaks, they bounce back off any object in so many milliseconds. Then the bat does some sums in its little 'ead, and knows it'll fly into a bell-rope if it doesn't bank to port a bit sharpish.'

'Clever little chaps,' Tarrant conceded. 'Do you have to squeak?'

Willie frowned and lifted a monitorial hand. 'No barracking, please! This dingus sends out ultra-sonic waves that bounce back. You hear bleeps and they vary according to the

52

size and distance of the object. You can even get a good idea of shape, once you've worked a few hours with it.'

Modesty said: 'Could you move through a house at night without showing a light?'

'Sure, Princess. Good for jungle work too, even in daytime. You can register someone moving, even if you can't see 'em. Could be useful anywhere in the dark, though.'

'What's the range?' Tarrant asked.

'Hundred foot maximum with this, but I reckon I can improve on that.'

'And could you rely on it for aiming a shot successfully in darkness?'

'The Princess could.' Willie shrugged ruefully. 'You know me and guns. I only collect 'em—handguns, anyway. Give me a pistol and I'll likely blow me foot off. But I'd reckon to put a knife in the middle of anything mansized at forty feet, throwing blind with this thing.'

'Let's see it work, Willie.' Modesty slipped down from the stool and padded through the door into the long combat room. The two men followed. Willie stood in the middle of the *dojo*, closed his eyes and turned round several times.

'Okay, Sir G. You start prowling around.'

Feeling a little foolish, Tarrant began to tip-toe in a half-circle round Willie, keeping as far away as the width of the building would allow. Willie's hand moved and a finger stabbed accurately at Tarrant. The finger followed him as he went on. When he stopped and circled back it stayed with him like a needle following a magnet. When he began to move closer the finger dropped gradually.

' 'Bout fifteen feet now,' Willie said. 'Twelve . . . ten . . . eight. Now you're moving back again.' He opened his eyes.

'Good enough,' said Tarrant. He was deeply impressed. 'I wonder if our Ministry of Defence boffins would be interested? There's quite a bit of close-quarter jungle action in south-east Asia these days.'

'Well . . . I'd rather not, thanks, Sir G.'

Modesty smiled. 'Willie likes to keep his gadgets in the family.'

53

'He's probably wise.' Tarrant moved across and sat down on the bench beside Modesty. He looked at his watch and wondered about the next move. It was half past four. All day long he had been waiting for an approach, an opening. So far it had not come, and he was disappointed.

He thought of the piece of yellow paper with crude black printing in his wallet. If he produced it now, how would Modesty react? Possibly in the way he wanted her to, but he could not be sure. Better to be patient and hope for an approach, or at least the hint of an approach, from Modesty. Or from Willie Garvin, acting as her mouthpiece.

Tarrant's mind drifted back, remembering the day when he had first set out to use Modesty Blaise. That was not long after she had split up *The Network* and retired to England, to the penthouse in the West End, and Willie had bought his pub on the river here. Both were rich and both had found boredom in retirement.

Willie was the first to break. He had slipped away to hire himself out as a mercenary in a banana-state revolution. But Willie Garvin without Modesty Blaise was like a lamp disconnected from its source of power. Unhappy, uninterested, he had been captured and sentenced to death, a prospect he had accepted with lethargic fatalism.

It was then that Tarrant had set out to blackmail Modesty into helping him on a strange and complex assignment; but at the last moment, on an inspired hunch, he had thrown away his lever and freely given her the information by which she had been able to snatch Willie safely out of danger.

And Tarrant's hunch had paid off. She had taken on the assignment. He could remember her saying to him: 'How did you know that I hate blackmail—but that I'm a compulsive payer of debts?' He could remember, too, the end of that assignment and the counting of the dead. It had been the closest thing. He felt a little cold at the memory of it.

But the new job couldn't possibly be as bad. He thought about that and decided he was being honest with himself. No, it couldn't be as bad. It wasn't even a job yet, only a misty hunch.

54

He sighed faintly and came back to the pr⟨esent⟩. ⟨He⟩ vanished into the workshop to put away t⟨he⟩. Modesty had lit a cigarette and was smokin⟨g⟩ side.

'Well . . .' he said slowly. 'It's been a fas⟨cinating⟩ me. Have you any further plans, or am I already out-staying my welcome? I beg you to be honest.'

'I don't like complete honesty.' She was in a tranquil mood, a little faraway, and she spoke almost absently. 'It often excludes courtesy and it can sometimes be quite cruel. Not hurting people is more important.'

Tarrant looked at the *dojo*, then at the kongo lying on the table, and laughed. She was surprised at first, but as she followed his thoughts a quick urchin grin lit her face.

'All right,' she said. 'But that's not the kind of hurting I mean, and you know it.'

'Yes.' He inclined his head, wishing the grin had lasted longer. It was a rare expression of hers, and it delighted him. 'But in answer to my question, are you going to be honest with me or courteous?'

'Both. When Willie and I have had a work-out we like a quiet evening. After he's taken a shower we'll have some tea and read the Sunday papers. Then we'll go out in Willie's boat. He'll spend an hour or so fishing, and I'll just lie in the boat and doze. If you wouldn't find the programme tedious, we'd love you to come.'

'I'm a fisherman,' Tarrant said simply. 'In fact you promised me some fishing, now I come to think of it. Can Willie lend me a rod?'

'I've got a dozen you can choose from, Sir G.' Willie had returned from the workshop. 'You can select your own weapon.'

Modesty stubbed out her cigarette. 'You'll be wanting a shower, Willie,' she said. 'I'll go and get some clothes on. Give me ten minutes.'

She stood up and padded into the big shower-cubicle, her fingers unknotting the scarlet sash of the robe.

e boat was moored under the shade of a big beech
ich leaned out from the bank. Modesty Blaise lay propped
on cushions, her eyes half closed. The sun was almost down
now. In the boat aft lay a basket with two or three small
roach, a two-pound perch, and a fat ten-pound carp.

Tarrant was using a split cane rod and fishing Norfolk
style, with two hooks. Willie was ledger fishing. His rod was
held in a sleeve fixed inside the gunwale of the boat, and a
piece of dough was stuck on the line between two runners, so
that he would see the movement of the line if it ran out. He
was leaning back against the far side of the boat, smoking
idly.

It was half-an-hour since anybody had spoken.

'How's trade these days, Sir G?' Willie's voice was quiet
and unconcerned.

'Up and down, Willie. You know how it goes. Last week
was bad, but that was the first man I've lost this year, so I
mustn't complain.' He paused, watching his float. 'I've been
luckier than Léon Vaubois.'

Vaubois was the head of the Deuxième Bureau in France,
a friend of Tarrant's as well as a colleague.

'Must've shaken 'im when Bigorre and Castellane were
nabbed,' said Willie. 'Not very nice finding your own blokes
are busy working underground for the OAS instead of getting on with the job.'

'Very unpleasant,' Tarrant agreed bleakly. 'The job's hard
enough without having to keep looking over your shoulder. I
don't know how Léon copes—but he showed no tensions
when I saw him last month.'

'He'll cope,' said Modesty. 'I put Vaubois in a class of his
own.' She opened her eyes and saw Tarrant smile, his gaze
still on the float. 'That's not a discourteous comparison, Sir
Gerald.'

'I agree. It's simply honest. And true.'

'You underrate yourself. I put you at the same level but in
a different class. Vaubois works by logic, you work mainly by
instinct. You each have powers the other can't match, but the
results come out about the same.' She eased her shoulders on

the cushions and added: 'That's not a snap judgment, you know. You were both under the microscope when we were running *The Network*.'

'I'm all for the old instinct,' Willie said. 'Look at that Gabriel business you brought us in on, Sir G. That was just a hunch to start with.'

'Yes.' Tarrant felt a thread of excitement stir within him. 'But my masters don't share your view, Willie. They like facts. I rarely spend men and money on hunches ... not officially, anyway.'

There was a pensive silence. Modesty's eyes were closed again. She said: 'You can't blame them. But it must be frustrating for you sometimes.'

'Sometimes, yes. Very.' There was a hint of emphasis on the last word.

'Nothing recently?' Willie asked, and put his cigarette over the side.

Tarrant reeled in his line, made a fresh cast, and settled down again. He said: 'You mean now?'

'Yes, he means now,' Modesty said, and opened her eyes. 'Is there something?'

Tarrant relaxed, feeling a strange blend of exhilaration and regret. The opening had been given, and he was fully aware of it. He pursed his lips and gave a doubtful shake of his head.

'No ... I've got nothing in your line at the moment.' He timed his pause, and added: 'Not really.'

'When you say not really ... ?' Modesty let the question hang in the air.

'Oh, I just mean there's a foolish thing nagging at me. But that's nothing new.' Tarrant gave a short, self-conscious laugh. 'This one's even more tenuous than that last affair.'

Modesty sat up slowly, re-arranged the cushions, and lit a cigarette. 'Can you talk about it?' she asked.

'There's not much to talk about.' Tarrant passed his rod to Willie and took out a black leather wallet. 'I'm afraid you'll find nothing very exciting in this.' He drew out the piece of coarse yellow paper and passed it to her

It was a pamphlet eight inches by five, inviting all politically mature people to attend a meeting of The Friends of Kuwait Freedom Society at a lecture-hall in Gossley Road, N.W.8. The head of the Free Kuwait government, Es-Sabah Solon, would address the meeting.

Modesty read the pamphlet carefully and passed it to Willie, who returned Tarrant's rod and began to read.

'Es-Sabah Solon sounds an odd name,' she said. 'Part Arab, part Greek. How does he come to be head of the Free Kuwait government?'

'There's no such thing.' Tarrant shrugged. 'Just this man Solon and a few hangers-on. The Kuwaitis are very content under their present enlightened rulers. I could start calling myself head of the Free Outer Mongolian government if I cared to. It's meaningless.'

'But Solon must present some kind of case, surely?'

'He claims direct descent from the original Es-Sabah family which first settled in Kuwait back in the eighteenth century,' said Tarrant. 'The place was just an unnamed patch of desert then. The present ruler, as you probably know, is Sheik Abdullah, descendant of the first Emir. Es-Sabah Solon claims a better title to the place and has some complex and completely phoney family tree worked out to prove it.'

'All that side of it's just the dressing,' Willie said, looking up from the pamphlet. 'What's the real caper, Sir G?'

'I don't know that one exists, Willie.'

'All right. What's your hunch about, then?'

'Kuwait,' said Tarrant. 'When you see the place now it's hard to realise that the oil only started gushing sixteen years ago. Today they load tankers at the rate of about forty thousand tons of crude oil every twenty-four hours. And the land holds a quarter of the world's known oil reserves.'

'My life,' said Willie, impressed. 'It could be a fair old caper, that.' He tapped the pamphlet. 'But this load of old cod's-wallop won't get anyone anywhere. It's just a laugh. Crackpot stuff.'

'We were in Kuwait for a few days about four years ago,'

58

Modesty said. 'It was no breeding-ground for revolution then, and I wouldn't imagine it's changed now.'

'Only for the better,' said Tarrant. 'It's a wealthy, well-governed little country.'

'So this man Solon with his freedom movement is just a joke, as Willie says?'

'Yes.' Tarrant looked at his float. 'It makes my Minister laugh, and it makes the Kuwaitis laugh. But it doesn't make *me* laugh. I seem to be the only one without a sense of humour.'

There was a long silence. Tarrant was aware that two very perceptive minds were assessing what he had said.

Modesty nodded towards the pamphlet Willie held. 'There must be more to it than this. Even for a hunch you need at least two items to complete the circuit.'

'Very true,' said Tarrant, and left it there.

Willie reeled in his line. As he prepared to lay the rod down in the boat Modesty held out her hand for it. He passed it to her. Stretching out her arms full-length at an angle, the butt of the rod gripped in both hands, she lowered the tip slightly until it just touched a leaf on a low-hanging branch above Tarrant.

Three times she lifted the rod away, and three times she lowered the tip delicately until it touched the same leaf. Willie watched her with interest and approval, giving a little nod of satisfaction each time.

'Would it be inquisitive to ask what you're doing?' Tarrant asked politely.

'I'm thinking.' Her eyes were intent as she touched the leaf again.

'Yes. But I'm curious about what you're actually doing, my dear.'

'Oh . . .' she gave a little laugh and handed the rod back to Willie. 'Just trying out something we thought up a while ago. An academic exercise. Nothing to do with what I was thinking.'

'I see. Or rather I don't. You leave me feeling a little baffled.'

'I'm sorry. I didn't mean to. Would you object if Willie and I went along to this meeting of the Kuwait Freedom Society?'

'I'd be delighted to know what you think of it. But may I ask you to be unobtrusive? Just as a precaution.'

'We're always very cautious, Sir Gerald. Will you be there?'

'Yes. But not on view.'

'Then perhaps you'll join us later at the penthouse, and tell us the other half of your hunch.'

'The meeting runs from eight till nine tomorrow evening,' said Tarrant. 'Shall I come to you soon after ten?'

'Yes. That should be about right.'

Tarrant's float bobbed, and he struck smoothly. For a minute there was no sound except the click of the reel and the flapping of the fat perch as he drew it alongside the boat. When he had unhooked the fish and tossed it into the basket Tarrant said: 'There's only one snag. I don't see how Willie can be in on this.'

'Eh?' Willie stared indignantly.

'I'm thinking of Melanie.' Tarrant's voice was urbane. 'Dark girl with the big mouth. You mentioned that you're taking her to Le Touquet tomorrow for a few days.'

Willie grinned and relaxed. 'Ah, that's all right,' he said. 'She's basically an eater. I mean food. Goes more for the food than the romance. It won't break little Melanie's 'eart if I call the trip off. I'll send 'er a bunch of violets and a pork pie instead.'

FOUR

IN a high, vaulted room of the ancient palace, Liebmann was finishing a lecture to a recent intake of men. They sat on folding benches, facing the huge screen on which a series of slides had been projected.

'. . . so by sixteen hundred hours,' Liebmann was saying as

he laid his pointer down on the table, 'all vital points will be in our hands; the airport, of course, and the seaport, Mina al Ahmadi, the barracks, the radio station, the police posts, and the whole of Kuwait City. All organised resistance, such as it is, will have been overcome long since.'

He looked at the map for a moment, then back to his audience. 'This ends phase four of Operation Sabre-Tooth, and you will then in theory come under the command of the new government, which will be flown in two hours earlier. But in fact the command structure will remain the same. The government will be concerned only with the political aspects of the situation. Are there any questions?'

A long-jawed Pole with crew-cut hair stood up.

'What is to be the function of the Flying Infantry after they have completed their part in phase one?' he asked in careful English.

'One section will assemble here at Jahra Gate, as a reserve,' said Liebmann. He picked up the pointer and touched the map now showing on the screen. 'The other section will be split up in pairs to patrol the city—that is, to control any unorganised resistance which may arise.'

'We shall have precise instructions?'

'You will have precise instructions on everything, Potocki.' The words were as cold as snow-flakes. 'This is a general briefing only, as I told you at the beginning.'

A fair-haired man with languid eyes and very full red lips stood up languidly. His name was Cogan, and six years earlier he had been cashiered from the British Army for beating an African native to death. Liebmann had cautious hopes of this man as a possible deputy commander. Despite Cogan's upper-class English manner he was tough and quick-thinking. He could well make a good leader of the kind Karz insisted on.

'The military side is charming,' Cogan said. He spoke with a well-bred drawl that was quite unaffected. 'It works. But we can't discard all pretence of interest in what happens next, Liebmann.' He waved a hand towards the map. 'We're all going to be there, where the shit's flying, so you can

61

hardly call it Unsound if we ask about the political moves. The British are bound to react, so are the Yanks and some of the Arab countries. How do we come *out* of it? And when?'

'Karz will brief you fully on this in due time,' Liebmann answered. 'For the moment I will give you a short outline. First, the whole operational method is designed to create confusion. The sixteen big air-freighters we shall use will consist of eight Lockheed Hercules' and eight Antonov An-12's. The anti-tank mines we shall sew around the perimeters of the city and port are British. The scooter-transport is Czech. The small fast scout-cars, modified for our own needs, are German. Our small-arms weaponry relies on the Armalite AR-15 with all its versatility as an automatic-rifle, a bipod machine-gun, and a grenade thrower——'

Liebmann broke off and shrugged. 'These examples are sufficient. Our aim is confusion on the political side. It is arranged that certain countries will at once denounce the operation as an American-backed coup. Absurd, of course, but a number of the new African countries will echo the cry.'

He put his hands in his pockets and looked towards Cogan, who had sat down now.

'You mention reaction,' he went on. 'There will be reaction, certainly. The Americans will waste time in hot denials. The British will run round in circles and argue fiercely among themselves on television programmes. Meanwhile Es-Sabah Solon will make a broadcast, announcing the take-over by his government and denying all foreign backing. He will speak of neo-colonial oppression, stooges, oil-masters, and the suffering, down-trodden people. His people of Kuwait.'

Liebmann's lips thinned in the semblance of a smile.

'Certain major countries, having first attacked the Americans for this coup, will then make a *volte-face*. They will give immediate recognition to the new government. A number of the young African countries will follow. Propaganda to this end has been carefully prepared. Es-Sabah Solon will invite a United Nations commission to Kuwait, to observe the elections he intends to hold. This will create a climate in which no major western power will make any counter-move against us. But the commission will not arrive because the standard delaying tactics will then be put into operation.'

Cogan laughed. Liebmann lifted a hand and continued.

'This brings us to twelve days after the coup,' he said. 'On the thirteenth day there will be a sudden crisis in one of the world's danger areas. It could be Berlin, or Malaysia, Cyprus or Formosa. I do not know where, and it is unimportant to us. All that matters is the crisis itself, to switch world attention.'

'Very nice,' said Cogan. 'One sees the pattern, and again it works. The rest of the world goes merrily on and our *fait accompli* remains just that. But we can't hold Kuwait down by force indefinitely. We want to draw our money and go home.'

'The internal arrangements will march in step with the external,' said Liebmann. 'The new government must secure backing from within. Some already exists—we have a small but well-organised fifth column there. If the government can secure only ten percent of the people, the *right* ten percent, there is no problem. A satisfactory police state can quickly be established.'

'How will this ten percent of the people be secured?' Cogan asked.

'By money and patronage, naturally. The oil revenues amount to over one billion dollars per year. With a quarter of that, one can buy all the support needed. A few undemocratic persons will be eliminated, of course. The press and radio will be at work all the time, in highly skilled hands. Those countries which depend upon Kuwait oil will quickly decide to negotiate with the new rulers. Within six weeks the country will be running quietly under the new regime. And then, Cogan, we can draw our pay and go home.'

Liebmann stopped speaking and looked round at the seated men. Some had listened closely, but most of them showed little interest. The political aspects meant nothing to them. He looked at Cogan and raised an eyebrow.

Cogan opened his mouth, then closed it again and shook his head.

'Quite right,' said Liebmann with a skeletal smile. 'Don't ever ask who our paymasters are, Cogan. That *would* be Unsound.'

Karz stood on a low shelf of rock near the side of a minor valley which branched west from the main valley, opposite the palace. His hands were clasped behind his back, and his stance was so immobile that he might have been carved from the rock on which he stood, a giant troll turned to stone by the coming of dawn.

He was watching a group of men fifty yards away being instructed in the handling of a one-man gun with a long barrel and a huge but lightweight cylinder under the breech. It was a weapon based on the Avroc forty-millimetre cannon, firing rocket-driven shells, self-loading from the drum magazine.

'Was the briefing satisfactory?' Karz said without turning his head. Liebmann, at his elbow, nodded. 'Yes. They grasped the plan readily. They are all experienced men.'

'No questions?'

'Nothing significant. Cogan, the Englishman, asked about the political follow-up.'

'Inquisitive?'

'No. He was intelligently concerned to know how the situation would be developed to a point where our forces could withdraw.'

'You explained?'

'In bare outline.'

'The men were satisfied?'

'Only five were interested. They were satisfied. I recommend a study of Cogan over the coming weeks. He has possibilities as a leader.'

A rocket-shell hissed from the 40 mm. cannon and burst against a tank-silhouette painted on the rock wall three hundred yards from the firing-point.

Karz said: 'Is there a message from the Recruiting Officer concerning Blaise and Garvin?'

'It just came in.' Liebmann unfolded a message slip on coarse buff paper. 'He agrees their value but doubts that a lever can be found to coerce them. On the other hand, if a sufficient lever *can* be found, he submits that no preliminary test of their capabilities will be necessary.'

Karz stirred, turning the massive head to look at Liebmann with reptilian eyes. 'His submission is rejected. In choice of commanders I delegate judgment to no man. Not even to you, Liebmann.'

'And if he can discover no lever?'

Karz looked at the training group again. He said slowly: 'This woman. This man. Their background. It is full of strange motivations and complexity.' The broad flat nostrils flared suddenly. 'Where there is complexity, a lever must exist. I know it, Liebmann, I smell it. You will instruct the Recruiting Officer to find it.'

The two men stood in silence for several minutes. On the far side of the firing range, where the minor valley widened, a dozen manlike shapes, grotesquely swollen, came into view. They were soaring through the air together in a great floating stride, like spacemen on a low-gravity planet. The shapes touched down a hundred paces on, then at once lifted again in another giant stride and passed out of view.

'We require a further thirty jump-suits for the Flying Infantry sections,' Liebmann said.

'You will have them tomorrow unless there is a freak storm.' Karz studied the hot clear sky. 'The Controllers are sending in two aircraft. Forty tons of stores.'

Liebmann nodded. A thought took shape in his mind, and he reviewed it carefully before speaking. At last he said: 'Are you satisfied with your budget for this operation, Karz?'

The lizard eyes blinked once. Karz said: 'Are you asking me how much it is?'

'No. Only if you are satisfied.'

'I have the equivalent of one hundred million dollars.'

Liebmann calculated rapidly. Forty-five million of air

transport; fifteen for weapons, ammunition, explosives; something over thirty million for payment to the mercenaries; a million or two for feeding and maintaining the tiny army throughout the training period and the operation; four million for the shipping arrangement and overheads. That left a small contingency reserve.

'It's a very good budget,' he said. 'I'm surprised at the amount.'

'You think it a large sum?'

'Yes.'

'The English spend as much in a week or two on gambling. It is cheap. A nothing when the outlay is balanced against the return.'

'Yes. The return is enormous. Better than the Tibet affair.'

'Far better. Our part of that occupied two years, and my budget was three times as large.'

Liebmann thought about the Tibet affair. It had contained some interesting aspects, but in the main it had been a matter of hunting and slaughter, which became tedious. This operation, with a compact army composed entirely of mercenaries, was infinitely more satisfying.

He folded the message slip and put it back in his pocket.

'I'll send your orders off at once,' he said. 'To the Recruiting Officer, about Blaise and Garvin.'

The lecture hall was old, small and shabby. It held seats for two hundred people. At one end was a low platform with faded curtains which remained permanently open because the runners had rusted and jammed. At the other end was a blank wall pierced by two small square holes, close together. Behind the wall, raised well above the floor-level of the hall, was the projection box.

Tarrant watched his man from The Department, Boothroyd, sorting and arranging the slides to be shown. The projection box was equipped with a Kershaw filmstrip and slide projector, and a Bell-Howell movie-projector with a four-inch lens.

66

Tarrant had studied a number of the slides. They were carefully selected to show Arab people in conditions of poverty, squalor and oppression. It was unlikely that any of the shots had actually been taken in Kuwait, but that was unimportant. Most of the people attending this lecture would believe anything they wanted to believe.

The audience would be made up of cranks, fools, foreign students, fervent idealists, and crackpots; there would be one or two people with very cold clear minds, comrades detailed to see if this could in any way provide grist for their mills; and perhaps there would be the odd heckler.

Tarrant thought wryly of the difficulty Jack Fraser, his lieutenant, had found in arranging for a man from The Department to handle the job of projectionist here this evening without arousing undue curiosity. It was the little things that were so damn difficult, Tarrant reflected. But Fraser had managed it smoothly.

Moving to the observation hatch, Tarrant looked down. The entrance to the hall lay at the far end, to the right of the platform. That made things a little difficult for Modesty and Willie. They could not slip in unobtrusively at the back. He wondered what they would do. Come in when the slides were showing and the hall was in semi-darkness, perhaps.

But Modesty, in particular, might well be noticed by one of the people with cold clear minds. In a place like this she would stand out like a race-horse in a cattle show.

Tarrant surveyed the hall. The two front rows were empty. About fifty people sat patiently on the wooden chairs. At intervals, more were entering singly or in pairs. Curious, thought Tarrant, that he had not yet seen a group of three or more.

A weary looking man came in and sat down at one end of a row. He took out a short-hand note-book, rested it on his knees, then leaned back as if closing his eyes to doze until the lecture started. The local reporter.

An Indian student with three or four books under one arm moved briskly along the right-hand aisle. He looked round, edged his way along a row of seats to a chair in the middle,

67

sat down, opened one of the books, and began to read intently.

A couple entered. The man wore a brown jacket which was part of a suit, and grey flannel trousers. A dull red tie hung over an off-white shirt with thin blue stripes. Greying hair showed beneath the cloth cap jammed firmly on his head. He had a tea-stained, untrimmed moustache and a beer-drinker's belly. He walked with a slight backward-leaning gait, belly thrust forward aggressively.

'Union man,' thought Tarrant. 'Brother Bloggs will now read the report from the Executive Committee.' He looked at the man's wife with sympathy. She was a sallow creature with wire-rimmed spectacles, walking nervously a half-pace behind her masterful husband. She wore a drooping black top-coat despite the warmth of the evening. Her hands appeared to be in thin brown gloves. On her head was a po-shaped cloche hat in dark felt.

'Home made,' Tarrant guessed. 'She goes to millinery classes on the evenings when the master is out at meetings.' He lifted the field-glasses which hung at his neck.

The man was pushing ponderously along one of the rows. His wife followed. With the magnification, Tarrant could see her lips move slightly as she murmured nervous apologies to those already seated. Her husband stopped and she bumped into him. He looked at her with angry contempt and jerked his head in command. She sat down, shoulders hunched like a frightened rabbit.

The man surveyed the hall with vague hostility, turning round slowly. For a moment he appeared to be looking directly at the hatch beside the projector. Tarrant felt a moment of uneasiness, then relaxed. He knew that he could not be seen. He had tested that possibility a good two hours ago.

Brother Bloggs put the tip of his little finger into his ear and wriggled it about irritably. Then he turned round, sat down, folded his arms, and leaned back, a picture of sturdy proletarianism.

'God Almighty,' Tarrant said softly, his voice awed.

68

Boothroyd looked up from his work. 'Anything wrong, sir?'

Tarrant moved to a chair and sat down, shaking with silent laughter. 'No,' he said at last in an odd voice, 'there's nothing wrong. It's just that I've spotted a couple of people I know rather well.'

Half-an-hour had gone by.

A grey-haired and eccentric M.P. had introduced Es-Sabah Solon.

Es-Sabah Solon had introduced his Minister of Foreign Affairs in the Free Kuwait Government, a man called Ridha Thuwaini.

The audience had applauded thinly.

The slides had been shown, accompanied by an impassioned and bitter commentary by Ridha Thuwaini, which had evoked somewhat heartier applause.

And now Es-Sabah Solon himself was speaking. He was a man of middle height in a medium-grey suit and a white shirt, with thick black hair and a sharp nose set between fiery eyes. His English was accented but clear. He gave an impression of smouldering fervour combined with reason and integrity. His appearance and manner were strangely at odds with the absurdity of his theme.

With professorial confidence he had shown on the screen some complicated charts of lineage to prove his title as the true ruler of Kuwait. He had referred to the shameful pictures already shown, as proof that his suffering people were crying out for liberation. And now he was talking in cryptic terms of the future.

'Tyranny holds the seeds of its own destruction.' His voice was low-pitched but carried clearly to the back of the small hall. 'Oppression produces the *will* and the *means* to secure liberation. One day . . .' he paused and surveyed his audience slowly, 'one day *soon*, my friends, the oppressors and their stooges will feel the weight of our anger. We are not without strength. Slowly we are building an army of dedicated men to take what is rightfully ours, so that the fresh winds of

69

freedom can blow through the little country we love.'

Es-Sabah Solon placed the palms of his hands together and spoke with slow emphasis.

'Will you support us? I believe you will. But you ask me —how? I will tell you. We do not ask for money.' A faint stir of approval rippled through the audience. 'We ask only for your goodwill! We ask you to work for us, to create a climate of opinion in which our aims will be seen to be the honest, true, and democratic aims that they are. Will you write to your representative in Parliament—*your* Parliament, the Mother of Democracy? Will you write to the Press? Will you bring motions in your unions and in your party meetings —no matter what that party may be?'

With each question Es-Sabah Solon clapped his hands softly together, for emphasis.

'Will you help us to tell the whole world that we *exist*? That we have a great and good cause? And when the time comes, when we strike our great blow for the four hundred thousand prisoner-population of Kuwait, will you then acclaim our work with all your might and be every means?'

He stretched his arms wide.

'You are free people. I ask you to help *my* people, who are in chains.' He was silent for a long moment, then added in a voice unsteady with emotion. 'I do not think you will fail them.'

There was a patter of applause. Es-Sabah Solon sipped a glass of water while the grey-haired M.P. asked if there were any questions.

A man with a white face and bitter eyes stood up, cleared his throat nervously, and said: 'I'd like to ask the gentleman what he meant about an army. Does he mean that he's prepared to use *violence*?'

'No!' Es-Sabah Solon was on his feet, voice firm and tinged with indignation. 'The Free Kuwait Government will *never* initiate any act of violence. What must be made clear is that war already *exists* in Kuwait—war between the helpless, unarmed people and their foreign-backed rulers.' He shook his head gravely. 'If those poor people . . . the men, the women, the little children, cry out for help, then we cannot deny them whatever defence we can provide.'

Somebody clapped loudly. The white-faced man sat down, looking vaguely baffled.

The Indian student stood up and spoke rapidly, his clipped words running together. 'I do not understand your assertion which you have made as I understand it that the Free Kuwait Government possesses armed forces. It is certainly a well-known fact which everybody knows that to sustain armed forces requires considerable finance. How do you account for this anomalous position? And where could such an army be based?'

Es-Sabah smiled with a touch of admiration.

'There speaks a shrewd and practical young man,' he said. 'His question demands a straightforward answer, and I will give it. Over the past two years my Government and I have travelled the world, speaking to all people as we have spoken to you tonight. Everywhere we have won support—everywhere! We ask for no money, but it is pressed upon us by rich and poor alike.'

The audience stirred uneasily. Was there to be a collection after all?

'You ask how we can support our army,' said Es-Sabah Solon, 'and I answer that *you* and all the men and women of goodwill are supporting us *now*—with your thoughts and your sympathy and your understanding.'

The audience relaxed.

'You ask if our army exists? I answer, yes. It exists in the hearts of the volunteers who have said they will give their blood for us when the time comes—volunteers of every race, colour and creed. But we pray that this army may never be needed. That our people shall throw off their chains without bloodshed. And that the aggressors shall fall under the weight of their own evil.'

There was a round of applause. Watching through the hatch, Tarrant caught his breath slightly, for as the Indian student sat down the cloth-capped head and thickset body of Willie Garvin were rising. For a moment Tarrant frowned,

71

then relaxed. This was right. Brother Bloggs would never miss a chance to hear his own voice.

'Mr. Chairman.' The voice was gruff and abrupt. 'As a member of the British proletariat, I would like to say on their be'alf that you 'ave our monolithic support. I intend to raise this matter at the next meeting of our union branch committee, in which I 'ave the honour to 'old a position of some influence. And I shall leave no stone unturned in persuading my fellow-members that a motion should go forward at the next Congress, pledging the support of the workers in any attempt to overthrow the decadent an' war-mongering clique 'oo at present 'old the people of Koo-white under their iron 'eels.'

Willie looked about him with aggressive satisfaction, wiped a finger across his untidy moustache, and sat down.

The grey-haired M.P. said: 'Ah ... thank you.'

Brother Bloggs jabbed an elbow into his wife's arm. She began to clap. It was taken up in a desultory fashion, then petered out.

In the projection box, Boothroyd flickered a furtive glance at his chief. He was a young man, very low in the hierarchy of The Department, and until this evening Sir Gerald Tarrant had been little more than a name to him, a remote being whom the old hands in the higher grades referred to as 'the squire' or sometimes 'the head boy'.

He was a likeable old bastard, Boothroyd decided, and wondered what was amusing him now. Tarrant stood with his back to the wall beside the observation hatch, eyes half closed, wearing a small dreamy smile of pleasure. He was, in fact, memorising the scene, memorising Willie's words, for later retailing to his assistant, Jack Fraser.

'..."*Oo at present 'old the people of Koo-white under their iron 'eels,*"' thought Tarrant, rejoicing. 'Jack will love that. But dear God, how does Modesty keep a straight face?'

FIVE

THE LIFT halted and the doors slid open. Tarrant stepped out into the foyer, then stopped short. Weng was standing in front of him, a finger pressed to pursed lips. Tarrant's eyebrows lifted in query. Weng took the hat and umbrella from him and with a suppressed smile pointed across the foyer to the big room beyond.

The skilful lighting glinted on black and white and gold, the motif of the décor. The glorious rugs, which always struck deep chords in Tarrant, were scattered pools of rich and glowing colour.

Modesty Blaise was on her hands and knees, a head-scarf bound over her eyes. She wore dark green silk trousers and a sleeveless black silk blouse with a low scoop-neck. Her feet were in open sandals with plaited gold straps. Her hair was again piled in a chignon on the crown of her head.

The only jewellery she wore was a heavy bracelet of exquisitely carved jet. Tarrant knew that she had carved it herself in the fully-equipped lapidary workshop established in one of the smaller rooms of the penthouse.

She had a figure that could wear slacks, thought Tarrant, even kneeling as she was now, beside one of the Barcelona chairs, her head cocked, listening intently. In one hand she held a rolled-up newspaper.

On the other side of the room, Lucille squatted on her haunches in a pink nightdress. She too was blindfold and held a club of newspaper. Willie Garvin, in dark slacks and a pale grey open-weave cotton shirt with a drawstring neck, crouched in the middle of the room on one knee, a handkerchief round his eyes. Tarrant could see the small black radar-device clipped on his right ear. Under one of Willie's hands lay a loosely-crumpled ball of brown paper. In his other hand was a rolled newspaper.

Tarrant stood still, watching. Modesty backed round the chair, feeling her way. Silently she emerged on the other side. Lucille crawled slowly forward, then paused.

73

Willie edged sideways, and the crumpled brown paper rustled under his hand. Modesty registered the sound and began to crawl forward warily. Lucille pulled her blindfold down so that one eye was showing. Rising a little, she scuttled forward like a spider, the rolled newspaper lifted.

Willie's head snapped round. He said: 'Cheat!' His long arm swung and the club of newspaper thwacked against the side of Lucille's head. The child said 'Ow!' indignantly and fell over sideways in her belated attempt to dodge. Willie pulled off his blindfold and knelt up, looking at her.

'Cheats never prosper,' he said with pious severity.

'What happened?' Modesty lifted her blindfold and looked at Lucille. 'Did you peek, darling?'

'Yes, she did,' said Willie. All three were kneeling up now. 'I knew it from the bleeps. She couldn't've come in that fast without looking.'

Lucille said plaintively: 'He hit me hard that time, Modesty.'

'Now don't stir it up,' said Willie, and grinned. 'You can't hit anyone hard with a newspaper.' He rose, picked up Lucille, and tossed her across his shoulders like a yoke. 'But that's what 'appens when you get caught cheating, see?'

'He means that's what happens when you cheat,' Modesty amended hastily. She saw Tarrant standing in the wide foyer and got to her feet with a smile. 'I'm sorry, Sir Gerald. We didn't hear you arrive.'

'You were concentrating on other things,' said Tarrant, and came down the steps into the room to take Modesty's hand. Lying across Willie's shoulders, Lucille said politely: 'Good evening.'

'Ah, hallo Lucille.' Tarrant heard the false joviality in his voice with despair. 'Have a nice game?'

'Yes, thank you.'

'Good. Well—ah . . .'

'Bed,' said Willie cheerfully. 'Come on Lucy-love. Say goodnight to Modesty and Sir Gerald.'

'Goodnight, Modesty.' A cool kiss on the cheek. 'Goodnight, Sir Gerald.' Awkwardly Tarrant gave the small hand a pat. Willie moved off with his burden and disappeared along a passage leading from the foyer.

'Do sit down while Weng and I tidy the place up,' Modesty said, and began to push some of the furniture back into place where it had been moved to make room for the blindfold game.

'I'd rather wander round if I may,' said Tarrant. He strolled across to the broad curving shelves in the corner.

The lion clock after Caffieri had gone, together with the Sèvres plates and several other pieces he remembered. They had been replaced by a Dutch friendship goblet, a pair of George II Corinthian pillar candlesticks, and a group of Japanese *netsuke* carved in ivory.

Weng gathered up the newspaper clubs and went out to the kitchen.

'I'm afraid I'm not good with children,' Tarrant confessed as Modesty came to stand beside him. 'And I find Lucille particularly baffling.'

'In what way?'

'She's very withdrawn. The way she looks at one is disconcerting. Even with you and Willie she seems . . .' He hesitated. 'I don't know. Wary, perhaps? Lacking in warmth? Not very affectionate, all things considered?'

Modesty looked at him curiously. 'Why should she be affectionate? Willie's given her a comfortable life for the last three years, and I've helped a little. But she was probably much happier in the old life, for all its squalor.'

Tarrant stared. 'Happier?'

'Yes. It was a life she knew and understood.'

'But she has security now. Isn't that what children are supposed to need most? She has you and Willie behind her.'

'That's the point, perhaps. We're behind her but we can't ever be really with her, not in a family sense. And this other kind of security,' her gesture took in the penthouse, 'it doesn't mean very much. In fact it weakens your springs if you're not careful.'

Tarrant smiled. 'Most people are ready to let their springs

75

be weakened under such pleasant conditions. You're a little different, perhaps. But I would have thought Lucille would adapt—and at least feel some degree of gratitude.'

'But why, if she's not happy? We do the best we can, but in a way it's a pity we can't put the clock back. It would probably have been better for Lucille in the long run if Willie hadn't picked her up that day when her parents were killed.'

Tarrant was shocked. 'You're being very hard, surely?'

She laughed, looking at him in surprise. 'I'm only saying what might have been best for her. It's odd for you to talk about being hard.'

'For me? But why?'

'Because you're a very hard and ruthless man, Sir Gerald. You have to be.'

'On the contrary, I should be, but in fact I'm a sentimental old gentleman.'

'That's even worse. It means you have to be harder still, because otherwise you might let sentiment affect your work.' Mischief danced suddenly in her eyes. 'I have a friend who's a sentimental old gentleman and who runs some cryptic department in the Foreign Office. But I don't think he's going to let sentiment prevent him making use of me, if he can.'

Tarrant sighed. '*Touché*,' he said ruefully. 'But perhaps he's only doing it because he believes you rather want him to make use of you. Couldn't you, in a sense, be using *him*?'

'I'm sure he can take care of himself. And he's not really so old.' She put a hand through his arm and moved towards the deep-buttoned chesterfield. 'Now, what will you drink?'

'Thank you. But I won't have one just now.'

'Have you eaten?' When he hesitated she went on: 'No, you haven't. Willie and I have been busy this evening, too, so I've had Weng make up three trays of cold chicken and salad. I thought we could eat informally while we talked—or would that be too barbarous?'

'It would suit me admirably. By the way, I'm well aware that you and Willie were busy this evening.'

'You were in the projection box?'

76

'Yes. But I only spotted you when Willie looked straight at the hatch and put a finger in his ear. It reminded me of the radar-gadget. Tell me, did you have rubber pads in your cheeks?'

'Yes. It's the simplest way to change the shape of the face.'

'Willie's declaration of support for the Cause was a gem. You must have found it difficult to hide your appreciation of it.'

'No.' She looked at him soberly. 'I wasn't just wearing drab clothes and a different face. I was tired and self-conscious and a little bit afraid of my husband. We wouldn't play a thing like that for laughs, not after you'd asked us to be unobtrusive.'

Willie came into the room looking apprehensive. 'Lucille's not finished 'alf those lessons she was supposed to do during the 'oliday, Princess. She just told me.' He ran a harassed hand through his hair. 'That Mother Bernard, she'll 'ave my guts for garters.'

Modesty began to laugh.

'S'all very well, Princess,' Willie said plaintively, 'but she frightens me to death.'

'You'll just have to send a letter saying how pleased you feel she'll be that Lucille has managed to get through half her holiday task. And enclose a donation to that new library fund the school sent a circular about.'

Relief swept the clouds from Willie's brow. '*Keep me as the apple of an eye; hide me under the shadow of thy wings,*' he said gratefully. 'Psalm seventeen, verse eight. Are we going to eat now?'

'Yes. Will you give Weng a hand with the trays? Then he can go off to that discotheque he's so keen on.'

Tarrant looked at his watch. 'Would it be convenient to put on the television in about ten minutes?' he asked. 'Our friend Es-Sabah Solon is being briefly interviewed.'

'On television?' Modesty stared. 'The Kuwait ambassador won't like that much.'

'It's something of a comedy programme and I pulled a few wires to get him on it. They call it *Some People* . . . and they

77

interview odd characters with quaint ideas. Solon will be on early, just for two minutes, after a Flat Earther, I believe.'

'What's funny about the idea of a Flat Earth?' Willie asked, moving towards the kitchen. 'You don't believe all that rubbish about it being round, do you?'

Fifteen minutes later, as Tarrant finished the last morsel of an excellent chicken salad, Es-Sabah Solon came on the screen. He said little they had not heard already that evening, but on one point the suave interviewer tried to pin him down.

'Do you say that this Army of Liberation actually exists and that it will one day attack Kuwait, Mr. Solon?'

'Not *attack*.' The answer came sharply. 'It will *defend* Kuwait against those who now occupy my country.'

'But it will have to go there to do so, surely?'

'It will go there, if need be, to defend the people against their oppressors.'

'And does this army exist, not just as an idea, but in terms of men and materials?'

Es-Sabah Solon pursed his lips. 'I do not think this is the proper time for me to give a full answer to that question. I would need the approval of my Cabinet, and I am sure they would not approve of any revelation which might hamper our plans and delay the coming of freedom and democracy to our little country.'

'Thank you, Mr. Solon.'

The camera closed on the interviewer's face. With a faint smile he said: 'That was Es-Sabah Solon, who claims to lead the Free Kuwait Government. And now we turn to Mr. Henry Tollit, of Surbiton, who claims to have fairies at the bottom of his garden and who has taken a number of photographs to prove it.'

Modesty thumbed the remote control button to switch off the set and said: 'No, sit still, Willie.' She collected the trays, went out to the kitchen, and returned with a small trolley set out for coffee. When she had served Tarrant and Willie she poured a cup for herself and settled down again at one end of the chesterfield.

'This Solon business is still no more than a joke so far,' she said, looking at Tarrant. 'What's the other factor in your hunch?'

'Mercenaries.' Tarrant looked down at his coffee. 'We do keep an eye on these people who crop up wherever there's trouble. Some of them are all right. They did a good job in the Congo—ask the people they pulled out. But there are quite a few who'd cut anybody's throat for a fiver. And a surprising number of these have just faded out of circulation recently. Nobody knows where they've gone.'

'You mean just our own blokes? British?' Willie asked.

'All nationalities, so far as I can check.' Tarrant stirred his coffee and looked apologetic. 'My feeling is that Solon might be crying "Wolf" to conceal the reality of his Liberation Army. And also to prepare the ground for world reaction after the army strikes.'

There was a long silence. Tarrant felt a touch of relief at seeing no immediate stare of incredulity from Modesty or Willie. They were reflecting soberly. Now and again they glanced at each other as if in some curious telepathic exchange. The silence lasted a full three minutes.

'But you'd need a proper base somewhere in striking distance, Princess,' Willie said at last, as if continuing a discussion.

She nodded. 'That would be the main snag. Apart from the backing, of course—and the backing is more of a question than a snag.' She looked at Tarrant. 'Russia, China—or both, I suppose?'

'It could even be both,' he agreed. 'They can fight on the ideological front but at the same time co-operate very closely in practical matters——' Tarrant broke off and stared. 'Are you accepting this idea as possible?'

'It's more in Willie's field than mine, but he thinks it makes reasonable sense so far.'

'My masters don't agree. They say an enormous operation of this nature couldn't possibly be prepared in secret.'

'What's enormous about it?' Willie said with scorn. 'Given the weapons you can get today, one man carries the firepower you needed a *tank* for in the last war. Look at the Stoner rifle an' machine-gun system the Yanks are developing—six weapons in one, with interchangeable components. Look at Redeye and the M79 and the Avroc gun. Kuwait's only a little place. No army to speak of. One battalion of the right blokes with the right weapons and transport could knock it off in twenty-four hours.'

'You think it would be a simple military operation?'

'Simple? Jesus, no! You'd need weeks of paperwork just on the battle-plan, and good Intelligence. You'd need the right men and the right weaponry and a few really red 'ot blokes in charge. Then you'd 'ave to be able to put them on the spot at the right time, with all the equipment.'

Modesty said: 'That brings us back to the big snag. A base within striking distance.'

'You can strike from a long way off these days, Princess,' Willie said thoughtfully. 'I can't see just how that bit works, but I don't reckon it's impossible.' He grinned suddenly at Tarrant. 'Look, you can get a better opinion than mine on this. I'm no general.'

'I've taken an expert military opinion,' Tarrant said. 'It corresponds roughly to your own.' He thought of the long bookshelves in Willie's living-room. One whole shelf was occupied by well-thumbed books on combat, weaponry, battles and campaigns. He added: 'I'm not surprised.'

Modesty said: 'Are you afraid of a *fait accompli*?'

'Yes. This is the age for that sort of thing.' He made a small uncertain gesture. 'I'm also afraid that my imagination may be running away with me.'

'It could be,' she agreed. 'Are there any other factors?'

'I'm not sure.' He gave a wry shrug. 'Once you start building a theory you can make anything fit in. But the C.I.A. believe that Solon had a secret meeting with a Soviet official in Istanbul, and Léon Vaubois tells me Solon was in contact with a Chinese Embassy man in Beirut. They don't attach great significance to it. Solon is trying to build himself up as the ruler-in-exile of Kuwait, so these people may feel they can make use of him as a nuisance value, anyway.'

'We still got no other explanation for the cut-throat boys disappearing,' Willie said.

'That's the big factor.' Modesty signed for Tarrant to help himself to a cigar from the humidor at his elbow as she spoke.

Again there was silence. Tarrant lit his cigar carefully, then sat back waiting for further questions or comment. After a while he became conscious that no more was going to be said. Modesty Blaise and Willie Garvin were simply looking at him.

'Ah ... well.' He sat up a little, frowning at the tip of his cigar. 'The thought did occur to me that if somebody is recruiting the cream of the mercenaries, then your names might well have been set down on a list somewhere at some time.'

'They'd be recruiting the dregs, not the cream, Sir G.,' Willie said politely.

'It's all in a point of view. I'm not talking in terms of morality. Let's say that for an affair like this the people concerned would have to recruit the most dangerous and experienced men they could find who were willing to serve on such an operation.'

'We may have figured on a long-list,' Modesty said, her eyes thoughtful, 'but that's about all. I've never been for hire, and neither has Willie since he joined me. That was a long while ago.' She looked at Tarrant with a hint of puzzlement. 'We've never been approached, if that's what you're asking. And I don't think we shall be. We're just not in that kind of orbit.'

'I know.' Tarrant relaxed, looking with a regretful air at a Braque still life on the wall. 'I can't think of any way that you could contrive to move down into the right orbit, where you *might* attract an approach ... and I couldn't possibly expect you to do such a thing, anyway.' He drew on his cigar. 'That really is a splendid Braque.'

She did not answer. The only sound in the room was the soft, precise tick from the Japy Frères movement of the French ormolu clock.

Modesty Blaise stubbed out her cigarette. She leaned back

81

in the corner of the deep chesterfield and put her hands behind her head. Tarrant saw that her eyes were open but unseeing, focused on some far-distant point. With gentle pleasure, void of desire, he dwelt on the smooth swell of her breasts beneath the silk blouse.

She had a magnificent body. Tarrant knew, for he had seen it once. Pictures flickered suddenly in his memory.

A studio in old Cannes ... Willie's knife hissing across the room to bite deep into a gunman's arm ... Modesty lying with thumbs cruelly bound, speaking the word that held back the second knife, poised for a death-throw ... Willie lifting her, and the slashed housecoat falling away to her waist.

The scenes were printed on Tarrant's memory in colour, and for this he was grateful. Few pictures in the files of his memory had retained the quality of colour. He was grateful, too, that the urgent fire of younger days smouldered only gently within him now. He could look at his memory-picture of her with a pleasure untinged by desire. And he could look at her now, not regretting that the smooth matt tan of her body was hidden from him, but enjoying the different pleasure of light and shade and the way the silk moulded itself to her shape.

Willie Garvin tapped him on the knee and moved quietly towards the plate-glass door beside the huge window. Tarrant rose and followed him out on to the terrace. Willie lit a cigarette and leant on the stone balustrade, contemplating London at night.

'What exactly is happening?' Tarrant asked politely.

'You're a crafty old bastard, aren't you, Sir G.?' Willie grinned as he spoke.

'I'm not sure that I qualify on all three counts. But you haven't answered my question.'

'She's thinking,' said Willie. 'In top gear.' He looked at Tarrant. 'I've only seen her go like this about four times, ever. You've really pressed a button somewhere.'

Tarrant drew the fresh night air into his lungs and counted the stars in Orion. They were all present, he noted with approval. Neither man spoke for a while. Modesty Blaise and

Willie Garvin both had a rare gift for companionable silence, and this was one of their qualities which Tarrant never failed to enjoy.

A thought occurred to him, and he said: 'Do you think the Gabriel affair you managed for me might have blown you with your old contacts?'

'No.' Willie shook his head. 'The rumour went round that Modesty was after that ten million quidsworth of diamonds 'erself—and only missed out because Gabriel got under our feet. It was a big enough take for her to make a once-only comeback from retirement.'

'That's very good. How did the rumour get started.'

'We started it. Just drop a word or two in 'alf-a-dozen of the right places and the thing freewheels on its own.'

'Is my social contact with Modesty a danger?'

Willie considered. He said: 'Not worth worrying about. There's only a handful of people who know you run The Department, and they wouldn't wonder about 'er keeping in touch. The way they see it, if she's in business it's an asset and if she's not it don't matter.'

The door to the big L-shaped terrace opened and Modesty came out. Her eyes held a new sparkle, and there was a controlled eagerness in her walk as she moved to join the two men. She was as close to showing excitement as Tarrant had ever seen her.

'Willie,' she said, and put her hand over his as it rested on the coping, 'I think we might be able to manage it. There are two or three things that can work for us if we're quick. Do you want to try?'

'That bunch of violets and the pork pie didn't come off too well with Melanie,' he said, 'so I'm between girls. Only thing is, can we do it in time? If someone's recruiting mercenaries, we don't know 'ow long it's going to last.'

'That's an x-factor, and we can't do anything about it. But I think we can put ourselves in the right orbit pretty fast. And we'll be trying out that idea you developed, the one you showed me a few weeks back, remember? First you see it, then you don't.'

'Blimey!' A happy grin lit Willie's face. 'I was only doodling. Never thought we'd get a chance to work it for real.'

Tarrant listened without comprehending, and decided to stay with the main question. 'How long will it take to get yourselves set up?' he asked.

She rested her forearms on the coping and looked out over the park which stretched away to the south. 'Two weeks, I hope. And then, if your hunch is right, Sir Gerald, I think we'll be going down the mercenary pipeline to see what's at the other end.'

Tarrant looked at the bare arm close to his hand, at the long neck rising from the blouse, and the firm, lovely lines of breast, waist and thigh. He thought with a pang of grief how vulnerable was human flesh and bone, and he felt the familiar touch of sour distaste for himself and for his work.

'I hope to God I'm wrong,' he said.

SIX

IT was hot in the great valley. The caps of snow on the lower ridges had grown smaller, but the distant and towering peaks still lay under their eternal blanket of white.

Sarrat sat on a rock beside Hamid and watched a small truck with a long trailer move past. The trailer was piled with food-stores unloaded from the big Hercules which had landed on the airstrip below the lake half-an-hour earlier.

The truck halted and a team of men began to load hand-trolleys, wheeling them up the ramp into the side of the palace where the refrigeration plant was established.

Fifty yards away, under the shade of light awnings, some thirty women lay on rush mats or stood in little groups talking. They were of many nationalities, mainly Asiatic but with a good proportion of Latin and fair-skinned Europeans. Their ages ranged from under twenty to the mid-thirties. All

84

were clean, well-groomed and well-fed. The care and main-
tenance of the *seraglio*'s occupants was laid down as being of
prime importance.

Some of the women wore thin silk dresses, others beach
shorts and shirts. A few wore swim-suits, all of modern cut
and fashion. One girl lay on her back in the sun, arms and
legs spread, eyes closed, completely naked.

Sarrat grinned as he looked towards the group. That was
Leila, the French-Chinese girl from Bangkok. She was a
nymphomaniac. Surprisingly, she was nowhere among the
favourites with the men. New drafts coming in would be told
of Leila's great appetite and fantastic variations. They would
rub their hands, try her once, and later boast coarsely and in
detail of all they had achieved. But they would not book her
for an all-night again.

Leila kept stirring now as she lay in the sun, turning a
little from side to side, hoping to catch the attention of the
men as they passed by.

Sarrat thought of his own experience with her. After three
hours, himself sated, he had become so enraged by her per-
sistence that he could readily have knocked her senseless. But
that was impossible. Karz allowed no damage to personnel of
his Women's Section, as he called it. One man had faced The
Twins and died for an infringement of that iron rule. And so
Leila had persisted—more than that, she had finally hinted
threateningly at what might happen if she raked her own
body with her long nails and screamed for Maya, the
madame.

Sarrat sweated as he remembered the rest of that night and
all that she had made him do in her frenetic search for satisfaction. He could raise a grin about it now, and enjoy the
thought of others suffering the same humiliation, but it had
not been amusing at the time.

'You have been with Leila?' he said to Hamid. The Arab
made a faint grimace of scorn and held up one hand with
thumb and finger a little apart.

'One short-time,' he said. 'She is no good for a man.'

'But she has much——' Sarrat slapped a palm against his

85

bicep and winked encouragingly. He hoped to lure Hamid into an all-night booking with Leila. The short-time gave her no chance to become really difficult.

Hamid wrinkled his jutting nose. 'No man can give that one pleasure, Sarrat.'

'What matter?'

'It matters nothing—if you are a monkey. For a man it is failure. It unmakes him in his pride.'

Sarrat laughed, his heavy body shaking. 'You bloody Arabs,' he said.

Hamid shrugged. They sat in silence, watching the men as they worked and the women at ease under the awnings. Not all the women were here. The full strength of the *seraglio* was just over fifty. Most were volunteers, to the extent that they had taken an unspecified job, knowing only what their work would be, in return for a large sum of money paid into a bank in advance.

On the whole they were not curious about the purpose of this strange little army, but were content with their situation. A few, perhaps ten in all, were not volunteers. Three at least had been bought as slaves in Saúdi Arabia, and Sarrat knew there were two Hungarian girls and three Chinese who had been political prisoners in their own countries. For them, once the life here had been accepted it was no doubt better than the life they had left.

Hamid said: 'Karz will not consider making a promotion to commander yet?'

'No.' Sarrat slapped at a fly on the back of his neck. 'He waits for word on Blaise and Garvin.'

Hamid massaged the butt of the M-16 rifle lying across his knees and shook his head. 'It is foolish. Who will follow a woman?'

'She is formidable.'

'But she is a woman.'

'Karz sent to the Controllers for her record. A full dossier came in yesterday on the Dove.' This was the twin-engined de Havilland Dove, the six-passenger aircraft which plied as a runabout from the valley, where it was based, to Kabul in the south, and north to a point unknown to any except the two pilots and Karz.

'He still wants this woman?' asked Hamid.

'More so, now that he has read her dossier.'

The Arab stared into space for a while. 'Has there been further news from the Recruiting Officer?' he said at last.

'A message yesterday.'

'Good or bad?'

'Both. He says the woman may have connections with a man who may have connections with British Intelligence.'

'Ah. And the good?'

'Something has occurred with Modesty Blaise. There are a dozen rumours. Suddenly she is on the move, restless.' Sarrat gestured with a muscular hand. 'France, Athens, Beirut, all in a few days.'

'For what reason?'

'She gambles. This is not new. But she gambles for great sums in the *salles privées*. This is new.'

'Why is it good?'

'Karz speaks of a lever. This new thing of hers is a weakness. Karz says that any weakness may provide a lever.'

Hamid spat, and his lean fingers caressed the rifle. 'May...' he echoed scornfully. 'Karz should choose two good men and promote them.'

Sarrat did not answer at once, and when he did it was in a voice too low for the men working nearby to hear. 'Hamid, this is your first time with Karz, heh?'

'Yes.'

'Then remember what he told us at the beginning. I have been with him before and I have heard it three times. The men we lead are animals. There are very few of our kind, yours and mine, Hamid, who can mould and lead a section of these men in the way Karz demands.'

'Pah! There are many who can lead.'

'Not who can lead wolves like these. And not in this kind of operation. Most men have ties with a country or some foolish cause.' Sarrat grunted with contempt. 'They are not like us.'

87

Hamid reflected. 'We may get the woman and she may fail. The man also.'

'That is for Karz to worry about.' Sarrat grinned and got to his feet. 'Leave it to him, Hamid. With or without Blaise and Garvin, he will have all things ready when the day of Sabre-Tooth comes.'

Willie Garvin held the blonde girl tightly until her warm body had stopped shaking. He kissed her, gently this time, then turned on his side and lay with his head propped on one hand, watching her. The bed-covers lay in a rumpled heap on the floor.

The early evening, Willie reflected, was really his favourite time for it. Later they could take a cab from her flat, dine at *Ehmke*, where he would once again test the theory about oysters, then on to St. Pauli and a nightclub; a few drinks, a little dancing, and a stroll up Davidstrasse and along the bright, narrow parade where the girls sat in shop windows on display, waiting for the occasional customer from among the throng of sight-seers; and so home to bed again for a couple of hours before he had to unwind himself from Ilse's arms and legs to reach the airport in time for his plane.

Ilse opened her eyes and patted his cheek. 'I'm glad you came, Willie.' Her English held an American inflexion.

She got out of bed, brought cigarettes and two ashtrays from the dressing-table, then lay down on her back beside him again.

'Wish I could stop on for a bit,' he said.

'You have to go?' The match burned down almost to her fingers as she stared at him in regret.

'M'mm. Sorry.' He blew out the match and lit his cigarette from hers. 'But I don't 'ave to go till two in the morning, so we can make an evening of it.'

'Ah, that's fine. But why must you go then?'

'Got to see a man in Rome.'

'A man?' She winked at him without resentment. 'I bet he's got these on him.' She patted herself twice.

'Why would I go to Rome for that, when I've got you 'ere?'

'Because you like a change. And you like dark girls best, not blondes.'

'Who says so?'

'I say so. It's because of Modesty, I expect. How is she, Willie?'

He took his time blowing out a long feather of smoke, then said shortly: 'She's all right.'

'Well you needn't say hallo to her for me. I don't like her too much.'

'Why not? She treated you pretty good, Ilse.'

'Maybe that's why. You want to notice, Willie—you do people favours and they don't like you.'

'Some people.'

'Oh, I don't really not like her. I'm just a little jealous, I guess.'

Willie said nothing, frowning up at the ceiling. Ilse turned on her side and propped herself on one elbow, looking at him. 'Hey, Willie. That was a funny way you said "All right", just now when I asked about Modesty. Is something wrong?'

'Nothing really. I'm just a bit worried.'

'About Modesty?'

'M'mm. I don't know what started it, but she's suddenly acting sort of wild. Been gambling a lot.'

'But she never did that. I mean, not heavy gambling, did she?'

'Not when there was plenty of other things to keep 'er busy.' Willie sighed and shook his head. 'But it's different now. The way she's been going on, it's . . .' he hesitated as if veering away from something close to disloyalty. '. . . well, not very sensible, you might say.'

'She loses?'

'Up and down. But it's the way she gambles. Really plunging.'

Ilse studied him with intelligent eyes. Once she had been a small cog in *The Network*. Her job had simply been to associate with financiers and industrialists, a listening post to

89

pick up fragments of information. What use Modesty Blaise made of that information she did not know or care. She received her assignments from Bauer, who was Modesty's branch manager in Germany, and she gave her reports to him. She thought they were probably used for industrial espionage, where the return could be very high.

Because Ilse had a glacial beauty which challenged men to thaw her, the work had been easy. She rarely had to sleep with a man to learn what she wanted to know, and even then the choice was her own. If she reported failure on an assignment, no questions or pressure came down through Bauer.

It might have been different now, with Bauer in sole charge. That was why, when Modesty split up *The Network* and retired, Ilse had chosen to be paid off rather than to stay on under Bauer. She now owned a half-share in a thriving hotel-restaurant and led a pleasantly comfortable life. Bauer owned the other half-share and she saw him often, but only for business. She would pass on any casual gossip which might interest him, but had made it plain that she would take no more assignments.

'You know what I think, Willie?' she said, and put a hand on his chest. 'Maybe Modesty doesn't like to have no work to do, and she would be glad if she lost all her money and had to start again.'

Willie stared in astonished disbelief, but before he could speak she went on quickly: 'No, don't tell me it's silly. Maybe she doesn't really know that she feels like this, and it's just a sort of . . .' her English failed and she frowned in annoyance. 'A sort of thing you can't help doing, you know?'

'A compulsion?'

'Ah, yes. That. A psychological thing.'

'Could be, I s'pose.' Willie inhaled gloomily on his cigarette. He was well satisfied. Unless he told Ilse not to, she would speak of this to Bauer, and the word would run on through the grapevine. He had already set it going in Paris, and tomorrow he would be in Rome.

There he would be meeting Calvanti, to sell three sculptured rubies for Modesty, magnificent stones carved by her

90

own hands in the lapidary's workshop set up in her pent-house. And by good fortune, Tasso would be over from Athens. It wouldn't be long before everyone who mattered knew the story.

Willie felt a touch of relief that after Jeanette in Paris yesterday and Ilse here today he would have no bedroom duties in Rome. Awareness of his relief brought a sudden wave of alarm.

'Jesus,' he thought. 'I'm slipping!'

Ilse had got up and put on a white silk-velvet dressing gown. Already she had the remote, frigid look which belied her potentialities.

Willie said anxiously: 'Do they still do those marvellous oysters at *Ehmke*?'

She looked at him in mild surprise. 'Sure, Willie. Why?'

'Oh . . . I was just wondering.'

She came and sat beside him and he felt the firm touch of her long fingers as she leaned over and looked down into his face. Warmth and excitement flared anew within him.

She said: 'You looked so worried just then, Willie.'

'I'm not any more.' He rolled quickly off the bed and stood up, grinning at her. 'No, it's all right, Ilse. I'm fine.'

Only the most carefully selected clients were allowed to play in *la petite salle privée*. It was small only by comparison with the main gambling rooms which lay on the other side of the thickly carpeted corridor on the upper floor of the casino.

The room was of panelled oak, with an intricately moulded ceiling, very lofty, and three huge chandeliers. The big arched window which looked down over Beirut to the sea was hidden now by deep red velvet curtains. Black carpet covered every inch of the floor. Around the long, kidney-shaped table were a dozen oval-back satinwood chairs in the style borrowed from France by Robert Adam. Two massive ottomans and a deep-buttoned sofa of the last century stood round the walls. In one corner a hatch gave access to a small bar.

There were a dozen men in the room. Modesty Blaise was the only woman. She wore a long silk gown in burgundy, with a fine mesh yoke. Diamond stud earrings sparkled at her ears. White gloves in French nylon satin reached to above her elbows.

Smoke hung in a thick hazy layer against the ceiling. The room was very quiet, with the hushed atmosphere of concentration which might attend some moment of high drama . . . a birth or a death or a duel.

This was a duel. Five of the men were seated, the rest were standing. Among them were two South American millionaires, a Greek shipping magnate, a South African diamond king, two oil sheiks and a French industrialist. The tension was acute, yet each one of these men had gazed with impassive eyes at the turn of a card which would win or lose him thousands of pounds.

Modesty Blaise sat on the right of the man who held the bank. He was an American, under forty, with a hard brown deeply-sculptured face and thick black hair. The slate-grey eyes were set wide, and heavy creases ran from his nose to the corners of his mouth. The face was not conventionally handsome, but there was no mistaking the power in it. He was a little above medium height, with very broad shoulders under the white tuxedo.

His name was John Dall and in twenty years he had built or acquired a complex of industrial enterprises, an empire which set him among the dozen richest men in the world.

A little behind Modesty stood a tall Levantine with a smooth, beige-coloured face and glossy black hair sleeked back. This was Jules Ferrier, the director of the casino and also its owner. For once the passionless mask of his face showed signs of uneasiness.

Dall's hands rested on the sabot containing the six packs of cards, recently shuffled and stacked by the croupier. At his elbow was an ashtray on which lay a black cigar with a short cane-tube mouthpiece penetrating the butt. In front of him was stacked the biggest pile of plaques ever seen even in this room, where the bank limit was the enormously high equivalent of twenty thousand pounds.

Eight times Dall had put up the limit. Eight times Modesty had called *banco* . . . and lost.

Jules Ferrier moved forward and murmured: 'Forgive me, Mam'selle Blaise. You have already much exceeded your banker's draft.'

She glanced at him coldly. 'I am not a stranger to you, Jules. Do you question my credit?'

'No, no, mam'selle. But I . . . I can allow you no more plaques. I am responsible for settlement to Mr. Dall, you understand.'

Modesty looked at Dall and said: 'Do you doubt my substance, Mr. Dall?'

He picked up the cigar and drew on it. 'No, ma'am.' The voice was deep and a little abrupt. 'You lost eighty thousand dollars to me yesterday, and I made a few long-distance calls after last night's play. I like to know who I'm dealing with, and I've a fair idea how much you're good for.'

She held his gaze and said: 'Then let's make this a private matter. Put up all your winnings and I'll call *banco*.'

'No, mam'selle!' Ferrier protested quickly. 'I cannot permit this.'

'Don't be stupid,' she said shortly. 'If Mr. Dall and I decided to toss a coin for the lot it would be no business of yours as long as I cover your plaques. I'm asking him if he'll accept my note on this bet.'

Dall put his cigar down slowly. He said: 'I guess you could meet that kind of loss, Miss Blaise. But you'd be a little pushed. I gamble for fun. I wouldn't break my neck on it and I don't enjoy seeing other people break their necks. Especially a woman.'

A flicker of contempt tugged at the corner of Modesty's mouth. She looked round the room, at the intent faces, then back at Dall.

'Don't waste your chivalry on me, Mr. Dall. If you'd prefer not to risk your winnings, just say so. I shall quite understand.' The last words were as quietly spoken as the

93

rest, but they held an undertone that cut like a whip.

Dall's lips thinned and his slate-grey eyes narrowed a little.

'As you please, ma'am,' he said impassively. Turning the shoe, he slipped the first card from its mouth. Three more followed. The croupier neatly scooped up Modesty's two cards on his spatula and dropped them face down in front of her.

She looked at them, laid them down again, tapped a gloved finger on top of them and said: 'A card.'

Dall slid one out and the spatula dropped it beside her hands, face up. It was the four of diamonds. Quietly, with no hint of drama, Dall turned his own two cards face up. A queen and an eight. A little murmur ran round the room.

'You'll need nine to win, ma'am,' Dall said flatly.

Modesty Blaise smiled with her lips only and flicked over the two face-down cards. A ten and a three. Her total count was seven.

'Not quite good enough,' she said in a neutral voice. 'Thank you for an interesting game, Mr. Dall.'

Ferrier moved forward, snapping his fingers in a sign to the huissier to gather up the bank. 'If you would come to my office now, Mam'selle Blaise? You also, Mr. Dall. The house is responsible for the unsecured plaques—but not for the last bet, of course.'

Modesty picked up her handbag and preceded Ferrier to the unobtrusive door in the corner which led to his office. Dall ground out his cigar slowly, then followed. Ferrier held the door open for him to pass through. It closed behind them. The tension in the *salle* relaxed. Men spoke, shrugged, signalled to the waiters for drinks.

The croupier gathered the used cards with his spatula and pushed them into the cylinder in the centre of the table.

'*Qui veut la banque?*' he asked.

In Ferrier's office Modesty took the chair that he held for her. Dall perched on the arm of a low couch. Ferrier sat down behind his desk and dabbed gently at his brow with a white handkerchief. The huissier knocked and entered. He emptied the pile of plaques from a cloth bag on to the desk and went out again.

Dall relaxed, looked at Modesty, and lifted one black eyebrow in a query. She smiled, and it was like sunlight sparkling on water.

'You were splendid,' she said. 'I'm truly grateful to you.'

'More fun than I've had in a long time.' Dall's strong, Red Indian face creased in a slow smile. He said to Ferrier: 'How was that sabot rigged?'

Ferrier gestured apologetically. 'The croupier who shuffled the cards and made up the sabot stacked the first run of deals, m'sieu.'

Dall's gaze became quizzical. 'You worry me, Ferrier. I was watching and I didn't spot it.'

'My *inspecteur* would have seen it, m'sieu. That is why I took over from him tonight. Please believe that the gaming in this house is honest. Tonight was an exception.'

'I believe you. But is the croupier safe?'

'He won't talk.' It was Modesty who answered. 'He's Jules's younger brother.'

'All nicely sewn up,' Dall said appreciatively. 'But how did you get this character to co-operate?' He nodded towards Ferrier.

'Jules is an old friend.' Modesty left it there, but Ferrier shook his head, a smile touching his pale-beige face.

'There was a time when I worked for Miss Blaise,' he said to Dall. 'That was in a casino in another country. When she ceased to be in business herself she gave me backing to set myself up here.'

'You'd earned it.' Modesty lit a cigarette. 'And you've built this place up from small-time to big-time on your own.' She looked at Dall through a coil of smoke and said quietly: 'If you claim payment for my gambling debt, Mr. Dall, I won't argue.'

His eyes narrowed with anger for a moment, then he relaxed. 'I guess that's your way of telling me this set-up we arranged wasn't just for kicks. You didn't have me break my vacation and fly in here for no good reason. Right?'

'I believe it's for a good reason.'

'It wouldn't have to be.' He got to his feet and stood with hands in his pockets, looking at her with frank curiosity. 'I'd have come here just to see you, ma'am. We had dealings two or three years back, but I only saw your representative in New York then.'

'I hope you found our services satisfactory.'

'A lot more than that. I offered you a deal. One of the I.E. boys had got hold of some data on a new antibiotic drug that my research team at Dall Chemicals had spent two million dollars developing. We weren't sure just how much he'd got, but we knew he was on his way to the Harbstein people in Europe with it. You picked him up for us before he got to them. You found that what he'd got was worth maybe twenty times what I'd offered you for the job. You could have gone to Harbsteins yourself and sold it. You could have put a pistol to my head for a bigger deal. But you sent all the data back to me—at the agreed price. Just like that.'

She smiled into the slate-grey eyes. 'I've always been slightly honest, in my fashion.'

He laughed, a strangely soft laugh for a man with so hard a voice, then shook his head regretfully. 'I'd like to ask you out to dinner with me, ma'am, but I guess that would make this evening's performance look kind of phoney.'

'I'm afraid it would.' There was genuine regret in her own voice. 'Perhaps there'll be another time when it won't matter.'

'Make it so, ma'am.' He took her hand in a firm grasp, and she could feel the power and virility in him. 'I have three or four homes, but you can always reach me through my New York office if I'm out of town. They have instructions. Drop by and visit any time you're free. Or call me again. You've called me once, and I came running.' He smiled, and the hard face held a sudden youthful charm. 'But don't feel indebted.'

'Thank you. I'll do as you say.' Her answering smile did not tell whether she meant that she would visit him or that she would not feel indebted.

His nod accepted the ambiguity without resentment, and he said: 'I guess whatever you're doing must be big. Take good care of yourself. I'll be thinking about you.'

He released her hand, nodded to Ferrier, and moved towards the door. As he went out his face was impassive once again.

SEVEN

SHE came from sleep to wakefulness in the space of one slow indrawn breath, and knew that there was another presence in the room. Her suite lay at the front of the hotel, no more than a mile from the casino she had left two hours earlier.

She stirred slightly, as if in sleep, and her hand slid beneath the pillow to grasp the little kongo which lay there. Restlessly she turned on her back, the other hand outflung to hang over the edge of the bed. In the darkness her fingers closed quietly on the lipstick case which stood close to the lamp on the low bedside table.

The lipstick case was a product of Willie Garvin's. It could shoot a slug of compressed tear-gas, sufficient to disable a man at six feet. She curled her fingers about it and felt for the press-switch of the lamp with her thumb.

The switch clicked and she was sitting up in the moment that soft light bathed the room.

The man sat in an easy chair by the curtained windows. He was in a light fawn jacket and dark trousers, a white shirt and a plain maroon bow tie. His hair was thick, dark, and rather long, but carefully groomed. His eyes were blue-green and humorous, set in a tanned face with a long jaw, a face with that oddly powerful attraction so often produced by a mixture of Irish and Spanish blood.

Propped on the hand holding the kongo, Modesty felt a familiar quiver prickle through her body, like tiny molecules of heat under the skin. She tightened her mind against it and said: 'Hallo, Mike.'

97

'Hallo, there.' His voice was mellow, with the barest hint of a brogue. 'I see you still sleep raw—even alone.'

His eyes studied her naked body with amused approval. It was as if he were reviewing something known long ago and finding it better than he remembered. She made no move to cover herself but said: 'Yes. Will you pass me that robe?'

He rose, picked up the robe of white spotted nylon over nylon taffeta which lay across the foot of the bed, handed it to her, and returned to his chair. 'You slept in your clothes for the first half of your life and you don't ever want to sleep in any kind of clothes again. Wasn't that it?'

She nodded. The kongo was under the pillow again now, and the lipstick was on the bedside table. Pulling the robe about her, watching Mike Delgado, she felt the old pang beneath her breast and knew that her pulse had quickened. It angered her, and she said almost curtly: 'Which way did you come in?'

'From the balcony.' A lazy hand indicated the curtains. 'I could have rung you or knocked. But old habits die hard, you know.' The blue-green eyes glinted with humour.

'Do they? I haven't found it so.'

'Ah, you're retired, of course. But you still sleep raw.'

She shrugged the point aside, took a cigarette from the gold case on the bedside table, and lit it. 'And you still don't smoke?' she asked.

'Virtuous as ever.' He had a way of manipulating his long jaw which gave him a fleetingly clerical air. It had always made her laugh, and she laughed now, but the slight tension remained within her. Behind the tension, which was a physical thing, her mind worked smoothly as she weighed possibilities and balanced values.

Mike Delgado moved in the general areas she had set herself to probe, and his contacts were many. It was possible that he could confirm Tarrant's hunch, at least to some degree. But Mike was a man who pursued only his own advantage. If she asked him outright, she would never know whether the answer was true or false. Even if he knew nothing, he might lie as a matter of policy while he made his own

98

inquiries to see if he could find an angle that would work for him.

She did not resent this. It was part of a game she had played too long herself to have any justification for resentment.

But even if a direct question was out, Mike was potentially too useful to discard. She wondered if his presence here was a factor that weakened Tarrant's hunch; if an army of mercenaries was being assembled, Mike Delgado's name would surely stand high on the list of possible recruits. But no . . . he was very much a solo man. Serving with the cut-throat boys, as Willie called them, was not Mike's meat. Like her, he was in the wrong orbit.

But he had ears in many orbits, and it would be well worth while keeping some kind of contact with him. She smiled inwardly, with wry self-knowledge, as she thought what kind of contact that would be.

And there lay the danger. If the job went hot, if Tarrant's nightmare really existed, then this was no time to heed the quickening warmth that stirred within her. It was no time for involvement, and she knew that she could not let Mike take her without involvement.

It was five years or more since she had last felt the touch of his hand and the weight of his lean body upon her, but now it might have been yesterday. She had known other men through the years . . . not many, not few. With them she had given, and been given, warmth and joy and the great leap to the summit and the glowing peace of fulfilment. But of them all, only three had carried her beyond the summit and into a blazing golden world of the eternal moment, when it seemed that the body's very essence was on the verge of being unmade.

Of these three men, Mike Delgado had been the first, and in so being he had secured some small part of her as his own. It was not a one-way hold: she knew that her mark was upon him, too. For this reason she had never offered him a place in *The Network*, and for the same reason he would have refused such an offer. Where she could acknowledge the tenuous hold and keep wary watch upon it, Mike Delgado feared it as something which might in the end threaten his total lack of scruples.

His voice broke in on her thoughts. 'You're not so skinny as you were at twenty-one.'

'Is that bad?'

'Not at all.' The hint of brogue strengthened with the phrase. 'Being all bone and whipcord was a bed-time handicap you rose above magnificently. I'm sure you'd be even better now.' He went on smoothly, without pause. 'And how's Willie Garvin?'

'He's fine.' She flicked ash into the ashtray on her lap. 'Are you in Beirut on business?'

'Hardly.' His eyes crinkled. 'I'm resting at the moment after a very successful performance in Macao.'

'Gold?'

'Ah now, darling, have a heart. Did I ever ask *you* that kind of question?'

'I'm sorry. When did you find out I was here?'

The humour faded from his face and he leaned back in the chair, watching her. 'An hour ago. Not long after you'd lost a fortune to Dall.'

She nodded without surprise. There had been a dozen or more witnesses to the game, and news of Dall's tremendous coup was the kind of news that would travel fast. She wanted it to.

Mike said: 'What the hell got into you?'

She smiled. 'Did I ever ask *you* that kind of question?'

'I've never done anything crazy enough to invite it.' He looked at her with quiet compassion and she wondered if it was real. 'The rumours are pretty wild. I first heard you'd lost half a million and by the time I'd walked from the bar to the street it was a million.'

'Pretty wild. If you're talking in pounds I lost well over three hundred thousand all told. The deal went against me nine times in a row—and it was double or quits on the last deal.'

He whistled softly and said, 'Christ!'

100

She nodded towards the door which led into the living-room of the suite. 'There's a drink in there if you'd like one.'

'Thanks.' He got up and moved to the door. 'I could use it after that. What about you? Red wine?'

'Not now. Unless you hate drinking alone.'

For a moment laughter came back into his face and he said: 'I don't mind doing anything alone. Almost.'

He went into the other room and put on the light. She heard the clink of glass, and half a minute later he came back carrying a long brandy and soda with ice. Passing the chair by the window, he sat down on the edge of the bed.

'That's a lot of money,' he said. 'How does it leave you?'

She put a shade of bitterness into her smile. 'Not quite broke, but pretty badly bent.'

'You've got quite a place in London, I hear. And there's the house in Tangier.'

'I've already arranged to borrow on them. I may have to sell.'

He drank half the brandy and soda. He would finish it in one more pull, she remembered. Now he was looking at her again with curious eyes.

'So what are you going to do, Modesty?'

'Well, I'm not going to look for a rich husband or a rich lover. And I'm not going to start living in a three-room flat.'

'So what are you going to do?' he repeated.

'You mean in the way of work? Like the old days?'

'Yes.'

'Have you any suggestions?'

He was silent for a while, running a finger thoughtfully over his upper lip. At last he shook his head. 'I'm sorry. Nothing occurs at the moment.'

'I thought not.'

'How's that?' He was puzzled.

'You wouldn't bring me in on any job you'd got lined up, and I wouldn't want you to, Mike.' Her voice was light, her manner friendly. 'We don't need each other.'

'Ah now, d'you think I've no concern for you?'

'I'd be hurt if you hadn't.' It was a lie. Concern from him would have surprised her. 'But I've looked after myself for a long time. For always, Mike. Whatever I've lost I'll make good in my own way.'

He drank the rest of the brandy and soda, put down the glass, and said: 'Soon?'

'Very soon.' Her tone was mellow and her face quiet, but there was a sudden aura of unshakeable will and power about her.

'So you have something lined up.' Mike Delgado smiled. 'That's my girl. I'll ask no questions.'

'You'd get no answers.'

'Naturally.'

He picked up her hand, took the cigarette butt from her fingers, stubbed it out in the tray on her lap, and moved the tray on to the side-table. Still holding her hand he moved closer to her, sitting on the edge of the bed, his body turned towards her.

He said: 'It's been a long time.' Gently his free hand took the frothy lapel of her robe and lifted it back over her right shoulder, then slid the other side back over her left shoulder. His hand touched her brow, her cheek, her neck, and moved gently down to cup her breast.

She felt the growing sweet-sour ache in her loins, and then her mind clamped down like a shutter of steel, severing every thread of physical sensation.

Mike was looking at her body. He said: 'Yes . . . you have grown up, my sweet.'

'I was always grown up. Look at me, Mike. No, at my face.' She held his eyes and said very quietly, very deliberately: 'Not now.'

'No?' His gaze was amused, void of resentment. 'Tell me why not.'

'Many reasons. First, because I say so. Second, because it's not the moment. Third, because I don't play games when I've work to do.'

'Work to do?'

'I told you. I've lost a fortune. I'm going to get another.'

102

His eyebrows quirked upwards. 'So it's that close?'

She had not moved or resisted, and his hand was still upon her. She looked at him thoughtfully for several seconds, then said: 'I'll be in Lisbon one week from today if all goes well. Join me there if you're free, and maybe we'll have occasion to celebrate.'

His hand released her. He pulled the robe back over her shoulders to cover her, then sat with both hands resting on his knees, smiling.

'When will you be leaving here?' he asked.

'I'm not sure. Probably tomorrow evening. Ring me in the morning and we might have lunch.'

'I'll do that.'

'Goodnight, Mike.'

He got to his feet, a tall man moving with easy grace. At the window he turned and looked back at her. 'Good luck, sweetheart.' The curtains stirred, she heard the click of the window-latch, and then he was gone.

Slowly she relaxed. After a while she picked up the phone and spoke to reception. 'Yes—a car ready in forty-five minutes for the airport. You can send up for my bags in half-an-hour. And let me have all flight schedules out of Beirut, please.'

She put down the phone, got out of bed, and began to empty the wardrobe and drawers for packing. It was useful to have let Mike Delgado know that she had a job lined up, but there was also an element of risk in it. Mike would be curious, wondering if he could find an angle of his own. Better for her to vanish now, taking the first plane out on a short flight to anywhere. Mike could find her in Lisbon a week later. That would be soon enough.

In less than ten minutes her three bags were packed and her travelling clothes were laid out ready on the bed—a light two-piece, a fresh bra, the combined pantie-stockings she always wore, flat shoes and a headscarf.

There was time for a quick shower. As she put on her shower-cap she remembered with impatience that there was no more than a sliver of soap in the bathroom and she had

103

forgotten to tell the maid. Opening the small overnight case, she took out a rather large Guerlain gift-box Willie had presented to her a fortnight earlier.

Presents from Willie came as no surprise. She had long since given up protesting. But this one had puzzled her a little. Willie's gifts always had some unusual quality about them; from America he had brought her an antique Derringer, made in the 1860's, a Williamson .41 calibre with an ivory stock and beautifully chased gold butt-plates. This was a collector's piece. For Willie, the gift-box seemed ... very ordinary.

It felt heavy in her hands as she went through into the bathroom, but her thoughts were running ahead and she was only vaguely surprised to find that it held no more than two small bars of soap, a tin of talc, and some body mist. The box seemed deeper than it needed to be. She pulled out one of the bars of soap, springing it from beneath two stiff tongues of cardboard.

Adjusting the shower, she stepped under the gushing rose. As the first warm jets flooded down over her body a chord of music sounded in the bathroom, followed by a rippling arpeggio. She spun round, staring. The small clear sound had come from the Guerlain box.

There was a pause, then a creamy-smooth announcer's voice said: 'And now, for all *clean* people ... *Music To Wash To*.'

Her wide eyes filled with laughter. Still watching the box, she reached out and turned off the shower. The voice was Willie's, one of the several he could produce perfectly when he cared to put aside his natural cockney.

The next chords were from a full orchestra, the opening bars of Chopin's *Polonaise in A*. But the fourth bar consisted of a perfectly-timed gurgle from an emptying bath. Then, incredibly, the music was modulated by a rhythmic bubbling; not an accompaniment, but a sound integral with the notes and chords.

In some way Willie had used the principle of the speaking violin or speaking-piano, where a voice over a micro-

104

phone is used to modulate the output of the instrument itself, so that the music takes on an eerie robotic voice of its own. But here Willie had used sounds instead of voice.

There was the rhythmic scrubbing, the hollow gurgle of the waste, the abrupt splash of a gushing tap, and the squeak of a rubber duck, all blended with happy wit into the *Polonaise*.

She stood with glistening wet body, her hand still on the shower control, head bent a little to capture every nuance. From time to time laughter shook her, and her eyes were alight with pleasure. She wondered how many hours Willie had spent in recording, composing and blending all the fantasy of sound on that miniature tape concealed in the base of the Guerlain box. It lasted for two minutes, then clicked off.

She drew a long breath and exhaled, thinking that one day she must play this for Tarrant. It would enchant him. She turned on the shower again and let it beat on her relaxed body. The small, aching tension roused in her by Mike Delgado was gone now, wiped away by laughter and pleasure and warm affection.

She thought about Willie. The day after tomorrow he would be in Rouen, lying on the table in Georges Brissot's surgery. Not a pleasant two hours for him, but very necessary.

Ten minutes later she was dressed, sitting on the bed and going through flight schedules while the night porter carried out her bags.

EIGHT

THE Director of the Musée Mattioret hid his irritation with an effort.

'Believe me, M'sieu Ransome,' he said politely, 'we are conscious of our responsibility. When you return to Paris you may reassure M'sieu Leighton on that point. The security arrangements for the Watteau are excellent.'

The man sitting on the far side of the desk in the Director's office leaned back and said tiredly in French: 'I'm sure that's so. I'm not arguing with you, m'sieu. But I'm not arguing with Mr. Leighton, either. He hired me as his personal representative to come down and check. He's entitled to do that. The Watteau is his picture.'

Ransome's French was fluent but with no rhythm or inflexion except for the American twang and the Anglo-Saxon vowels which grated on the Director's nerves.

The man wore a dark blue blazer of transatlantic cut, fawn trousers and a cream shirt with a long pearl-grey tie. He was tall, with rather short black hair as if a crew-cut were being allowed to grow out. His face was bronzed, his eyes coffee-brown, and both cheeks bore round patches made up of hundreds of pin-point black dots, as if at some time he had suffered a severe powder-burn from a gun exploding close to his face. The bridge of his nose was angular, jutting in a distinctive peak.

The Director did not like this man Ransome, but could not afford to show it.

He said: 'Certainly M'sieu Leighton is entitled to re-assure himself. He is the owner of this great painting, discovered here in our town. The Watteau has enormous value and we are most grateful that he has allowed us the honour of exhibiting it in our little *musée*,' he gestured modestly, 'when the great galleries of Paris must have been clamouring for the privilege.'

Ransome looked at his watch and said nothing.

'But I do not understand M'sieu Leighton's sudden anxiety,' the Director went on. 'He has allowed us to show the picture for six weeks before he takes it home to the United States. There are only two weeks left now. What has caused his feeling of alarm so late in the day?'

'I didn't ask him any questions,' Ransome said. 'That's not my job. But if I had to guess, I'd say he might have heard some rumour that an attempt will be made to steal the painting.'

The Director lifted his shoulders with a touch of pained

amusement and said: 'A rumour.'

Ransome was silent for a while. At last he said politely: 'I'm not an art expert, so perhaps I haven't grasped the situation correctly. Will you tell me a little about this picture?'

'Gladly, m'sieu.' The Director was pleasantly surprised. Perhaps this man Ransome was not such a boor after all. 'Antoine Watteau painted his pictures in the early years of the eighteenth century—pictures of the ladies and gentlemen of French society, set in Arcadian landscapes. Some of his works were lost in the original, such as this *Fête Dans Les Bois*.' He gestured towards a television set in the corner of the room.

This was a closed-circuit television, showing the section of the *musée* where the picture was hung. It took in the whole of the wide alcove and the three or four people who stood behind the barrier-cord, studying the Watteau. Ransome did not trouble to look round. On the screen, the painting itself was no more than a small rectangle.

'A number of engravers of that period reproduced Watteau's work,' said the Director, 'and so you will find engravings of *Fête Dans Les Bois* in many museums. The original was painted for Le Duc de Charentin, and it hung in the great Paris house of the family until the Revolution.'

'What revolution was that?' Ransome asked.

The Director winced and looked at the ceiling. 'The *French* Revolution, m'sieu! An affair which took place towards the end of the eighteenth century. In it, many great aristocratic families were destroyed, the Charentin family among them. It was always believed that this picture, with many other treasures, was also destroyed at that time. We shall never know how it was brought out safely from Paris to the Chateau Brunelle.'

He turned in his chair to look out of the window. Three miles away, on the long green ridge overlooking the town, stood a small chateau.

'It was only a few months ago that the chateau was put up for sale and all the effects were auctioned,' went on the Director. 'Your M'sieu Leighton attended that auction. He

107

bought a single lot, a number of old pictures which had lain in an attic room for more than a century and a half. They were rubbish, filthy with the dust of all those years.'

The Director turned back to Ransome. 'M'sieu Leighton had them carefully cleaned. They were still rubbish—except for one picture.' He leaned forward dramatically. 'Watteau's *Fête Dans Les Bois*, undamaged, preserved by its thick varnish, in perfect condition! On the back of the canvas, in one corner, was the red seal bearing the coat of arms of the extinct Charentin family.'

The Director spread his hands. 'It is the art discovery of the century, m'sieu, a genuine Watteau, one metre long by two thirds of a metre deep, immediately authenticated by the greatest experts. Ah, there can be no mistaking that delicate, magical colouring——'

'How long is it since any Watteau painting was put up for sale on the open market?' Ransome broke in suddenly.

The Director blinked and pondered for several moments. 'Not at any time within my memory,' he said at last.

'And what would this *Fête Dans Les Bois* fetch?'

'Ahh, who can say?' The Director gestured again. 'It is a priceless thing, m'sieu. A million and a half dollars, *two* million, perhaps! One cannot put a ceiling to the possible bidding.'

Ransome nodded. 'So let us agree that M'sieu Leighton is entitled to worry about any rumour, however groundless, that an attempt to steal the picture might be made.'

The Director drew in a long breath and let it out slowly.

'You do not understand, m'sieu,' he said. 'One's greatest fear for such a picture is the possibility of fire, not of theft. That is why you see fire precautions everywhere throughout the *musée*. That is why the picture is so hung that it can be easily lifted down if fire were to break out.'

'So I understand.' Ransome referred to a small note-book. 'It could also be easily lifted down by a thief.'

'It is a priceless thing, but it is a famous picture, not a block of gold,' said the Director stiffly. 'To whom would a thief sell such a picture?'

'He would have sold it in advance of the theft,' Ransome said. 'For half its value. To a ... a gloater.' He used the English word, thought for a moment, then added: *'Celui qui couve des yeux.'*

The Director lifted expostulatory hands. 'The unscrupulous millionaire who will keep stolen pictures hidden in a cellar to enjoy them for himself alone? Ah, I do not think such exist.'

'They exist,' Ransome said flatly. 'I could name maybe three—but I won't. I could name one who never even looks at what he's got. Having it is all that matters.'

The Director shook his head in doubt and bewilderment. 'You know more of these affairs than I, m'sieu.'

'That's why Mr. Leighton's secretary rang to say I'd be coming along,' Ransome said patiently, and looked at his watch again. 'Would you care to give me a rough idea of the security arrangements before we go down and take a look?'

The Director picked up a pencil and began to make meaningless lines on his pad. 'First there is the closed-circuit television,' he said, indicating the set. 'While the *musée* is open this office is never vacant. If I am not here myself, then my assistant is here.'

'And the other arrangements?'

'I think you must have some knowledge of them, m'sieu. They were mentioned in the newspapers to deter any foolish amateur attempt. As you see, the painting hangs in an alcove, in a small section of the *musée* which we cleared for the purpose. No person is allowed into this section carrying a stick, or umbrella, or anything with which damage might be done.'

'How close can they get to it?'

'No closer than three metres. There is the usual barrier of heavy silk cord, and an attendant is present at all times. There are also three gendarmes on duty, two at the exit and one patrolling the outside of the *musée*.'

'Inspector Faunier mentioned an electronic alarm.'

'You have spoken with him also?'

'I like to check everything twice.'

'I see. Yes, there is an arrangement of that nature. I understand it projects a number of beams, so that anything which passes the unseen barrier will cause alarm bells to ring in several different parts of the *musée*.'

'How high is this electronic barrier?'

'I am sure the Inspector must have told you. Two metres.' A wintry smile touched the Director's lips. 'It extends from the floor to a height of two metres. Sufficient, I think?'

Ransome nodded grudgingly. He took a heavy gunmetal cigarette-case from his pocket, lit a cigarette, and put the case down on the desk. 'You'll be closing in a few minutes now. I'd like to see the arrangements and make a test——'

He broke off. The Director was staring past him. Ransome turned. The picture on the television screen was a flickering mass of lines and distorted fragments. The Director rose and crossed the room. He fiddled with the controls for a while, but without result.

'A fault,' said Ransome. 'You must have it attended to, m'sieu.'

'First thing in the morning, before we open,' the Director assured him, frowning. He fiddled a little longer, then gave up and switched the set off. 'No matter. The set is not used at night, of course, and we shall be leaving the office now.'

Ransome said: 'Will you ring down to the attendant and tell him not to go off duty until I've seen him?'

The Director shrugged. Henri, the attendant on duty, would be around for half-an-hour after the *musée* closed, checking all door and window alarms. But it was not worth arguing with this American. He picked up the telephone on his desk and pressed one of the four buttons on it.

Henri strolled across to the big arched entrance of the special section. It was five minutes to closing time and the last few visitors were drifting away. There were far fewer than there had been during the first three weeks of the exhibition. Often the *musée* was empty half-an-hour before the doors were closed.

The woman was still here though, still studying the Watteau and jotting down notes in a tiny notebook. Each time she completed a note she would open the big shoulder-strap handbag hanging from her shoulder and put the notebook away. Then she would study the painting anew for a while, open the handbag, take out the notebook, write in it, and put it carefully away again.

A school-teacher, thought Henri. Not bad legs, he decided critically. And a very neat backside. But she was thick round the middle and had a small pot of a stomach. Her face was sallow, too, and there was the dusky hint of a moustache on her upper lip.

A pity, thought Henri. She could have been quite good if she had taken a little more care with her figure, and if she had dressed in something other than that dreary brown nylon mack. It matched the headscarf she wore, with the fringe of mouse-brown hair showing along her brow. The spectacles didn't do anything for her, either. Altogether, it was a waste of a neat backside.

The phone in his little cubicle along the passage rang briefly. Without haste he went out through the archway and entered the cubicle. Settling himself on the tall stool there, he picked up the phone.

Modesty Blaise took one sweeping look round the small hall and stepped back from the thick cord barrier across the alcove. Taking the weight of the heavy handbag under her right arm, she slid aside a small flat cap low down on the forward end of the bag and drew out a thin, nozzle-ended tube.

She let the handbag hang from her shoulder again and continued to draw out the tube with both hands now. It kept coming as section slid from section like a telescopic antenna. The tube was made of a very light alloy, and in five seconds she held the full ten-foot length of it in her hands, a tapering, perfectly-machined piece of metal. At the nozzle end were two short metal whiskers an inch long, set at an angle. The butt-end of the tube swelled into a wide metal grip with a small button on it and an even smaller aperture beside the

111

button. Into the grip was bonded one end of a length of rubber tubing. The other end disappeared through the hole in the bag.

Very carefully Modesty gripped the metal tube in both hands as if it were a fishing-rod, and lifted it high above her head so that it sloped up and away from her.

She moved slowly towards the barrier. Seconds were ticking away on the clock in her mind, but her movements were unhurried. The tube must be kept over two metres from the floor, otherwise she knew the alarms would sound. Delicately, with her arms at full stretch above her head, and standing as close to the barrier as she dared, she brought the nozzle-tip towards the top left-hand corner of the Louis Quinze gold frame.

When the two fine steel whiskers were touching the canvas and the edges of the frame-corner a tiny light glowed in the aperture of the grip, and she knew that the nozzle was positioned exactly. Her thumb pressed the button beside the aperture and held it down.

There came the faintest sound of hissing as an atomised spray issued from the nozzle, fed from the long metal cylinder which lay in the bottom of her handbag.

Thirty-five seconds.

In the office above, the Director said: 'Certainly, Henri. I realise that you would not consider yourself off-duty until you had attended to the routine security precautions. But the gentleman with me,' he favoured Ransome with a frosty smile, 'wished me to make sure that you would remain. H'mm? Yes, of course. We shall be down in a few minutes.'

Ransome held out a hand and said quietly: 'Let me speak to him, please.'

'To Henri?' The Director stared. He said into the phone: 'Wait, Henri.' His eyes were still on Ransome, and now his annoyance was plain. 'Really, m'sieu, he can tell you nothing I have not already told you. There is little point in your talking to him now.'

'I like to talk to everybody,' Ransome said bluntly. 'The Inspector, you, Henri—everybody concerned with this matter. It may not be the way you think I should do this job, but Mr. Leighton pays me to do it my way.'

The Director's lips thinned. Without a word he passed the phone across the desk and sat back.

Ransome took the phone and spoke into it. 'Henri? My name is Ransome, and I'm acting for Mr. Leighton, who owns the Watteau. I'll be down to see you in a few minutes but I want to know something now. Who's watching in the exhibition hall while you're answering this phone?'

Nobody was watching in the exhibition hall. Modesty Blaise moved the faintly hissing nozzle along the bottom edge of the frame. Without lifting the steel contact-whiskers from the canvas she released her thumb-pressure on the control button.

All round the edge of the picture there was now an opaque, creamy-white strip an inch wide. Even as she watched, the gloss faded to leave a dry matt surface—in a colour which had been carefully matched to the plaster wall against which the painting hung.

Sixty seconds plus. Not much above the best time she had made during a dozen rehearsals in a garage in Paris the day before. The next part, blanking out the main area of the picture, would go much more quickly since there was no danger of spraying over the edge of the frame.

She began to move the nozzle more freely in steady sweeps back and forth, ignoring the growing ache in her extended arms. Vaguely through her concentration a part of her mind was listening to the sound of Henri speaking on the phone. She could hear him now, even though the cubicle was some ten paces along the passage, because his voice was steadily rising.

In the office on the upper floor of the *musée* Ransome said: 'I'm not accusing you of neglecting your duties, Henri. I'll take your word for it that from where you sit now you can see anybody who comes out of that hall. And I know they couldn't get to the painting while the electronic alarm system is on. At least, they couldn't *steal* the painting, but it might be possible to damage it in some way——' He broke off,

113

listening impatiently, tried to cut in again, and succeeded only on the third attempt.

'Yes, I know they'd have to be mad, Henri, but there are plenty of crazy people about. All right, so there's only some school-teacher woman there at the moment, but I'm not talking about *this* moment. Will you please try to take in the simple fact that——'

He broke off again, jerking the phone from his ear as it crackled with noisy indignation from the other end. When the phone fell silent at last he resumed doggedly.

The Director sat back, his good temper restored. This Ransome had more than met his match. For himself he could not be troubled to argue with the man any further. But Henri would delight in it. When it came to a heated argument Henri was inexhaustible. He would wear this Ransome down without even extending himself.

Modesty Blaise clicked the last two sections of the telescopic tube back into her bag alongside the pressure cylinder. She looked at the Watteau. Already the slight gloss from the last few sweeps of the spray had faded. It was as if she were looking right through the empty frame to the wall behind it.

She slid the little cap over the hole in the fore-edge of the handbag and moved slowly towards the arched entrance. The notebook and pencil were in her hands, and she was jotting absorbedly as she walked.

Henri slammed down the telephone and glanced across at her with enraged eyes as she appeared. She stood still, finished writing, then put the notebook away and moved briskly on through the larger hall which led to the exit. Henri's eyes followed her, but his mind was gnashing on greater things. Vaguely a blend of word-picture-symbol vision connoting 'backside' floated across his mind. Then it vanished and he gave himself up to the joys of hatred, composing vitriolic phrases in readiness for M'sieu Ransome.

It was two minutes later when the Director appeared at the foot of the broad stone stairs. A tall dark-haired man was at his shoulder. Henri emerged from his cubicle and waited for them to approach.

So this was Ransome, he thought. A typical American. The way he spoke French was an affront to the ears. Henri rejected the scathing irony he had been composing. He would be cool and remote, a little patronising perhaps.

'Ah, Henri,' said the Director. 'This is M'sieu Ransome.'

Henri inclined his head by a millimetre and said coldly: 'A pleasure.'

'The Watteau's through there?' Ransome nodded towards the wide arched doorway.

'Yes. If m'sieu will be so good as to follow me.' Henri turned with dignity and led the way. The Director brought up the rear. Once in the smaller hall they had to turn right to come to the front of the cord barrier.

'Voila, m'sieu,' said Henri, and gestured casually, his eyes on Ransome's face. 'Now I will cut off the main alarms and demonstrate how the alarm in this room——' He stopped short. Ransome was staring rigidly past him. The Director's face was grey and frozen.

'Is this a joke?' Ransome said hoarsely.

Henri whirled, staring at the wall. The angled lights played on an empty frame.

'It—it is impossible!' he said in a shaking voice. 'Impossible! There was only the woman here! The alarm would have sounded—she could not reach the picture without steps! How could she cut it out?' His voice rose higher with every phrase. He started to move forward but Ransome caught his arm in a hard grip.

'How long since she went?'

'Three minutes . . . four . . .' Henri put a hand to his head. 'But it is impossible.'

'She can't have got far and I don't want all the alarms going off to warn her,' Ransome said in a low, fierce voice. 'Get hold of the gendarmes. Tell them to start looking for her. She must have a car somewhere near—in the square, perhaps. *Run, damn you!*'

Henri set off at a dazed run, his feet echoing through the empty *musée*. Ransome turned to the Director. 'How do you switch off the alarms?'

115

The Director closed his mouth with a visible effort and looked at Ransome with horrified eyes. 'There . . . there is a control-board,' he gulped. 'I have the key here.' On shaking legs he moved round the end of the alcove and unlocked a metal panel set in the wall

'Cut the main alarms,' Ransome said in a taut voice. The Director threw three of four switches with a trembling hand. Ransome moved to the cord barrier and leaned forward. At once a bell sounded from Henri's cubicle.

'All right! Cut that one as well! At least the thing was *working*!' Ransome's tone was shot with anger and bafflement. The bell stopped, and the Director rejoined him at the barrier.

'Don't go any nearer!' Ransome snapped. 'I want two big dust sheets and some tall steps. Hurry, please!'

'Dust sheets? Yes . . . yes, of course.' The Director drew a hand across his damp brow. 'But the police, m'sieu? Should we not call Inspector Faunier at once?'

'Get the dust sheets.' Ransome had control of himself now, but his voice was like iron. 'I'll call Faunier from the phone in the cubicle while you're about it. Go *on*!'

Modesty Blaise sat in the great dark church which dominated one side of the square. It was six minutes since she had left the *musée*.

Even today the church seemed too large in proportion to the town, and it had been built three hundred years earlier. Here, in the corner of the rear pew at the side, she was almost invisible in the dim half-light permitted by the narrow stained-glass windows. There were no more than eight people scattered in the pews ahead of her, and they were absorbed in their own affairs.

Kneeling, she drew from beneath the seat a large navy-blue beach-bag of woven straw which she had hidden there half-an-hour earlier. Inside, it were smart white shoes, a white denim hat with a narrow brim, lipstick, impregnated cleansing tissues, and a pocket mirror with a low-wattage bulb on one edge fed by a tiny battery fixed to the back.

She slipped off her headscarf, and the fringe of mouse-brown hair came away with it. Underneath the brown nylon mack she wore a pale blue denim dress with a white leather belt. Reaching up under her skirt she dragged out the padding of blanket material over her stomach, resettled the dress and drew the belt tight.

The mack and the headscarf, the black handbag, the flat shoes and the padding—all went into the beach-bag. Opening the packet of impregnated tissues she bent low and switched on the tiny mirror-light. Sixty seconds later the sallow make-up and the shadowy moustache had been cleaned from her face. She applied fresh lipstick, studied the result, then put the mirror into the beach-bag.

Her hair had been pinned up loosely under the headscarf. Now she rolled it quickly into a top-knot, pinned it firmly, and drew on the denim hat.

One minute later she was in the church porch, the beach-bag on her arm, talking to a tubby, amiable priest and asking him the best way out of town for the village of Bournisse. He walked with her across the square to where her grey Citroen was parked, his hands making signs in the air as he described the route.

A gendarme on a motor-cycle swerved round them, head turning and eyes darting anxiously as he scanned the strollers and the cars in the square.

Modesty settled herself behind the wheel, listened carefully as the priest repeated his instructions, thanked him with a dazzling smile, and drove leisurely away.

In the *musée*, the Director came into the small exhibition hall carrying two large folded dust-sheets. His colour had returned but he was still shaken and perspiring. Ransome had unfastened the heavy cord barrier. He took one dust sheet and spread it carefully over the floor leading up to the wall where the painting hung, unrolling the sheet ahead of him.

'There may be some clue on the floor. It must be preserved for the police,' he said.

'You have spoken with Inspector Faunier?'

'Of course. He is sending two detectives at once. I am to

117

take the frame of the picture to his headquarters so that it may be tested for fingerprints.'

'He is not coming himself?' the Director said blankly.

'For the moment he is more concerned with establishing a cordon to prevent this woman leaving town with the picture,' Ransome snapped. 'Where are the steps I asked for?'

'Henri is bringing them——' the Director broke off as Henri appeared with a tall pair of wooden steps.

Ransome said: 'Please keep well back.' He took the steps, moved gingerly over the dust sheet, and set them up below the picture. Returning, he took the second dust sheet, climbed the steps, and carefully draped the sheet over the whole frame. Lifting the frame from the wall, he rested it on top of the steps and wrapped the dust sheet completely round it before descending with his burden.

Henri and the Director trotted unhappily beside him as he strode along the corridor.

'You have a car, m'sieu?' said the Director.

'Yes. Parked just outside your staff entrance.'

'Shall I ask one of the gendarmes to accompany you?'

'I hope,' Ransome said grimly, 'that at this moment the gendarmes are using their best efforts to accompany the woman who has stolen M'sieu Leighton's painting.'

NINE

WILLIE GARVIN towelled his hair vigorously, looking in the mirror above the chipped sink. There were two damp pads of cotton-wool plastered on his cheeks. Putting down the towel he leaned close to the mirror and lifted one of the pads, peering beneath.

With a nod of satisfaction he pulled the pad off. The cotton-wool was smudged and speckled with black, but there was now no sign of any powder-burn effect on the skin. He checked the other cheek and peeled off the pad.

The bridge of his nose was no longer peaked and angular. There was now only a short, skin-deep cut to show where he had removed the wax that Dr. Georges Brissot had injected under the skin. A coagulant had sealed the little cut, and in a day or two it would be healed.

Midnight was ten minutes away. He had only one more thing to do to become himself again.

Willie had laid out of sight in the back of Modesty's grey Citroen during the five-hour drive to this small flat at the back of an antique shop on the outskirts of Paris. The car Willie had used as 'Ransome' lay abandoned off the road in some woods only five miles from the *musée*. That was where Modesty had been waiting to pick him up.

He swirled the black foamy water in which he had washed the dye from his hair and watched it vanish down the waste of the sink. Now came the moment he had been putting off. He picked up a little rod with a suction cap on the end, leaned close to the mirror again and gingerly plucked out the brown contact-lenses which covered the blue irises of his eyes.

You could probably get used to slipping the damn things in and out, he thought, but he wasn't used to it and he hated it. He put the lenses in a padded box and picked up a large gunmetal cigarette case.

This was the case he had laid down on the Director's desk. The major part of it consisted of a one-watt power unit operating a transistorised oscillator. The oscillator had sent out a train of pulses from a multivibrator at a frequency very close to that of the line timebase of the closed-circuit television set in the Director's office, destroying the picture.

There was room for only four cigarettes in the case. One remained. He took it out, lit it, then ran a comb through his damp hair and went into the other room.

Modesty, wearing gloves, was working with a soft moistened brush on the painting. Only a few square inches of the powdery, cream-coloured coating remained to be cleaned away.

She looked up and smiled. 'That's better, Willie love. The

119

powder-burn looked rather dramatic, but I didn't like the nose.'

'I didn't go for it much meself,' Willie admitted. 'How's the painting?'

'Fine. That concoction of yours comes off beautifully. No damage at all.' She continued brushing carefully, pausing to rinse the brush in a basin of water from time to time. Willie sat smoking, watching her as she worked.

'Good to get a chance of using that idea,' he said after a while. 'It's all right cooking up a caper in theory, just for a giggle, but it's nice when you can try it out.'

'Yes. And it was handy having this one ready. A good one.' She looked up. 'As good as your best, Willie.'

'Mine? It was your idea, Princess.'

'That's the easy part. You make it work.' With a damp rag she wiped away the last vestige of the creamy colouring. 'Now let's see what we've got.'

Willie put on a pair of gloves, propped the picture up on the table so that it leant against the wall, and they both stood back.

Fête Dans Les Bois showed elegant ladies and gentlemen in eighteenth century finery, picnicking in a forest glade.

'Do a picture like that today,' said Willie, 'and the only place you'd get it shown would be on a chocolate box.'

'You don't like it?' She was surprised.

'I think it's great. I just meant the subject and style are wrong for today. But that kiddy Watteau could really paint. Look at those colours, Princess ... and the way 'e uses 'em.'

'Yes.' She lost herself in the painting for a while, then went on slowly: 'The whole effect is ...' she shrugged. 'I don't know.'

'Nacreous,' said Willie, and she laughed. He had a habit of producing the occasional surprising word.

'You've been reading good books again,' she said. 'But you're right. It shimmers like mother-of-pearl.'

'I pick up a lot reading the music critics in the papers,' said Willie, and grinned. 'They slay me.'

'How do you mean?'

Willie closed his eyes, concentrated for a moment, and began to quote: 'The content of these passages is opaque rather than glassy in this hermetic little work, with laconic solo interludes, spare in texture yet with a nacreous veneer. To say that the performance of such a work demands no small degree of incisive brilliance would be an absurd litotes——'

'Ah no, Willie. You're making it up. Not litotes!'

He opened his eyes. 'Honest, Princess. I looked it up and it's an ironic understatement, like saying—um—John Dall is not exactly a poor man, for instance. You should read these music critics. They're a real gas.'

'I must try them. And that reminds me—so was your Wash-tub Polonaise. A gas, I mean.'

'Ah, you opened the Guerlain box, then?'

'Yes. That tape's a gem. God knows how much work you put into it, but I loved every second of the result, Willie.'

He grinned contentedly, moved to an ancient wine-cupboard in the corner of the room, opened a bottle of red wine, and poured two glasses.

A pair of shabby armchairs stood near the old-fashioned black stove against one wall of the room. Willie pulled them forward a little, picked up the glasses and handed one to Modesty.

They sat with their wine, quietly looking at the picture, savouring the relaxed contentment that followed a time of tension. After a while Modesty said: 'Did you ring Weng about Lucille?'

'M'mm. All okay, Princess. He put 'er on the plane and rang the school the same evening to make sure she'd arrived safe and been met in Tangier.'

'No trouble with her?'

'From what Weng said I got the idea she was a bit narked about you and me not being there to see 'er off.'

'Did he tell her we'd be flying out to see her in a few days?'

'Yes, but that didn't stop the sulks.'

Modesty shrugged resignedly. 'She'll get over it.'

'I don't reckon she was that much bothered about us not being there. She just likes a chance to put it on a bit.'

Willie got up and spread a folded blanket on the table. He laid the picture face down. The stretcher was of oak, with a single cross-bar, and was held in the frame by short corner-strips of metal over rubber wedges. Willie unrolled a small wallet of tools. He unscrewed the metal strips and eased the stretcher out of the ornate gold frame.

'Can you get the canvas off without breaking that seal on the back?' Modesty asked.

'Sure, Princess.' He selected a miniature forked jemmy and began to work very carefully on the first of the many tacks holding the canvas.

A quarter of an hour passed in silence.

Modesty said: 'Willie, I haven't had a chance to tell you before, but Mike Delgado turned up in Beirut.'

Willie glanced at her, then resumed his work. 'Turned up? 'Ow did it look?'

'It looked as if he just happened to be passing through.'

Willie removed the last of the tacks along the upper side of the stretcher. 'Could be useful, Delgado on the spot when you lost that lot. He'll blow it around.'

'It made quite a few newspapers anyway.' She put down her glass. 'I've said I'll meet him in Lisbon. It seemed worth keeping contact.'

Willie reflected, rubbing his chin with the handle of the little jemmy. 'Delgado's bound to have an angle,' he said at last. 'Not the thing we're after, but he might've heard a whisper. Yes . . . it's worth keeping contact.'

'You mean he's bound to have an angle of his own if he turns up in Lisbon to meet me?' Modesty got up and moved to stand beside Willie as he bent over the painting again.

'Sure. You know the way he plays it, Princess.'

She smiled and tapped Willie gently on the shoulder with one long finger. 'I don't know if you're feeling tired or if you're just being ungallant, Willie. His angle could be *me*.'

Willie rested his hands on the table and shook his head slowly in self-condemnation.

'I'm naïve,' he said. 'That's my trouble, Princess. I'm naïve.'

She laughed and went through into the other room. In one corner stood a large open crate holding a dozen white plaster statuettes packed in straw. Each was a little over two feet tall. They were vaguely oriental and highly grotesque, dramatic only in their crude lack of taste. The crate was addressed for collection from the docks at Lisbon by a nonexistent company. One of the statuettes was in two pieces, the head broken off clean from the body by a sharp blow.

Modesty picked up the two pieces and went back into the room where Willie was working. He removed the last of the tacks, eased the canvas away from the stretcher, and carefully tested its pliability.

'Will it roll without damage?' she asked.

He nodded. 'As long as we don't roll it tight.'

Two minutes later the canvas lay coiled in a loose cylinder four inches across, secured by three pieces of tape. Modesty held the body of the broken statuette while Willie slid the rolled canvas into it. The break, though jagged, was clean, and when she settled the head back in position the two parts fitted snugly together.

She went back into the room where the crate stood. Willie followed. He watched as she laid the statuette alongside the rest in their bedding of straw.

'Right, Willie.'

He spread a thick layer of straw over the whole surface, picked up the heavy wooden lid, and began to nail it in place.

'Let's 'ope old Tarrant's managed to fix up his end of this caper,' he said.

René Vaubois of the Deuxième Bureau stroked his well-shaven cheek and looked out of his office window at a pigeon perched on the branch of a chestnut tree. The pigeon was watching him.

With the scrambler phone to one ear, Vaubois got up, opened the window, took a biscuit from the drawer of his desk, and crumbled it along the window-sill. As he closed the window the pigeon alighted and began to feed.

'But my dear friend,' Vaubois said into the phone with courteous reproach, 'I feel you should have told me this earlier. For thirty-six hours now the police have been obsessed by this affair of the Watteau.'

Tarrant's voice came apologetically over the line. 'I'm sorry about that, René, but I couldn't tell you what I didn't know at the time.'

Vaubois did not resent the lie, since he appreciated the necessity for it. Tarrant was not trying to deceive him, only showing proper understanding of his position. Vaubois was very glad he had not been told earlier, for this would have placed him in a difficult situation.

He said: 'The man and the woman—they were Modesty Blaise and Willie Garvin, of course?' He did not pronounce the name 'Weelee', as most Frenchmen would. Vaubois' English was immaculate, and only the precision of it betrayed that this was not his mother-tongue.

'I've no idea about that, René.' Tarrant's voice was bland. 'Those two have retired, of course, but this does seem rather like their style. All I can tell you is that I've had this anonymous tip-off and I felt I should pass it on to you.'

'It is a police matter, Gerald, not a concern of the Deuxième.' Vaubois smiled, watching the pigeon, as he went through the verbal formalities.

'I realise that, René. But in view of the very odd nature of the tip-off I felt I should speak to you first and rely on your judgment.'

'I understand.' Vaubois looked at the jottings on his pad. 'You say that if a particular crate falls from the back of a particular shipping-agent's truck as it enters the freight depot in Paris, and if this crate is examined for damage to contents then the missing Watteau will be discovered intact.'

'So I've been anonymously told, René.'

'And it will be impossible to trace the crate or its contents back to the sender?'

'Yes.'

'And you express the wish that a journalist should happen

124

to be on the spot at the time of the discovery, so that the news will make the newspapers?'

'Yes.'

'This will alert the guilty persons, you realise, and they will make no attempt to collect the crate at its destination.'

'I do realise that,' said Tarrant. 'It's disappointing for the police, but the main thing is that the Watteau will have been recovered. Do you think you can make the necessary arrangements?'

Vaubois sighed. 'You really are a bloody nuisance, Gerald,' he said politely. 'It is much more difficult to put in two men as loader and driver on this truck than to arrange for a safe-breaking or the stealing of an ambassador's briefcase.'

Tarrant's laughter came over the line. 'I know, René, I know. It's always the little things that give us headaches. But can you do it?'

Vaubois completed a sketch of a nude girl on his pad. 'Yes. Leave it to me, my dear friend. I will arrange that all credit accrues to the police. But you are still a bloody nuisance.'

'I'm most grateful to you.' Tarrant meant it. The two men always helped one another when possible. And at those times when the shifts of politics made them temporary antagonists in the strange undercover world they inhabited, they contrived to duel without quarter yet without loss of personal esteem.

Vaubois sketched in a chastity belt on the girl and looked at the result with distaste. He said: 'Why is she doing this, Gerald? First the affair in Beirut—a fortune lost. And now a theft which is not a theft. I find it hard to deduce any purpose from this.'

'Try not to speculate, René,' Tarrant said gently. 'I'll tell you about it as soon as I can.'

'Very well. But may I ask now if you are speculating yourself, Gerald? Is she playing a hunch of yours?'

There was a moment's silence, then Tarrant said: 'I'm speculating—yes.'

'If Modesty Blaise is playing this for you it must be big.'

'I may be wrong, René.'

'But if you are not wrong?'

'Then it's big. Very big.'

Vaubois watched the pigeon fly away. He said: 'You know, I have never met her. I would like to do so, one day.'

'I've heard her speak of you. With admiration. I know she would be very pleased, René. I'll try to arrange it.'

'Thank you. I shall look forward to it—if you don't manage to get her killed first, Gerald.' Vaubois spoke lightly, then was angry with himself as he heard the touch of heaviness in Tarrant's reply.

'Yes, René. If I don't manage to get her killed first.'

Mike Delgado said: 'Congratulations.'

He lay on one side of the bed, half-covered by a sheet, looking at Modesty Blaise. She was still asleep, lying on her front with her head turned towards him, breathing slowly and evenly, her body soft and relaxed, her face young, content and vulnerable.

The bedroom windows of the villa stood open. The white shutters were closed, and the early-morning sun slanted through the louvres to lay gold stripes down her tanned back and along the sheet that covered her to the waist.

The villa was perched on a gentle slope. Behind lay a wooded hill of jacaranda, eucalyptus and dwarf pine. Below ran the road between Cascais and Estoril, bordering the Tagus.

Delgado put a finger on the tip of Modesty's nose, pressed gently, and said again: 'Congratulations.'

She grimaced in waking, drew back her head, opened her eyes and said: 'M'mmm?'

He grinned. 'I just said congratulations.'

She turned on her back, put up her arms and stretched, kicking back the sheet and tensioning every muscle of her body like a cat rousing from sleep. Relaxing, she lifted her head a little and looked down the length of her body.

'Look, I've got gold stripes on me.'

'Very fetching.' He pushed himself on to an elbow and began to trace one long curving strip of sunlight with his fingertips. Her eyes, wide awake and touched with exuberant humour now, watched his face.

The fingertips slid across her flat stomach and curved over her hip, where the golden stripe disappeared.

'It's like one of those children's picture-puzzles,' he said. 'Mister Bunny is trying to find the way home to his little house. It is very difficult. Can you find the right path for him to take, kiddies?'

He traced another stripe which carried his hand over the outer curve of her thigh.

She said: 'Mister Bunny's not doing too well.'

'Mister Bunny thinks the puzzle's been rigged. Move over this way, about four inches.'

'That would be cheating.'

'This Mister bloody Bunny specialises in cheating.'

'I know.' She picked up his hand and rested it between her breasts. 'What time is it?'

'On my wrist.'

She turned his hand and looked at the wrist-watch. 'Five past eight.'

'Is that important?' he asked.

'No. But I've got an appointment later today with Willie Garvin. There's something we have to arrange.'

'To do with collecting the Watteau?'

Her eyebrows lifted. 'What Watteau?'

'Just any old Watteau that might have disappeared recently. Who's your buyer, darling?'

She said equably: 'Mister Bunny should know better than to poke his little pink nose into my business.'

He grinned. 'I seem to remember you've told me that before.'

'Then stay told, Mike.' Her tone was amiably casual.

'All right. But allow me to say I'm very glad. The idea of you being broke didn't please me at all. And choosing Lisbon was good thinking. You can transact in gold—no restrictions on it here. Is Willie pleased?'

'I think he's enjoyed himself over the past few days. He didn't like the idea of my being broke, either.'

'I can imagine.'

She frowned slightly as if searching her memory, and turned towards him. 'You were saying something to me when I woke up just now. What was it?'

'Congratulations.'

'Oh. The Watteau again?'

'No. Personal congratulations.'

'On what?'

'On the progress you've made since the last time we were together like this. Last night was quite an experience.'

She lay back, her face quiet. Leaning over her he looked down into her face with curious wonder, and when he spoke again the soft brogue was more pronounced than usual.

'It's five years,' he said. 'Even then you had a lovely flame in you for the giving and the taking, sweetheart . . . but now there's more . . . ah, there's gold in the flame and a long, long cry of joy——'

She broke in softly: 'Don't you know when to be quiet, you green-eyed bog-trotting mick?'

He stared for a moment, startled. 'D'you think I'm giving you the blarney?'

'No.'

'Then why be quiet?'

She shook her head slowly, smiling a little as she looked up at him, then lifted her hands and linked them behind his neck. 'It's to have and to be and to do, Mike. Not to talk about.'

'Ah. . . .' The blue-green eyes above her understood and accepted. 'Well, then.'

Their bodies merged and the slits of sunlight through the shutters began the long dance, shifting and curving and breaking in a hundred patterns upon them.

It was ten o'clock when Modesty came out of the bathroom, belting a pale yellow nylon housecoat about her. Through the open door of the living-room she could see

128

Mike's back. He was dressed in blue beach slacks and a matelot shirt, and stood by the table set for breakfast, looking at a newspaper in his hand.

A little pile of half-a-dozen other newspapers lay folded on the table, airmail editions from abroad. They had been brought in by the Portuguese girl who went with the rented villa. She was in the kitchen now, preparing breakfast.

Modesty called: 'Five minutes to dress and I'll be with you.'

She was moving towards the bedroom when Mike said: 'Wait.' There was an odd flatness in his voice. She turned back into the living-room. He was by the door now, facing her. In silence he held out the newspaper. She gave him one quick glance and took it.

The newspaper was *L'Aurore*. A headline on the front page screamed: LE WATTEAU RETROUVÉ! She stood very still, her eyes scanning the opening bold-type paragraphs.

Mike said: 'The bloody crate fell off the back of the truck and broke open. There were big statuettes inside. Some were smashed. The Watteau was hidden inside one of them.'

He watched her as she went on reading. Her cheeks held their colour but her face might have been chiselled from marble. At last she handed him back the paper, turned away and went into the bedroom. He followed her, closing the door after him. She was sitting on the bed, hands in the pockets of her housecoat, looking out through the window that now stood with shutters wide.

'Can they trace the crate, forward or back?' he said.

'Not back. Not forward now. If the Press hadn't got on to it they could have let the crate go through and alerted Lisbon to pick up whoever collected it. But not now. I ought to feel lucky.'

He lit a cigarette and gave it to her. A moment ago her eyes had been blank. Now they were intent, not looking at anything, but hard with concentration.

'Lucky,' he said softly. 'Christ. I wouldn't call it that.'

'I made a mistake.' The anger in her voice was against herself. 'I should never have sent the thing on.'

'It was the best way.'

'No!' She turned to stare at him. 'It was the safest way, not the best. I should have brought it out myself, with Willie. That's what we'd have done in the old days. But I slipped, Mike. I've gone a little soft.'

'You?'

'Yes.' She rose and began to pace slowly, forearms across her stomach, hands grasping her elbows. The cigarette clipped in her fingers did not tremble. 'I'll need to get my edges honed before I try again.'

'Try again?'

'What else?' She looked at him. 'But I've got to get back in form before I try anything big. Take some knocks and get hardened up, the way I used to be.'

'So what will you do?'

'I'm not sure.' She stopped pacing and stood in front of him. 'I wouldn't mind what it was, providing it's tough and pays my way for a bit.' She shrugged and laughed shortly. 'Oh, don't worry, Mike. I know you're a loner and I'm not asking to cut in on anything you might do.'

'I've got nothing lined up anyway.'

'Maybe not. But you have your ear to the ground. I've lost touch a little. Do you know of anything going that might interest me?'

'You'd work for somebody?'

'For a time, if I have to.'

He stood in deep thought for a full minute, then shook his head. 'I'm always picking up rumours, but you can seldom tell if they're firm.'

'If you come across anything firm, and you think it might suit, let me know.' She went to the window and stood looking out, smoking thoughtfully.

After a while he said: 'What do you aim to do right now?'

'Today?'

'Yes.'

'I'll ring Willie in case he hasn't seen the papers yet. Then I aim to be on my own.' She paused, and added slowly: 'We celebrated too soon, Mike. It's over now.'

130

'You want me to move out?'

'I'm sorry—yes.'

'I can't help in any way?'

She smiled at him, and now some of the tension within her had passed. 'You're surely not offering me a hand-out?'

'No.' He smiled back at her without apology. 'That wouldn't suit either of us, darling.'

'It certainly wouldn't. So what kind of help?'

'Only what you mentioned just now. If I hear of anything I think might interest you I'll need to get in touch. Where can I make contact?'

'I'll be here for another two days as planned, then I'll be going to Tangier.'

'With Willie Garvin?'

'Yes. His young stray, Lucille—she's expecting to see him.'

'Ah, yes. And what will you be doing?'

'Lucille expects to see me, too. But I might also have to start arranging to sell the house there.'

'You'll miss that. You've had it a long time. But at least it should fetch plenty to give you some working capital.'

'It had better fetch plenty. I told you, I've borrowed on it. But you can ring or cable me there any time in the next three weeks—unless Willie and I pick up the sort of job we want on our own.'

'Okay.' He got up. 'Can I have breakfast before I pack?'

'Don't be silly.' There was affection in her smile. 'I'll come and have some with you.'

'And a last swim afterwards?'

'No. Afterwards you just drive away, Mike. There's something I have to do this morning.'

Humour touched his eyes. 'You don't still go in for contemplating your navel?'

'Why not?' she said without resentment. 'I still use yoga techniques when I want to wipe out tensions and get myself balanced. It works.' She moved to the door. As she opened it she looked back at him and a swift urchin grin lit her face. 'It'll make a change from you contemplating it, anyway.'

131

Two hundred yards from the villa, just off the main road, a man looked up from the newspaper he was reading as he sat behind the wheel of a parked car—a Simca. He wore a light-weight fawn suit, a cream shirt with a matching tie, and a soft cream poplin hat with a narrow brim. His face was thin and dark.

He looked at his watch, glanced towards the villa almost hidden among the trees, then returned to his newspaper. It was already uncomfortably hot in the car, and it would grow hotter still, but he would wait indefinitely to carry out the special task he had been given.

Discomfort was a very small matter compared with the displeasure of the master he served.

TEN

MODESTY BLAISE lay on a rush mat spread on the sand. The sun was still strong, though the hottest hour of the day had now passed. There were not more than a dozen people on the little beach east of Cascais, and the nearest group was well over fifty paces away.

Mike Delgado was gone—to Lisbon perhaps, or to the airport. She had not asked his plans. At lunch-time she had rung Willie Garvin at his Lisbon hotel.

"Allo, Princess. Looks like our old mate worked it okay with his oppo.' He was referring to Tarrant and René Vaubois.

'Yes. It's going well enough, Willie. But I don't think Mike's going to give us any lead.'

'You tried 'im?'

'I made it plain that we're in the market. He didn't react.'

'M'mm . . . you'd think he'd get to know about a party like that, sooner or later.'

'Maybe it's too soon. Maybe there isn't a party. Or maybe they're very smart. They couldn't afford to let anyone really

132

know the score until after he was committed—and under their hand.'

'That's a point. So what 'appens now?'

'We'll go on to Tangier in two days as arranged. I've told Mike he can reach me there. If he doesn't know anything himself, at least he'll spread the word that we're in the market. If the right ears pick it up, we may get an approach.'

'Okay. You doing anything tonight, Princess?'

'No. But don't worry about that, Willie love. I'm sure you're heavily involved.'

A chuckle. 'Trouble is, this one's a romantic.'

'That's good, isn't it?'

'*A* romantic. She wants me to spend the evening listening to one of these *fado* singers wailing about unrequited love. Too lugubrious for my liking.'

'You've been reading the music critics again. All right, what shall we do that's not lugubrious?'

'Well, we better not walk around looking cheerful after what's in the papers. The wrong people might notice—if they're around. What about a little sail down from Estoril to look at the Boca do Inferno?'

'Fine. I'll cook you a supper at the villa afterwards.'

'See you at the Estoril marina, then. About seven?'

'About seven.'

In the afternoon she had put on black and white check gingham shorts and shirt over her midnight blue one-piece swimsuit and walked down to the beach, to swim for an hour and to lie in the sun.

Eyes closed, feeling the warmth soak into her body, she thought about Willie Garvin. She was pleased that they would go sailing together this evening. Being with Willie was always good. She thought of the day, many years ago now, when she had bought him out of a Saigon gaol—a hard, muscular and dangerous man, seemingly empty of humanity; a man with a dull, blurred mind twisted by resentment and suspicion.

She had seen him fight in a terrifying Thai-style contest a week earlier, in an open arena where the Oriental Boxing

Federation were trying to introduce this ferocious form of combat to Vietnam. She had been awed by his speed and power, but that alone would not have tempted her to buy him for *The Network*. She remembered the moment soon after the knock-out of his opponent. . . .

He was looking along the aisle of the open-air arena as he pulled on his tattered shirt, and she glimpsed something in his face—a look of soul-weariness and grey despair. Following his gaze she saw the two policemen moving down the aisle. When she looked back at Willie Garvin all the bitterness and hatred had returned.

She saw the two policemen halt in front of him and speak curtly. He did not resist when they led him away. As he passed close to where she sat their eyes met. Perhaps he saw something in her face, for again the shroud of sullen anger fell momentarily away. He shrugged his big shoulders, and she saw a flash of humorous resignation in the blue eyes. Then he was gone.

She remembered being uncertain whether to bribe him out of trouble or forget him. It was those two brief glimpses of another and different man within him that decided her. And so she had bought him out and taken him back to Tangier with her, and over a period of no more than six weeks she had seen the old Willie Garvin die.

She knew, and had known almost from the beginning, that in some ways the new Willie Garvin had a better mind than hers. His skills were varied and of high quality. He absorbed knowledge without effort, and possessed almost total recall of anything he had heard or read. The new Willie Garvin walked tall and was a happy, confident man. She knew that she was the catalyst which had changed him, and in the early days this had troubled her, for she also knew that he lived by and through her, as if she were the source of his being.

She had never completely lost this sense of responsibility for him, but over the years dependence had become more mutual. They had fought and bled and won together, succoured each other in bad times, and tended each other's wounds when the bad times were over. For the first time in

134

her life she had found somebody she could dare to lean on, and to Modesty Blaise this was a gift beyond all purchase-price.

Other men she cherished in a different fashion, fully and with joy in the bodily consummation of an exciting relationship—but always transiently, because in the end she could belong only to herself. All these men together counted as nothing to her beside Willie Garvin.

Yes. It would be good to go out with him tonight. They would be quite alone in the sailing-dinghy, able to relax and talk—not about the job in hand, for there was nothing to be said. They could only wait now.

She decided she would get Willie going again on the writings of music critics. His exposition on that had been all too brief——

Somewhere close to her a voice said: 'Hallo.'

She opened her eyes. A man was squatting about a yard away, wearing a blue shirt, open-toed sandals and khaki shorts. He was in his mid-twenties with an angular face, dark hair and small hard eyes. He smiled and said in accented English: 'Do you like to come for a trip in the boat with my friend and me?'

The man was Italian or Sicilian, judging by his accent. The first immediate thought that this was a simple attempt at a pick-up on the beach she rejected as soon as her eyes opened. There was a quality in the man's attitude that set the sensitive alarms within her jangling. She knew trouble had found her. At the back of her mind there was surprise, for if this was the approach she had been trying to attract it had come impossibly soon and in an unexpectedly menacing way.

She raised herself on one elbow, looked at the man, then turned her head to look at his friend, who sat idly with a leg doubled under him, a crumpled cotton hat in his hand. The friend was a little taller but of the same stamp. A few yards from the water's edge bobbed a two-berth convertible cruiser. One man was aboard, another stood knee-deep in the water, holding the bows to keep the boat from grounding.

Modesty said: 'No. I don't wish to ride in your boat, thank you.'

The man nodded across her at his friend. 'Emilio wants very much. He say it is necessary.'

Emilio smiled with his lips but his eyes were very wary. He moved his hand and she saw that the crumpled hat screened a silenced gun. It was a Smith & Wesson Centennial, a snub-nosed hammerless revolver with a grip safety-catch. The front of the trigger-guard had been cut away. His finger was on the trigger and the grip safety-catch was depressed.

Watching his eyes she made a three-second analysis of the situation. She wore only the swim-suit and a pair of light sandals. Her hair was not piled in the chignon which on occasion contained a hidden kongo. The tear-gas lipstick was in her bedroom at the villa. There was no gun in her handbag, which lay inside the big straw beach-bag with her shirt and shorts. The handbag contained a small compact and a manicure set, lipstick, cigarettes and lighter, some money and two handkerchiefs.

Her only weapon was the large clasp of the handbag, a thing of black polished wood with two small hemispheres at the ends; it was gripped by a clip on the other side of the bag and could be jerked free to become a kongo.

The spokesman said: 'We go now.' He rose and stepped back. Emilio remained as before, the screened gun in his hand. She knelt up and lifted her hands to brush sand from her body. At the first movement the gun twitched a little. The spokesman, still smiling, said in a vicious whisper: 'No! Hands by sides and move slow. Very slow. Face to me, all the time.'

She got up. 'Do I take my things?'

He glanced round the beach, hesitated for a moment, then said: 'We take.' Quickly he scooped up the beach-bag and the rush mat. With a nod ordering her to follow him he moved towards the boat. She knew that Emilio was walking behind her, the hidden gun pointing at her back. Lowering her head she slid her eyes round to follow the shadow he

136

threw obliquely on the sand. He was keeping two arms'-lengths away from her—a good professional distance which permitted no easy countermove.

The man ahead splashed into the sea, waited for her, and smiled widely again for the benefit of any onlookers as he gave her a hand up into the boat. A gesture indicated that she was to sit on the port side amidships. Emilio took his seat facing her. The gun showed clearly now, hidden only from the shoreward side by the hat in his other hand.

The spokesman climbed aboard and the man holding the bows followed. She looked at him and said in Italian: 'The name is Forli, isn't it?'

He half-grinned and slid his eyes away from her.

Emilio spoke in Italian to Forli, his eyes never leaving Modesty. 'You know her?'

'I have seen her once in Catania. Four years ago. I was with Vecchi then, and she had business with him.'

The fourth man started the engine and the boat roared out in a long curve away from the beach.

Modesty said: 'Vecchi will be unhappy concerning this. He is an old friend.'

'Vecchi has his own problems.' Emilio smiled, his long mouth stretching back like the mouth of a crocodile. 'Vecchi is dead.'

The boat was heading west, parallel to the shore and half-a-mile out.

'A cigarette, please,' Modesty said, watching the shore, checking her position. Forli moved a hand to his pocket but Emilio froze him with an obscene curse.

'Keep away from her,' he said. 'You understand, imbecile? Don't go close to her. Not you, not anybody.'

Modestly filed away a fragment of knowledge in her mind. Whoever was behind this must be well-informed about her. He had sent four men to pick her up, and he had warned them that she was highly dangerous.

The spokesman opened her beach-bag, then the handbag, and began to check every item with meticulous care.

137

It was half-an-hour later that the launch idled into a rocky cove, its fender bumping gently against a crude wooden jetty. She was taken up a winding path through scrub and trees to a track where a car with a driver waited. The spokesman's name was Ugo, she had discovered now. On his orders she sat in the front between the driver and Forli. The other three sat in the back, Emilio in the middle, his gun touching her bare neck.

In ten minutes the big car drew up outside a large and ugly villa of pink and blue ochre. It stood alone in a high clearing amid a forest of umbrella-pines. A small red Fiat was parked on one side of the villa. Ugo gave orders. She got out and her captors closed about her. The big car moved off down the dirt road. She was taken along the side of the house and across the back to a broad terrace.

Four men sat in the room which opened on to the terrace. They were playing gin rummy. Three of them, though they had the look of the city about them, were in casual beach-wear. The other wore a lightweight fawn suit and a cream shirt with a matching tie. On a sofa behind him lay a soft cream poplin hat with a narrow brim. His face was thin and dark.

Two of the men in beachwear were Forli types, strong-arm thugs with little intelligence. The third was chunky with broad shoulders. Thick thighs emerged from crumpled shorts and tapered to small feet. Scanty black hair was combed sideways in thin strands across an almost bald skull. His eyes were cold and quick-moving. She marked him as dangerous —more dangerous than Emilio, who had been her first choice so far.

This grading was a subconscious thing, quite automatic. It was also very important, for a golden rule applied to combat against more than one opponent. When the time came, if it came, you took the danger-man first and took him fast.

He looked at her, spatulate fingers toying with the cards, hairy forearms resting on the table. 'I am Gerace. You hear of me, yuh?'

'Montlero's man?'

138

'Thass right. Montlero send me with some boys. So now you know we don't play small game, yuh?'

She nodded. Montlero had been big in the American hierarchy of gangsterdom. Deported four years ago to his home in Sicily, he still controlled a number of rackets in certain areas of the States. He also operated powerfully in Sicily and Italy.

She said: 'You've told me who. Now tell me why.'

Gerace lifted an eyebrow. 'You think you got no enemies?'

'Perhaps. But Montlero charges top prices. This would be a forty thousand dollar job.'

The man grinned. 'Maybe somebody don't like you more than he like forty thousand dollar.'

She was baffled but her face gave no hint of it. With a shrug she said: 'What happens now?'

'When I get word you find out what happen. Maybe tomorrow, maybe day after.' He gestured to Ugo, who put the beach-bag and its contents on the table, the manicure set a little apart from the rest.

'No weapons,' he said in Italian. 'Just the nail-file and scissors.'

Gerace put the cigarette lighter on top of the manicure set. 'You want her to start a fire maybe?' he said. He pawed over the other items then thrust them carelessly into the beach-bag with her shirt and shorts. 'Okay.' He picked up his cards.

Emilio took her by one arm, his gun pressed into her ribs. Forli gave her the beach-bag and gripped her other arm, watching her nervously. Together they took her out into a hall where a staircase led to the upper floor. Ugo followed.

When the door had closed behind them Gerace looked at the man in the lightweight fawn suit and said: '*Bene?*'

The other nodded. '*Bene.* Now you wait and see if they find the way out. It is arranged?'

'Yes.'

'Give them forty-eight hours.'

'And after that time?'

'The job is finished. You let them go, you kill them, what you like.'

139

Gerace rubbed his chin with a thumb. 'She has money to pay. Much money.'

'Not now. She has gambled stupidly.'

One of the other men spoke, sorting his cards. 'Better to kill them. Save trouble later.'

Gerace passed the tip of his tongue over fleshy lips. 'The woman has a fine body and much spirit,' he said musingly. 'We could use her first.'

The man in the fawn suit gave a little shrug. 'Only after forty-eight hours. That is the contract.' He looked at his watch. 'We finish this game, and I go.'

Modesty mounted the stairs with Forli beside her and Emilio behind. Her mind was busily occupied. From the first moment of sighting the villa she had been making mental snapshots of everything she had seen of its layout. Passing along the side and then across the terrace she had seen a large iron grille, four feet long by three feet deep, bolted to the rendered brickwork so that it completely covered one of the upper windows.

Now she was moving along a wide passage which would bring her to that room with the barred window.

The original door had been removed and stood against the wall of the passage. A new door had been substituted. This was of solid wood, looked very thick, and was hinged to open outwards. There was the brass escutcheon of a mortise lock on the door, and four holes had been drilled down the side opposite the hinges, each hole almost half-an-inch in diameter.

Ugo had moved on ahead. He stood waiting, holding a little cardboard box containing a spanner and four long screw-bolts with hexagonal heads. In the other hand he held a 9mm. Luger with a four inch barrel. A couch stood at the end of the passage, some ten paces beyond the door.

Ugo put down the cardboard box, took a key from his pocket and unlocked the door, keeping his weight against it. He jerked the door open and sprang back with the same movement, gun levelled at the doorway. Then he relaxed a little and said: 'Okay, Emilio.'

140

Emilio's gun prodded Modesty's back. She went into the room. Willie Garvin, in maroon swim-trunks and monk sandals, leaned with one shoulder against the frame of the window, looking out. The shutters were flat back against the inner wall and there was no window as such, only the bars of the grille.

On each side of the room stood a low iron bunk with a thin mattress and three folded blankets. A door led off to one side. It was open, and she could see a lavatory and a wash-basin. There was no window, only a small vent.

On the floor in the main room stood a cardboard box containing two loaves of bread and a number of packages. Beside this was a wooden chair bearing two china mugs. Otherwise the room was completely bare.

As she heard the door close behind her Willie turned from the window, a small absent-minded smile on his lips. He gave a little nod, as if something expected had now been confirmed, and said: "Allo, Princess.'

'Hallo, Willie.' She put her beach-bag down on one of the bunks. 'Been here long?'

'Couple of hours.' His voice matched her own quiet murmur. 'I wasn't sure which way to play it, but I reckoned they'd be bringing you along. Been no chance yet to play it different, anyway.'

'No. Same with me.'

There came a sound from the door. She saw that a new and very thick frame had been fitted. The faint sound was that of a screw-bolt biting into wood. She remembered the four holes drilled in the door. Ugo, or one of the others, was busy now with a spanner, screwing the bolts home so that the door would be held immovably to the solid frame.

She looked towards the cardboard box and said: 'Food?'

He nodded. 'And there's water in the tap.'

Modesty had the same absent expression now. It was as if they both spoke from the surface of thought while their minds were busy with other matters.

'Reckon it's anything to do with what we're after?' he said.

141

She shook her head and moved to stand beside him, looking out of the window. 'I can't see it. Wrong approach for anyone wanting to hire us, surely?'

'It's what Gerace said, then. Someone paying off an old score?'

'It's possible.' She gave a little shrug. 'If it's not what we want, I'm not interested in staying around to find out about it.'

'Right.'

A decision had been made, and now they could concentrate on immediate matters. Modesty opened the beach-bag and took out the handbag within. The kongo clasp had not been detached. She tapped it, glancing at Willie, and he gave a nod of satisfaction. Opening the handbag she took out the lipstick, looked round the room, then moved to the bare wall to one side of the door. Willie followed her.

Outside, the long bolts were still being screwed home.

Modesty drew a thin horizontal line on the wall and said in a whisper: 'Forty feet?'

He thought for a moment, then nodded. Quickly she sketched in the rear elevation of the house—the terrace and the french windows, the kitchen door to one side, the three upper windows and the roof.

Moving to a new space she began, more slowly this time, to draw a plan of the ground floor. At the side of this she marked an oblong with a circle in it. This was the little red Fiat she had seen parked there as she was brought round to the back.

From time to time she glanced at Willie for confirmation. Once he took the lipstick from her and marked a door in an interior wall. She knew that he would have observed every detail, as she had done. From what they had seen between them, inside and out, much that they had not seen could be accurately deduced. This was something she had taught Willie to do long ago, as a necessary principle of their profession.

In silence she sketched a plan of the upper floor. There was one area which neither of them could fill in with certainty. She marked a dividing wall with a query on it, then began to draw a larger-scale, detailed plan of the big lounge which opened on to the terrace, blocking in a layout of the furniture.

When she had finished Willie gave a final nod of agreement. For five minutes they stood in silence, studying the plans, only vaguely aware that the screwing-in of the bolts had ended and that the sound of footsteps was fading along the passage.

Modesty moved back to her bunk. She stripped off her swimsuit, took the shorts from her beach-bag and began to put them on. Willie turned from gazing at the plan and said softly: 'Finished with this, Princess?' He neither looked at her nor avoided looking at her. There were no mysteries between them.

She nodded and threw the swimsuit to him. He bundled it in one big hand and began to scrub the thin coral-coloured lines of lipstick from the wall. She put on her shirt, buttoned it, and sat down on the bunk.

Distantly there came the sound of a car driving off. That would be the Fiat. She patted the edge of the bunk and Willie sat down beside her.

He said: 'I've 'ad a good look round while I was waiting.'

'Anything?'

He frowned. 'Yes ... but I dunno what to think about it. Look.' He got up and lifted the end of the mattress. 'These bunks are made so they bolt together. The crossbar at the top of the legs just drops home with a sort of cap at each end fitting over the top of each leg. The legs themselves are bolted to the frame, see?'

She knelt down, bending low to follow his pointing finger, and saw the domed head of a thick bolt passing through the tubular iron leg and the angle-iron of the frame, with a square nut on the inner side.

She nodded and knelt up, looking at Willie, asking no questions. There must be four bolts to each bunk and he would have tried them all—because it was routine to explore everything minutely in a situation like this. He would have

143

examined the lavatory and the cistern, the wash-basin and the vent and the grille barring the window. If there had been any carpet or lino on the floor he would have lifted it to examine the boards beneath.

'All eight bolts screwed spanner-tight except one,' he said. 'Over 'ere.'

He moved to the other bunk and eased off the cross-bar, then knelt and began to unscrew one of the nuts at the head-end of the bunk. Modesty gripped the corner of the frame, taking the weight as he drew out the bolt and lifted the short tubular leg clear, then she lowered the corner gently until it rested on the floor.

Willie held the leg for her to see. The hole through which the bolt had passed was about three-quarters of an inch square.

'Why that size and shape?' she said quietly.

'I dunno. You'd think it would be round. But that square 'ole is just the size of the nuts that bolt that grille on outside the window.'

She stood frowning in thought. The iron bed-leg could easily be slipped through the grille. With a little manoeuvring, arms reaching out through the bars at the side, it would not be too difficult to get the square hole over the head of a nut and unscrew it from the bolt grouted into the wall, using the leverage of the bed-leg as a spanner.

In two hours you could get all four nuts off. Blankets tied together would do for lowering the heavy grille to the ground below. Climb down the blanket-rope, and away.

Willie was watching her intently. She shook her head and said: 'No. It's too good. That's what they want us to do.'

He nodded, pleased. 'That's what I reckoned. But why?'

'I wouldn't know, Willie love. But let's not do it their way. We'll do it our own way.'

'Okay. What time d'you reckon?'

'If that bed-leg thing was really set up for us, they'll be expecting us to try something after dark. So we'll make our move before then. Let me think about it for a bit, Willie.'

'Right.' He reassembled the bunk and stretched out on his

144

back, hands behind his head. Modesty lay on the other bunk.

'How many picked you up?' she asked.

'Four.' He nodded down at his body, naked but for the swim-trunks and sandals. 'Picked me up off the beach just like this. I was with Luisa.'

'The *fado* singing fan?'

'Yes.'

'She saw them take you?'

'No.' He grinned. 'Next best to *fado* singers she likes ice-cream. Crazy about banana-flavour. I was just on me way along the beach to get 'er another and the quartet joined me. All nice and friendly, you know?'

'I know. What were they like?'

When he had described them she nodded. 'The same four who picked me up later.'

'Busy afternoon for 'em. But it's a nice technique, Princess.'

'Yes. We'll have to remember it.'

She closed her eyes. Her body was relaxed but in her mind there was a light, splendid tautness. This was the pleasure of the climber facing the overhang, of the sky-diver waiting to jump, of the big-game hunter stalking the tiger. This was her stimulant, and she was neither glad nor sorry about it. She simply accepted it.

Long ago, in the days when she was a small wild creature without even a name, in the days of the war and the long lone journeys through the Balkans and the Middle East, this sensation had been raw fear; but even before puberty it had been transmuted by long familiarity into the stimulant that it was now.

As a climber studies the route ahead, peering with intent eyes to judge the problems to be mastered, so she now made her assessment of the task that she and Willie would face.

Four men had picked them up. Another four had been playing gin rummy when she arrived. The Fiat had driven away; deduct one man at least. Seven, then. Unless there were others in the house she had not seen. She doubted this.

They would probably have dinner around half-past eight or nine, then settle down to play cards. That would be the best time to take them, when they were all together. A scattered fight through the house against men with guns would be almost suicidal.

She thought about the couch on the landing. Was it for a guard? There seemed little point in guarding the passage when the door was fixed immovably by the screwbolts. Perhaps the couch was simply a matter of accommodation, a place for one of the men to sleep.

She opened her eyes and said: 'How long do you think it will take to get into action, Willie?'

He looked reflectively at the bare wall. 'About forty minutes, give or take ten.'

'Can you manage it quietly?'

'Sure. I got a lovely idea for that. I'll need about thirty minutes to get set for it.'

'You can have a couple of hours. We won't be starting till nine.'

'Yes.' He had been following her earlier thoughts and reached the same conclusion. 'Hope they're all in the big back room, and take 'em there?'

'You from the kitchen, Willie. Me from the hall.'

'Best way. There'll be seven of 'em.'

'Yes. I'll use The Nailer.'

'Right.'

There was silence for several minutes. Willie turned on his side to face her and said: 'Princess, I been meaning to ask. How you getting on with *Alice in Wonderland*?'

'I can't quite make up my mind.' She frowned at the ceiling. 'If I'd read it when I was small I'd probably see it quite differently. But reading it now, knowing it's a classic, knowing Carroll was a bit of a weirdie, I keep looking out for the symbolism and psychology of the thing.' She paused, reflecting. 'I think I like the verses best, but I don't like Alice. Why doesn't she get frightened more?'

'Well, it's like a dream, I suppose. You know, not real for the kid.'

146

'At her age I got more scared by dreams than anything else.'

'Me too.'

'Did you read it when you were small, Willie?'

'My auntie read it to me,' he said reminiscently. 'In ten-minute spells between customers.'

She knew about Willie's 'auntie', the woman who had purported to look after him when his unmarried mother had died.

'I didn't think she was the kind who would read to you, Willie.'

'Only when she was tight, and only between customers. Then she'd go sort of maudlin. When she was sober she'd more likely thump 'ell out of me for not being asleep.' He grinned cheerfully. 'I liked that better than *Alice in Wonderland* wafting on a gin-laden breeze. At least it taught me 'ow to duck before I was six.'

He got up off the bunk and said: 'Plenty of time, but I'll just go and get me gear ready.'

He went into the lavatory, leaving the door open. She followed him and stood in the doorway to watch. Kneeling down, he gripped the rather long, curving waste-pipe under the wash-basin, holding it by the metal trap at the bottom of the U-bend. Bracing his other hand against the wall, he heaved suddenly.

The lead pipe bent sideways a little, at the point where it entered the basin and at the point where it ran out through the wall.

'Willie Garvin is a good boy and can go to the top of the class,' she said.

He grinned, then thrust hard at the pipe, bending it in the opposite direction. For five minutes she watched the rippling and knotting of his powerful shoulder-muscles as he bent the pipe back and forth. It was a task for a very strong man, and one who knew how to use his strength. Between each thrust and pull his muscles relaxed completely. There was no scrap of energy wasted.

The pipe broke off just under the sink. Taking it in both

147

hands he waggled it easily back and forth until it broke again at the point of entry into the wall.

'For my next trick,' he said, 'I shall need the assistance of a young lady from the audience.'

They went back into the main room. Willie loosened the leg on his bunk, but did not unscrew the nut completely. Because the bolt was long, there was now an inch of play between the leg and the angle-iron of the frame.

'You 'old the piping in the gap so the middle of it comes between the leg and the frame, Princess.'

She obeyed. Willie gripped the top of the leg and pushed on it steadily, using the leverage to crush the lead pipe between the leg and the frame. Again and again he pushed hard, and Modesty saw the middle of the piping slowly flatten into a solid bar.

'Okay, Princess.' She took the length of piping away and handed it to him. The flat section in the middle was about three inches long, swelling out at the edges in a lozenge shape.

Willie began to rub the middle of the lozenge against a corner of the iron bed-frame, cutting a thin groove at first which quickly deepened as threads of the soft lead were chiselled away. After a while he turned the pipe over and made a similar groove on the other side.

When he was satisfied he bent the pipe back and forth several times. It broke at the groove, leaving him two short lengths of lead pipe with flared chisel-edges. The brass waste-pipe was in the middle of one length.

'Nice 'eavy stuff, lead,' he said.

'Yes.' She took one of the pieces and weighed it in her hand, her eyes very thoughtful. 'We could make more use of it.'

He looked at her quickly. 'You got an idea?'

'I think so. But not for now. For another time, Willie love.'

Willie tightened the loose leg of the bunk and stretched himself out comfortably again. Modesty took the other bunk.

'Did I ever tell you about that Japanese girl pearl diver I used to know?' he said.

'Pearl diver? No, she's a new one, Willie.'

'Lovely girl, she was. But she was always practising 'olding her breath. She could do it for minutes on end, and she used to practise at the funniest times.'

'Not in bed?'

'So help me, Princess. In bed. Frightened the life out of me, first time she did it. Talk about creepy.'

She laughed. 'All this time and I'm still not sure whether you make these girl-stories up, Willie.'

'I don't make 'em up,' he said simply. 'I reckon there must be something about me that attracts bizarre girls.'

Gerace stirred his coffee.

'Listen,' he said. 'I don't want anything to go wrong. If Blaise and Garvin are very smart, they'll be working on that grille tonight after dark. If they're just smart, they'll get to it tomorrow night. If they're not smart enough . . .' He shrugged. 'Then we have some fun, maybe.'

He looked round at the men sitting at table with him in the villa's dining room.

'You clear up here, Forli.' He gestured at the table. 'When you finish in the kitchen, you go up to the passage.'

'What do I do there, Gerace?' Forli asked anxiously.

'You lie on the couch and read a dirty book, I think.' Gerace grinned. 'But you listen a little. Maybe you hear some noises and you can tell they are doing something with the leg from the bunk.'

Gerace lit a cigarette and inhaled. 'From ten-thirty on, there must be one man in the big room at the back, and one in the garden. With guns.'

Ugo said: 'Why this? If they find the way out, we must let them go, yes?'

'You are a fool, Ugo,' Gerace said with contempt. 'Yes, we let them go if they find the way out. But suppose they do *not* go? Suppose they think we are all asleep, and come into the house?'

149

'Garvin is death with his knives,' Forli said uneasily. 'And Modesty Blaise——'

'Garvin does not have his knives,' Gerace cut in. 'The woman has nothing. But even so they are dangerous. Therefore two men will be awake at all times as I have said. Emilio, you will arrange the shifts.'

'From ten-thirty onwards?' said Emilio.

'Yes.' Gerace got to his feet, looking at his watch. It was nine-fifteen. 'Come,' he said, 'we play a little poker. I am tired of gin rummy.'

ELEVEN

THE sun had not yet set. In the sealed room the shutters were closed now. The two bunks stood on end near the middle of the room, leaning together at the top so that they supported each other. They were lashed with strips of blanket, and the two mattresses had been thrown over the top of the inverted V to make a more comfortable platform.

Willie was crouched on top of the structure, close to where a long flex hung down with a lamp on the end of it. The light was switched on.

Willie placed the chisel-edge of one length of lead piping against the plaster of the ceiling about eighteen inches from the flex. Using the other length as a hammer, he struck the butt-end of the lead chisel sharply.

There was hardly any noise as lead met lead, but the chisel-edge drove a quarter of an inch into the plaster. Modesty was moving about, clattering the china mugs, running water into the basin and catching it in a mug as it flowed through the broken waste-pipe, pulling the lavatory chain, and generally making a reasonable amount of innocent noise.

Willie continued his work. Five minutes later he pulled the first piece of plaster away from the laths above. He nodded to Modesty, and she slammed the lavatory door as Willie snapped two of the brittle laths with a blow from his

150

lead hammer. He pushed his arm through the hole and located the nearest joist.

The run of the joists was from the window towards the door. Willie lightly marked out a rectangle on the ceiling with the point of his chisel and set to work again. In twenty minutes he had chipped and broken away a rectangle of plaster fifteen inches wide and two feet long. The width was as great as the distance between the parallel joists would allow.

Some of the laths had broken. Willie used a blanket to muffle the snapping of those that remained, and Modesty set the noisy lavatory-cistern roaring again as he did so.

Willie knelt up and turned sideways to ease his broad shoulders between the joists. A moment later he had disappeared into the loft. Modesty saw his face in the rectangle for a moment as one long arm reached down to draw up the flex and lamp which hung only six inches from one end of the hole.

She picked up her beach-bag and mounted the improvised scaffolding. Carefully she hoisted herself up through the gap and stood with legs straddled, feet resting on the joists.

Willie was moving warily across the loft. She lifted the lamp as high as the flex would allow, to give him more light. After a few moments she saw him turn and give a thumbs-up signal.

He had found the access trap.

She moved across the joists and knelt beside him. The trap was simply a hinged wooden flap about three feet square. Willie lifted it an inch, put his head down and peered through. They were at the end of the broad passage, a little beyond the head of the couch. He eased the trap a little higher and signalled for Modesty to look.

Forli was lying on the couch, a little forward of the trap. She could see the back of his head and shoulders above the upcurving end of the couch. He was reading a paper-back book.

She signalled Willie to lower the trap again, frowning a little. It would be easy for one or other of them to drop down and put Forli out, but the trap would have to be fully opened for that; the hinges might squeak; the drop would have to be made as a standing jump, and that might be noisy. Forli needed time for only one loud shout of alarm.

Willie tapped her arm. In the dim light she saw him make a circle of finger and thumb. He moved away to the hole cut in the ceiling and vanished down through it. When he returned two minutes later he was carrying both lengths of lead piping.

She started to shake her head. Willie could throw anything with unfailing accuracy. He could put Forli out easily enough, but the lead falling to the floor would make a heavy thud.

Then she saw that he had tied a strip of blanket, half-an-inch wide and seven or eight feet long, to the heavier piece of lead with the metal trap in it.

He lay flat as she eased open the access flap . . . an inch, three inches, eight inches. The hinges did not squeak. Now the gap was wide enough for him to edge forward so that half his body extended over the edge of the framed hole. She rested her weight across the back of his thighs to support him.

Willie Garvin judged his distance and threw the chunk of lead with a quick downward flick of the wrist. It took Forli solidly on the back of the skull. The man barely moved. His arms simply fell so that the book rested on his lap. The piece of lead dropped on the rounded top of the couch and slithered off. Willie jerked at the strip of blanket in his other hand. The lead stopped short a foot from the floor and hung swinging like a pendulum.

Willie drew in the strip of blanket, and Modesty opened the trap wide. He sat up and turned so that his legs dangled through the opening. Easing himself forward, he hung by his hands and dropped lightly to the floor. Modesty tossed the beach-bag and the two pieces of lead down to him in turn.

When she lowered herself through the opening and dropped soundlessly beside him, Willie was already searching Forli. The man carried no gun on him, but in his trouser-pocket was a flick knife with a haft of bone and steel. The four-inch blade slid out at Willie's touch. Modesty watched as he stood with dust streaking his body, resting the knife across the tip of one finger to test its balance. After a moment he nodded, pushing out his lower lip ruefully. He was not enthusiastic about the knife, but it would do.

She lifted one of Forli's eyelids, then felt his pulse. He was concussed. How badly she could not tell, but he would give no warning for a good fifteen minutes, and that was her only concern. There was no need to tie him up. The action would be over, one way or another, within the next five minutes.

The stairs led down to a hall with the front door to the right and three other doors leading off, one of them to the big back room. On bare feet now, so that their sandals would not slap on the floor, they moved down the stairs.

The door to the back room was closed. They could hear talking and the clink of a glass. One of the other doors stood partly open. According to the plan of the house imprinted on their minds, the wall in this room was common to the kitchen. Willie went into the room first, the knife held by the tip of the blade between a thumb and two fingers. Modesty followed a pace behind. She had left the beach-bag up on the landing, but she carried the kongo in one hand and a piece of the lead piping in the other.

They halted, looking for what they hoped to see. It was there. A door in the common wall, leading into the kitchen. Willie crossed the room, eased the door gently open, and peered inside. The kitchen was empty. He left the door ajar and returned to Modesty. She had taken off her shirt and was naked to the waist, ready for The Nailer, the device which would give them a priceless three-second advantage.

She gave him the piece of lead. The kongo was gripped in her right hand. She put her left hand on his shoulder and leaned forward, her lips close to his ear. 'On a count of twelve, Willie. From . . . *now*.'

At her last word Willie moved away. She watched him go through the door into the kitchen. Turning, she went out into the hall. The seconds ticked away precisely in her head. She walked through the hall and curled her fingers round the handle of the door.

Eight seconds, nine seconds . . .

She opened the door wide and stepped inside quietly and without haste, pushing the door shut behind her. With wrists bent, the backs of her hands resting on her hips, she stood still. Her face wore a bright inquiring smile.

Five men sat at the round table—Gerace and Ugo, the two thugs and the man who had driven the boat. One man stood by the bar over to her right, refilling a glass. Emilio.

Six blank faces stared towards her. Six rigid bodies made a frozen tableau.

The men were nailed.

Ten seconds . . .

The kitchen door opened quietly and Willie stepped into the room. He carried the hunk of lead pipe in his left hand, the knife in his right. No head turned towards him.

Modesty snap-shotted the scene in every detail. Two guns on view, Emilio's under his arm in a shoulder holster, Gerace's also in a holster but hanging on the back of his chair. That made Emilio the danger-man. The two thugs would have been facing Willie if their heads had not been turned towards her. Ugo faced her directly across the table. The boatman and Gerace had their backs obliquely towards Willie.

Eleven seconds . . .

She took two unhurried steps obliquely forward, leaving Emilio on her right flank, apparently ignoring him.

Twelve seconds. A man loosed pent-up breath. The tableau flickered and stirred.

Modesty took a long swerving stride. The bottle dropped from Emilio's hand and he snatched for his gun. Her leg swung with the whole impetus of her body behind it. Her toes were arched back and the ball of her foot hit Emilio squarely on the solar plexus with the explosive energy of her hundred and thirty pounds behind it.

The boatman was toppling sideways, the short length of

154

lead bouncing from the side of his head. That throw would have been for Gerace, but he was in line with Modesty and a miss might have caught her.

Willie's body followed the throw in a feet-first flying dive that took him hurtling across the surface of the table. His feet lashed out at the two thugs and one big hand swung like an axe to chop at Gerace. But the man was fast. He rode the blow, falling sideways with his chair.

Emilio was out, his body crumpling, glass crashing as he slithered down against the bar. Modesty spun away from him. She saw one of the thugs reeling dazedly towards her, and dropped him with a quick, economical side-jab of the kongo below his ear. The other thug was on his hands and knees, head wobbling, trying to rise. On the edge of her vision she saw Willie jerk Ugo upright with his left hand and drop him with a four-inch jab to the jaw from the heel of the same hand.

Willie had not used his right so far. It held the knife.

Gerace was on his side on the floor, teeth showing in a death's-head grimace, hand scrabbling for the holstered gun which now lay on the floor by the overturned chair.

Modesty relaxed and walked towards the man on his knees, knowing that the business was over. Eight seconds had passed since she had entered the room.

She heard Willie Garvin say sharply: "Old it, Gerace.' An instant later there came a faint thud and a strangled yelp of agony.

Willie said: 'I told you.'

The thug had managed to rise from his knees and was swaying on rubbery legs. She hit him sharply twice, once on each arm, then pushed him towards an easy chair that stood a little way from the table. He flopped into it, arms hanging limp and helpless, like wet string.

She looked across the room. The thrown flick-knife had pierced the fleshy part of Gerace's forearm, pinning it to the floor. Willie stood over the man now. He bent down, jerked the flick-knife free, and picked up the gun which lay just clear of the holster.

Painfully Gerace lifted his dripping arm from the floor and hugged it to his stomach. His face was pale now, his eyes blank with shock.

Willie said: 'Well, that's that bit then, Princess.' There was a contented look on his face. She smiled at him and moved to pick up Emilio's gun. Willie went out of the room and returned a few moments later with her shirt. He held it for her as she slipped it on.

'Look after things here, Willie love. I'll check through the place.'

'Okay, Princess.'

She went out and began to work her way methodically through the whole house, searching every room. There were no letters or papers to explain why she and Willie had been picked up. In two of the four bedrooms she found guns. Forli, on the couch in the passage, was still breathing. He stirred as she bound his hands tightly with a strip of blanket.

On her way down the stairs she heard a sudden yelp from the back room. She ignored it and went out of the front door. There were no cars on the dusty driveway, and the garage at the side was empty. Behind the garage stood an old four-wheeled carriage with elliptical springs. It was in the barouche style with a half open body. For many decades it must have been preserved with care, for the coachwork and wheels were still sound, but now it had been left to rot and already the marks of two or three seasons' weather lay upon it.

She went round to the back of the house. There was no garden as such, only a stretch of scrubby grass with encircling trees beyond. A small wooden shed stood near the trees at the farthest point from the house. She checked it carefully. Inside were some old buckets, a rusty felling-axe, some coils of thick rope, and a wheel-barrow.

Twenty minutes after she had left Willie she came back into the room by way of the terrace windows. Inward laughter swept through her. One of the thugs had been stripped to his underpants and Willie was wearing his florid Bermuda shirt, slacks which were two inches too short for him, and

156

pointed leather shoes in white and tan with plaited toe-caps.

Of the six men, five lay on their backs on the floor, hands resting on their heads, thumbs tied tightly together with twisted strips of cloth. They were all conscious now and lying in a row, but no man was moving.

Surprisingly, Gerace lay insensible on the sofa. His right forearm was swathed in a thick bandage made from a ripped table-cloth. Willie sat on the edge of the table, smoking, toying with the flick-knife. Three guns lay on the table together with a brimming saucer, a bottle of Dettol, and a reel of thread with a needle stuck in it.

'What happened to him, Willie?' Her head indicated Gerace.

'I thought I'd better put a few stitches in the arm, Princess.' He nodded towards the reel of thread. 'Better than nothing. But it's a bit tricky, using a straight needle.'

'Did he faint?'

'Not exactly.' There was a hint of apology in Willie's voice. 'The stupid burke started 'ollering and jerking about so I chilled 'im for a bit. He'll be round soon, though.'

'Good. I want to talk to him.'

Willie offered her a cigarette from the packet on the table, and lit it from a slender gold lighter she had never seen before. It had come with the clothes, no doubt. She sat down in the easy chair and stretched out her legs, watching Gerace. The eyes of the men lying on the floor flickered back and forth in uncomprehending fear, watching this strange pair smoke in peaceable silence.

'Bit late for that sail we were going to 'ave,' Willie said at last, regretfully.

'I don't know. It's nicer at night. But they don't seem to keep a car here, Willie.'

'Nothing?'

'Only a carriage. Like one of those things in the Coach Museum in Lisbon, but not so ornate. No car.'

'Pity.'

'Yes. You'd better bring down the one upstairs, Willie love.'

'He's alive?'

'He was coming round when I last saw him.'

Willie went out. He was gone longer than seemed necessary and it was three minutes before he returned with Forli over his shoulder. Forli's eyes were open now. Willie put him down beside the others.

Gerace stirred, and Modesty went across to the sofa where he lay. She pinched his ear sharply. After a moment or two his eyes opened. Understanding came slowly into them. His lips parted in a feeble smile, half fearful, half hopeful. The fear did not surprise her. She had often found that the professional hatchet-man fought well only up to the moment of defeat; beyond that point he was no stoic.

She said: 'What was it all about, Gerace?'

'I—I don't know. This is the truth.' His voice was ingratiating, inviting sympathy and professional understanding from the enemy. 'Montlero has a good offer to do this job. He sends me with a few boys. It's just a job—you know?'

'I know. When you see Montlero, tell him that if I haven't killed him inside a year he can sleep easy again. I never bear grudges for long.'

'A year . . .' Gerace's smile grew sickly. Then another implication in her words dawned on him and he brightened, nodding vigorously. 'When I see him again? Sure, sure—I tell him.'

'I meant *if* you see him again, Gerace. Now tell me what the job was.'

He started to make a placating gesture, then winced and held his bandaged arm. 'But I told you. I don't know, Modesty——'

The knife that had been in Willie's hand flashed past within an inch of Gerace's ear and buried itself in the back of the sofa. Gerace went the colour of dirty milk.

Willie said: '*Miss Blaise*, you bloody little crumb.' He walked across and recovered the knife, his face taut with genuine anger.

'Sorry! Okay, sorry!' Gerace said frantically. He looked at Modesty again. 'I don't know, Miss Blaise. We come to

158

Lisbon, we meet a contact, the man you saw here with us. We don't know his name. He puts the finger on you and on—' he gulped and corrected his imminent error, '—on Mr. Garvin. All we must do is take you and hold you here forty-eight hours. We rent the house, we fix up the room and then we . . . we do the job.'

'What was supposed to happen after forty-eight hours?'

'We let you go, Miss Blaise,' Gerace said virtuously. 'The job is finish.'

Willie Garvin laughed. It was not a humorous laugh.

'Is true!' Gerace said with desperate conviction. 'I swear on my mother's grave!'

Modesty looked at Willie, a tiny frown of query between her eyes.

'The forty-eight hour bit's true, Princess.' He jerked a thumb towards Forli. 'I had a chat with that one before I brought 'im down. Same story. Except we were supposed to get out using that bed-leg as a spanner. And if we didn't, Gerace could do what 'e liked with us after that.'

'I don't see it,' she said slowly.

'Nor me. You want to follow it back? Go after the contact bloke?'

'No.' She spoke for Gerace's benefit. 'We'll maybe ask Montlero himself.' She moved to the table and stubbed out her cigarette. 'There's no phone laid on here, Willie. It looks as if we'll have to walk.'

'A good seven or eight miles to Cascais, I reckon.'

'Never mind. It's a nice night.'

'These shoes aren't too comfy, and you've only got sandals. Mind if I take a look round? I got 'alf an idea.'

She suddenly knew what was in his mind, but hid her laughter, knowing it would please him to surprise her. 'All right, Willie.' She picked up one of the guns. 'You go and look around.'

The coach creaked and lurched slowly on its way, moving more smoothly now that it was on a metalled road. The sun had set long ago, and it was almost two hours since the coach

159

had begun its journey down the long dusty track from the villa.

Gerace sat on the coachman's seat, his bandaged arm hidden under a mack draped about him like a cloak. Emilio and Ugo were the lead-horses, with the other four men behind them in two files along the single shaft, all connected by a single rope knotted about each man's waist. They leaned against the hauling ropes, hands raw, shoulders aching as they fought the slight but long slope up to the final descent into Cascais.

Their minds had long since become empty of thought. Panting, straining, mouths open, they sweated on in the curious apathy that exhaustion can bring. The first half-hour on the long winding track running down from the villa had been like something out of an old Keystone Cops film.

Three times Gerace had been late in applying the brake, and the carriage had ploughed slowly into the human horses. Insults had been screamed. God and His Mother and His Angels had been called upon. Theories on the laws of motion, impetus, kinetics, and the conservation of energy had been advanced in crude lay terms and bitterly disputed. When Gerace, the discredited leader, tried to weld his team into a working unity, he had been invited to perform sexual assaults upon himself which even the stone-carvers of ancient Pompeii had never dreamed of.

But now the flame of rebellion had died to cold ashes. By trial and error the team had fallen into the least unsatisfactory system for combining to perform their task. Any glimmering thoughts of relief or escape were long since extinct.

It was only important now that the strain on the ropes should remain steady; that the fool immediately behind should not tread on your heels; that the ape in front should keep his feet out of your way; that the clown on the seat should brake sufficiently on the down-slopes but not too much; that curious observers should be satisfied with the curt answer from Ugo, who spoke a little Portuguese, that this was a wager performed for charity.

160

Modesty Blaise was asleep, leaning sideways, her head cushioned against Willie's shoulder. The lurching of the coach did not disturb her. For half her life she had never known the comfort of a bed, and she could sleep at will under any conditions.

Willie Garvin leaned back in the corner of the coach, watching Gerace's back and the heads of the human horses beyond. There was a gun tucked down beside him, and the flick-knife was jabbed into the front of the seat so that it lay within an inch of his dangling hand.

'I'm not too 'ot with a gun,' he had warned the team cheerfully at the outset. 'So if there's any trouble I'll let Gerace 'ave it first with the knife. Then I'll just 'ave to do me best with the gun, so let's 'ope I manage to shoot the one who's acting frisky, and not someone else, eh?'

There had been no trouble.

Willie inhaled the warm night air. He was replete with contentment. This was a time he savoured, the aftermath of action, a time of peace when the nerves lay relaxed like sleeping athletes yet the senses remained wholly sharp and the world was splendidly clear.

There had been many times like this in the years since Modesty Blaise had entered his life and remade the world for him. The action tonight had been brief and, as it happened, undemanding. There had been other times, harder times, of long and savage action, of hurt and pain and wounds to be tended, yet the aftermath of peace and contentment was always the same.

He thought about a man he had known long ago; another Willie Garvin, who had never found that peace, who had found little joy in anything until that vividly remembered day when a dark girl of twenty, looking like a princess, had faced him across a table in a Saigon gaol and said: 'You're leaving now, Willie Garvin—with me.'

In the semi-darkness of the coach her head shifted on his shoulder and re-settled. She gave a sleeper's sigh, and then her breathing was steady again.

'Oh, Christ,' Willie Garvin thought with deep humility,

161

and wondered at the marvel of it all. She was infinitely above him, though she would never have it so. Her mind had a lucidity and her spirit an impregnable strength that he could never dream of matching, but she seemed strangely unaware of this difference in them. There had been nobody to remake the world for her, as she had remade it for him; yet out of a childhood which he flinched from imagining she had emerged as . . . Modesty Blaise.

He felt no envy of Mike Delgado or any other man who had possessed her in that way. In a hundred ways he, Willie Garvin, possessed her far more fully than any of them, because by heaven-sent fortune she had chosen to create him, and the bonds forged by that act of creation were as hoops of steel compared with the silk-thread bonds which sometimes, briefly, held her to other men.

Willie Garvin looked out of the coach. Gerace was using the brake now, and the human horses were relaxing, plodding wearily down the slope to the lights of Cascais.

He reached across his chest and patted Modesty's cheek gently. She did not stir from his shoulder but her voice was wide awake as she said: 'Are we there, Willie?'

'Just about. Cascais in five minutes. We'll be able to pick up a cab to the villa.'

'It can wait while I change and get packed. Then we'll go on and collect your stuff at the hotel.'

'Okay. We moving out, Princess?'

'Yes.' She touched his ear, and he knew she was speaking for Gerace to hear. 'Listen. I've figured a marvellous way to get hold of Montlero, right on his home ground. Then we'll get him to tell us who hired him to set up this job. And why.'

Willie made his laugh soft and chilling. 'I'll take care of making 'im sing. All you need is a button-'ook and a box of matches——' he broke off, then resumed hopefully. 'You don't reckon Gerace 'ere might know the answers after all?'

Gerace shuddered visibly.

Modesty said: 'I don't think so, Willie. And anyway, it's Montlero I want to see wriggle.'

'He'll wriggle all right,' Willie said with gruesome relish.

He knew they would not be heading for Sicily. But Gerace and his men would be on the earliest plane they could catch. And Montlero would sweat for a long time to come.

At ten o'clock the next morning a man in a lightweight fawn suit moved from room to room through the empty villa Gerace had rented. There was a puzzled expression on his face and a gun in his hand.

It took him some time to unscrew the bolts holding the door of the sealed room. When at last he entered he stood staring at the hole in the ceiling for a full minute. The grille over the window was still in place.

An hour later, in Lisbon, he sent off a coded cable to an address in Barcelona.

TWELVE

TARRANT eyed the papers on his desk. There were three newspaper cuttings about Dall's coup in the casino in Beirut at the expense of 'the wealthy, beautiful and enigmatic member of London society, Modesty Blaise'.

Enigmatic was a sub-editor's word, Tarrant thought. You couldn't be sued for it. As for London society . . . that would amuse her.

There were many more cuttings about the theft and recovery of the Watteau. René Vaubois had done extremely well there, Tarrant acknowledged. He decided to send Vaubois a packet of *Swoop* to feed his pigeons. It would delight Vaubois to discover that the English actually bought packets of special food to give to wild birds.

Lastly there was the single pale-green sheet containing the report from his man in Lisbon. It was brief and not very informative.

Tarrant sat back and looked at Fraser, his number two. Fraser was a slight man, nearing fifty. He wore spectacles and had the humble manner of a Dickensian bank clerk. It was a manner which had served him admirably through long years of field work.

'What do you think, Fraser?' Tarrant asked.

Fraser looked down diffidently at the carpet. 'The Beirut affair appears to have every sign of credibility, Sir Gerald. The theft—' he corrected himself with a swift, furtive look, '—or perhaps I should say the *putative* theft of the Watteau was also very satisfactory.'

'Yes. Putative. That's very accurate.' Tarrant waited for Fraser to compose a smile of doglike gratitude. 'And what about this?' He flicked the sheet of pale-green paper.

'It seems to be a little unspecific, sir.' Fraser said with great caution, lifting his voice at the end so that the phrase became a tentative question rather than a statement.

'I suppose it's a bit woolly,' said Tarrant, 'but you're expecting rather a lot, Jack.' The use of the Christian name told Fraser to drop the role he played from long habit and speak plainly.

Fraser took off his glasses and began to polish them. 'A lot?' he echoed. There was contempt in his voice.

'Yes. Our chap in Lisbon had to work almost blind. Don't be too hard on him.'

'I'd geld the bastard with a blunt knife,' Fraser said simply. 'You tell him to observe and report. He observes sweet sod-all, and reports that he *thinks* something happened between Modesty Blaise and a bunch led by Gerace who happened to be in Lisbon at the same time.'

Fraser put on his glasses again and continued grimly. 'He doesn't know *what* happened, or where either of the parties of the first and second parts have gone now. He also mentions Delgado, and doesn't know where *he's* gone. He further mentions and describes a man he hasn't been able to identify, but who drives a small red Fiat. Christ, my half-witted mother-in-law could do a better job for us, and she's been dead five years.'

'You did instruct him not to get in the middle of anything,' Tarrant said reasonably. 'Observing under those conditions isn't easy—as you well know.'

164

'We don't pay people to do easy things,' Fraser said stubbornly. He dropped into an armchair and lit a cigarette. Tarrant found the irritable scowl on his assistant's face almost comical, and yet he sympathised. Fraser would have observed without getting in the middle. He had a priceless knack for that sort of thing. Because it was a gift, he had no understanding for people less able.

'I don't think Lisbon matters much now,' Tarrant said. 'She'll be going on to Tangier with Willie. That was the original idea.'

'Unless the approach has been made already.' Fraser drew on his cigarette, then looked at it with hostility. 'Another fourteen mercenaries have vanished from circulation in the last two weeks—and that's just from our own lists. There could be five times as many.'

'She had to get into the right orbit for an approach to be made,' said Tarrant. 'Lisbon would have been too soon—less than twenty-four hours after her failure to get the Watteau. Her putative failure,' he added, straight-faced.

'I'm not sure what you're worried about,' Fraser said. 'She's set herself up. We can only wait and hope something happens. God knows we're used to waiting and hoping.'

Tarrant got up and walked to the window. He stood with hands in his pockets, looking down on Whitehall. 'I'm worried about communications,' he said at last. 'We've assumed that if an approach was made she could let us know about it and we'd find some way to keep track of her and Willie through the pipe-line. But it may not work out like that. And we've set up no system of emergency communication with her.'

'I'm not sure that she'll like the idea,' Fraser said doubtfully. 'But if she's at her place in Tangier you can ring her and fix something.'

'No.' Tarrant shook his head. 'I want you to go out there, Jack.'

'Me?' Fraser was astonished, but there was an undertone of eagerness in his voice. 'I'd have to be regraded for that.'

'It wouldn't be official.' Tarrant turned from the window.

165

'None of this is official so far, anyway. You take three weeks' leave, starting tomorrow, and you do what you like with it.'

Fraser got up and stubbed out his cigarette in the big ashtray on the desk. There was a new alertness in his movements. He said: 'I've been behind a desk for the last five years.'

'You feel you may have lost something in that time?'

Fraser thought carefully, then said: 'No. Do you?'

'That's something only you can judge. I'm not giving you a directive, you understand. But I can think of nobody who could do this kind of job better, or even half as well.'

Fraser nodded. Without vanity, he held the same view. A slight grin touched his thin face. 'Modesty Blaise won't thank you for putting me in.'

'I know.' Tarrant's voice was dry. 'She'll no doubt express her views in a very caustic fashion. Your best tactic is to agree with her, Jack, or even anticipate her. Complain of me with weary resignation as an old fool who's given you stupid orders.'

'How will that help?'

'I think she'll shut you up and co-operate.' Tarrant smiled. 'She's remarkably loyal to her friends.'

Liebmann stood looking across the landing ground at the northern end of the valley, a stopwatch in his hand. Thirty-seven men on small, powerful scooters were moving across the flat valley-bottom.

They wore American-style steel helmets and very light breast- and back-plates of plastic armour. Beneath their uniforms they wore similar articulated plates to cover the stomach and scrotum. The armour would not stop a direct hit, but it had already been proved of high efficiency in preventing minor casualties and in giving a sense of security which had a powerful effect on morale.

Each man carried a Colt AR-15 rifle air-cooled, magazine-fed, semi- or fully-automatic. Each scooter was fitted with brackets bearing a recoil-less 40-mm. cannon, and panniers for ammunition.

As the phalanx reached the far side of the valley Liebmann pressed the button on the stop-watch. He turned to the huge relief mock-up of Kuwait, which spread over a quarter-acre of ground, and walked to where The Twins stood by the port area of the mock-up.

'One minute forty-six seconds,' he said, his voice high and cool.

Lok jotted in a notebook. As he turned a page the pencil dropped from his fingers. Chu glanced sideways at him with smouldering eyes and said: 'Clumsy bassar'!'

Lok's eyes glittered with hatred. He did not answer but started to bend down. Chu stood firm, and the flexible leather bar joining their shoulders strained and twisted. Lok lifted a hand as if to slash at his brother's face. He did not complete the slash. Neither twin ever completed such a move, for beneath all the seething animosity there lay the grim knowledge that a fight begun would mean death for one or the other. And death for one meant screaming madness for the survivor.

Liebmann looked at Chu and said: 'Lok, make a note that Hamid's section must improve that time by eight seconds.'

Again Lok bent to recover the pencil, and this time Chu went with him sullenly.

In the early days here, Liebmann had wondered if Karz was right to use The Twins. Then he had seen the exercise for securing Kuwait airfield. The Twins led the parachute section which would make the first drop. Themselves, they used a double 'chute and harness. Training for the actual drop had taken place in another area, Liebmann did not know where. But the main part of the exercise had been rehearsed here in the valley. Then he had seen The Twins as Karz saw them. They led their section with ruthless drive and power, welding it into an irresistible thunderbolt of fire and speed and destruction.

In action The Twins were one man, as Liebmann had seen during the disciplinary killings. More than one man, they were one superman at such times. If Liebmann had been capable of pity he would have pitied them for the horrible

167

burden they bore at all other times. As it was, he simply noted it with interest.

Liebmann looked at his other watch. In fifteen minutes an air freighter would be landing with twenty tons of ammunition—mortar-bombs, rockets, grenades, anti-tank mines, plastic explosive, and the standard .223 ammunition for the AR-15 weapons system, all to be carefully unloaded and placed in the great cave which lay under the ridge of rock forming the valley's end.

Beyond this ridge lay the lake, its waters gently debouching over a twenty-foot wide spill at the eastern end of the half-mile ridge and speeding down a short stretch of rapids into the quiet river which ran sluggishly in its deep bed round the edge of the valley-wall. The cave was ideal as an ammunition store. The lake kept the whole ridge cool, and the interior of the cave was painted with Synthasil to prevent any dampness seeping in.

Liebmann bent to the small pack-transmitter standing on a nearby rock and lifted the microphone. 'Hamid. Get your section clear of the strip now and have them standing by ready to unload ammunition in fifteen minutes.'

Liebmann put down the mike. As he did so a pen-shaped receiver clipped in his shirt pocket bleeped three times. He said to The Twins: 'Karz wants me. Remember to tell Hamid about that timing.' He turned and walked towards the jeep standing by.

Karz was sitting at the long table in his office adjoining the Control Room. He put aside a file as Liebmann entered, and picked up three message-forms clipped together.

'There is new information from the Recruiting Officer,' Karz said. 'Certain things have occurred which make Blaise and Garvin accessible to an approach.'

Liebmann allowed himself the slightest of shrugs. 'Surely that means very little. Time is passing, Karz. The Engineer Section and the Mobile Reserve Section are being formed now. Leaders must be appointed very soon.'

'I agree.' Karz laid down the message. 'Fortunately the things which have occurred no longer matter. There will be

168

no need for a cautious approach. The Recruiting Officer has found a lever. The approach will therefore be in the nature of a command.'

'You insisted that an efficiency test should be run on Blaise and Garvin. That will take time to arrange.'

'The Recruiting Officer arranged that matter beforehand, in order to save time. A high-grade test was run. They passed with formidable ease.' There was an unusual touch of satisfaction in Karz's eyes. He slid the long message across the table to Liebmann.

There was silence while Liebmann read it through carefully. 'I see.' He looked up at Karz. 'But the Recruiting Officer also states his belief in the possibility that Blaise and Garvin may in some way be connected with British Intelligence.'

'Yes.'

'This makes them Unsound.'

'I have never expected them to be otherwise. If the hold is strong enough the rest has no importance.'

'You believe the hold will be strong enough?' Liebmann nodded down at the message. For once there was the merest hint of concern in his emotionless tenor voice.

'Yes.' Karz rested a hand like hewn stone on the file at his elbow. 'This is a dossier I required the Controllers to supply. It contains all known facts about the woman Blaise and about Garvin. But there is also a detailed evaluation of them by a team of psychologists.' The big head nodded slowly. 'The hold will be more than sufficient.'

'They will resent duress.'

'Of course. Resentment without the power to express it causes me no concern.'

'You believe they will lead well?'

'They will have no choice. The lever will be in our hands until the end.'

'I understand that. I was asking if you believe they have the qualities to lead a section.'

Karz lifted his hand slightly and dropped it on the dossier again. 'It is all here, Liebmann. The conclusion is positive.'

'Very well.'

The stony eyes fixed on Liebmann grew cold, and something brutal stirred in their depths. 'You should have brought these two to my attention earlier. This was a serious omission.'

Liebmann stood still, savouring the tremor of fear that flickered within him. He waited several seconds, then said: 'How soon will they be here?'

'In eight days or less.'

There was finality in Karz's voice. The sloe-black eyes went suddenly blank. Liebmann knew that Karz had finished with the subject, withdrawn his mind from it. His thoughts were occupied by some other aspect of the massive and complex operation. He might sit for five minutes or five hours like this, until his mountainous mind had crushed the problem out of existence.

Liebmann found he was still holding the message in his hand. He read it once more, then put it down on the table and went quietly out of the room.

THIRTEEN

A scent of mint tinged the warm air that hung over the hillsides of Tangier. To the west of the town, looking out across the straits to the Spanish coast, lay the area called The Mountain, where lavish villas and miniature palaces stood each in quiet isolation on the pine-clad slopes.

Fraser picked his way slowly through the trees. He wore a cheap crumpled cream jacket and grey flannel trousers, maroon socks and new yellow sandals. His nose and brow were pink from recent sunburn. A moderately good camera hung at his shoulder. Beneath the jacket he wore a limp cream shirt, a diagonally-striped tie, and a thin droopy sleeveless pullover.

Now he could glimpse the swimming-pool through the trees, and the house beyond. The pool was twenty metres long and five wide. The whole garden was screened by a rectangle of dwarf pines. Within the ring of pines a mass of bright colours glowed from well-kept flower-beds. He saw, as he drew nearer, that the flower-beds consisted of vast concrete troughs sunk deep in the ground and filled with rich soil. On the broad tiled surround of the pool stood a swing-couch under an awning, several garden chaises-longues, and two tables with huge articulated sunshades mounted above them.

The house made him sigh with pleasure, though he could see only the back of it now. It was two floors high, but very wide, with white walls and a terra-cotta roof. Broad casement windows opened on to a patio, hemmed on two sides by thick white walls pierced by a series of trefoil arches. A belt of rich green grass lay between the open side of the patio and the swimming pool.

A man of about fifty, in a white jacket and dark trousers, was setting out glasses and fruit-juice on one of the tables. His hair was black but flecked with grey. He might have been of any Mediterranean or North African nationality, or one of the many blends of race that Tangier abounds with.

Fraser clutched his guide-book and walked hesitantly out from the trees. The man looked up, stared, then continued transferring the contents of his tray to the table. With a feeble smile Fraser cleared his throat and moved forward.

'Er . . . excuse me,' he said in a rather vague, shaky voice. 'Do you speak English? English?'

The man straightened and looked at Fraser politely. 'Yes, sir. I speak English.'

'Oh . . . good.' Fraser rubbed a hand across his eyes. 'I wonder . . . would it be all right if I just sat down for a minute?'

'I am sorry, sir. This is a private residence.'

'Yes. I—I know.' Fraser put a hand on the chair nearest to him as if to steady himself. 'But I'm feeling a bit groggy. I'm afraid I wandered away from the coach. Taking photographs, you know.' He swayed, and blinked dazedly, 'Then I thought

171

I'd take a short cut down into the town, but it's been a bit too much for me. The sun. . . .'

Fraser's voice trailed away in a mumble and he took a lurching step forward. A hand caught his arm, steadying him, lowering him into a chair beneath one of the big sun-shades. 'Yes, you have had too much sun, sir. Drink, please.'

Fraser groped for the glass of cold fruit-juice, muttered his thanks, and began to drink. The voice said: 'Drink slowly, sir. I will fetch mam'selle.' Fraser heard the soft footsteps moving away across the matt tiles. He did not look up, but finished the drink. Slowly, head slumped forward, he began to take off his jacket and pull-over.

There came the sound of voices and he lifted his head. Modesty Blaise was coming towards him along the side of the pool, followed by the man in the white jacket. She wore a pale blue one-piece swimsuit and white beach sandals. There was a towelling beach-jacket over one arm and a white swim-cap in her hand.

As Fraser looked up he saw the quick flash of recognition in her eyes, and then it was gone.

'I'm sorry you're not feeling well,' she said.

'I do apologise,' he mumbled with painful embarrassment, starting to get to his feet. 'I was with the coach party, you see, Madden's Tours, and——'

'Please sit down, and put your feet up.' She turned to the man beside her. 'Moulay, ask Mr. Garvin to bring some ice, salt-tablets, and another jug of fruit juice—quickly, please.'

'I will bring them myself, mam'selle.'

'No. I want you to drive down to the hotel where this gentleman is staying. Find the courier for Madden's Tours or leave a message to let him know that the gentleman is quite safe. We'll drive him down later, when he's feeling better.' She turned to Fraser. 'Which hotel is it? And what name shall he say?'

'Hotel Mauritania. Er—my name's Swann,' Fraser said apologetically. 'But really, you mustn't put yourself out, Miss.'

'It's no trouble. Moulay has to go down into town for me anyway.'

'Mam'selle?'

'Yes. Will you call in at Conti's, say I'll be there for a fitting tomorrow at three, and take along that sample of material I picked out for the other dress. But go to The Mauritania first.'

'Yes, mam'selle.' Moulay inclined his head and moved away.

'No messing,' thought Fraser with some pleasure. 'Jesus, if I wasn't with Madden's bloody Tours and if my cover wasn't dead solid all the way through, she'd take the Old Man my head on a platter.'

He watched Moulay vanish into the house and said softly: 'It all checks. I'm not a new boy at this, you know.'

She stood looking down at him impassively. 'So I've heard from Tarrant. But I've only seen you in your shrinking Civil Servant role before.'

'I do this one just as well. Shrinking book-keeper on holiday in foreign parts.'

He heard a car start up and move off. Willie Garvin came out of the house and across the patio carrying a silver ice-bucket, a packet of salt-tablets, and a jug of fresh fruit-juice still frosty from the refrigerator. He wore royal blue very short boxer trunks, sandals, and nothing else.

'Look who's here, Willie,' Modesty said in a neutral voice.

Willie Garvin glanced at Fraser and put the things he carried down on the table. Kicking off his sandals he sat down on the edge of the pool with his feet dangling in the water, squinted up at the sun, and said: 'Christ on a bicycle.'

'I'm sorry.' Fraser looked at Modesty with apparently honest regret. 'I feel this is unwise just as much as you do. I tried to argue the Old Man out of it, but he insisted.'

'Tarrant gave you orders to make contact?' Modesty said. Fraser could not tell whether she was angry or not, but he noticed that Willie Garvin had his head turned to watch her and was keeping quiet.

'I'm afraid so,' Fraser answered, and gave a wry shrug. 'It's foolish in my opinion. I sometimes think his grip isn't quite what it was.'

'Do you?' Her voice was very soft but he noticed that Willie Garvin closed his eyes and seemed to hold his breath. 'Do you?' she repeated. 'And just who the hell are you to——'

She broke off, staring at Fraser in silence for long moments, then suddenly laughed and sat down on one of the chaises-longues. 'You did that very well,' she said. 'He told you to play it that way, of course?'

Fraser held a blank look while he made up his mind whether to persist with the play. Then he grinned suddenly. 'Let's say I don't really think he's losing his grip.'

'Good. You can tell him it was the right bait but I didn't bite.'

Willie opened his eyes and kicked up water with one foot, frowning a little. 'I still think it's dodgy making contact with us, Princess.'

'So do I.' Her face was serious again and she was still looking at Fraser. 'Tarrant must have had a good reason.'

'Communications,' said Fraser. 'He's worried that you might just disappear like the rest of the people who've gone out of circulation.' He went on quickly before she could speak again. 'If you get an approach and then try to contact us you're likely to be blown. Tarrant thinks it's better to have somebody on your tail. An approach won't tell you much. You've got to go down the mercenary pipe-line to find out what we want to know. You need a man outside to keep track of you.'

'He'll 'ave to be good.' Willie's voice was not enthusiastic.

Fraser looked at him and said amiably: 'I *am* good.'

There was a long silence. Modesty roused herself from thought at last and said: 'I don't like it much, but I suppose it makes sense from where Tarrant sits. How will you work, Mr. Fraser?'

'As you like to work yourself, Miss Blaise. In my own way.'

A grunt from Willie, but Modesty gave a little nod of acceptance. 'All right. How do you want us to let you know if anything happens?'

'It's possible that you'll be able to ring me at The Mauritania without any difficulty. If I'm not there, leave a message for Mr. Swann to call at Barclays Bank about some traveller's cheques he cashed.'

'And if we're not able to ring?'

'That's my worry. I'll be pretty close most of the time.'

'You're alone?' she asked sharply.

'Yes.'

She relaxed, and saluted him with her eyes. 'You must be very good, Mr. Fraser.'

'I've made mistakes, Miss Blaise—but fewer than most people in my line.'

She smiled. Tarrant had told him about that smile, or tried to. It was very rare, but it came from right inside her and lit up her face with laughter and warmth and the sudden intimacy of a feeling shared.

'Fewer than most,' she repeated. 'Yes. That's the secret, Mr. Fraser.' She picked up the white swim-cap from the table and her face became sober again. 'But this is all a little academic at the moment. Nothing may happen. Or something may happen and you may just make one of your rare mistakes, and lose us.' Her tone took any offence out of the words. 'If so, and if we have a chance to get word out somewhere along the pipe-line, or at the end of it, what do you want us to do?'

'A cable to *Mercycorps*, London, will reach us,' said Fraser.

'To *Mercycorps*?'

'It's the Association of International Mercy Volunteers, for giving emergency help anywhere in the world—floods, earthquakes, epidemics, and so on.'

'But in fact The Department has a piece of it?'

'Yes. All *Mercycorps* messages come to us first. Most of them are the real thing. Our people only use it as a last resource.'

175

'We can't carry around paraphernalia for cipher or code. Any message would be in free cryptic.'

'Yes. Don't worry about that. The Department will sort it out. Sign it "Doctor Rampal".'

'To *Mercycorps* from Doctor Rampal. It carries a nice aura of urgency.'

She stood up, put on her swim-cap and slipped her sandals off. Her feet were strong, a little broad for elegance, but well-shaped. A walker's feet. He remembered hearing from Tarrant that she had walked from Greece to Persia before she was eleven, and in those days she had no shoes to wear.

Moving across the tiled surround of the pool she put her hands on Willie's shoulders, pushed him off the edge, and dived in after him. They began to swim unhurriedly up and down the length of the pool. Willie's crawl had little style, but it was steady and rhythmic, giving an impression of limitless stamina. Modesty's stroke was a little smoother but otherwise similar. Fraser thought it likely that one had taught the other. They seemed to have imparted their various skills to each other very thoroughly over the years.

A telephone bell rang somewhere close by, an extension bell mounted near the pool. The two stopped swimming and trod water. Modesty said: 'I'll go, Willie. It's probably Conti's about the fitting.'

She took two strokes to the side of the pool and drew herself out with one easy movement. Picking up the towelling jacket she walked away across the stretch of grass and the patio, dabbing water from her body. Fraser watched her go into the house.

The bell stopped ringing. Willie Garvin resumed his relaxed swimming up and down the pool. Three minutes passed. Modesty came out of the house. She dropped her beach-jacket on a chair near Fraser and poured another glass of fruit-juice for him.

'You'd better drink,' she said. 'I think you really have taken a little too much sun. You're rather pale.'

'Whitehall pallor.'

'Perhaps. But get some liquid down you. I won't insist on the salt-tablets.'

'Thank you.'

She dived into the pool again. Fraser picked up the glass and watched as she waited for Willie then matched his stroke so that they were swimming dead level again.

Up and down ... up and down. The steady movement became hypnotic. Fraser settled back in the chaise-longue. She might have been right about him taking too much sun, he thought. His head felt a little muzzy. Now there seemed to be four people swimming in the pool. That was strange. He closed his eyes for a moment. . . .

Modesty stopped at one end of the pool and said: 'Willie.'

He stood up, chest-deep, shaking the water from his hair. 'We've only done 'alf-a-mile, Princess. I thought——'

He broke off, staring. The look on her face was one he had never seen before. It held a blend of anger and shock, bitter self-reproach and a strange distress. He looked quickly towards the figure of Fraser, sprawled in the chaise-longue.

'He's out,' she said tautly. 'I slipped a knock-out pill in his drink.'

She drew herself out of the pool. Willie followed and stood looking at her. He said: 'The phone-call?'

'Yes. Just a voice. A man's voice.' She hesitated. 'Willie, they've got Lucille.'

'Got Lucille?' For a moment his face was blank, then his eyes focused with total concentration on a point in space. She waited for him to juggle with the mass of speculations and probabilities, as she had done ten minutes ago. When he looked at her again there was ugliness in his eyes.

'So that's 'ow they're playing it?' he said, and his voice held the slightest of tremors. 'We set ourselves up for an invitation. But we don't get invited. We just get told.'

'It looks like it. I don't know when they picked her up or how.'

'The kids get a free afternoon on the beach today.'

'That would make it easy. It could have been done by boat.'

177

'Gerace again?'

'No.' The shake of her head was positive. 'This is the people we were after, Willie. But they've come after us.'

'What did the bloke on the phone say?'

'He said they'd got Lucille. That I was to ring the school and say Lucille had felt ill and taken a cab home, here. That I had to leave for France tomorrow and might take her with me for a check-up. He said that you and I were to be on the corner of Rue du Mexique and Rue des Vignes in one hour. A suit-case apiece. No funny business. Whoever picks us up there won't know where Lucille is.'

'All nicely worked out.' Willie rubbed a hand across his face. 'Did you get on to the school, like he said?'

'Yes.'

'The voice didn't ring a bell?'

'No. Fair English, foreign accent. It could have been anyone. We've no lead. No lead at all.'

Willie pushed his hands back over his hair, squeezing the water out, and said softly: 'Oh Christ, Princess. . . .'

She put a hand on his arm in distress. 'Willie, I'm sorry . . . I brought this on her.'

'No!' He was shocked. '*They* brought it on 'er, those bastards!'

'They play to different rules. God knows we've tangled with their kind often enough before. I should have seen it could happen.' Her voice was quiet but in her eyes there was bitter contempt for herself.

Very gently Willie Garvin put his hands on her shoulders. It was rare for him to touch her except in time of need or action. 'We should both 've seen it, Princess. But we didn't. So let's forget that part—please?' Though he was comforting her he was asking for comfort himself. 'It's 'appened now. They've got the kid. They've put the screws on us. We can only start from there.'

'I know, Willie. All right. No more feeling sick with ourselves.'

'Good.' His hands tightened a little on her shoulders and a touch of desperation crept into his voice. 'So what do we *do*, Princess? How do we play it?'

Now he was asking for something she could not give—a move, a riposte, a way out of the trap. And even in asking he knew that it was impossible.

'It's . . . not very good, Willie,' she said. 'There's only one way we can play it. We do as we're told. We play it straight until we know the score. Then we wait for an opening—and do what we can.'

He let her go and dropped his hands to his sides. 'It's a long shot, Princess. Too long. There's got to be another way.'

'There isn't,' she said flatly, and held his gaze. In the silence she saw him slowly absorb the inevitability, saw him shut hope and uncertainty from his mind with a deliberate effort as he accepted that no miracle was possible.

Now he had followed her into a realm where hope and fear and imagination were all set aside, where Lucille became only a factor in a grim equation to which no answer could yet be seen.

Modesty relaxed a little, relief sweeping through her with the knowledge that Willie had not failed to find the only mental posture from which they could hope to fight.

'Sorry,' he said, and a ghost of the old grin touched his lips. 'I was off-balance for a minute.'

'So was I. And Fraser couldn't have helped. That's why I put him out. It's one thing for us to take our chances, but Lucille's in it now, and she didn't ask to be. We have to play this one for her.'

'She'll be scared,' said Willie softly, 'scared out of 'er poor little stupid wits.'

'I know.' Modesty's voice was harsh. 'People who do this kind of thing are for killing.'

She turned away and walked to Fraser, lifting one of his eyelids. He was unconscious and would remain so for a good two hours. 'Put him to bed in your room, Willie,' she said. 'Then we'll get packed.'

'What do we take?'

'Nothing too tricky. Not the special boots or any major stuff.'

'My knives? Your guns?'

Her lips twisted. 'Yes. I'd say whoever wants us will expect that.'

Half-an-hour later they sat in the big living room, dressed and with two suit-cases packed. Moulay had returned and been given instructions concerning Fraser. Willie had rung for a cab to take them to their rendezvous.

Moulay could be trusted to reveal nothing to Fraser or anybody else. He had been with Modesty for five years and was well-used to strange happenings.

Modesty got up and walked to the open windows, looking out over the garden. She said: 'It's a bad way to start a caper. All the initiative's on the other side. We can lose this one, Willie. So can Lucille. So can Tarrant.'

'If that's the way it's written.' Willie spoke with acceptance, not despair. 'You're sure this is to do with the Tarrant business? Couldn't be an ordinary snatch?'

'No. It hasn't got the feel. This is for something bigger.'

'Us?'

'I believe so.'

'It's making a big deal of it. They could get plenty of others.' He came to stand beside her.

'Yes. Plenty of hired hands, maybe.' She took the cigarette he had lit for her. 'Accept Tarrant's hunch as right. A *fait accompli* take-over of Kuwait. It needs the cut-throat boys, it needs massive backing and planning, it needs equipment, mobility and fire-power. Given all that, what would worry you most, Willie? You know your battles better than I do.'

Willie nodded soberly. 'It's a text-book answer, Princess. Leaders. Just a few, but they're 'ard to come by.'

'Not easy to find outside regular armies?'

'Not even inside. Ninety percent just get by okay. You'd need to do better than just get by for this caper.'

'And we qualify?'

He thought for a moment, then said: 'For anyone who knows the full record—yes.'

'I think anyone running this would be able to get the full record on us.'

180

He exhaled cigarette smoke and looked out at the pool, not thinking about Lucille, deliberately starving his imagination. This was something he had learned from Modesty. He knew it would be hard during the first hours but would grow easier as the barriers hardened and the pattern of thought became set.

There was a tap on the door and Moulay entered.

'The cab you ordered is here, mam'selle,' he said.

'All right, Moulay. Take the bags out, please.'

When Moulay had gone from the room she said: 'Willie . . . just now I said we could lose this one. Forget it.'

'Someone always 'as to lose, Princess,' he said slowly. 'It could be us this time.'

'No. *Not* this time, by God.' Her eyes flared dangerously. 'It's not going to be cheap. I can feel it. But I *won't* lose this one.'

Willie stared at her, feeling new strength and purpose tingling through him. He spun his cigarette out of the window. 'All right, Princess,' he said quietly. 'Let's go an' win it.'

FOURTEEN

THE Dove's engines groaned in the thin air. A white crag reached up from a ridge no more than three hundred feet below. Now the note changed as the Dove banked away from the crag and slid down the far side of the ridge to level out at twelve thousand feet.

The Gipsy engines settled to a steady roar as the Dove altered course and flew east, following the line of the next ridge which lay three miles north.

Modesty sat in the front port-side passenger seat. Willie was on the starboard side. The back-to-back seats immediately behind them were empty. In the two remaining seats, aft and facing forward, were the two escorts.

Modesty wore black denim trousers and shirt, with a thick

white pullover. Willie was similarly dressed except that his pullover was grey.

It was six days since they had left Tangier—at dusk and in a small sea-going launch. Before they were landed at Casablanca the next day they had been given false passports, a number of airline tickets, and a complex itinerary to follow. Contacts met them at each point of change. They knew none of the men who quietly checked them through, any more than they had known the men who crewed the launch.

Twenty-four hours ago they had reached Kabul, and next morning they had been driven to the airport by the two men who sat behind them now in the de Havilland Dove. The escorts were hard-faced men, one Spanish, one she could not place—a Slav perhaps. Both were in civilian clothes and looked out of place in them.

They had eyed her curiously from time to time, but spoke little and shook their heads in answer to questions. The pilot was Russian, she thought, the co-pilot Chinese. Even among themselves the four men spoke nothing but English. It was probably their only common language.

Modesty knew that their general direction was a little east of north. Throughout the flight the sun had confirmed this, but she would have known anyway. The long lone wanderings of her early days had developed a mental compass in her head.

In the hotel in Kabul, she and Willie had borrowed a map and studied it. Afghanistan lay in an irregular triangle between Persia, Russia, and Pakistan. And at one point, beyond the north-eastern tip of the five-hundred mile Hindu Kush range was the narrow finger of the Pamir region, ending in a fifty-mile border with China. To the north, beyond the mountains, lay the dusty plains which stretched to the Russian border.

The Dove had not passed over the greatest heights of the Hindu Kush. It could not make such an altitude. The bigger aircraft, the Ilyushins which plied between Kabul and Termez, and the DC-6's, these could go over the top in a straight line. The old DC-3's and 4's had to fly through the

Salang pass, and even this forced them to nineteen thousand feet. The Dove had taken neither route. It had flown northeast on a strange and mazy course leading ever deeper into the vast, convoluted heart of the mountains.

She wondered which border they would cross to reach their destination. Willie Garvin turned his head and looked across at her. The same question was in his mind. Another hour or two would take them behind the Iron or the Bamboo Curtain. She gave him a minute shrug and looked out of the window again.

It was the first time she and Willie had exchanged a glance since leaving Kabul. On take-off, and for the first ten minutes, Willie had sat staring absently through the open door to the cockpit. And then, since crossing the first low ridges of the mountains, he had been gazing out of the window.

There was no low cloud, and visibility was good. She knew that throughout the flight Willie had been recording the route in his mind as if on film. For what it was worth, she had been doing the same thing. She did not quite have Willie's gift of a photographic memory, but her sense of direction was better. Probably the exercise was worthless, but they had long since learned that to know your way in and out of anywhere was always of possible value.

From a higher altitude she had looked down on a wild tangle of ravines and broken ridges, with here and there the mirror-gleam of a lake and the silver threads of tumbling rivers. Now there were no considerable peaks close by, and they were flying between two massive ridges.

The Dove turned to port. It seemed that they were flying head-on into the grey ridge, but the ridge was broken by an overlap and the Dove turned easily through the half-mile gap, losing height slowly now. The pilot was still flying as if through a colossal and increasingly complex maze.

She sensed sudden tension in Willie and turned sharply to look at him. The Dove banked steeply once more and broke out of the grey walls.

A valley lay below, a deep four-mile long gash in the heart of the range. It narrowed to a bottle-neck in the middle. On two sides sheer walls hemmed it in. At the northern end lay a big lake, almost circular. From it ran a river, not through the middle of the valley but along the eastern wall. At the southern end the narrow river vanished into a jumbled tangle of rock, great slabs as big as city blocks piled in a fantastic barrier. Here, at some time long past, the sheer valley-side had shed its monstrous skin, and countless tons of rock had fallen.

The Dove came round in an easy circle, keeping above the confines of the valley, at an altitude where the sheer walls fell back in long slopes to distant ridges above.

Modesty saw the rows of camouflaged huts and vehicles, the dot-like figures of moving men. As the aircraft dropped lower she caught her breath for a moment at sight of the palace tucked away between two massive spurs. So this was the end of the journey. This was the springboard for what Tarrant had feared. And it was on neutral ground, in an area where spy-plane or satellite cameras would never seek.

The Dove swept low over the lake, crossed the long hump of rock, and dipped towards the landing strip. There was a slight bump as it touched down. The roar of the engines dwindled, and the Dove taxied on. Ahead, thirty feet of the bottle-neck was occupied by the river curving round its edge. The remaining width consisted of a broad road. As the Dove came to a halt, a truck drove through the bottle-neck and headed towards it.

Karz said: 'You have much to do in only a few weeks. You will receive a general briefing on Operation Sabre-Tooth today, and a detailed briefing of the work of your particular sections tomorrow.'

He sat looking across his long table at Modesty Blaise and Willie Garvin. They had taken off their sweaters now. Liebmann stood to one side, watching with remote eyes.

Modesty turned her head a little. She saw that Willie was looking at Karz with a strange expression. He was impressed by Karz, enormously impressed. That was little to wonder at. She was impressed by Karz herself. The cold, stone-like creature had a titanic presence. It was easy to fear him. It was difficult not to fear him. His personality attacked the human spirit, evoking a strange and nightmarish sense of smallness in everyone about him.

Modesty Blaise felt herself becoming a child again in his presence. And there, strangely, she found help, for it was as a child that she had fought her most frightening battles alone. Now, inwardly, she bared her teeth and summoned up the strength that counted no odds but was simply a wild-animal refusal to succumb. Outwardly her face showed no emotion.

She said coldly: 'First things first, Karz.' In the brief pause she sensed that Willie had jumped inwardly as if some growing and hypnotic spell had been broken. His recovery could have been measured in fractions of a second.

He said brusquely: 'Too bloody true.'

She rejoiced, and went on: 'We want to see the child.'

Karz held her eyes for a full half-minute, then abruptly gave a little nod of approval, as if he had tested her and not found her wanting. He said: 'The child is not here. She is in another country.'

'How do we know she's alive?'

'You will know when this matter is ended. I tell you she is alive and safe. If you prove Unsound, she will die. A brief radio message will ensure that.'

'Why should we believe she's not dead already?'

'Because she is my lever. Without the child I cannot rely on you.'

'She could still be dead. All you need is that we believe she's alive.'

'I do not work in that way. But I take your point. In one week from today I will arrange for you to speak briefly to her over the radio-telephone. And each week after that.'

'All right.' Modesty's voice was brisk. 'But there's something else. Suppose we do our job, and suppose the operation fails just the same. What happens to the child then?'

'Sabre-Tooth cannot fail.' Karz spoke as if pronouncing an immutable law.

Modesty Blaise said: 'Why not?'

'Because I control it. I do not fail. Ever.'

'I'll accept that. But you're not immortal. An aircraft can crash in the first wave. A bullet can go astray. Anything can happen. I'm asking you again—what happens if we do our job but the operation fails?'

'Then you will either be dead or in prison.'

'And the child?'

Karz half closed his eyes, studying her. At last he said: 'I will tell you how I work. I make no empty threats and I make no false promises. If you prove Unsound, the child will die. If you perform your work well, then no matter what the result of the operation the child will be returned to Tangier in the same manner that she was taken.'

'Alive and unharmed?'

'Yes.'

Willie gave a little sigh, and Modesty relaxed. It was pointless to hide their relief. If Karz doubted the strength of his hold over them their danger would be immediate. So would the danger to Lucille.

Now was the time for the next move. She jerked her head towards Willie and said: 'When the time comes, let Garvin speak to her over the radio-telephone. He seems to think he's got more right than I have.'

Willie took the cue smoothly. It was not a new gambit for them. Apparent hostility between them made the opposition less watchful and suspicious.

'Now look,' he said to her grimly, 'don't let's start arguing again about who's to blame. We've both been worried bloody sick because we didn't know the score. Now we do. So let's just forget the why's an' wherefore's—and keep our noses clean. Got it?'

She stared at him coldly. 'You've changed. You're forgetting your place.'

'My place is the same as yours now.' His voice was bleak. 'I run E-section. You run R-section.' He looked at Karz. 'Right?'

'Correct.' Karz's eyes dwelt on Modesty. 'When will you take over? I can allow you twenty-four hours.'

'I'll take over my section now,' she said curtly. 'It's likely to be eventful, and I intend to get it settled straight away.'

Liebmann said: 'There need be no difficulty. The men in your section have been instructed to take orders from you as they would from Karz.'

'Cancel the instruction,' she said, thin-lipped, looking at Karz. 'What the hell's the good of a commander who needs that kind of backing?'

'No good.' Karz leaned back in his chair. 'Liebmann was in error. No such instruction has been given.'

'I see. Are you going to run any more of these little tests on me?'

'You will always be on test.' The heavy voice brought out the words with slow emphasis, like ponderous blows from a club. 'The work of your section is entirely your responsibility. The same applies to Garvin and his section. Failure to reach the required standard will be considered Unsound. You will now see the Recruiting Officer and he will give you copies of our Regulations. Read them carefully.'

His eyes went blank and distant. Liebmann stirred, opened the door and said: 'This way.'

They followed him along a narrow corridor in the H.Q. section of the palace.

'Commanders have a separate mess,' he said. 'They sleep with their sections. There is a separate cubicle for each commander in his hut. When you have finished talking to the Recruiting Officer I will take you to your respective sections.'

Liebmann stopped outside a wooden door set in a unit-built partition. Modesty said: 'You mean you're still recruiting?'

'No. It is finished except for documentation.' Liebmann indicated the door. 'He will be taking over a section now that he has returned. I will wait for you by the transport.'

He walked away. Modesty rapped once with her knuckles on the door, opened it, and walked in. Willie followed and closed the door behind him.

Mike Delgado rose from behind a desk across one corner of the room, smiling. She moved quickly to keep between him and Willie, one hand behind her, fingers splayed in an urgent signal.

Delgado said: 'Hallo, sweetheart. Welcome to the club.'

Behind her Willie said softly: 'You bastard . . . you slimy, cold-gutted bastard.'

She was thankful to hear his voice. It meant that he had somehow controlled the explosion of murderous fury. Delgado looked past her with amused protest. 'Ah, be your age now, Willie, for God's sake. You've played with the big boys long enough to know the score. You win a few, you lose a few, and it's no good getting sore.'

'I've marked you down, Delgado,' Willie said. His voice rasped like a file. 'Sometime this lot's going to be over. Then I'll 'ave you.'

Delgado laughed. 'Cool off, Willie, or you won't be around for long. Just play ball and you'll get the kid back safe.'

Modesty said: 'Safe. But not the same.'

He lifted an eyebrow at her. 'We all have our rough patches. She'll just have to take it. Don't tell me you're surprised at me.'

'I was. But only for a moment,' she said slowly. 'I'm not, now that I think about it. There's nothing in you to stop you doing this. If you wanted us, why didn't you ask?'

'Because you have scruples, darling. Some scruples, anyway. I'd never have got you on this job without having a screw to turn. Admit it, now.'

'I admit to being a fool. That business in Lisbon with Gerace . . . it was a test, wasn't it? And you laid it on. You were the only one who knew I was going to be in Lisbon at that time.'

'You and Willie did brilliantly, my sweet. I was very proud of you.'

She shrugged contemptuously. 'You've been in on this from the beginning?'

'Almost.'

'I thought you worked alone.'

'I'm not a fanatical isolationist. There'll be a hundred angles in all this when the show's over. And I have been working alone. I've had the sole responsibility for recruiting. Now I take over a section. There's nothing lonelier than commanding a section in this set-up. You'll find that out.'

He had been speaking a little tautly, but now he relaxed and indicated two wooden chairs. 'Sit down and I'll go over one or two points with you.'

Willie remembered not to hold the chair for her, and she felt a touch of guilt at having felt a moment of anxiety. He slumped down without waiting for her to sit, and lit a cigarette. He did not offer her one. Delgado registered mild surprise, then flickered an eyelid at her and grinned.

'Operation Sabre-Tooth,' he said. 'Karz chose the name. It's a little florid maybe . . . but very apt.' He tilted back his chair and spoke as if quoting. 'The sabre-tooth tiger was no bigger than a European bear, but because of its speed, its power, and its armament, which consisted of its long and daggerlike upper canines, this creature could pounce from hiding and destroy huge pachyderms with a few quick slashes of those fearsome tusks. That is how we shall subdue Kuwait, like the sabre-tooth tiger———'

'Get to the business,' Modesty cut in abruptly. 'I've got work to do.'

Delgado leaned forward and rested his forearms on the desk. 'Yes, you have indeed, darling. A section to take over. All right, let's not waste time. First, you each earn fifty thousand pounds sterling for the job. And you'll get it. Believe me, this is run as an honest business. Second, you needn't worry about repercussions afterwards. The political side of the operation is going to be the smartest piece of work ever, and it'll be mounted on a world-wide basis.'

Willie Garvin reached across Modesty without a word and crushed his cigarette out in the empty ashtray on the desk.

Delgado watched with interest, then went on: 'Third, you can't allot your pay to any kin; if you die, in action or otherwise, your share goes into the bonus pool. Fourth, there'll be an airlift for the wounded and first-class hospitalisation.' He grimaced at the word. 'Sorry about that, but we create an American flavour here. It's all part of the big bamboozle.'

'Karz spoke of the Regulations,' Modesty said. 'I take it we're not just one trusting and united family?'

'It depends.' Delgado took two small printed booklets from a pile at his elbow and slid them across the desk. 'Just a question of staying in line. Anyone who steps out of line is considered Unsound.' He paused, and added: 'We kill them. You'll probably see an execution sometime over the next week or ten days. I think you'll find it technically very interesting.'

Modesty picked up one of the booklets, folded it, and put it in the pocket of her shirt. 'I've been given R-section. What does that mean?'

'You'll be fully briefed. In a nutshell, Willie's is a combined assault and engineer section, striking from the airfield to link up with the seaborne group hitting the port. Preparation for massive demolition there, as a threat against any hint of armed intervention by the British, the Americans, or whoever. Then on to the oil installations to prepare more demolition as an additional threat——'

'I asked you about my section, not Garvin's.' She spoke as if Willie was not in the room.

'There seems to be quite a rift in the lute,' Delgado said, amused. 'All the better. Just remember that Karz likes a little friction between his commanders, but no open quarrels. Now we'll come to your section, sweetheart. R-section is the mobile reserve and functions as what Karz calls the semicircular canals.'

'Again, please?'

'Semi-circular canals. It's another apt analogy. These canals in the human ear give us our sense of balance. An army has to keep its balance throughout an operation. If anything goes a little wrong somewhere—and something always does—then the Mobile Reserve comes in fast, fast, fast to put it right. I'm in charge of the transport for that, among other things—small hot-rod armoured cars.'

'Weapons?'

'You can go into that later. The general brief is that you hit very hard, take no prisoners, and observe complete ruth-

190

lessness. Karz rates this job as vital, and he's right. It's the one section that won't know exactly what it will have to do until the time comes.' He gave her a smile that was full of charm. 'You've got the toughest bunch of all, individually. You'd better make a good section of them.'

'Is there anything else?'

'I don't think so, at this stage. Oh yes, you'll have to wear the regulation uniform. Willie can draw his from the stores. For you, I've had one made.'

She said: 'It had better fit. I'm not going to try leading a section looking like a clown.'

'You won't.' Delgado's blue-green eyes twinkled. 'I know your measurements, darling. I've a marvellous tactile memory.'

He looked at Willie. 'Anything you want to know?'

'I'll find out what I want to know without a lot of yap.'

Modesty stood up. 'I'll go and meet my section now. Liebmann's waiting to take me along.'

'I'll join you.' Delgado rose. 'It could be amusing.'

'There'll be trouble, certainly.'

'Sure there will. You're a woman. I think somebody has to get slapped down hard. It could be you.'

'That's amusing?'

Delgado's face held no concern, only a cool, pleasurable touch of excitement. He said: 'I only know you in bed, sweetheart, and I'm intrigued to see this other side of you. No hard feelings. You don't necessarily dislike the man on the tight-rope but you're fascinated to see if he falls off.'

'And if I fall?'

He looked at her ambiguously. 'That's up to Karz. I expect he'll find some kind of job for you here.'

Willie Garvin dropped off the jeep outside the two E-section huts at the southern end of the line. He lifted off his case and set it down on the ground. There were some twenty men of the section standing or sitting around outside the huts. Two of them knew Willie and hailed him.

He greeted them curtly and said: 'Where's the others?'

The big Italian answered. 'Training with the gas-bombs. The rest of us have done the course.'

'All right. Hump that bag inside. I'll get settled in and talk to the section later.' He looked round at the men watching him, gave a brief general nod, and walked into the hut.

A Welsh voice said: 'Going to be a batman are you, Gio?'

The Italian grinned sardonically. 'No, Taff. I just make sure I keep my teeth in my head. Better for you to do the same.' He picked up the bag and followed Willie into the hut.

Liebmann let in the clutch and the jeep moved on three hundred yards to the R-section quarters. Here there was one large hut sleeping forty men. The section was off-duty. A dozen men were lounging outside.

Liebmann got down with Modesty Blaise. Delgado stayed in the jeep, leaning back in one corner, watching casually.

'This is Modesty Blaise,' Liebmann said. 'She will command this section.'

Some of the men grinned. Some stripped her with their eyes. One or two faces grew wary.

Modesty said shortly: 'You'll soon get used to it. I'll talk to you in a moment.' She went through them into the hut, and Liebmann followed. Inside, men were sprawled on bunks or sitting in little groups playing cards. There was a table down the centre of the hut, bearing coffee-stained mugs, some tattered magazines, cleaning materials, and a number of well-thumbed weapon manuals. At the far end was a partition with a door leading through into a small separate cubicle. In the middle of the hut on one side there was a wooden notice-board on the wall.

Most of the men had stripped off their shirts. Some wore singlets, some were bare to the waist. Every man's clothes and person seemed clean, even though some of the uniforms were now faded and well-worn. This was something laid down in the Regulations which Modesty had flicked through briefly during the short journey from Delgado's office.

Liebmann spoke again in the same clear high voice, cutting through the murmur of talk. 'This is Modesty Blaise. She will command this section.'

The reaction was slow and in some cases studied. Heads turned, hands toyed with cards, men stopped moving about. The hut became still. The faces showed the same variety of expressions as those of the men outside.

Modesty looked round the long hut in an unhurried appraisal. She said again: 'You'll soon get used to it.' A man laughed, then cut it short. She ignored him. 'Line up outside. I want to talk to you.'

She turned without waiting and went out. Liebmann followed her. She moved clear of the hut and stood ten paces from the jeep, watching the door without impatience. A man appeared in the doorway, hesitated, then strolled casually out; two more followed, then a group of four with grins on their faces. The trickle continued for a while, then ended.

Modesty looked at the last man out and said: 'Is that all?' The man shrugged. She moved towards the hut and went inside. Two men sat on a bunk, playing cards—or pretending to. A third, on the other side of the room, lay on his back with hands behind his head, eyes half-closed.

The tendrils of her instincts reached out, measuring, appraising. The two men playing cards were a little taut, a little unnatural in their absorption. The man on the bed was relaxed. She waited. After perhaps fifteen seconds one of the two card-players flickered a quick glance towards the man lying on the bunk.

Now her instincts were confirmed. This was the unofficial leader of the herd. This was the man she must lock horns with.

He was a little under six feet, very muscular, with thick black hair showing on his chest above the circular neck of his singlet. He had long arms. His thinly-fleshed face was broad and angular in bone-structure beneath a cap of very short-cropped hair.

Modesty walked forward until she stood at the foot of the bunk. She picked up a half-filled mug of coffee from the table, looking down into it, and said: 'Name?'

He opened his eyes a little wider, looked at her without interest, and answered: 'Brunig.'

'Outside, Brunig.' Her hand jerked and sent the coffee in a long jet over his head and shoulders. She dropped the mug and moved briskly towards the door. 'You too,' she said to the staring card-players as she passed.

There came the creak of the bunk and a quick patter of composition-soled boots on the floor of the hut behind her as she emerged into the open. The crowd outside had swollen. Men from other huts had appeared. She did not look for Willie Garvin. He would not be there.

She was three paces beyond the door now, looking ahead, her face showing nothing of the fierce concentration within her. She heard the different sound of a boot grinding on gritty rock—Brunig's first foot-fall outside the door. He was close now and coming fast.

Smoothly she dived forward, forearms angled flat in front of her to cushion the impact. As her arms touched the ground her legs were half drawn up, her head turned to sight over her shoulder. Brunig tried to swerve. He was too late. Her booted feet shot out in a mule-kick, taking him squarely on the chest.

He came an inch clear of the ground with the impact, and flew backwards through the door. From within there came the sound of his fall. She straightened up, turning and backing to give herself more room.

Brunig would come again. She could have crippled him or laid him senseless with a different placing of the kick. The men knew it. Brunig knew it. But that was not what she wanted. That could have been a one-shot move, a fluke.

The kongo lay tucked in a squeeze-pocket of her slacks, but she left it there. This must be done without the kongo.

Brunig came out slowly this time, breathing fast, his face mottled with anger and shock. The two card-players followed him and moved quickly away to one side.

Now the thing must be ended quickly. It would be, anyway. This kind of fight could never become a long, scrambling affair of alternate knock-downs and advantage. She knew Brunig must be strong and very skilful. He would have to be, since he was certainly the kingpin of this tough section.

Her mind moved ahead. She had to win conclusively yet without causing Brunig too much loss of face. He was an important man in the section.

He moved in with one foot slightly forward, crouched a little, well-balanced, hands held rather low and half-clenched, ready to strike with fist or edge. She walked straight at him, with arms folded loosely across her breasts. The unorthodox move confused him, worried him. He hesitated, looking for the trick, then shaped to dodge a kick which did not come. Another pace and she was within reach, her arms still loosely folded. His right hand slashed edgewise at the side of her neck.

She blocked it with the point of a suddenly lifted elbow to the inside of his wrist. The impact was audible. The slashing blow was deflected clear of her shoulder and his teeth bared in a grimace as pain erupted through his arm. Her other hand smacked viciously across his face and then she was out of distance again—just out of distance of those long arms. But even as she moved back his right foot lashed out in a quick counter, driving for her groin. This was the move she had manoeuvred for and invited.

She jumped two-footed, only an inch clear of the ground and six inches back, bending a little to take Brunig's rising ankle against the crotch of her crossed forearms. As her arms yielded like shock absorbers to the impact, her hands curved to grip heel and toe of the boot and she wrenched the foot round in a swift, explosive twist.

Brunig cried out wordlessly. His arms flailed and his standing foot jerked clear of the ground as he spun on the axis of the held leg to save the tendons. He hit the ground face down, arms spread. She was beside him, dropping with both knees on the middle of his back. There came a great 'huff!' as the breath was driven from his body.

Dazedly he lifted his bloodied face. She reached forward and took him by the upper lip just below the nose, pinching the flesh between finger and thumb in the simplest but most painful of finger-grips. Still with one knee on his back she drew his head up and round, her other hand poised to chop at his exposed larynx.

Brunig's choking gurgle of agony grew shrill as he saw the hand lifted to strike. His head quivered as he made an effort to shake it. He beat the ground with his hands and a distorted cry of 'No!' came from his gaping mouth.

She let his head fall, stood up and stepped back. He lay panting, body heaving as he fought to drag breath into his lungs.

Modesty said quietly: 'All right, Brunig. Fall in with the others. I want to talk to you.'

An incredulous murmur was released from the watching crowd. Somebody laughed. Modesty whirled like a cat, glaring with hard, slitted eyes. This was an opening that pleased her, but her face showed only anger.

'Who laughed?'

There was an almost schoolboyish exchange of hesitant glances, then a dark stocky man with a round face said uneasily with a heavy accent: 'I just laugh. Dat is all.'

'You laugh at Brunig?' Her eyes were like black chips in which cold flames of anger shone. She glanced to one side and said to nobody in particular: 'Get a bucket of water and a towel. Quick.'

A man detached himself from the ring of watchers and went round to the back of the hut. A minute later he reappeared with a bucket of water. Another man had gone inside and brought a towel. There was complete silence while she waited. Modesty looked unblinkingly at the round-faced man throughout.

She soaked the towel in the bucket and knelt over Brunig, turning him on his back. With brusque but not brutal movements she swabbed his face with the sopping towel, then carefully felt his ankle. He lifted his head, staring at her blankly.

'I don't think there's any serious damage.' Her voice was without rancour. 'Stand up and try that leg, Brunig.'

He was empty of fight. His face held only bewilderment

196

shaded with suspicion. Slowly he got to his feet, tried the leg gingerly at first, then walked a few paces back and forth, limping slightly.

'Well?'

He looked at her, suspicion fading now, leaving only perplexity. 'Is not bad,' he said slowly. 'Okay soon.'

She swung round on the stocky man. 'You thought it was funny. Will *you* fight Brunig?'

He hesitated, sullen-eyed, then shook his head.

'All right. Don't laugh at a better man again.' As she walked towards the door of the hut she glimpsed Brunig's face. He was still out of his depth, but there was no enmity in him now. She had unseated him as herd-leader but prevented him being made an outcast; under her, he was still top man. Now she would confirm that.

Turning in the doorway she faced the ring of men. She had to lift her voice only a little to be heard, for it was very quiet. 'Any men from other sections, clear off,' she said tersely.

The crowd stirred, hesitated, and began slowly to break up.

She said: 'You know who's who, Brunig. Get the others out of it. I want just us here.'

'Us,' thought Delgado. 'That's very good. She's got them, by God.' He glanced at Liebmann, who stood leaning against the jeep's bonnet, and said very softly. 'Will do?' Liebmann's head turned. For once there was a spark of interest in the empty eyes. He gave a slight nod.

Brunig prowled round the ring, uttering a short command now and again, watching the men drift away. At last he looked at Modesty. 'Is okay now. Just us here——' He broke off uncertainly, not sure how to address her.

'You call me Blaise.' She paused. 'In twenty-four hours I'll know the routine here and we'll be starting work. All I want to know right now is if you're satisfied with conditions.' She had deepened her voice subtly and was using a touch of transatlantic form and accent in her speech.

Liebmann stiffened at her last words. There was a long silence. A man with a soft American accent said: 'A beef

197

might get a man tabbed Unsound around here.'

'I'll be a bloody unsound section commander if I don't make sure you've got good conditions to train under. Speak up.'

'Liquor,' said another man. A Scottish accent.

'What's the ration?'

'A bottle per man per week. I could do that in a day.'

'Forget it. One bottle's enough. I don't want to hear about it again.' She looked round the ring. 'Anything else?'

'Airstrip guards and general fatigues.' It was the American. 'We're catching twice the duties of other sections.'

She looked straight at Liebmann and said: 'Why?'

It was a moment or two before he answered. Delgado was entertained by the realisation that she had tilted Liebmann off-balance.

'Until now the section has not been fully established and has been engaged only in basic training,' Liebmann said coldly. 'A higher proportion of routine duties has naturally fallen to them.'

'We're established now. Who allots routine duties?'

'I do. You may put in a request to me.'

'I've put one in. If nothing's done about it in twenty-four hours I'll take it to Karz.'

'That would be unwise.'

'It might. Or it might be unwise for anybody who stops my section getting their full time on training. We'll let Karz decide.'

For the first time Delgado saw Liebmann's smile. It was a death's head smile. Some rare emotion swept Liebmann. It could have been anger or fear or a blend of both, yet there was pleasure in it simply because it was a feeling, a plucking of emotional strings.

'The matter will be seen to,' Liebmann said, and got into the jeep. It moved away. The men of R-section ignored its departure. They were wholly absorbed in studying their new leader.

She watched the jeep go, gave a sudden humourless grin, and said: 'Well, we shook that bastard a bit.'

198

There was brief laughter and a murmur of satisfaction. She looked round the ring of faces. Their respect was won, and with it such loyalty as they were capable of. It was a tenuous link and could easily snap. These were the cut-throat boys, each man an egocentric creature for whom good or bad was defined solely by what was good or bad for him alone.

She felt nothing for them. If her grip slackened they would turn upon her as lions on a fallen tamer. But in this first crucial confrontation she had achieved dominance and created some sense of unity. It was a first step on a journey in which both the route and the end were still hidden. No speculation was possible yet. She and Willie Garvin had agreed that. They could only play the roles that had been forced upon them and wait for whatever the whims of chance might offer.

She said: 'Listen. And listen carefully. I'm not a bloody fool. Having a woman among you could make for problems. Some of you are wondering if I can be made, so I'll tell you the score and you can stop sweating. I can't be made. Not here, not while this job lasts, and not by you.'

Her words eased a thread of tension in the group. She went on in the same harsh flat voice which left no room for doubt in their minds. 'We're going to work. I'm going to drive you so hard you'll be too tired most of the time to think about hauling your ashes. And if you're not too tired, I understand you've got it on ration in the *seraglio*. Is that right?'

'It's like the whisky,' said the American voice sadly. 'The ration's kind of small for us big boys.' There was a ripple of laughter, an amiable sound.

'Like the whisky,' she said. 'You'll have to make do with it.'

She had not laughed with them, and there was no femininity in her now. Her posture as she leaned casually against the wall of the hut was mannish.

They would probably think she was a lesbian. That suited her well. 'Have someone bring in my case, Brunig,' she said, and went into the hut.

FIFTEEN

THAMAR, the Georgian, moved his knight and said: 'Check.'

Modesty studied the board. She was a pawn up, but Thamar's sacrifice had gained him the attack. Either she would be checkmated in four, or she would lose a rook.

'Your game,' she said. This was one of the many she had played against Thamar over the past ten days, and she had yet to win. Thamar was a master.

It was late evening and they were in the section-commanders' mess. Willie Garvin, The Twins and Sarrat were playing poker. The game would not last long—not with The Twins sitting in. They were turned slightly towards one another, each holding his cards carefully, darting suspicious glances at the other. Soon they would quarrel and the game would break up.

Brett, the Englishman, was in the *seraglio* which occupied a complete wing of the great rambling palace. Hamid had taken his section out on a night exercise, with Liebmann observing. Delgado was on duty in the control room.

Karz stood with his back to the long curtained window, hands clasped behind him. He did not eat in the mess, but sometimes in the evening he would spend half-an-hour there. By tradition his presence was not acknowledged. He would stand unmoving except for an occasional slow turn of the head as he transferred his brooding stare from one person or group to another. Finally he would go plodding out like some monstrous troll brought to life, saying no word.

Modesty knew many things now that she had not known ten days ago. Some she knew as fact, others she had deduced.

The valley lay in the eastern ranges of the Hindu Kush, at about four thousand feet. Between the valley and the plains far to the north and to the south lay a maze of huge peaks and ridges, valleys and ravines. Nobody knew whether there was a way out through that maze other than by air. Around the lake to the north the ground sloped up gently at first for a mile or two, forming a vast and partly wooded basin, then lifted almost sheer and became bare rock with more ravines and valleys leading off.

At the southern end the river disappeared under the mass of a riven mountain. At one time, perhaps a thousand years or more ago, the river must have offered access to the valley from the distant plains; and so some long-dead Khan had caused his summer palace to be built here ... five thousand hands, perhaps, working for five thousand days, in an era when time was of little consequence.

Two transmitters were housed in a prefabricated building on one side of the landing ground, beyond the bottle-neck. They were remote-controlled from the H.Q. section of the palace. The slender aerials were mounted high on one of the long slopes near the arena.

The logistics of the operation were staggering. Every two or three days at least one big aircraft, a Hercules or AN-12, would land and disgorge war-stores. They came in over the top and lost height circling the great basin around the lake until they were low enough to make their final approach to the landing-ground. Their take-off and climb was made in the same fashion. Modesty had been told that the valley itself was barely visible from twenty thousand feet and above. Only the lake could be seen.

The fire-power of each section was enormous. Each category of weapon was standard in itself, but the sources were many. There was the AR-15 weapons system from the United States; recoil-less rifles from Russia; Czech grenades and French mortars; German and Italian radio equipment; British anti-tank mines and radio-controlled rockets.

She had seen the two sections of Flying Infantry, both under Thamar, exercising in their jet-suits, practising amid the vast tangle of valleys and around the mock-up street of houses set up along the far shore of the lake.

The suits were a little different from those she had seen in photographs of the Bell rocket-belts developed for the U.S. Army Transportation Research Command. Delgado had told her they were fifty percent more efficient. These jet-suits bore no marks of origin. They had three jet-nozzles instead

201

of two, and carried two racks across a plastic breast-plate for grenades and ammunition.

Three men, with this mobility, and with AR-15's adapted to launch 75 mm. grenades or simply used as machine-guns with a cyclic rate of over seven hundred rounds a minute, could easily control a dozen city blocks.

No heavy transport would go with the airlift. A small Fifth Column had been established in Kuwait over the past year, and a dozen commercial trucks would be conveniently standing near the airfield ready for seizure. The ten scout cars for her own section would go by air, so would the hundred-odd fast scooters and six 105 mm. air-portable cannon. Four of the great freighters would carry nothing but H.E. and ammunition.

But the light tanks, and all the reserves and stores to sustain the occupation after the first twenty-four hours, would be carried by sea on a twenty thousand ton cargo ship, arriving innocently in the port of Kuwait a few hours before the first parachute section dropped on the airport.

Only one section of the Liberation Army would go by sea—Brett's section, which was to be air-lifted out of the valley six days before D-Day, to embark for the sea-borne operation. How the transfer would take place, and where they would be embarked, she did not know. But she knew that D-Day was to be September 11th, in just under six weeks' time, and that H-hour was 0500.

She watched Thamar setting out the pieces for a new game. He was different from the other men here. She had no feeling for him, but she could acknowledge the difference. The Liebmanns and the Sarrats and the Delgados—all were men who had rejected every scruple, had emptied themselves of compassion. Thamar was a robot who had never been aware that scruple or compassion existed.

She glanced round at The Twins. They had started quarrelling, hissing filthy words at each other. Karz watched them without interest. The game broke up. Sarrat stretched, grinning, then moved to an armchair and picked up a magazine from a pile beside it.

Lok drew a pad towards him and began very carefully to sketch an exploded diagram of a 105 mm. cannon. Chu lit a cigarette and stared blankly into space.

Three days earlier Modesty had seen the first disciplinary execution. A Turk from Hamid's section had damaged one of the women—Leila, the nymphomaniac. He had knocked her down, breaking her jaw. She had been flown out in the Dove, and next day the Turk had died in the arena under the metal-gloved hands of The Twins.

He had chosen to fight with a sabre, and tried to slash through the linked pauldrons, to cut The Twins apart. The blade had not even reached that six-inch flexible link. And then The Twins had hammered him to a senseless pulp with their steel hands before taking the sabre to him.

She had watched impassively, caring nothing for the man's death but loathing the Roman-holiday manner of it with a deep and bitter intensity. Willie, she knew, would be feeling the same, though his face had shown no more emotion than her own.

And now the two linked brothers who had fought as if with one mind sat simmering with hatred for one another.

Karz stirred, moved to the door and went out. Willie Garvin sat shuffling the cards idly, his face thoughtful. He did not look at Modesty, but she saw him rub a finger along his upper lip and knew that in a few moments he would have something to say to her.

This was rare. When they met in the mess or in the course of their work they were brusquely hostile. This was an accepted thing now, and nobody cared, since their work was good.

Modesty had steadily tightened her grip on R-section since that first day. She drove them hard in training. Her own strength and stamina was a challenge to them. When they toiled, heavy-laden, on a toughening-up exercise, she was with them, burdened as they were, grim and panting but lashing them on fiercely by word and example.

She was hard and lean, her face weatherbeaten, hands brown and ungroomed, nails chipped. She knew they speculated about her, perhaps indulged in sexual fantasies, but she had met no problems on that score. She was out of bounds to them and the barrier had never even been tested. There was a curious streak of pride in them now. At first they had been the butts of many caustic jokes by other sections, but that had quickly passed. Now her men boasted about her. To be in Blaise's section was something of a cachet.

She had learned much from them. Her own ability with a handgun or rifle overlapped only slightly on this more massive form of combat, and the use of small-arms for warfare was something they knew better than she. This did not reduce her in their esteem, for she quickly absorbed all that was valuable and her basic skills of hand and eye were readily adapted to new weapons.

Willie Garvin had met no problems. He was known to at least a score of the men in the valley, and many more knew him by reputation. Also, he was a master of the weapons, for he had fought with the Legion and as a mercenary before that, and the whole subject was his special study. With revolvers and automatics he had no skill, yet strangely this lack did not extend to the rifle, machine-gun or heavier arms.

He ruled his section with grim confidence and with rough justice. They considered him a hard bastard, but this they accepted and in fact preferred. When the pins started hitting the primers it was a good thing to have a hard bastard in charge.

Modesty had last spoken to Willie three days ago in Liebmann's office. She had been called there after Willie had visited the radio-room for the promised contact with Lucille.

The conversation between Modesty and Willie had been curt, for Liebmann was present.

'You spoke to her?'

'Yes. Only about 'alf a minute.'

'It wasn't intended to be a social chat. Are you sure it was Lucille?'

'It was her all right. Conditions must've been good. She came over clear enough.'

'What did she say?'

204

'What she was allowed to say, I suppose. Just that she was all right. She 'adn't been hurt. When was I coming to get her? Then she started crying.'

'Lucille, crying?'

'What d'you expect?'

'I only meant she doesn't cry easily.'

'This isn't easy for 'er. She's scared stiff.'

'All right. But at least you're sure she's alive?'

'Yes.'

Modesty had nodded curtly and gone out of the office. No word had passed between them since.

Now Willie wanted to speak to her. Not here, in the mess, but he wanted to set something up so that they could talk. It wasn't surprising. She wanted to talk to him freely herself, but they had made themselves rigidly preserve the atmosphere of hostility for a long period, so that it would be accepted as genuine.

Thamar moved his king's pawn out. A hand tapped her shoulder. She glanced round, looking up at Willie.

He said: 'I want a word with you.'

'What about?'

'I 'ad the houses booked for my section Tuesday morning.' He was speaking of the mock-up street used for practice in house to house fighting. 'You saw Liebmann and switched it to the afternoon.'

'I know. I needed the houses myself for the morning. R-section has got an exercise on that night, and I've got to rest them in the afternoon.'

'Look, I've got bloody problems, too!'

'Then solve them.'

'I will. I'll see Liebmann and get the thing switched back. If 'e won't play I'll go to Karz.'

'Oh, for Christ's sake!' she said angrily. 'Let's settle it ourselves. There's no point in making a big deal of it. We can work something out.'

'Suits me.' His voice was terse. 'When?'

'Tomorrow morning sometime.' She gestured irritably towards the patient Thamar, who was listening stolidly. 'I don't want to talk about it now.'

'What time tomorrow?'

She looked down at the chessboard as if already withdrawing her attention from him. 'I'll be taking a truck-load of dummies to set up in the houses tomorrow at ten. You can drive up with me and help.'

'Thanks. I got a section to run.'

'So have I. A section not a one-man band. I'm letting Brunig put them through their paces tomorrow morning. It'll do him good. Will your lot fall apart if you're not there?'

'Don't fret about my lot. They can manage on their own. I'll see you at the stores, ten o'clock.'

He turned away, nodded to Sarrat and The Twins, and went out.

There were clouds over the valley and the air was close and humid. Willie drove the truck with the pile of limp dummy-men in the back, tattered and repaired from the bullets which had riddled them in earlier practices.

Modesty sat beside him. She did not speak until they had bumped up the long curving slope of rock at the western end of the ridge and reached the flat ground which ringed the lake.

'It really was Lucille, Willie love?'

He relaxed, let out a long breath, and nodded. 'Sure, Princess. It was just the way I said.'

'Then she's alive, but we don't know where.'

'I've been thinking about that. Probably somewhere over the border, north or east. Tashkent maybe, or Kashgar.'

'A long way out of our reach, then.'

'A long way.'

She lit two cigarettes and passed him one. The truck moved steadily on along the broad flat shore of the lake.

'What do you want to do, Willie?' She knew he would have thought through every aspect of the situation. She had done so herself, and reached a grim conclusion.

'We got to make up our minds who we're going to work for,' he said slowly. 'There's Lucille, there's us, and there's

206

Tarrant. If we reckon on keeping Lucille alive, then we've got to go right the way through with Sabre-Tooth.'

'Yes. All the way to Kuwait, and whatever happens there.'

'But if we ditch Lucille, we could maybe figure a way out of 'ere.'

'Could you fly that de Havilland Dove, Willie?'

He shrugged. 'I've never flown one before, but I've 'ad plenty of flying-time on a Beech-18, and there's not a lot of difference. All I need is ten minutes to look over the controls. I was watching the pilot when we took off from Kabul, and I got a fair idea of the layout, but I couldn't see everything from where I was sitting.'

'What about finding the way out through that maze of mountains? It's all below peak-level and you can't go over the top.'

'I'd sweat a bit. But as long as it was daylight I reckon I could manage.'

She said: 'So if we can get hold of the Dove, we fly out and just send a message to Tarrant. Sabre-Tooth won't come off. And Lucille dies.'

'That's for sure.'

'So what do you want to do, Willie?'

He was silent for a long time, and when he spoke his voice was tired. 'I'll tell you something I've never told before, Princess. About Lucille. I'm fond of the kid—you know. But I've never really clicked with 'er. I've tried, but I s'pose I'm not much good at it.'

'I haven't been much good at it either. Does this make any difference?'

'No.' He glanced at her. 'I just wanted to tell you, but it makes no difference. I can't stand kids bein' scared or hurt. Any kid. Most of 'em are right little brats, but they're still kids.'

'So you want to play this for Lucille? You want to go right through with it?' She spoke quietly, head turned a little to watch him as he drove. For once she could not guess what was in his mind.

'No,' he said, and hunched over the wheel, staring bleakly

207

ahead. 'There'll be kids in Kuwait, too. Plenty of 'em. And you know the orders for the first twenty-four hours, Princess. Get the ambassadors and any outsiders locked up tight, quote, for their own safety, unquote, an' then control by terror.' He shook his head. 'Think of Brett and The Twins and Sarrat—any of 'em. Think of your lot or my lot, going in with that kind of order from Karz. There'll be bloody butchery. Kids and all.'

He swung the truck round in a long curve and brought it to a halt in front of the hundred-yard long mock-up of timber-built houses. Switching off the engine, he turned and looked at her. His face was quite calm. Whatever battles he had fought within himself over the past days were ended now, and the outcome was settled.

She said, looking ahead of her: 'Lucille or the rest.'

'That's what it comes down to, Princess. It's not us, or Tarrant, or Kuwait, or anything like that. It's one or a few hundred—in kids. Simple as that.'

'Have you thought that you might feel different if Lucille was your own, Willie? Or if——' she hesitated. 'Or if it was me?'

'Yes,' he said simply. 'I reckon I'd feel different all right, but I reckon I'd be wrong.'

She nodded. 'It looks as if we've worked it out the same way.'

'We usually do.' He rubbed his eyes with finger and thumb. 'When do we try for the Dove, then?'

'We don't, Willie love.' She flicked her cigarette out of the window. 'There's just one way we can play this to give all the runners a chance—the rest, and Lucille, and Tarrant. And us.'

His head jerked round and he stared incredulously, sudden hope flaring in his eyes. Gradually he relaxed, leaning back in the corner of the cab with his brown face beginning to crinkle in a grin.

'How do we work it?' he said. She looked at him without response The grin faded and became a puzzled stare. Her gaze was hard and direct, with a touch of warning in it. He

208

had seen that look rarely, but he knew its meaning. Her mind was made up, diamond-hard; she expected opposition, but she would have none of it.

She said flatly: 'You won't like it, but don't argue. I mean that.'

He rubbed a hand across dry lips, alarm dawning in his eyes, and said: 'Tell me.'

She spoke quietly for three minutes, without expression. As he listened his face began to work, the muscles of his jaw twitching and flexing, shock draining some of the colour from his cheeks.

'No!' he said hoarsely when she had finished. 'Oh Christ, no, Princess!'

'It's the only two-way bet we've got.'

'But you can't make it! You'll never come through all that lot!'

'Which bit of it? The Twins?'

He shook his head, blank-eyed. 'I dunno .. maybe. But *after* that.'

'I've had worse things happen to me. It's only a bad time.'

He closed his eyes for several seconds and opened them again. 'But ... after *that*, Princess. Jesus, you can't fly the Dove, and you can't hope to get out on foot!'

'Who says I can't get out on foot? I've got good feet and a good sense of which way to point them. The men who built that palace came in on foot, up the river. That way's blocked, and all I've got to do is find my way round the block.'

'You might 'ave to circle out for fifty miles through all this tangle of bloody mountains to find your way round!'

'What's fifty miles? Time's the only problem. I've got to get out in time to warn Tarrant about D-Day.'

He shook his head dazedly. 'For God's sake, Princess——'

'That's all, Willie. No more argument.'

He wanted to look away from her but her eyes would not let him. At last she saw the beginnings of hopeless resignation begin to creep over his face. Satisfied, she opened the door and got down from the truck, turning to look at him with a dry little smile.

209

'Don't sweat about it, Willie love. At least we've got half a caper on now. We had nothing before.'

He crossed his arms on the wheel rested his head on them for a few minutes, then lifted it again and looked at her, lips twisted in a ravaged grin.

'We should 've stayed in crime,' he said wearily.

SIXTEEN

THE two radio transmitters were housed in a hut near the small power-house which lay midway along the northern section of the valley. They were operated from the receiver room in the palace by remote control cables.

A man was permanently on duty in the transmitter hut, with a phone link to the operator in the receiver room.

It was two-thirty in the morning, half-an-hour after the last change of shift, when Modesty Blaise moved silently along the valley wall towards the transmitter hut. Two guards patrolled along the foot of the long ridge, covering the ammunition store and the Dove which stood in the open at the end of the runway, but their beat was almost a mile away from where Modesty stood now.

A shadow moved, and Willie Garvin touched her arm gently. There was no need for speech. All that lay ahead had been planned the day before, during the two hours they had spent alone together in the mock-up street-fighting area.

Modesty wore the Colt .32 at her waist. The kongo was in her hand. She gripped Willie's arm for a moment, then moved on to the door of the hut. Very carefully she gripped the handle and turned it, easing the door open. No light shone out, for black-out conditions were preserved in the valley against the bare possibility of over-flying aircraft. A heavy curtain hung from floor to ceiling on a curved rail encompassing the door.

As she closed the door behind her there came the scrape of a chair in the room. Her entrance had been heard. She pushed the curtain aside and moved forward with a little gesture of reassurance, saying: 'Relax, it's only me.'

She knew the technician by sight but not by name. He was a dark-haired Greek with a shiny face and small sharp eyes.

'What is wrong?' There was a hint of suspicion on his face.

'I've been out checking the guards. They're from my section tonight. Did you know there's smoke coming from your power-cable conduit just outside?' She gestured towards the transmitters behind the Greek, where the cable entered through a conduit at floor-level.

'Smoke?' He turned to follow her gesture, and as he did so she took one long pace forward and struck with the kongo just below his ear. He crumpled at the knees, and before he hit the floor she was at the side of the hut, tapping gently on the wall with the kongo.

Willie was outside, listening. Five seconds later he came in, drawing the curtain across behind him. Modesty bent over the unconscious man, slipping an anaesthetic nose-plug into one nostril. Willie moved straight to the transmitters. There were two of them, both one-kilowatt Telefunkens. One was for working, the other a reserve.

He unplugged the remote control cable from the key socket of the reserve seat and plugged in the local key. Modesty came to stand beside him, watching as he noted the frequency-setting on the dial. He was wearing thin cotton gloves.

She took a slip of paper from her pocket and laid it on the bench at his elbow. It read: *'Mercycorps, London. Attention Dr. Letts. Ref. operation on Petty Officer S. Pepys 528625 your diagnosis positively confirmed. Patient will require massive antibiotic pre-op dosage. Please supply.—Dr. Rampal.'*

Willie was setting the transmitter to a frequency of five hundred kilocycles, the distress frequency on which every ship at sea maintained constant listening watch. Even a small ship carrying only one radio officer would have an alarm system to warn him if a message began to come through on that frequency during the hours when he was off duty.

S.O.S. would prefix a message from a ship in dire emergency. The XXX prefix that Willie used was of lower priority but more in accord with the message being sent. A number of ships over a wide area would pick it up. It might well be viewed with suspicion as the work of some crank, but it was addressed to *Mercycorps, London*, and had a sufficient ring of authentic urgency to ensure that some captains at least would decide to pass it on.

A British ship would route it through the Commonwealth Network, to Bombay or to Mauritius, and thence to London.

Willie was tapping the key now, sending slowly at about fifteen words a minute. He repeated the prefix and the message three times, then switched off the transmitter and replaced the remote-control cable in the key-socket.

Modesty moved to the unconscious man, took the anaesthetic plug from his nose, put it on the slip bearing the message, and set a match to the paper. When the plug of wool and the paper had burnt to ashes she ground them into the tin on the bench, used as an ashtray.

Willie finished resetting the frequency to its original reading. Throughout the whole operation he had worked with quick, precise movements, his face completely impassive. Normally at times like this there would have been a hint of zest and sparkle in him, an outward sign of the stimulation that came when the caper was on and the tight-rope of danger was being walked.

But not this time.

He turned in the chair and looked at Modesty. 'That's it, then. You can reckon a hundred to one it'll reach Tarrant. And it won't mean anything to anyone else.' His voice held no more emotion than his face, and she knew that he was simply working like a machine programmed for a particular job to be done.

'All right.' She kept her eyes on the man on the floor. There was nothing of comfort that she could say to Willie now. Words would only bring the danger of breaching the mental barrier he had set up to seal off all feeling.

She had built up her own wall within her. It was a means of protection, an assurance of continued efficiency, that they always used to some degree in any caper. But she knew with bleak certainty that they had never before needed it as urgently as they would need it now and in the days immediately ahead.

Five minutes passed in silence, then the man on the floor stirred and sighed.

Modesty nodded.

Willie stood up, facing her, within arm's length.

Briefly she met his eyes and allowed herself one small smile. Then her hand leapt out and her nails raked down his cheek.

Talo, the Greek, came muzzily up from the sick dark sleep enfolding him.

There was noise . . . a man shouting . . . the sound of a fierce struggle . . . a thud as a body hit the wall of the hut.

As vision cleared he saw the overturned chair, the ashtray contents scattered on the floor. The door of the transmitter-room stood wide open and the curtain had been flung back. Talo lifted his head, staring.

Garvin . . . and the Blaise girl. They were fighting like wild-cats. She was hurled back. Her hand was flashing down to her holstered gun, but Garvin came in fast. His shoulder slammed into her midriff and his left hand clamped on her wrist. She went down beneath him, writhing, trying to bring the gun round. Garvin's hand jerked and twisted. A gasping cry broke from her lips and the gun dropped to the floor, slithering across the room towards Talo.

The Greek was on his knees, staring dazedly. For an instant Willie Garvin's head turned to him. '*She was at the bloody radio, getting set to send a message!*' he panted in a rasping voice.

Tightening the hammerlock on Modesty's arm, he hooked his free hand about her throat from behind. 'You bitch! You twisted, creeping bitch! I'll bloody kill you——!'

His voice was cut off abruptly. Talo did not see exactly what happened, only the quick twist of Modesty's body and the upward lunge of her free arm, then Willie Garvin was rolling aside with one hand clutched to his throat, turning on his back with feet raised to ward off attack as Modesty came upright.

Talo lunged for the gun and his hand closed on the butt. As it came up to the aim, Modesty stopped dead, looking at him, her hands half raised.

'Hold it,' Talo said harshly. 'You move, by God I kill you.'

There was complete silence for several seconds. Talo stood up, the gun steady in his hand. 'You okay, Garvin?' He did not take his eyes from Modesty. She stood frozen, unmoving.

Willie Garvin got slowly to his feet, a hand massaging his throat. 'I'm okay,' he said huskily.

Modesty spoke in a low, urgent voice to Talo. 'I'll make a deal. Kill Garvin. The story can be that I found *him* trying to get a message out. Name your own price——'

Talo laughed shortly. 'You crazy? I already got a deal, Blaise. I work for Karz, I get paid. I work for you, I end up against The Twins.'

'The Twins...' Willie echoed softly, and moved across behind Modesty to reach the phone. He picked it up, his eyes resting balefully on her. 'You'd be a lot better off if I'd broke your neck just now.' He spoke into the phone: 'Garvin 'ere. Give me Karz. Emergency call.'

It was warm and close in the control room, but Liebmann felt a pleasurable chill.

Karz, shaved and dressed, was seated at his desk. The Mongol face showed no emotion, yet from that massive form there seemed to emanate a glacial coldness which filled the whole room.

It was three in the morning, only twenty minutes after Garvin's phone-call from the transmitter hut. Modesty Blaise stood facing Karz across the desk. Her hair was loose and dishevelled, her hands were bound behind her back with insulated wire.

Karz said: 'You were attempting to send a message. Who to?'

She shrugged indifferently. 'Does it matter now?'

'Answer the question.'

'To an old contact of mine in Bombay. A ham radio operator. He works these hours every night for as long as I've known him.'

'The content of the message?'

'All this.' She gestured around her with her head. 'A rundown of the operation. I'd condensed it to just under a hundred and fifty words.'

'On paper?'

'In my head.' She spoke with the dull unconcern of one knowing that neither lies nor truth would make any difference in the end.

'Your contact would pass this to the British Government?'

'And the American Government. I included that in the message I was going to send.'

'The purpose of this betrayal?'

'Money. Saving Kuwait would be worth almost anything to either Government. I would have got ten times what you're paying me.'

'Perhaps. And after you had sent the message, what then?'

'I was going out on foot, along one of the valleys west of the lake.'

Karz's eyes narrowed a little. 'You know that is impossible. No person can escape from this area on foot.'

She shrugged. 'I'd give myself a fifty-fifty chance of making it.'

'A pack of iron rations was found outside the transmitter hut,' Liebmann put in quietly. 'Enough for two weeks.'

Modesty looked at him with contempt. 'Two? I could spread that over five. I'd be living on roots and grass and anything that swims in the rivers or crawls on the ground before I got through. But I've lived that way before.'

Karz nodded slowly. 'I recall the details of your dossier.

You have lived hard before. You will not have the opportunity to do so again.'

She saw his eyes flare with sudden hatred for a moment, and knew that he was hating her because she was lost to his carefully constructed army. To Karz she was more valuable than a full section of men; all his commanders were. Now he would be forced to promote a new commander from the ranks. A potential weak link.

'She has trained Brunig well.' Liebmann, too, was following his master's thoughts. 'He is of very different calibre now. There is also Cogan.'

'That can be considered later.' Karz was impassive again, still looking at Modesty. 'You did not overlook the fact that by your actions you were bound to cause the death of the child?'

'Lucille?' Anger touched Modesty's voice. 'She's Garvin's concern, not mine. I played along with him for old time's sake, but he's grown too big for his boots. I don't owe him anything. I don't owe the child anything.'

Karz sat looking through her for a long time. 'Take her away, Liebmann,' he said at last. 'Then bring in Talo and Garvin.'

Talo's story was brief. The woman had come into the transmitter hut, distracted him by saying that the cables were short-circuiting, and knocked him out. He had recovered in time to see Garvin and Blaise fighting all over the transmitter hut.

Twice Willie tried to interrupt as Talo told his story, and twice Karz silenced him with a curt word.

'Now,' Karz said as Talo finished. 'Do you confirm this account, Garvin?'

'Yes! And I——'

'How did you come to follow Blaise there?'

'Look, never mind that!' Willie's face was shiny with sweat. Words burst from him in a torrent now, and he would not be stopped. 'What about the kid? That's all *I* care about! That bloody woman don't give a damn what 'appens to Lucille—obvious, isn't it? I warned Delgado about 'er

216

days ago. I *told* him! She was all right till she dropped that load of loot gambling in Beirut. Okay, so we try picking up the Watteau, and it goes wrong. Ever since then she's been dead queer. You've seen the way she acts with me——'

'*Be quiet!*' It was only by raising his voice that Karz was able to stem the angry flow of words at last. Willie drew a deep breath and wiped a hand over his sweating face.

'You suspected she was Unsound?' Karz asked in his normal voice.

'Yes. I mean, I knew if she fancied chancing 'er arm at something she wouldn't worry about the kid getting done in.'

'So you followed her tonight?'

'That was luck. Thamar's duty officer and I sat up till two playing chess with 'im. I saw Blaise slipping along by the last of the section 'uts on me way back, so I followed.'

'Go on.'

'Well, she went to the transmitter 'ut. I saw her go in and waited 'alf a minute, wondering what she was up to. Then I went in meself. Talo was strewn out on the floor and she was just getting settled in front of the reserve set.'

'She sent no message?'

'She didn't get a chance. I went straight at 'er. We were fighting thirty seconds after she'd gone into the 'ut. Now look—*I* stopped 'er, Karz! Remember that. *I stopped 'er!* Otherwise you'd 'ave this whole operation blown wide open by now. *So what about Lucille?*'

Willie leaned forward a little, forcing himself to hold the look of mingled anxiety and challenge, though he knew there could be only one answer.

Liebmann, by the wall, was watching Karz curiously. On form, Karz would have the child killed. But the situation was no longer simple. The Blaise-Garvin partnership had split wide open, and Garvin had undoubtedly saved the whole operation from disaster. Again, Karz had lost one commander in Modesty Blaise. He could ill afford to lose another.

'The child will remain unharmed,' Karz said after a long

217

silence. 'Always providing, Garvin, that you yourself remain Sound.'

'I reckon I've proved that,' Willie Garvin said grimly. 'And what about that bitch Blaise?'

'She will provide the usual entertainment.' Karz glanced at Liebmann. 'What hour is convenient for all sections tomorrow?'

'Fourteen hundred hours. It will only delay the afternoon training programme by half-an-hour at most.'

Karz got up and walked to the door.

'Give warning to The Twins that they will be needed,' he said.

Big Ben chimed the hour of ten. It was raining in London on this summer morning.

Tarrant sat watching the Minister seated behind his big desk and wondered how many more times he was going to read the short message.

The Minister was a new man, Roger Selby, recently moved up in a Cabinet reshuffle. He was forty-eight, languid in manner, and had a cool practical mind. In the House he was a formidable and quick-witted debater. Behind his desk he was methodical. He had the ability to go to the heart of a problem and to make a firm decision, ignoring peripheral details. This was a quality Tarrant usually approved of, but there were occasions when it produced the wrong results.

Sometimes those troublesome and complex details added up to more than the apparent heart of the matter, and it required a man of imagination and no little intuition to perceive such an occasion when it arose. Tarrant did not think that the Minister measured up on this count.

Selby laid the message down. 'This was received last night by several ships in the Indian Ocean and the Persian Gulf?'

'Yes, Minister. It reached me at eight o'clock this morning. I sent it over so that you could see it as soon as you came in.'

'How do you construe it?'

'First, if I may ask, have you studied the report I attached to the message, giving you the background?'

Selby picked up a foolscap sheet from his desk and ran his eye down it. 'Yes. You suspected that the Kuwait Liberation Army was something more than a thing of Es-Sabah Solon's imagination. Mercenaries have been disappearing into nowhere. You put in two of your agents——'

'Forgive me,' Tarrant interrupted, 'but Modesty Blaise and Willie Garvin are not agents of ours, or of anybody else.'

The Minister looked at him. 'We won't split hairs, Tarrant. I've met Modesty Blaise briefly on one occasion, at a social affair, and I know about the two of them. I've read up the files on that Gabriel operation.'

'I felt I should make the point clear, Minister. We don't employ them.'

'We could hardly afford to,' Selby said drily. 'However, they obligingly agreed to put themselves in line for employment as mercenaries, and in due time they disappeared.'

'Yes.' Tarrant had left out of his report any reference to Fraser and the affair in Tangier. At first it had baffled him when Fraser had phoned, inconsolable, to tell of waking from a drugged sleep to find Modesty and Willie gone. But then Fraser had checked on Lucille at the school; René Vaubois had consequently checked on the story that Modesty Blaise had flown to France with Lucille for a medical overhaul, and Vaubois had found the story false.

From that time on, Tarrant had been tense with alarm and uncertainty on several counts. Now, out of the blue, had come the coded message routed through *Mercycorps*.

'. . . three weeks and no trace of them,' the Minister was saying. 'So you assume that they entered this mercenary pipeline, got to the end of it, found your theory was correct, and have now sent this message. Is that right?'

'I believe so.'

'Then please construe this message for me.' Selby read it out. '*Attention Dr. Letts. Ref. operation on Petty Officer S. Pepys 528625 your diagnosis positively confirmed. Patient will require massive antibiotic pre-op dosage. Please supply. —Dr. Rampal.*'

'The operation is the blitz attack on Kuwait,' said Tarrant. 'She confirms my diagnosis, or theory, about that. The mention of massive pre-op antibiotic dosage clearly means that to prevent this thing it will be necessary to have very strong forces on the spot in defensive positions before the operation—of which she gives the date.'

'She does?'

'Yes. In free cryptic. The supposed number of the imaginary Petty Officer is the key.'

Selby looked up from the message. 'Apart from the fact that S. Pepys might be Samuel Pepys, the noted diarist and a naval gentleman to boot, I can see no significance in this. I'm sorry if I appear stupid.' He did not sound sorry.

'We had to give it some thought ourselves,' Tarrant said politely. 'Pepys gives the idea of a diary. So does Letts. They're among the best-known publishers of diaries in this country. So we assumed Modesty was working from a Letts pocket diary, and we studied one. It gives the exact time of sunrise and sunset for each Saturday of the year. You have to split the number she gave, 528625. Sunrise is at 5.28 and sunset at 6.25 on Saturday September 11th, a little over five weeks from today.'

The Minister frowned and put the message aside. 'It might have fallen on another day of the week,' he said.

'They would have found some way to convey it, Minister. Modesty Blaise and Willie Garvin are very resourceful, I assure you.'

'And you take this seriously?'

'The message is plain and the signature puts it beyond any doubt that it was sent by Modesty Blaise.'

'That hardly answers my question.'

'On the contrary, Minister.' Tarrant allowed a hint of his annoyance to show.

'I see.' Selby was unruffled. 'The message is from Modesty Blaise, therefore you take it seriously.' He paused for a long while, then added: 'I think you may be right.'

Tarrant's heart sank. There was an intonation that told him Selby thought nothing of the kind. Now would follow a

220

few polite evasions to save Selby the need for saying point-blank that Tarrant was wasting his Minister's time.

'What I doubt,' Selby went on, 'is that Modesty Blaise has the capacity to assess the military aspects of this matter. I rather fancy it will be no more than a Bay of Pigs affair, a ramshackle effort that won't get very far. Certainly I'll recommend to the Prime Minister that we put some of our forces in Bahrein and Aden on a forty-eight hour alert in due course. If there *is* any trouble, Kuwait will call us in as they did before, when the Iraquis were putting troops along the border a few years back.'

'My point is,' Tarrant said carefully, 'that this attack may *not* be a ramshackle effort. It could well be that Kuwait won't get the chance to call us in, and the whole thing will be militarily concluded within a matter of hours. Modesty Blaise evidently thinks so, and she's not an alarmist.'

Selby thought for a while, then shook his head. 'The logistics would be too formidable.'

'I've talked about a theoretical situation of this kind with General Sperry,' said Tarrant. 'He's in the same class as Liddell Hart and Fuller as a military expert. And he agrees that with present-day mobility and fire-power, a highly trained task force of battalion strength could well carry through the operation in twelve hours.'

'He may be right,' said Selby. 'But the core of the matter is this, Tarrant. The whole thing is built up around an idea of yours which is improbable, to say the least, and is confirmed only by an enigmatic message from we don't know where by a woman who's not in our employ and whose background makes her reliability highly dubious.'

'I feel that may be over-simplifying the matter, Minister.'

'No. Just simplifying it, Tarrant.' Selby smiled amiably. 'I can't put troops into Kuwait until we're asked to. I can't throw our rather meagre forces into chaos by ordering preparations on the scale that would be required if your theory were correct. You know how thinly stretched we are.'

'I do,' said Tarrant. 'And I therefore believe we should alert Kuwait, which will do little if any good at all, and also alert the United States, which may do quite a lot of good.'

'They'd laugh at us.'

'I think not. They have far more resources than we have, and they can afford to spend time, money and people on checking unlikely but unpleasant possibilities. I'd like your permission to inform the C.I.A. And I don't mind being laughed at.'

'Perhaps not.' Selby's voice was cool. 'But I object to Her Majesty's Government being laughed at.'

Tarrant got to his feet. There was no room for further argument. Roger Selby was a shrewd, confident political animal. He had weighed up the risk to himself of taking action and of not taking action, and he had made up his mind. In theory Selby put the country first, his party second, and himself third. But he was fully convinced that the first two would be best served by the continued ascendancy of the third. Therefore he had chosen the lesser risk.

Tarrant wondered where Modesty Blaise and Willie Garvin were at this moment, and what they were doing; how they had got the message out, and what had happened to the child, Lucille. Whatever the answers, whatever they had done or risked or suffered, it had all been in vain. He felt suddenly very old.

'Suppose this improbable thing happens?' he said.

Selby gave him a charming smile. 'Then no doubt my head will roll, Tarrant. It would also be likely to roll if I took the action you recommend and this improbable thing didn't happen. Frankly, I believe a forty-eight hour alert as from September 8th will take care of the situation. But let me know if you get another message, of course.'

'We won't,' Tarrant said flatly. 'Modesty Blaise wouldn't imagine that we'd need telling twice.'

Selby ignored the near-rudeness of the answer and maintained his smile. 'Then perhaps your Modesty Blaise and her chap Garvin will manage to confound the enemy on their own somehow,' he said lightly. 'As you've said, they're very resourceful.'

Tarrant felt his throat closing up.

'It's expecting rather a lot of them,' he managed to say, then turned and walked out of the room.

Ten minutes later, in his own office, Tarrant stood looking down on Whitehall as he reported the result of the interview to Fraser.

Fraser adjusted his spectacles and swore liberally. 'So we just sit on our podgy arses and watch it happen,' he ended. 'Do you think it would do any good if you went to the P.M. direct, over Selby's head?'

'No.' Tarrant turned from the window. 'He'd have to back Selby. And the whole thing's so damnably tenuous, Jack.'

'Not to us.'

'I agree. But why not to us?'

Fraser stared. 'Well—because of that message.'

'Yes. A message from Modesty Blaise. We know her form, so we know what the message is worth, and we're convinced. How the hell do you convince the politicians? To them she's just a very enigmatic young woman with a definite but un-proven criminal past who seems to like doing a bit of un-official work for me.' Tarrant shook his head. 'You can't convey to them what she really amounts to.'

'They know what she did in the Gabriel affair.'

'Words on paper.' Tarrant shrugged. 'It's unreal, like a citation for the V.C. "... and in the face of heavy fire Captain Blank single-handed destroyed two enemy machine-gun posts." Fantastic if you know from experience what it means, but if not you can see something ten times better on tele-vision any week.'

Fraser rubbed his chin. 'All right, so it's just a message. But there was all that happened before it.'

'Apart from what I told Selby, all that happened before the message was that Modesty Blaise and Willie Garvin slipped you some knock-out drops and disappeared. And a child who was Willie's protégé disappeared as well.'

'Don't remind me about the knock-out drops,' Fraser said gloomily. 'Christ, when I think how I sat there and told her how smart I was——'

223

'Forget it,' Tarrant broke in sharply. 'You couldn't have dreamt she'd have the screws put on her through the child. She didn't think of it herself. And you did damn well picking up that foxy trail over the next couple of weeks.'

Fraser had wandered over to a map spread on a table in the corner of the office. He tapped a finger on Persia. 'A dead-end at Teheran,' he said grimly. 'I'd say they were taken over the border into Turkmen.'

Tarrant came to stand beside him, looking down at the map. 'They may not be behind the Iron Curtain,' he said vaguely.

Fraser looked at him with interest. 'What makes you say that?'

'To be honest, I've no idea.' Tarrant frowned as if annoyed with himself. 'And it doesn't help anyway. We have to assume they're behind the Curtain, so I suppose we should be prepared for the possibility that they may . . . they just *may* get out somehow.'

'How do we prepare for it?'

Tarrant was silent for a long time. He brushed a hand across the southern border of Russia, the whole sweep including Turkey and Persia and Afghanistan. 'There's precious little we can do on our own,' he said.

'Selby wouldn't let you bring in the Americans?' Fraser scowled. 'They've got people everywhere.'

'He said the Americans would laugh at us.'

'They might.'

'Yes.' Tarrant moved to sit down behind his desk. He took a cigar from his case and gave his whole attention to lighting it. There was a stubborn look on his face. Fraser waited, feeling a little stab of excitement. He knew that look. The old bastard was going to take the bit between his teeth somehow.

'It depends how the thing might be put to the Americans,' said Tarrant. 'Or perhaps *who* puts it to them. Now that chap Dall, the one Modesty got to come over and do his stuff for her in the casino at Beirut . . . he's a very big man.'

'In business, yes. He's got three or four different empires, I understand.'

'Business and government have closer ties in the States, Jack. The point is, he must think a lot of her.'

'As a woman?'

'No doubt. But I think he also has reason to know that she's a highly efficient professional.'

'You mean he'd believe the full strength of that message she sent?'

'He might.' Tarrant picked up one of the phones on his desk and spoke into it. 'Get me a personal call to John Dall, of Dall Enterprises Incorporated, New York. He won't know me, so if you have secretary-trouble try saying that I'm calling on behalf of Modesty Blaise. Say that in any case. If he's not at his office, ask that a message be sent to him, and that I'd be very grateful if he would call me on a very urgent matter. Have you got that?'

He listened, then said: 'Right.' Putting down the phone he leaned back in his chair and looked at Fraser. 'If Dall comes through, I want you out of the office while I talk to him. You're not in on this.'

'I'd prefer to be.'

'No. That's an order, Fraser.'

'Very good, Sir Gerald.' Fraser shrank into himself and blinked nervously, resuming his habitual role. 'May we deal with some other matters in the meantime? It will be early morning in New York. Our operator may have to wait a few hours before he can raise Mr. Dall's office.'

'Dall has interests spread around half the world,' said Tarrant. 'I rather think there'll be some kind of night staff on duty. However, let's have the routine reports. I'll take the latest from Vaughan on those Baltic installations first.'

Ninety minutes later the phone rang. Tarrant picked it up and said: 'Yes?'

He listened, with sudden surprise and satisfaction in his eyes. At last he said: 'At one-thirty? Thank you.'

Putting down the phone he looked at Fraser. 'We got through, Jack. Mr. John Dall is over here in Birmingham, on

225

business. His New York office rang him there and gave him my message.' Tarrant gestured towards the phone. 'That was one of his secretaries ringing from Birmingham to say that Mr. Dall is already on his way aand would like me to lunch with him in the private suite of his London office at one-thirty.'

'Ah . . . so you were right.'

'What about?'

'Dall. He must think a hell of a lot of her. My God, he's not wasting any time.' Fraser hesitated. 'But you could get the chop for this.'

'I know. It depends how Dall handles it and how the Americans react.' Tarrant's thoughts returned to his interview with Selby, and he felt renewed anger mounting within him. 'Selby's only reaction was to suggest with a light laugh that perhaps my Modesty Blaise and her chap Garvin might manage to confound the enemy on their own somehow.'

Fraser's thin face grew bitter. 'I wonder just what Modesty Blaise is doing,' he said slowly, 'while the Right Honourable Roger Selby sits in his ministerial chair making his bloody little quips.'

SEVENTEEN

THOUGH there were upwards of five hundred men gathered on the slopes which looked down upon the broad platform of rock, the silence was almost uncanny.

Modesty Blaise stood in the middle of the arena. She wore the uniform grey tunic and trousers of a commander, and the regulation boots. To her left was the brink of the twenty-foot drop and to her right the massed half-circles of men on the amphitheatre slopes.

Thirty yards ahead of her on level ground, a little apart from the main audience, Karz stood with hands linked behind him, head sunk between his shoulders as he surveyed her broodingly. Beside him stood The Twins, and just be-

226

hind, in a ragged half-circle were the rest of the commanders
—Liebmann, Hamid and the stolid Thamar; Sarrat, Brett
and Delgado.

And Willie Garvin.

The Twins were drawing on their black chain mail gloves.

Willie stood with arms loosely folded, his teak-brown face
a mask, watching her.

Karz lifted his head and spoke, his heavy voice reaching
every man clearly.

'This woman is called Blaise,' he said. 'She has been
proved Unsound. Though she held the rank of commander
among you, she has attempted an act of treason. For this she
will now die.'

Karz paused. The echoes of his voice faded and there was
no other sound. Tension was like a bow-string drawn through
the mass of men. Eyes turned from Karz to the figure in the
middle of the arena. She stood with arms hanging relaxed at
her sides, hair drawn back in a tight knot at the nape of her
neck.

Karz said: 'What will you fight with, Blaise?'

Her voice was flat but clear in the silence. 'I'll fight as I
stand.'

A murmur of incredulity rippled through the watching
men.

'You are permitted any weapon other than a firearm,' Karz
said.

'I know.' She looked at The Twins and lifted her voice a
little, giving it a harsh tinge of contempt. 'I'll fight as I
stand.'

The great Mongol head of Karz turned slowly and he
nodded to The Twins.

Lok looked at Chu with slitted eyes. 'Is nothing, this
woman wit' no weapon. I do the killing.'

Chu's lips drew back from his teeth. 'Don't tell me what
we do, you lousy bassar'! You t'ink I jus' walk along wit'
you——?'

'You will begin *now*,' said Karz in a voice like a glacier
cutting slowly through rock. The Twins were silent. For a

long second they glared venomously at each other, then their heads turned and they began to walk towards Modesty Blaise.

Liebmann watched them carefully. For once there was the tiniest lack of co-ordination in the two men linked by their leather pauldrons. By making herself seem an easy kill, Blaise had got The Twins into the arena at odds with each other. It was a good psychological move, but too expensive in Liebmann's view. He did not think it would outweigh her lack of any weapon.

The kongo had been taken from her, and there was not one hidden in her hair. He wondered if she had managed to conceal a spare kongo about her . . but there was little point in that. She could have had the weapon for the asking.

The Twins quickened their pace. It was almost as if they were racing each other to reach her. When they were six feet from her Modesty moved suddenly sideways with a long stride. For an instant The Twins jostled as both tried to face her. She changed direction with a quick, almost floating movement, then dropped. Her hands were on the ground and two booted feet shot out. Chu moved his leg fast, but one kick got home on the side of his right knee. Then she was rolling away and coming to her feet in the same movement, well out of distance.

Chu cursed, and Lok spat something in reply. The kick had not landed with full force, but it had been effective as a weakener.

Modesty circled The Twins warily. They were cautious now and turned back to back, waiting. She moved round to face Chu again, and abruptly darted towards him.

A growing roar of excitement rose from the watching men. They saw no detail, only an eye-baffling blur of movement. Modesty was chopping with the edge of the hand and stabbing with stiffened fingers; Chu was blocking and counter-chopping. She could not dare to block the frightful metal gloves, but could only duck and sway and block against wrist or forearm.

The close engagement lasted only four seconds, and of all

who watched it perhaps only Willie Garvin could have detailed the moves later. Then a little cry of exultation broke from Chu's grinning lips, and Modesty was backing quickly away, crouched a little, shaking her head to clear it. A great mottled welt down the side of her face showed where the chain mail glove had caught her a grazing blow.

Lok swung round eagerly to stand shoulder to shoulder with his brother, and together they moved forward smoothly. Now the fight became a chase. Twice she was almost trapped against the brink of the drop, and twice in a fierce flurry of kick and chop and rolling somersault she broke clear.

In almost every engagement she attacked low, going for the legs of the four-footed monster, and using her feet far more than her hands. To come to grips would be fatal for her with only two hands against four.

She was panting now, her tunic ripped, but The Twins were not unscathed. Both were limping slightly, and Lok's left eye was half closed with a great lump swelling beneath it.

'She's giving them a run for their money, the bitch,' Brett said tensely. 'They've never taken this long before. By God, she's fast. As fast as they are. But she's quicker with her right than with her left, d'you notice?'

Willie Garvin made no answer. He still stood with arms loosely folded. His tunic was unbuttoned from neck to midchest. The fingertips of his right hand were resting on the hilt of one of the two knives in the harness sheath under his tunic.

Fleetingly his eyes flickered towards Karz, measuring the distance for the throw. If things went wrong, if Modesty died, Willie had his moves planned. The first knife would take Karz in the throat, slicing through the jugular vein; the second would drop Hamid, only three paces away. Hamid carried his automatic rifle, as always. There were other men, variously armed, nearby. But with Hamid's rifle in his hands Willie was coldly confident that he could wipe out every one of Karz's commanders before he went down himself.

The Liberation Army would be a headless body. Who-

229

ever held Lucille could gain nothing by killing her, even as an exemplary lesson. She might live or die, but her chances were better than Modesty's or his own.

Willie's eyes had long since moved back to the battle. Modesty was backing round the inner edge of the arena. Anxiety tightened his stomach as he saw the first hint of sluggishness in her footwork, He wondered if she had left her big move too late.

The strategy so far had worked well. She had sown dissension between The Twins before the fight began; she had tested them and punished them; she had taken hard punishment herself, because this was inevitable. The fight must last long enough for a certain pattern to be established before she made her move, otherwise the element of surprise would be lost. If it had been made too early, with The Twins alert and suspicious, the move could well have failed. It could still fail, if she had left it too late.

'Now!' Willie thought urgently. 'Princess, for Christ's sake!'

Her bruised face gave no hint of desperation. But instead of cold impassivity there was now a burning, animal glare in her eyes. Over many years Willie had seen it only twice before. This was Modesty Blaise totally possessed by a ferocious and unyielding will to survive, all else stripped away.

Sudden relief pierced him as he saw her right hand reach up to the left shoulder of her tunic. She jerked savagely at the carefully weakened seam, and the whole length of the sleeve ripped away from the shoulder. Still backing, she gripped the cuff in her hand and flicked the other end at Lok's face as The Twins moved warily in.

The torn shoulder of the cloth barely touched his face but his head jerked back instinctively. There was a murmur of incomprehension from the mass of watching men. This was like a schoolboy playfully flicking a damp towel. The sleeve snapped out again and yet again as she retreated.

Chu laughed abruptly. The Twins increased their pace. Once more the sleeve flicked out, but this time she was holding the torn shoulder-end of it in her hand. Chu made no effort to dodge. The cuff hit his temple like the end of a whiplash. A gasping grunt broke from his lips and he staggered dazedly.

Only Willie Garvin knew why. Sewn within the double thickness of the shirt-cuff was a broad, flexible band of lead, two and a half inches wide, seven inches long in its curve round the wrist, and just over one-sixteenth of an inch thick, making over a cubic inch of lead. It had been squeezed into a solid chunk during the moments when she was holding the cuff in her hand and flicking with the harmless end of the sleeve.

Chu had been hit by a piece of lead weighing just under half-a-pound. Lok was off balance, dragged by the linking bar of flexible steel-cored leather as his brother reeled and half crumpled.

Again the weighted sleeve flashed out, catching Lok on the side of the face. A rising roar of amazement filled the amphitheatre, and deep within that sound there was a note of eagerness.

Twice more the lead struck home, not with full force for it was impossible to flick the heavy end of the sleeve with accurate timing and placing, but even so the four-legged, four-armed creature was staggering blindly now.

A defensively groping metal hand caught the end of the sleeve and clung desperately. Modesty let go and launched herself directly at The Twins, lunging between their inner arms.

She was between them, her face close to the pauldron link, in the only close-quarter position safe from any quick counter-blow. Her arms flashed out wide, hands curving in. There came a crack as the two shaven heads were smashed together, then she was away again and The Twins were swaying, sagging, barely holding their feet. She caught Lok's wrist and heaved, swinging the tottering pair in a half circle.

Now their backs were towards the drop which formed one side of the rocky arena—and Modesty was behind them. She jumped, a hand hooking round each throat from behind, her legs drawn up with the flat of one foot against the small of each back.

For a moment all was still, then The Twins fell back as one. Her shoulders hit the ground. She heaved with her hands and thrust with all the strength of the long, steely muscles in her thighs.

It was a reverse stomach throw, made from the rear. The Twins hurled over her in a backward arc, cleared the edge of the drop, and crashed down on to the jumble of rock twenty feet below.

An incredulous, swelling roar rose from the mass of watching men. It tailed away into a strangely hushed murmur. Because the brink of the arena curved, only Karz and his commanders could see The Twins now.

Modesty got slowly to her feet, moved to the edge, and looked down. The thick link between the pauldrons had snapped, and The Twins were separated. Lok's back was broken but he was moving, writhing by inches towards his brother, who lay sprawled with a leg twisted unnaturally beneath him, eyes open and staring.

Lok's groping hand found a rock the size of a grapefruit, and lifted it . . .

'You . . . bassar'!' Chu gasped viciously. 'You—' The rock smashed down on his skull. Lok gave a shrill laugh of joy, then his shaven head fell forward in death.

Modesty turned away from the brink, moving stiffly. Her back was savagely bruised from the necessary fall on the hard rock to make the final throw. One side of her face was agony, and her head throbbed with pain. Every muscle was slack from exhaustion. She looked towards Karz and his commanders. They were standing like statues.

Now . . . now, after all this, would come the moment of sharpest danger.

Karz turned his head and looked at Hamid.

'Shoot her,' he said. For the first time there was a core of passion in the iron-cold voice.

Hamid slowly unslung the M-16 from his shoulder. Willie Garvin's fingers took a tighter grip on the knife under his

232

tunic. He kept his eyes on Karz's neck, the first target, and lifted his voice.

'Do it later!' he said loudly. 'Knock 'er off just before we go. Why waste the cow when we can use 'er in the knock-shop?'

Karz's head swivelled to stare stonily at him. Willie met the look without yielding. 'What's the bloody difference, Karz?' he said stubbornly, angrily. 'Shooting's too good for that bitch! I say stick 'er in the knock-shop where the lads can 'ave a go at 'er!'

A low, rumbling murmur of approval echoed round the amphitheatre, and in that murmur there were threads of many emotions—excitement and desire, an unconscious feeling for the underdog who had won, the fascination of the thought that some among them would have the chance to possess this astonishing woman in one of the *seraglio* bedrooms. There would be the reports from the lucky ones, the gossip and comparisons, a whole new aspect of the eternal topic to discuss.

And underlying all this was a fine-spun thread of something akin to defiance. The men wanted this Garvin's way.

Liebmann heard that ominous note. He knew that Karz had heard it too. And Karz was hard-pressed as he had never been before. The Twins were lost. Blaise was unusable. His army was in danger of losing the tempered edge so vital to success. He could not afford to allow mass resentment at this stage. His problems of leadership were more than enough to cope with.

Nothing of this showed in Karz's face, but his head nodded slowly.

'It is a sound recommendation, Garvin.' He turned and spoke to Liebmann. 'Special precautions must be taken. Blaise is dangerous. You will make the necessary arrangements.'

EIGHTEEN

'SHE'LL liven up all right by the time I've finished with 'er,' said Willie Garvin.

He dealt the cards with a deftness born of long practice and picked up his hand. The day's work was over and he was in one of the E-section huts with his men.

'I do not think so, amigo,' said Gamarra. He was a big Bolivian with sunken eyes and a thin mouth. Half of his left ear was missing, bitten off during a brawl in a South American waterfront bar. He turned to a fair-haired man with a petulant face who lay stretched on one of the bunks near the table in the middle of the hut. 'She is no good, Zechi. Right?'

'She is like asleep,' the Pole grunted sullenly. 'Like you not got a woman to work on, just some big dummy.'

Three days had gone by since the fight in the arena. On the second night, when Modesty was declared available by Liebmann, Gamarra had booked her on his green card after a draw among the other applicants. On the third night, Zechi had been to her.

She was not available on the white cards. This was by Karz's decision. The fascination and excitement of the whole affair had done a lot for morale in the miniature army by combating the tedium of routine training. Karz wanted to prolong that situation for as long as possible.

One of the card-players, a Scot, pushed six gambling counters into the middle of the table. There was no money in the camp. These counters were an official issue and each would be worth one dollar when the great pay-day came.

'You want to watch it,' the Scot said. 'She might wake up an' ruin ye, or tak' an eye oot o' your haid. Christ, she made a mess o' them Twins, didn't she?'

'Her arms are strapped behind her,' the Bolivian said, grinning. 'If she tries to do something you can give her a bad time. There is no rule against doing damage to that one.'

Willie Garvin swallowed the bile that rose in his throat and stretched his lips in a grin. For the hundredth time he fiercely smashed the image forming in his mind, the image of his hands about Gamarra's throat, about Zechi's throat, crushing and twisting. There were other images he had fought to blot out during the long hours of the past two nights, when he had lain awake in his cubicle, knowing that Gamarra was with her . . . that Zechi was with her.

Every hour he grew more afraid that the besieged barriers of his mind were on the verge of crumbling, and that he would go berserk.

'I said gi'e me two,' said the Scot for the second time.

'Sorry.' Willie dealt the cards and put the two discards at the bottom of the pack.

'Garvin thinks about what he do with her tonight, he hopes,' Zechi said with something of a sneer.

'I'll liven 'er up all right,' Willie repeated. He was finding it more and more difficult to think of anything to say. 'It's one of 'er tricks,' he went on after a moment. 'She goes into a sort of trance. She can put 'erself right out for a bit. But I know 'er tricks.'

'You didn't know that one wi' the chunk o' bloody lead in her sleeve,' said the Scot. He looked at his cards with disgust and threw them in.

'I knew it.' Willie's voice was cold. 'I didn't know she'd fixed 'er uniform tunic that way, though. Crafty cow.'

The hand was played and the kitty of thirty-odd counters was scooped in by a silent Australian.

'Like a dummy,' Zechi muttered angrily. He was an evil-tempered man. 'You lift her up, she fall back. You twist her over, she lie like dead thing with no bones. You give her fist on mouth, she don't blink eye.' He looked resentfully at a freshly-scarred knuckle, then went on telling his experience for the third time in obscene detail.

'Ah, you're just an amateur, Zechi,' Willie Garvin broke in, and got to his feet, pushing the cards to the Scot. He knew that if he did not get away from these men now, at once, he would crack. 'Count me out. I got to go and see Delgado about tomorrow's exercise.'

Gamarra laughed. 'Make the most of tonight's exercise,

235

amigo. Even if she is like asleep, she has all the things a woman needs. They did not show when she wore uniform, but I tell you she is much woman, that one. Her body is something to see, by God——' He was starting an itemised description as Willie went out through the black-out curtain and the door beyond.

The sun was down and dusk lay over the valley. Willie stood dragging air into his lungs. His heart was pounding as if he had just run a ten-mile race, and waves of nausea swept him.

He waited for the pounding and the nausea to pass, narrowing his thoughts to focus only on what lay ahead. It was true that he had to see Delgado, but there were other things to be done first. He estimated that they would take half-an-hour. Say fifteen minutes in the office with Delgado, then an hour in the commanders' mess, because that was the natural thing to do. By then it would be ten o'clock . . . half-an-hour after the time when the men with the green cards could go to the *seraglio*.

Willie Garvin had a special card, a commander's priority, booking Modesty Blaise for the night. It was valid under the system for every sixth night, and he was weak with relief that this night had been no longer delayed. Another twenty-four hours and he would have broken.

His teeth showed in a snarling grimace of contempt for himself. *He* would have broken? God Almighty, what about *her*?

The *seraglio* consisted of some thirty rooms on three floors in a section of the palace which had been sealed off from the rest.

Maya, the plump middle-aged Eurasian woman who was the brothel's Madame, looked up from the wooden table which served her as a desk, and made a little tick in a well-thumbed register.

'You are Willie Garvin?' Her smile showed yellowing teeth.

'That's right.'

236

'We not have you come to us before.'

'No. This is special.' He grinned at her wolfishly.

'Ah, yes. The Blaise girl. Come now, I take you to her.' She waddled out and along a short passage. 'You are the last to arrive tonight,' she said. 'You come late.'

'I 'ad some things to do. Don't believe in rushing this sort of job, anyway.'

Maya giggled, her fat body shaking. She turned right and padded on towards a heavy door at the end of the corridor. The hinges squeaked faintly as she opened it. Beyond was a small square lobby with a single door leading off it.

'Is nice room,' Maya said, fumbling a key from a pocket in her skirt. 'And she is ready for you. We put strap on her one hour ago.' She looked at Willie warningly. 'Is only one rule with Blaise girl. Not allowed to take off strap.' Her voice dropped to a dramatic whisper. 'Is . . . *Unsound*, you understand?'

'I've read the orders, Ma,' Willie said impatiently.

'Okay. Toilet and ablution back along passage on left if you want. We ring bell at six-thirty. All men out by seven o'clock.' She unlocked the door and pushed it partly open, standing back for Willie to enter.

He looked at her. 'All right, Ma. I'm a big boy. I can manage on my own now.'

She giggled again, slopped away on sandalled feet into the passage, and closed the lobby door behind her. The hinges squeaked faintly again.

Willie Garvin drew a long, shaky breath and walked into the room, pushing the door shut behind him.

It was a fair-sized room with no windows. The ancient mud-brick walls had been hung with cheap, gaudy material. A four-foot divan bed stood against one wall. There was a worn easy chair and a small wooden table. On the table a large enamel jug of water stood in a metal bowl The light came from a single electric lamp projecting from the wall on a swan-necked bracket and bearing a pink lamp-shade.

Modesty Blaise lay on her side on the divan bed. Her arms were secured by a thick strap buckled just above each elbow and stretching for only six inches across her back, so that though her hands were free their movement was so restricted that she was virtually defenceless.

She wore a thin sleeveless dress in red nylon, fastened by three buttons at each shoulder so that it could be removed despite the strap holding her arms. The dress was her only garment. She looked clean, as if she had recently been taken to the showers. Her hair was loose and tied back with a piece of bright green ribbon.

One side of her face was yellow with the fading bruise made by the chain mail glove during her fight with The Twins. Her lips were parted a little. One side of her mouth was badly swollen by a recent blow, and a diagonal piece of one front tooth was missing.

Willie remembered the gash on Zechi's knuckle, but it brought no reaction within him. His mind was numb now, the nerves dead. He could think only of what must be done next, for she was shaking her head at him and pursing her swollen lips in warning.

Willie nodded, taking the cue and moving into his role like a programmed robot.

'All right,' he said harshly. 'Wake up, you bitch.'

He tossed his small-pack of toilet kit on to the table and moved across the room. Very gently he helped her to sit upright with her feet on the floor, and at the same time he uttered a string of sneers, threats and obscenities.

She nodded approval, her eyes warm and reassuring, then knelt by the end of the divan and pointed awkwardly with her head.

Wille slapped one hand hard across his other forearm and said viciously: 'That's a starter. You act dead on me, doll, and we'll see what 'olding your face down in a bowl of water 'll do.'

He knelt, lifting the divan a little and peering beneath it, knowing what to look for. In one corner of the wooden framework was clamped a small metal cylinder about the size of a cotton-reel.

A bug.

In his own small bedroom a hundred yards away, Delgado sat with the earpiece of the receiver held to one ear. His blue-green eyes were intrigued. The sounds from the room in the *seraglio* came through thinly but clearly.

It had been his own idea to check on Garvin in this way. A small doubt had nagged in his mind ever since the affair in the transmitter room, when Modesty had been caught attempting to send out a message. He had arranged for her to be moved out of her bedroom for an hour earlier in the day, so that he could fix the bug in position.

Now he heard her voice in the earpiece ... low, defiant, and filled with hatred. 'You guttersnipe, Garvin. You backstabbing rat. I dragged you out of the sewers and *made* you! And you've cut my throat for the sake of that brat Lucille——'

'*Shut your mouth.*' Garvin's voice, ugly with rage, accompanied by another heavy, slapping blow.

An instant of silence, then a gasping grunt from Garvin.

A curse, a medley of sounds, a crash and a scrambling struggle—abruptly the receiver went dead.

Delgado put the earpiece down, his eyebrows raised. At least Garvin had managed to rouse her. But she had fought back somehow, even though she had only her teeth and her bare feet to fight with.

Or had she? If she had managed to break that strap in some way, and taken Garvin by surprise ...

Delgado got to his feet. He had better go and check.

Willie surveyed the partly over-turned divan. A tangle of sheets hung over it. The bug was hidden from his view now. It was shattered by the kick he had just given it.

He turned to Modesty, a query in his eyes.

'That's the only one,' she said softly. 'I spent the whole evening checking. Delgado fixed it this afternoon, I think. It's bound to be him.'

'He'll probably be along 'ere soon, then.'

'Yes. Fix me up, Willie. But mark me first. A slap.'

There was sweat on his forehead and his eyes looked past her.

'Willie.' Her voice was hard and demanding. He looked at her quickly and swung his open hand at the unbruised side of her face. Her head jerked with the impact, then she smiled at him.

'Fine, Willie love. Now go ahead.'

He gripped one shoulder of her dress and ripped it away, half baring her body diagonally from shoulder to waist. Picking her up, he lifted her over the upturned divan and lowered her to the floor against the wall. He tipped the divan a little farther over on top of her, then moved to stand by the door, listening.

It came a minute later, the faint squeak from the hinges of the lobby door. Willie moved quickly to the easy chair and sat down on the arm of it, bent over a little, one hand to his groin.

The door opened. Delgado stood there with Maya behind him, her face startled and uneasy.

Willie looked up with a glare, still hunched as if in pain. 'What the bloody hell do *you* want, busting in 'ere?'

'Maya thought she heard a fight.' Delgado looked round the room and smiled blandly. 'It looks as if she was right. Where's our Miss Blaise?'

'There.' Willie jerked his head towards the divan and got painfully to his feet. 'She got clever, so I thumped 'er. She stayed clever and landed me one with 'er foot. Then I got mad.'

'I trust her footwork was only a near miss?' Delgado said, grinning. Willie ignored him, moved to the divan and turned it on to its feet, pulling it away from the wall. Modesty lay awkwardly on the floor, half on her back, her arms still strapped behind her.

Delgado said: 'Good evening.'

She did not look at him. Her eyes were fixed dully on Willie Garvin, and she seemed dazed. Willie moved round, picked her up roughly, threw her on to the divan and pushed it back against the wall.

Delgado looked at her with an interest untinged by any shred of compassion. She lay limply on the divan, her hair a tangle, dress ripped, the red imprint of an open hand blotching one side of her face.

'You know, Willie,' Delgado said mildly, 'I don't think she'll last very long at this rate. There's a special rule for her, of course, but I don't think Karz would be pleased if she got used up *too* quickly.'

'Don't worry, I'm not going to kill the bitch,' Willie said bleakly. 'But if she keeps acting up I'll keep belting 'er. You got any objections?'

'None in the world.' Delgado gave a little shrug. 'We all have our own way of doing things.'

'Right. So get out an' leave me to do this my way. You come busting in again and by God I'll belt you too, Delgado.' There was no mistaking the reality of the threat.

Delgado smiled at him thoughtfully. 'I fancy we'll tangle in the long run, Willie. But not for a while yet. That might be Unsound.' He looked at Modesty again. She rolled slowly, painfully on to her side and closed her eyes. Her mouth hung slack with exhaustion. Delgado shook his head with regret. 'You certainly chose the hard way, darling,' he said. 'Have fun.'

Turning, he went across the lobby and through the door to the passage, Maya waddling at his heels. There came the slight squeak of the hinges as the door closed after them.

NINETEEN

WILLIE GARVIN shut the door of Modesty's room. Methodically he cleared the small table and stood it on end at an angle, with one edge jammed under the handle of the door.

He drew one of the knives from the harness under his tunic. Modesty was sitting up on the edge of the bed now. She turned a little so that he could cut through the strap

241

holding her arms, then turned again to face him while he unfastened the stiff buckles above each of her elbows. His hands seemed strangely clumsy and it took him a long time.

At last it was done. Willie put the knife back in its sheath and sat down on the edge of the bed beside her, his big hands resting on his knees.

She drew up the torn shoulder-strap of her dress at back and front, and knotted it roughly. Willie was staring down at the floor. He did not speak.

Easing her shoulders, she gave a little sigh of relief. The bad time was over now. She could open her mind to what lay ahead and give free rein to her thoughts, because what lay ahead was good.

Willie would be feeling the same.

She leaned her head sideways against his shoulder, smiling a little, and said: 'Hallo, Willie love. Tell me in fine silver prose what everybody's saying along the boulevards these days.'

It was as if he had not heard her. She was suddenly aware that the muscles where her cheek rested against his arm felt like rolls of steel. Startled, she sat up and put a hand on his forearm. It was rigid. Even his face was like wood under her hand. Every muscle of his body was locked in unyielding contraction.

She stood up in front of him, her hands on the iron shoulders and whispered: 'Willie?' There was no response. The blue eyes were fixed on something a million miles away.

He did not resist when she prised his hands from his knees, but she had to use force. She leaned against him, pushing him sideways on to the divan, then lifted his feet so that he lay on his back.

She could see something struggling deep in his eyes now. He was trying to help her, trying to fight the great frozen hand that gripped him.

'Don't fight, Willie love,' she said softly. 'Just rest for a little while.'

Kneeling down beside the divan, she took one of his taut hands and held the back of it against her cheek. She put her

242

other arm across the shallow-breathing barrel of his chest and gripped his shoulder, feeling the sheathed knives under her forearm. His head was turned so that he faced her, staring through her. Gently she began to rub his hand against her cheek.

In the past few seconds a window had opened in her mind and she saw with horrified clarity the shocking burden she had laid upon him since that moment in the truck by the lake when she had set out her plans and forbidden all argument.

For her, the crude bodily violation and pain of the past two nights had been a loathsome ordeal; but she could take the memories of all her senses and drop them into some deep cavern of her mind, where in a little while they would dissolve and strike no chord ever again.

A bad time, but finished now, the memory already fading. Soon it would be erased completely, in the sense that she would have no feeling of being involved in what had happened.

But Willie . . .

She knew she was his talisman, the centre of his life. For three days he had gone about his work in the valley, hardfaced, making no slips, showing none of the pain and murderous fury that must have seethed within him, first at knowing what would happen to her, then what *was* happening to her, and finally at hearing all the filth spoken about her.

Gamarra, the big Bolivian of the first night—he would have been pestered by eager questions. So would Zechi, the malicious Pole of the second night. It happened that both were in Willie's section, and the two would have compared notes at length for prurient ears. They had enjoyed no more than a limp body, a flaccid and barely conscious woman in a self-induced partial coma. But they would make the most of their cachet as the first in the camp to have her.

Willie Garvin would have heard it all. His days must have been days of sick horror. And the nights . . . for two nights he must have lain alone in his cubicle, obsessed by the effort to fight off visions of what was being done to her as he lay there.

She doubted that he had slept. He was skilled, as she was herself, at closing his mind against the destroying claws of imagination; this faculty was one of the strongest weapons in their armoury. But not strong enough for him to bear the attack of the past seventy-two hours.

And she should have realised this from the beginning.

Willie Garvin had fought a vicious lone battle, and won—but only just. She knew he would have done all that he had to do, just as he had done everything as planned from the moment he entered the bedroom. Now reaction had set in.

It was a miracle that he had not gone berserk before this. With her mind opened now, she was appallingly aware of what she had done to him, and she marvelled that he had somehow managed to cling to his role.

'Oh, Willie . . . I'm sorry.' Her voice was a whisper.

He tried to shake his head, but it moved only fractionally.

Modesty hesitated. She held a sure and certain key to unlock him from the grip that held his mind and body in helpless inaction. It was a small thing, an inch or two of tape, hidden now in the hem of her dress. This would open the shackles . . . but if she used that key she would have failed him. Nothing would ever be quite the same again for Willie Garvin.

With her help, Willie had to win this one alone—and the hard way.

She wondered how best to help him. She could pretend anger. That might be the way to break through. He would hate to be the focus of her anger. Or she could pretend an amused toughness, mocking him gently for taking this so hard——

No.

She stopped thinking and let her instincts take over. Gently she forced his hand open and held the cupped palm against her bruised cheek.

'Willie . . . don't try too hard, and don't worry,' she whispered. 'Just rest, and listen to me. That's all.'

She saw something in his eyes, a hint of awareness and comprehension, perhaps.

'Look, it's over now, Willie,' she said softly. 'And I wasn't really there any of the time. You know that.'

She put his hand to her temple for a moment. 'It hasn't touched me here. I'm just the same.'

She spoke very quietly and clearly, pausing between each sentence, giving his numbed mind time to grasp her words.

'Willie, think what I'm saying to you ... we've never moaned when we've bought ourselves a rough ride.

'We bought this one, Willie love. Whatever happened, it was all in with the ticket.

'You've had the worst of it. I should have known that before, but I know it now.

'My bit wasn't funny. . . .' A spark of wry humour touched her eyes. 'But it wasn't a fate-worse-than-death, either!'

She pressed his hand a little tighter against her cheek.

'Listen, Willie. You know I never lie to you. I was a thousand miles away.

'It was nothing like when it happened to me long ago, when I was twelve. I was frightened then, until I passed out.

'And even that's gone now. I shut it out long ago. It happened to somebody else. So did this.

'I set this one up myself, Willie love, so it was that much easier. Now it's gone. Finished.

'We have to think about the next bit, and that's going to be my bad time, because I'll be the one who's wondering and worrying. About you.'

She stopped speaking and looked at him for a long time. Then she bent her head and rested her brow on his chest. Her voice did not plead. It was just a little sad, a little tired, as she said: 'Come back to me now, Willie. We've walked a long, long way together. I don't want to have to start walking on my own again.'

There were no more words to say. She stayed as she was, all thought suspended, quietly waiting. It was minutes before she realised that his breathing was deeper and that the cruel contraction of the muscles was yielding.

Relief swept through her, but still she waited, unmoving.

245

The sound as he let out a long exhalation seemed very loud. His hand moved from her cheek and rested about her shoulders, holding her. He cleared his throat and made three attempts to speak before his voice emerged in a husky whisper.

'Did you know ... did you know, Princess ... only about one whelk in four million is left-handed?'

Tension drained from her body. She knew he had won.

'Left-handed? No. I didn't know that. I didn't know whelks had any hands, Willie.'

'Not 'ands, Princess. Their shells are twisted right-'anded. You could work all your life with whelks, and the chances are you'd never see one with a left-'anded shell.'

'Only one in four million?'

'That's right.'

She felt his body relaxing with every moment that passed.

'It's an amazing thing, Willie.'

'I thought you'd like to know.'

'Yes. It's of no small importance.'

'Ah ... you've just made a litotes.'

The word made her want to laugh, but instead her body began to shake and she was silently crying. He held her for a full minute until the spasm passed. She lifted her head and looked at him, shocked. 'I've never done that before, Willie —not in the middle of a job. Only afterwards. Sometimes.'

'I know. It didn't do any harm, though. Gets you unwound. And this job's come out a bit different.'

'Yes.'

She got up and sat on the arm of the easy chair, watching him with a sense of overwhelming content.

Willie swung his feet to the floor and stood up. 'Let us join in singing 'ymn fifty-four, *Now With Stomachs Gently Rising.* . . .' He shook his head in disgust. 'Sorry about the Marlon Brando bit, Princess.'

'Sorry I snivelled, Willie love.'

He gave a quick shake of his head. 'No. That was all right.'

Picking up his small-pack from the floor, he took out the

246

towel and toilet-bag on top, then began to lay on the bed a number of objects hidden beneath—her belt and holster with the Colt .32; a plain black bra and pants; the kongo; her lipstick tear-gas weapon; a small phial of anaesthetic nose-plugs; half-a-dozen flat tins of iron rations; and a small flat wooden box she had not seen before.

His hands moved with unhurried efficiency now, and he talked quietly as he worked.

'I reckoned this lot would do to start with, Princess. Nothing's 'appened to stop us playing the caper the way we figured it. There's just the two prowler guards up by the Dove and the ammo store. I've cached your gear under that rock we picked out by the river—shirt, slacks, boots, sweater, a blanket, and a few odds and ends, all in a standard shoulder-pack.'

He sat down on the bed and took out cigarettes. When he held the match for her the flame was quite steady.

'Pity you can't fly that Dove out,' he said, 'but you've only 'ad twelve hours solo on a small kite and it's ten to one you wouldn't make it. I reckon you've got a better than even chance on foot.'

He looked at her, but when she did not answer he went on: 'Okay, so the guards change at three o'clock. We'll be up there by then, waiting for 'em. I've opened up one of the sealed doors that lead into this place, the one from the technical stores, so we can get out that way with no trouble.'

He looked at the end of his cigarette and said quietly: 'It's my section's night for guard duty, starting at nine, so it was me that fixed the detail and the shifts. The two going on shift at three a.m.—they'll be Gamarra and Zechi.'

He went on quickly before she could comment, still looking at his cigarette. 'After we've done 'em, we come back 'ere. You knock me cold an' tie me up. We'll make that bit good. It'll look like you got me with a kick, banged me napper against the wall, and managed to cut your strap with one of me knives. Then you go off the other way—not past the guards and the lake, but south along that small valley. They'll 'ave the Flying Infantry and 'alf the army out search-

247

ing north. Karz won't be too pleased with me, but 'e can't afford to lose any more commanders, so I reckon I've got a good chance of not getting the chop.'

He thought for a moment, then looked at her and said: 'Is that about it?'

'That's fine, Willie.' Abruptly, despite the swollen lips, her face was lit by the bright mischief of her urchin smile. 'Only we're not going to do it that way now.'

'Not?' He was alarmed for a moment, but the quick shake of her head reassured him.

'No. It's going to be much better.' Her voice was warm and eager. She lifted the skirt of her dress and picked at the hem. 'Everything's changed, Willie love. We haven't got a ball and chain round our ankles any longer. *We've got a fair caper at last.*'

She drew out the two-inch length of grubby white tape from where it lay hidden in the hem of her dress, and handed it to him. On the tape, printed in red, was the name *Lucille Brouet*.

Willie lifted his head and stared. 'It's one of her name-tapes,' he said hoarsely. 'She's got 'em sewn in all her clothes —it's a regulation at the school. Where d'you find it, Princess?'

'It must have come loose from something she was wearing, Willie.' Modesty leaned forward and put a hand on his. 'I found it here in this room. It was in the corner behind the divan.'

Willie Garvin sat very still, his eyes blank as his racing thoughts caught up with hers.

'We should've known,' he said softly at last. 'Of *course*, she's 'ere, Princess. Karz always makes an example if anyone goes Unsound. If it came to killing Lucille, he'd do it here, make a thing of it, so everyone could see he never bluffed.'

'And your radio-telephone call to her, Willie, that wasn't from somewhere over the borders. She could have been speaking over a portable transmitter here, only a few hundred feet from the control room.'

He nodded absently and got to his feet. There was puzzlement in his eyes. 'Princess . . . why didn't you tell me before, when I was making a nit of meself with the big drama bit?'

'You had to come out of it under your own steam, Willie, still believing that we were going to have to do this the hard way. I didn't want to feed you a lucky-pill to get you out of it.'

His look understood, accepted, and thanked her. He walked across the room and stood with hands resting on hips, looking up like a man studying a splendid sunset, drawing long deep breaths of pleasure. Carefully he put the flat of his hand against the massive mud-brick wall behind the gaudy chiffon and stared at her with one eyebrow lifted in smiling query.

'I could push this whole bloody wall over, Princess,' he said. 'Want me to show you?'

She laughed. 'I believe you. But leave it a while. We've got plenty to work out yet.'

'Okay.' He knelt and poured water into the metal bowl on the floor. While he washed the sweat from his face and dried vigorously on the towel from his small-pack, she took off her dress, put on the pants and bra, then slipped into the dress again.

'Right, Willie, let's start figuring.'

'Just a minute.' Willie put down the towel and took her face very gently between his hands, turning it first one way then the other to study her hurts.

'Zechi broke the tooth?' he said.

She thought for a moment. 'Yes. That was Zechi. But the lips don't hurt much now, and I'll get the tooth crowned as soon as we're home again.'

'Sure. You hurt anywhere else, Princess?'

'I pulled a thigh-muscle a little with that last throw on The Twins, but there's no more than a touch of stiffness now.'

'And . . . while you've been in this place?'

'I don't remember much. Honestly, Willie. I know I've got a few bruises, but nothing to slow me down.'

'I'd better check you over.' It was in the nature of a command, the only kind of command he ever gave her, and she was glad. It showed that he was himself again, and Willie Garvin looked upon himself as the judge and guardian of her fitness. There was good sense in this, for he was a natural and practised expert in all that it involved.

She slipped off the shoulder-straps and let the dress fall. He studied her with clinical eyes, noting new bruises on her body and a deep oval welt on one shoulder. He held up one hand and said: 'Use your left.'

Without shaping for the blow or telegraphing it she flashed out her left to strike with the *shotei*, or hand-piston form of blow, the heel of her hand smacking into his palm.

'Now the right.'

She struck with the other hand, very fast. He nodded his satisfaction, put his hands on her shoulders and turned her round. His fingers worked their way along the deltoid muscles, then down to the biceps and triceps.

He went down on one knee behind her. 'This leg, Princess?'

'Yes.'

'Put your weight on it.'

She obeyed. His fingers probed the thigh-muscles carefully, back and front. He straightened up and said: 'It's okay. Just the old rectus femoris wants loosening up. You'd better lie down.'

He cleared the objects laid out on the divan bed and she lay down on her back. For ten minutes he worked on the muscle, his fingers kneading away the slight stiffness. She did not talk, because she knew that his whole mind was concentrated into his fingers and that there was more than simple mechanics in his manipulation, a touch of magic perhaps.

'Right,' he said at last. 'Give it a try.'

She got up, walked across the room, and flashed the leg out in a sudden waist-high kick. She poised on the leg, bent it at the knee, then jumped from it.

'Fine, Willie. Thanks.'

He had watched her sharply throughout. Now he relaxed. She put on the dress and sat down beside him on the divan.

'How do we play it, Princess?' he asked.

She told him, and he listened intently. When she had finished he said: 'The first bit's the dodgy part—finding Lucille. This place is a warren and we don't know which rooms the women are using.'

'Lucille was in this room to start with, Willie. That's how the name-tab came to be here. Maya must be in charge of her. When I joined the company they moved her out to make a place for me. I'd say she's on the upper floor somewhere, out of the way.'

'We could get 'old of Maya and wring it out of 'er.' Willie spoke uneasily, without conviction. If Maya talked under threat alone it would be all right. But if she was stubborn . . .

Modesty shrugged, knowing his thoughts.

'No good kidding ourselves, Willie. Either you can do that sort of thing or you can't. And we'd balk. So let's forget it. We'll just have to risk searching the place——'

She stopped, for Willie was staring into space, his face absorbed. Taking the packet of cigarettes from his shirt pocket she lit one and sat waiting. A slow grin began to clear the concentration from his face.

'And now,' he said in the bland, rounded voice of a fashion-show announcer, 'we have a terribly smart little number here that I'm sure you'll simply adore.'

It was an hour after midnight when the telephone handset in Maya's office rang. She was dozing in her armchair. After fifteen years of experience as a Madame, the habit of cat-napping by night and sleeping for a few hours during the day was too strong to be broken.

Vaguely puzzled she heaved herself to her feet and picked up the phone.

'Karz,' said the stone-heavy voice. It was the way he always announced himself. 'You will check the security of the child.'

'The security . . . ?' Maya was more frightened than surprised. Karz terrified her. 'Yes. Yes, commandante. You mean—now?'

251

'At once,' said the voice. 'And ring me when you have done so.' The line went dead.

Maya wiped her face with the hem of her dress, picked up a flashlamp from the table, and went out of her office at a quick shuffle. She moved along a dimly lit corridor, turned left and left again, then mounted a flight of stairs to the second floor. From one or two of the rooms as she passed there came the sound of movement, from another a guffaw of laughter.

She moved on up a further long flight of stairs. Here there were no lights. She switched on the torch, flashing it ahead of her.

Modesty Blaise moved a dozen paces behind, on bare and silent feet.

Puffing, the woman made her way along a narrower passage. She passed a T-junction and moved on to a door at the end. There came the sound of a heavy bolt being drawn, then a second bolt. Modesty watched her enter the room. A dim light from within showed through the half-open door.

Modesty turned down in the blackness of the T-junction and waited, pressed against the wall. A minute later she heard the door close and the bolts slide home. The flashlamp beam bobbed along the passage and the heavy figure shuffled across the end of the T-junction.

Three minutes later Maya waddled breathlessly into her office and wound the handle of the telephone handset.

Only fifty yards away, beyond several intervening walls of the palace, Willie Garvin stood in complete darkness, his hand on a telephone which stood on one of the benches in the technical stores.

When the phone rang he lifted it to his ear and said with a foreign inflexion: 'Switchboard.'

'Give me Karz,' Maya's voice puffed. 'I have orders to call him.'

'Okay.' Willie flicked the mouthpiece of the phone twice with his finger-nail, gave the generator handle a half turn, waited two seconds and said: 'Karz.' The heavy, toneless voice was easy to imitate.

Maya's nervousness came over the line as she spoke. 'I have been to the child, commandante.'

'She is secure?'

'Yes, commandante——' Maya had been about to add, 'of course', but stopped herself in time. 'She was asleep. Quite secure.'

'That is all.' Willie put down the phone. Switching on a masked torch he unclamped the toothed terminal-clips from the section of twin cable stapled along the wall above the bench. An inch of the cable had been stripped of insulation and cut through to disconnect it from the exchange in the H.Q. section offices. Only his own phone had been connected direct to Maya's. He twisted the ends of the cut cable together to restore the line to the exchange, and moved to a heavy door in the wall, picking up his small pack which now bulged again.

This was one of several doors in the palace which were kept permanently locked to seal off the *seraglio* from all access except through Maya's office. He had dealt with the lock earlier that evening. He closed the door after him, moved along a short passage, and turned down one of the main corridors of the *seraglio*.

Modesty was waiting for him in her room.

'It worked, Willie.' Her dark eyes were alight with relief. 'A room up on the third floor.'

'Ah ... now we're rolling.' He looked at his watch. 'Quarter past one now. What time do we go and get 'er?'

'Soon after two, I think. By that time most of the customers here have settled down to sleep for a while. Did you pick up what you wanted from the stores?'

'Sure.' He patted the small pack under his arm, moved to the divan bed, and sat down beside her. 'Maya said on the phone that Lucille was asleep.'

Modesty thought for a while, frowning, then said slowly: 'We don't know how she'll react when we rouse her.'

'Eh? She ought to be 'appy as a lush in a brewery, once she knows it's us an' that we've come to take 'er out.' Willie's tone was faintly surprised and indignant.

'For heaven's sake, Willie—she's not *us*. She's only twelve and she's been scared out of her wits. She could easily go into screaming hysterics.'

Willie rubbed his chin. 'I s'pose so,' he said gloomily. Turning, he picked up the small flat box he had taken from his pack earlier. Inside lay a hypodermic syringe and four ampoules.

'I nicked it from the sick-bay this evening,' he said. 'That was when I thought we were still on the original caper, with you going out on your tod. There's a three-grain phenobarbitone solution in each ampoule.'

'What was the idea?'

'I reckon it'd be a good thing if you gave me a shot after you'd chilled me. Then when they found me in the morning I'd still be really out, so they'd figure you'd only been gone maybe an hour instead of three or four. No reason for them to wonder if I was doped and not just concussed.'

Modesty nodded. 'We might have a better use for it now. Keep it handy, Willie.' She picked up her belt, drew the Colt from its holster and checked it carefully. 'How did you get hold of this? And all my other gear—the clothes and the kongo?'

'That radio bloke lung on to the Colt after the punch-up we staged in the transmitter room. I bought it off 'im later for two green cards.'

'And the other stuff?'

'I just went to your section 'ut after you'd knocked off The Twins and took it.'

'Brunig and the others didn't argue?'

'Let's say they didn't try to stop me.' Willie smiled grimly. 'I probably looked a bit liverish.'

254

TWENTY

WILLIE GARVIN eased back the two bolts and opened the
door of the room on the third floor. A low-wattage lamp
hung in the centre of the room. There was a bunk along one
wall.

Modesty closed the door behind her. Together they moved
towards the sleeping child.

'Lucille . . .' Modesty spoke in a whisper, gently pinching
the lobe of Lucille's ear. 'It's us—Modesty and Willie.
We're here, darling. Everything's all right now.'

The eyes opened and stared blankly. The hair was a
matted tangle spread about the thin, taut face.

'It's all right, sweetheart.' Modesty slipped an arm under
the narrow shoulders and lifted Lucille upright. 'Look,
Willie's here too.'

' 'Allo, love.' Willie leaned forward. 'Right ol' pickle
you've been in, eh? Still, we'll soon be 'ome now.'

Lucille was shaking and in her eyes there was hatred and
terror. She gabbled in French, her voice a choking whisper.

'They took me away! You *told* them to take me away—
they said so! They put needles in my arm to make me
sleep!' Her voice was rising. 'That fat woman comes—she's
horrible! And I hear things, men and women, I hear them
come and go and I know one day they'll come to kill me——'

A small fist lashed out at Modesty's face. She caught the
wrist, imprisoning the arms against her body, and clapped a
hand over the child's mouth as Lucille drew breath to
scream.

'Willie. Be quick.'

He thrust the needle into the ampoule and carefully drew
the solution into the syringe. Lucille was struggling wildly.

'Let's 'ave one arm, Princess.' It felt like a stick in his
hand. He saw Modesty's mask-like face and knew that the
sickness in her eyes was reflected in his own. His fingers felt
for the tiny muscle, and the needle slid home.

To Lucille it must have seemed that the two adults were

monsters, crushing and suffocating and hurting her. Willie'
withdrew the hypodermic, still keeping his hold on the
skinny arm. After perhaps twenty seconds, which seemed to
endure for days, the frantic struggling grew weaker and at
last the small body went slack.

'Oh, Christ,' Willie said softly, and wiped the back of his
hand across a dripping brow. 'Poor little bint.'

Modesty stood up, the limp child wrapped in a blanket in
her arms. 'You go first, Willie.'

He drew a knife, holding it by the tip, and went on ahead
of her with the masked torch in his free hand, using it spar-
ingly. They met nobody on their way down through the
seraglio.

Two minutes later they passed through the door into the
technical stores. Willie slipped the knife back into its sheath
and led the way between racks and benches of equipment to
the outer door. He bent to unlock it with a metal probe.

'You okay, Princess? Want me to carry 'er?'

'She doesn't weigh a lot. Better for you to have your hands
free.'

He nodded. His knives were silent. She could not use her
gun without raising the alarm.

Outside the night was of black velvet, with high cloud
obscuring moon and stars. They moved away from the
palace, hugging the valley wall for two hundred yards before
starting the half-mile crossing to where the river ran in its
cutting on the other side. Modesty closed her mind to the
growing weight of her burden and kept her eyes on the
shadowy figure of Willie Garvin moving ahead.

It was warm and close. Even the dust beneath her bare feet
felt warm to the toughened skin of her soles.

The danger of their being seen was small. Somewhere a
man unable to sleep might be outside taking the air, but there
were no lights showing and vision was limited to little more
than twenty paces.

At last there came a time when Willie turned, took Lucille
from her arms, and laid the limp, blanketed form down
against a low rock.

'All right, Princess,' he whispered. 'You take a breather while I go and get your stuff.'

He returned three or four minutes later with a large pack over one shoulder. Modesty was lying flat on her back, breathing deeply. She stood up, unbuckled her belt, and stripped off the red dress. He waited while she put on the black shirt and trousers, the socks and the combat boots. The kongo went into a squeeze-pocket by her thigh, the lipstick tear-gas gun into her shirt pocket. She buckled the holstered Colt about her waist.

With every move she made, Willie Garvin could feel the black spectress of the past few days retreating from his mind. She stood facing him in the darkness and he felt a light touch as she punched him gently on the shoulder.

'All right, Willie love. Now let's go and push a few walls over, like you said. I'm me again.'

'So am I.' She saw the glint of his teeth in the darkness as he spoke.

When she picked up Lucille for the long trudge to the head of the valley he stopped her. 'We can make it easy for ourselves, Princess. This way.' He moved towards the river bank, which dropped sharply for a few feet to a narrow strip of gravel. Easing himself over the edge, he crouched by a shapeless bundle which lay just clear of the water.

She could not see what he was doing, but after a few seconds there came a soft hissing sound. The bundle expanded and took shape. It was a self-inflating rubber dinghy of the kind carried by aircraft.

'It'd just been repaired in the stores,' he whispered as Modesty handed Lucille down to him. 'I figured it might be the best way past the guard-'ouse—and a lot quicker for coming back if we'd played it the way we were going to.'

She wondered again at the meticulous way he had managed to keep polishing and perfecting their general plan through all the torment of the past few days.

The river current was sluggish throughout its whole length after the first short rush of the rapids from the lake. Willie slipped a paddle through a loop of rope at the stern of the dinghy and began to skull deftly, twisting the paddle from side to side in a smooth figure-of-eight movement.

The laden dinghy began to move slowly up-stream. Some time later, as they passed the guard-house set near the point where the river curved in sharply round the bottle-neck, there came the sound of scooters starting up. That would be Gamarra and Zechi going on shift. They would drive up the two mile length of the airfield, and the off-coming guards would use the scooters to return.

The dinghy moved on along the deep-cut channel and round the wide curve where the river bordered the valley. After five minutes they heard the growing then fading sound of the scooters as the two guards who had completed their three-hour shift returned to the guard-house.

The high clouds had thickened and it was darker than ever when they came at last to the point where the rapids made themselves felt. Willie turned the dinghy into the bank and steadied Modesty as she climbed out with the unconscious child.

Somewhere along the face of the ridge which extended westward across the valley the two prowler guards would be patrolling on a cross-beat from the Dove aircraft on the far side to the ammunition store in the middle of the ridge.

Gamarra and Zechi.

Willie said softly: 'One of us better stay with Lucille.'

It was unnecessary. She would not wake for two or three hours. But Modesty nodded. 'Yes. I'll stay, Willie. You do this bit.'

'Thanks, Princess.'

She saw him fumble in his pocket and carefully plug something into his right ear—the blind-man's radar device. Next moment he had vanished soundlessly into the darkness. She sat with the small limp body cradled in her arms, her back resting against the steep rise of the bank, glad for Willie that at last he could release the compressed coil-springs of action that he had held in check for so long.

Out in the valley Gamarra leaned against the rocky ridge near the thick wooden doors of the ammunition store. The natural opening into the great cave had been squared off with reinforced concrete to make a frame for the double doors. An automatic rifle was slung over Gamarra's shoulder. At his belt hung a masked flashlamp. He lifted it and shone it briefly on his watch.

Three forty-five. He had two cans of beer hidden near the Dove. Zechi didn't know about them. Gamarra decided he would have the first in half-an-hour and the second an hour later. Then there would be only forty-five minutes to go before the shift ended.

He moved on slowly past the big doors. This business of guards was a waste of time, he thought. It made sense to have a guard on the liquor store in the palace, but who would want to get to the ammunition or the Dove? Still, Karz had laid down the orders and that was the end of it.

On reflection, he thought idly, it was just possible that one or two of the men had flying experience, and if some fool wanted to desert then his only way out would be by the Dove. Even that would be a very slim hope.

Gamarra had come in with a draft of twenty or more in one of the big Lockheed Hercules aircraft, but he had heard men talking who had been brought in by the Dove. They had not enjoyed it. Apparently it was like flying through a big maze, well below the mountain tops.

His thoughts fluttered to another subject and a grin twisted his lips. He wondered how Garvin was getting on with that half-dead Blaise girl. . . .

The oscillator in Willie Garvin's ear began to bleep faintly. The sound grew louder. He moved a dozen paces to his left and lay flat on the ground, straining his eyes into the darkness. The bleeps told him that the man was coming towards him now, but obliquely, and would pass a little to his left.

His eyes picked up the tall, burly figure.

Gamarra.

Eight paces away, seven, six . . . in another moment he would be passing on and increasing the range. Willie came to one knee and his arm swung hard.

The beautifully balanced knife made the faintest hiss as it flashed through the air. He launched himself after it. Gamarra took one staggering pace with the knife buried almost to its hilt in the side of his neck. Powerful hands caught him as he fell, lowering him quietly to the ground. Vision fading, Gamarra stared uncomprehendingly into the face above him.

Garvin . . . ?

An icy, whispering voice: 'You should 've stayed away from Modesty Blaise, amigo.'

Gamarra died with the beginnings of fear and a blurred question forming in his mind.

Willie jerked the knife free, wiped it clean on the dead man's shirt, and moved on westward through the darkness.

Zechi was feeling sullen anger as he prowled through the scattering of small boulders along the ground at the foot of the ridge. He was sure that bastard Gamarra had got some beer hidden away somewhere and didn't intend to share it.

Zechi peered down among the rocks, wishing he could use his masked flashlamp more often. But that would only make Gamarra suspicious. A last look round the base of the big boulder standing ahead, and then he would move on. Already he had spent too much time at this end of the beat.

He rounded the boulder and lifted his flashlamp. Something hit his right shoulder a savage blow, and the whole arm went limp. His cry was cut off by a hand like a grapnel hooking round his throat from behind. Zechi's good hand came up to tear at it, and an arm flashed beneath his armpit. Another grapnel clamped behind his neck.

He was held with his sound arm imprisoned in the half-nelson. The hand at his throat moved slightly, the heel of it pressing in, the fingers hooking up over his jaw-bone, straining his head round. Even as he tensed to kick backwards a knee drove with numbing force into the back of his thigh, forestalling the move.

'Garvin,' an arctic voice whispered in his ear. 'Tell Gamarra I sent you. He'll tell you why.'

Willie Garvin's hands jerked hard. There came a sound like the snapping of a damp twig.

He slid down the river bank beside her. It was thirty minutes since he had left.

'Finished, Willie?'

'All settled.' He took Lucille from her arms. 'I spent ten minutes in the Dove 'aving a good look over the controls.'

'What about fuel?'

'Tanks full. Bring my small pack will you please, Princess?'

Ten minutes later Modesty passed Lucille up to Willie as he crouched in the doorway of the Dove, and climbed in after him, closing the door and switching on the masked flashlamp.

The four facing seats were designed so that each pair could quickly be converted into a couch. Modesty set up the port-side couch and Willie laid the sleeping child on it, securing her with two safety-belts.

Modesty said: 'She'd better have another shot of dope in about half-an-hour. I'll come back and see to it.'

'Okay.' He took the box containing the hypodermic from his pack and laid it on the floor.

They climbed down from the Dove, closed the door and moved along the face of the ridge towards the doors of the ammunition store. There was no lock, just one big drop-bar.

Inside hung a wide asbestos fire-curtain. Willie closed the doors and switched on the lights. The cave spread out widely from the mouth and bit a full fifteen paces into the hundred-and-twenty foot thickness of the ridge. The roof was solid rock, thirty feet of it. Together they surveyed the great mass of carefully stacked crates of anti-tank mines, 81 mm. mortar bombs, plastic explosive, 105 mm. shells, and the piled boxes of small-arms ammunition, grenades and rockets.

'Good ol' Tarrant,' Willie said softly.

She looked at him, a little surprised. 'Why?'

'I wanted a refresher on the latest stuff. Tarrant wangled me a special course with the R.A.O.C. Ammunition Organisation.'

'I didn't know.'

'It was while you were over in Bermuda. Those blokes know the score all right.'

'Good old Tarrant then.' Her swollen lips parted in a little smile. 'Just say if I can help, Willie. This caper seems to be all yours from now on.'

'About time. You've 'ad your share, Princess. Jesus, I was scared when you were up against The Twins.'

All the time as they spoke his gaze had been ranging thoughtfully round the ammunition store. Now he stripped off his shirt and said: 'Right. We'll shift some of this stuff to get the best out of it.'

The anti-tank mines were packed five to a crate, each crate weighing some eighty pounds. Willie broke open two of them and put the ten mines carefully to one side. 'About forty or fifty tons 'ere altogether,' he said. 'We'll get all the H.E. stuff we can manage stacked round that big pile of anti-tank mine crates at the back of the cave.'

For the next half-hour they worked steadily and in silence, shifting a little over five tons in that time, never pausing to rest. The clock in Modesty's head sounded a warning. She straightened up and drew a forearm across her wet brow.

'That's all we've got time for, Willie love. I'll go and give Lucille another shot while you start the clever stuff.'

'Right. I'll be getting this lot 'ooked up.' He turned to his small pack and began to lay out the items he had taken from the technical stores. A long coil of Cordtex detonating fuse; a few composition exploding primers and No. 27 igniferous detonators; three Switch No. 10 time-pencils.

Outside, Modesty was momentarily startled to find that the high clouds had cleared completely and the valley was now bathed in cold bright moonlight. It was unlikely that any chance observer outside the distant guard-house would be able to detect her moving figure, but she hugged the face of the ridge until the Dove screened her from view.

Lucille was still unconscious. Modesty gave her another intramuscular injection of the three-grain phenobarbitone solution. It was not like the last time, thank God.

When she got back to the ammunition store Willie was on his knees, cutting the Cordtex into various lengths. Round his neck hung something like a long limp sausage of yellowish putty. Plastic explosive.

'Lucille okay?' he asked without looking up.

'Yes. She'll be well under for a few hours yet.'

Modesty saw that he had now distributed eight of the ten anti-tank mines on top of different stacks of ammunition spread around the cave. The remaining two were on top of the main pile of mines and other H.E. stacked at the back of the cave, tight against the wall.

'Can I help, Willie love?'

'Sure, Princess.' He was distributing the lengths of Cordtex to each mine, and when he had finished he broke the plastic explosive in two, giving her half of it. 'Lay one end of the Cordtex over each mine and wind it round a bit, then tear off a chunk of P.E. and press it down over the Cordtex.'

'No detonators in the mines?'

He grinned. 'No, we won't need 'em except for the two on the main pile. You take the four mines on this side, I'll see to the others.'

When they had finished the task he gathered the free ends of the eight lengths of Cordtex together and moved to the main stack of H.E.

''Old the end for me a minute, Princess.'

She took them in her hands. 'What are you aiming for, Willie?'

'I want to make sure the 'ole lot goes up at the same time. These two mines will start it with this stack, and the Cordtex is an instantaneous detonating fuse, so it'll carry to all the other stacks and set off the mines on top.'

He tilted each of the two mines in turn, inserting a C.E. primer into the cavity and a detonator into the primer. Taking the ends of the Cordtex from her he wound them round both mines and secured them with lumps of plastic explosive.

'Two mines just to make doubly sure?' she said.

He smiled. 'It was you that taught me to be cautious, Princess. And I'm using three time-pencils.'

'How long will they give us to get clear?'

'This kind should give twenty minutes, but you can reckon plus or minus five. They're not that accurate.'

He picked up the time-pencils. They were in a casing of thin lead. When the glass phial within each pencil was crushed, acid would be released. The acid would eat into a metal strip, and when the strip gave way a spring-loaded striker would hit the cap and detonate the charge.

Willie crushed the ends of the time-pencils under the heel of his boot and pushed two of them into one mine, the third into the other.

Stepping back, he looked at Modesty and grinned. 'We'd better go and try our intrepid birdman act, Princess.'

'I can't think of anything better to do, Willie.'

They went out, easing the doors shut quietly, and turned west, moving along against the ridge for three hundred yards. Now they could turn to where the Dove stood only a long stone's-throw away, near the end of the runway which extended down the middle of the valley to the bottle-neck. To one side was a cluster of boulders, cleared when the runway had been prepared for the big freighter aircraft.

They were twenty paces from the Dove when a voice to their right said calmly: 'Hold it. Very still.'

Delgado's voice.

He was ten paces off by a big rock, holding a .44 Magnum revolver pointed at Modesty. Three men stood behind him with sub-machine guns held in casual but alert readiness. They were men from his own section.

Willie Garvin had not put his shirt on yet. It still hung from his hand. The black leather harness with the two sheathed knives lying in echelon across his left breast stood out sharply against his brown glistening body.

'Don't try the knives, Willie,' Delgado said. 'I know you're fast, but I can pull this trigger on Modesty even faster.'

He moved forward and halted six paces from Modesty.

'By the same token, don't even think about pulling that Colt on me, darling. You just couldn't make it.'

She did not answer at once. From the corner of his eyes Willie watched her hand, the one nearest to him. He saw the thumb and finger form a circle, with the other three fingers pointed straight down at the ground. His eyes moved and he forgot Delgado, giving his whole attention to the three men beyond.

'Well . . .' Modesty's voice was very mellow. 'What brings you out this fine night, Mike?'

'A nagging little hunch, sweetheart.' Delgado smiled. 'I could never quite believe that you and Willie had split up. My God, you made it look good though, I'll give you that. But I know you better than all the others. Much better, you may remember?'

She said: 'You're a very small reception party for us.'

'But adequate.' She could see his eyes sparkling with amusement in the moonlight. 'And I get the kudos this way. I can use a good mark or two in Karz's book. He seems to feel I should have known you might be Unsound in spite of Lucille.'

She was thinking that Delgado couldn't know about the time they had spent in the ammunitions store, or he would never have stood here relishing his triumph.

'So you checked my room in the *seraglio*?' she said.

'Not until just under an hour ago, and after an uneasy night, darling. And I found you gone. Willie likewise. So I gathered these worthy lads and we made quietly for the aircraft, just in case that was the idea. I was a little worried that you'd beat us to it.'

She gave a tired shrug. 'We came the long way round, by the river and across the valley. Then we had to wait quite a while before we could get the prowlers without any noise.'

'Too bad.' He gave a smiling sigh of sympathy but the Magnum did not waver. 'It just shows how much depends on small details.'

'Why don't you join us, Mike?' she said quietly. The question was asked only to make him believe that she had no other hope.

He chuckled. 'No thank you, my pet. I like to be on the

265

winning side. So do these stalwarts behind me, no doubt. And you can't win now, you know. You're a woman, with all the hindrance of little scruples.'

'Perhaps you're right.'

'I know I'm right. Why look now, I could shoot you and watch you die . . . and feel a little sad maybe, but I'd lose no sleep over it.' His smile grew gentle and his voice softer yet, with the Irish brogue sounding more strongly. 'But you'd find it hard to pull the trigger on me even if you held the gun, darling. D'you know that? I'm the man who first made you happy a long time ago, remember? Ah, sure you re-member. Wonderful Mike Delgado. You'd never be able to kill the man who taught you to fly to the stars, would you?'

Her shoulders sagged. 'That's something we'll never know for sure,' she said wearily, and half turned to look at Willie, her left flank towards Delgado. 'I'm sorry we didn't quite make it, Willie. . . .'

Her left hand came up in a small helpless gesture to draw Delgado's eye, and in the same instant her screened right hand moved in a smooth blur of speed. Her head turned to Delgado as the Colt .32 cleared the holster, and she fired across the small of her back—a trick shot with all the dangers of failure and all the virtues of surprise.

The sound of the Magnum followed the sharper crack of the Colt by a split second. She felt a searing pain across her left arm, high up near the shoulder. Delgado was falling. Something glinted across her vision and one of the three men with sub-machine guns reeled back on tottering feet, the black hilt of a knife jutting from his breast.

She threw herself sideways, firing as she fell. It was as if the single shot had hit both remaining men, for they went down together, one spinning round, his reflex action loosing a brief burst of fire high over the ridge as he died. The other simply crumpled, clawing feebly at the three-inch haft pro-truding from his throat. Willie's second knife had found its mark.

She got to her knees. Willie was checking all four men. He looked at Delgado last, then came towards her, tapping a finger to his chest. 'You got an outer, Princess—through the ticker.'

'It'll do.' Her eyes rested on the sprawled body. 'He died of vanity.'

Willie nodded. Then she saw the sudden alarm on his face as he realised she was clutching an arm that poured blood. The heavy bullet had ripped through flesh and muscle, gouging out a very deep two-inch long furrow. 'Get me aboard, Willie,' she said harshly.

Already lights were showing by the guard-house two miles down the valley. Three quick shots were fired to raise the general alarm. Willie Garvin lifted her up into the Dove and scrambled in after her. She lay with head swimming, gripping the wound with all the strength she could muster. Blood pulsed out from between her fingers. Willie knelt beside her, ripping a field-dressing from the thigh-pocket of his trousers.

'Put it down by me and get flying,' she said in a rasping whisper. 'Go *on*, Willie!'

He closed the door and went to the controls, shutting everything from his mind but the task ahead. It would be three to four minutes before the first men on scooters from the guard-house could cover the length of the valley. They would not know what had happened, only that shots had been fired. But they would know what was happening as soon as the Dove's engines started.

He switched on the instrument lights and the petrol cocks, then put on the master airvalve. With battery and generators switched on he reached down under the seat and operated the pump for priming the engines.

Forty-five seconds.

He opened each throttle slightly, flicked on the magneto switches, and reached out for the starter buttons. The port engine came to life, then the starboard engine. He pressed the brake lever on the control wheel to release the parking lock, and opened the throttle wider.

The Dove began to taxi forward. Now it was turning on to the runway. He opened both throttles wide. The engines roared and the Dove gathered speed. He wished there had been a few minutes' grace for a warm-up before taking off, but it was no good wishing.

The Gipsy engines did not falter. The air-speed indicator needle rose to seventy, eighty. . . .

Half-a-mile. He pulled back the control wheel. Two figures on scooters ahead were swerving aside, skidding to a halt, unslinging their AR-15's.

The Dove lifted smoothly. He pushed the knob above the fuel cock to retract the tricycle landing gear. Now the bottle-neck lay ahead, its walls sloping back as they rose. There was ample clearance. A row of holes appeared suddenly in the port wing-tip and there came a metallic thrum as a bullet hit some solid part of the fuselage.

He was through. The remaining length of the valley flashed below, and then he was lifting the Dove at fourteen hundred feet over the stepped heights beyond the southern end.

Willie Garvin let out a long breath and banked round in a tight circle to head along the narrow half-moon valley which branched obliquely from the main one. This was the next move in gaining height to climb out from among the lower ridges. He had watched the regular pilots of the Dove make several take-offs over the past two weeks.

Now the aircraft broke out from the confining walls and was above the mountain-hemmed forest that surrounded the lake. Here was the airspace where even the big freighters could circle to gain height.

Willie relaxed a little and looked over his shoulder. Modesty was sitting propped in the open doorway to the cockpit. The field-dressing was bound round her upper arm and she was knotting the ends with one hand and her teeth. But already the blood was soaking through and her face was waxen under her tan. The great yellow bruise on one cheek stood out sharply, and her swollen lips were colourless. The heavy .44 Magnum was a bad bullet to take a hit from.

He saw the broken tooth as she gave him a ghostly smile and crawled into the cockpit, dragging herself up into the co-pilot's seat on his right. Slowly and clumsily, using only her sound hand, she fastened the seat-belt.

When he looked at her again she had taken the kongo from her squeeze-pocket and was pushing it hard up into the armpit of her injured arm, against the pressure point there. She gripped the arm just below the dressing and held it tightly against her side.

'Stopped the bleeding?' he said anxiously.

'Enough.' Her voice was feeble. 'Can you find the way out, Willie?'

'It's a doddle,' he lied confidently, and banked in a wide curve over the northern edge of the lake, climbing steadily. 'What about when we're out, Princess? Kabul?'

She shook her head slightly. 'No. We . . . we don't know who our friends are there. Once you're out, fly south-west on the compass and head towards Kandahar. You can follow the Tarnak. The Americans are pushing a road out somewhere around there. Try to find it . . . and them . . . while your fuel lasts.'

'Right.' Willie looked down. They were three thousand feet up now. Below them the lake lay like a great mirror. 'It's about bloody time——' he began.

A vast spurt of flame shot out from the ridge, horizontally, as if an enormous gun had been fired. The forty tons of exploding ammunition had vented a minor part of its fury through the doors of the cave.

Willie banked again, in a tight circle this time, turning his head to watch the ridge. At first it seemed that nothing had changed. Then he saw a thin thread of silver moving away from the middle of the ridge and into the valley . . . a second and wider thread from another point. He tried vaguely to estimate the tonnage of water that the ridge held back, but gave it up as an academic problem, for now there were a dozen threads, broadening steadily.

Black lines showed against the grey-white rock of the ridge. He saw the black lines widen. As if in slow motion the whole length of the ridge seemed to spread out in fragments. In a great silver mass the waters of the lake began to spill into the valley below.

'Lovely,' said Willie with immeasurable satisfaction. 'Let bloody Karz try an' get that lot mopped up. Blimey, did you see the way that ridge broke, Princess——?'

He stopped. Her head was lolling sideways and her eyes were closed. Only the seat-belt prevented her from falling. The kongo lay on the floor. Her injured arm hung limply. Blood was welling steadily from the dressing again.

Willie Garvin swore in fright. For long moments panic swept him and fresh perspiration beaded his forehead. Modesty was losing blood. There was an auto-pilot on the Dove, but it might well be two hours before they were clear of the mountains. If they ever got clear. Two hours before he could dare to set the controls on auto and attend to Modesty's arm.

He made another climbing circle, smashing mentally and with hatred at his fear until it was dead and he could think coldly.

It would soon be dawn, and the Dove was an obedient little aircraft. Apart from three or four tricky bits on the route that was stored as if on film in his mind, he could fly well enough with one hand.

Reaching out, he positioned thumb, fingers and palm around her bandaged arm, then closed his big hand like a clamp.

'Jesus,' he whispered. 'Don't walk away from me now, Princess.'

Locking the muscles of his right hand, he forgot about it and focused all his attention on flying.

The first light of dawn lay over the valley. The lake had dwindled to half its size, with the waters now lapping at the edge of the shattered ridge.

The four-mile length of the valley was flooded. At the airfield end it had settled now to a depth of five or six feet. At the other end, beyond the bottle-neck, the depth ranged between two and four feet. The huts and the transport stood up from the great sheet of water, their reflections rippling upon it.

Here and there a few bodies floated. A group of men were gathered on the high ground of the arena, staring down, silent and lost. In the palace, women were wailing.

Many men had already gone, swimming or climbing to get clear of the flood, then setting off into the rising valleys which lay in a convoluted maze around the whole area. The two store-huts for the jet-suits of the Flying Infantry were flooded. The suits were useless.

Sarrat, Brett and Hamid were in the partly flooded food-store of the palace, making silent preparations for their journey. Thamar stood on the steps outside, a sub-machine gun slung over one shoulder, his face still blank with shock. He stared uncomprehendingly as the three men came out laden with heavy packs.

'What is this?' he said.

'We're going.' It was Brett who answered. 'What the hell d'you think?'

'But—you cannot leave!' Astonishment touched Thamar's heavy face.

'We can try. Sarrat reckons we can cut round west, do a little climbing, and pick up the river again further south. He might be right.'

'But you have no orders from Karz!'

'Karz?' Brett laughed without mirth. 'You can ask him for orders, Thamar. Here he comes.'

The square, burly figure was wading towards them, plodding like an automaton. They waited in silence for him as he mounted the steps. His face held no expression, but the pupils of his eyes were contracted to pin-points.

He surveyed the assembled commanders, and for a moment the weight of his massive personality touched them with fear. Then he spoke, and his voice was shrill and cracked like the voice of a schoolboy.

'The water must be cleared,' he said. 'I will expect the airfield to be operational by noon. Transport must be dried out. The radio station put in order.'

Fear was wiped away. Hamid smiled thinly, contemp-

271

tuously, and said: 'You had better give the necessary instructions to Liebmann.'

'Liebmann is dead.' The voice grew shriller yet. 'I have killed him. He refused to obey my orders. Buckets and squeegees . . .' The Mongol head began to rock from side to side like the head of a great doll.

Sarrat looked at Thamar and laughed. It was an ugly sound. 'Orders!' he said. 'You see?'

Thamar's face was crumpled with bewilderment, sorrow and distress. He brought the sub-machine gun up to point at Karz and cocked it with an automatic movement.

'Unsound,' he said incredulously. '*Unsound,* by God!'

The gun chattered in a long vicious burst.

TWENTY-ONE

'Am I to understand,' said the Minister, 'that you've heard nothing from Modesty Blaise since that cable she sent you from Istanbul nearly a month ago?'

Tarrant considered the question and decided that he could answer it truthfully, though his answer would have been the same anyway.

'Not a word, Minister.' Tarrant's face registered mild inquiry.

The Right Honourable Roger Selby took a copy of the cable from the file on his desk and read it aloud: '*Relax. Operation total washout. Please send five crates best Scotch to Dave Connolly c/o Dall-Pachmeyer Construction Inc. local office Kabul.*'

'Ah, yes,' Tarrant said reflectively. 'She signed that one "*Blaise*". As I recall, this confirmed your view that the cryptic warning she sent earlier was without substance. You felt that she had set up an imaginary windmill to tilt at and was now claiming to have demolished it. I have a copy of your memo.'

272

Selby's fingers drummed on the desk. 'You made no further inquiries after this second cable?' he asked.

'No. If you were right, Minister, there was no point. And if Modesty Blaise was right, then she had, as you once suggested, managed to confound the enemy on her own. She and her chap Garvin,' he added urbanely. 'However, I did send the whisky as requested. Not at The Department's expense, of course, but Modesty Blaise is a friend of mine and I'm sure she'll reimburse me when she turns up again. I shall be interested to learn just who Mr. Connolly is.'

'I can tell you that, Tarrant.' Selby's voice was cold, his eyes a little suspicious. 'The United States Ambassador called to see me an hour ago, and I can now tell you a great deal. Connolly is an ex-major of the United States Army, now an engineer in charge of a road-construction team in southern Afghanistan.'

'Ah, yes. I understand the Americans are doing quite a lot of that kind of work there,' Tarrant said approvingly.

'It appears,' said Selby, 'that a twin-engined aircraft made a semi-crash landing on rough ground close to the forward camp of the road-building team, where Connolly was in charge. The Ambassador quoted Connolly as saying that in the aircraft were Willie Garvin, Modesty Blaise, a young child named Lucille Brouet under sedation, and two or three pints of loose blood.'

'Whose?'

'The Blaise girl's. She'd been shot.'

'I see. This would explain the cable she sent from Istanbul, I imagine. Mr. Connolly must have been very helpful.'

'The whole of the Dall-Pachmeyer Construction people out there were extremely helpful. And so was the American intelligence network. There seems little doubt that they had all been warned by John Dall to look out for our two friends.'

Tarrant pursed his lips and considered the point.

'Russia is pouring aid and technicians into the north and America is doing the same in the south,' he mused. 'The whole country is a hot-bed of espionage, of course, crawling with agents. We have one or two of our own people there, and I did take the liberty of alerting them, just in case you had misread the situation, Minister. But I wonder why Dall alerted the Americans?'

'I hoped you might be able to answer that, Tarrant.' Selby's suspicion was overt now. 'I find this whole matter highly confusing. According to the Ambassador, this man Dall is extremely powerful. He holds a controlling interest in major firms of half a dozen different industries, he has the ear of people in high places in Washington, and he is apparently a friend of Modesty Blaise.'

Selby paused and flicked over the papers in the file. 'Yet I note that Dall was also the man to whom she lost a fortune only a short time ago. What do you make of that?'

'It's difficult to make anything of it, Minister,' Tarrant said apologetically. 'As you say, it's all very confusing. But Modesty Blaise tends to be a confusing person. I can only guess that if Dall had some idea that she was behind the Iron Curtain, then he would assume that her most likely way out would be over the southern border somewhere. So he warned his own people and American Intelligence in Persia and Afghanistan to look out for her.'

'She wasn't behind the Iron Curtain. She and Garvin were in some valley in the middle of the Hindu Kush. Apparently that's where the Kuwait Liberation Army was based.'

'The Kuwait Liberation Army?' Tarrant's eyebrows climbed. 'My theory was fact?' he said in astonishment. 'And Modesty's warning had substance?'

'Yes.' Selby's voice was curt. 'And I'm going to be greatly embarrassed in reporting to the Prime Minister on this. What I find quite outrageous, Tarrant, is that this woman sends *you* a cavalier message telling you to relax and send a man some whisky—but gives the whole damn story to American Intelligence.'

'We don't employ her, Minister,' Tarrant said blandly. 'And perhaps she learned that we'd ignored her warning. What story did she give them?'

Selby told him at some length. Tarrant listened with

apparent attention. He had already heard the whole thing from Dall. Even in Dall's account there were curious gaps which puzzled both men. Selby's story did nothing to fill those gaps.

'. . . so on the strength of what she and Garvin told them,' Selby was saying, 'the Americans put up a spy-plane. They located the valley and photographed it in detail, then went to the Afghan government. The Afghans threw up their hands in horror, which may or may not have been genuine. They vowed that the valley was unknown to them, and that any people there were squatters, not tenants.'

'Difficult for them,' murmured Tarrant. 'They get massive aid from both the United States and the U.S.S.R. No doubt they want to keep it that way.'

'Whether they knew or not isn't important,' Selby said impatiently. 'A joint Afghan-American investigation team was sent out. The Americans supplied an amphibious aircraft able to land in this flooded valley.'

'It *was* flooded? That seems to confirm what Modesty Blaise told American Intelligence.' Tarrant paused and added with inward pleasure. 'I mean, concerning what she and her chap Garvin had managed to do.'

'Everything confirmed it,' Selby said, tight-lipped. 'The investigation team found a number of bodies floating around; about fifty mercenaries and thirty women living above water-level in some ancient palace; a complete military base and a mass of documents including a full and highly complex plan of battle for a blitz on Kuwait. The operation was called *Sabre-Tooth.*'

Selby looked at some notes scribbled on a pad at his elbow. 'According to Major-General Reeve, the U.S. military expert accompanying the team, the armaments, transport, air-facilities and warlike stores were more than sufficient to implement the battle-plan.'

'So Modesty Blaise's assessment of the military situation was correct after all?'

'In the event, yes. We could hardly assume that at the time, but we were wrong.'

Tarrant let the 'we' go for the time being. He could deal with that later. Fraser was at that moment going joyously through the memo-files.

'What happened to the rest of the army?' Tarrant asked. There was a subtle change in his voice. It was still polite but no longer apologetic.

'Dispersed,' said Selby. 'The amphibious aircraft spotted several little groups of men moving through the surrounding valleys and mountains in all directions and at various distances from the base. Some attempt may be made to lift them out or guide them out, as opportunity offers. But Afghan opinion is that not more than a third will survive. Those that do will be deported to their own countries. The men and women who stayed in the valley are being lifted out now. No doubt we shall be getting one or two of our own nationals any day.'

'Yes.' Tarrant already had advance warning from his agent in Kabul that two Britons would be flown home within the next twenty-four hours. He had ensured that his department would handle their interrogation.

Selby sat back in his chair. 'All this,' he said grimly, 'comes to us by courtesy of the United States. It should have gone to them from *us*, Tarrant.'

'I agree,' Tarrant said shortly. 'But it seems that on Dall's recommendation they were prepared to place their bets on Modesty Blaise. And we were not.' He looked impassively at Selby and added: 'Dall must be a more persuasive man than I am.'

There was a long silence.

Tarrant sat remembering Dall's cold, angry voice over the line from the American Embassy in Istanbul: 'We whisked them out and Modesty's in our own hospital here. She's been patched up, but she's going to need a skin-graft on her arm and some dentistry. Garvin says she heals fast, and they both make light of it But they're both clamming up on some parts of the story. I don't know what happened, but if it was worse than what I've seen it must have been goddam ugly.' Dall's voice had sounded ugly, too. 'Christ, she went through

276

the mincer to get that message out, and for all the action your boss took she could have done it for nothing.'

'We haven't your resources,' Tarrant had said quietly.

'Okay, okay. And I know you put your own head on the block. Now listen. I want her to stay here in hospital while I have the best specialists flown over from the States. Garvin won't have it, and she goes along with him. They're flying out somewhere tomorrow, for God's sake. Garvin says he'll see to everything without any help, thanks. I can't talk him out of it, and when I talk to her she just says they always make their own arrangements and she'll call me when she's fit again. Can *you* talk any sense into them, Tarrant?'

'I'm afraid not. They're very independent.'

'Garvin acts like he thinks nobody but *nobody* can look after her except himself.'

'Yes, I can imagine. But just let it go, Dall. They do things their own way.'

'I don't get it. What's the score between those two?'

Tarrant had laughed, for Dall sounded like a baffled man who was quite unaccustomed to being baffled.

'That's a big question. I'm so indebted to you that I'd answer it if I could, Dall. Don't mistake Willie's possessiveness for that of a consort. It's only because she's hurt. If you're around with the pair of them for a while you'll get to know the score between them. To some extent anyway. Far better than I could describe it.'

'I don't look like having the chance to be around with them.'

'She said she would call you when she was fit again, and you can be quite sure Willie Garvin will be there. Will you ask her to call me, too? And give her my . . . affectionate respects?'

'Sure.' Resignation had sounded in Dall's voice. 'Sure, I'll do that, Tarrant. She asked me to send her love to you and her apologies to some guy called Fraser.'

In the Minister's office, Selby stirred and leaned forward. Tarrant came back to the present. He noted that Selby was smiling amiably at him.

'The P.M. will no doubt be calling for a personal report from you on this matter,' Selby said. 'I hope we can agree on the nature of the report you'll be putting in.'

Tarrant got to his feet. It was as he had expected. Selby had blundered and Selby wanted to arrange a white-wash. But Tarrant was out for blood.

He remembered Dall's description of Modesty's hurts. He remembered Selby's attitude after the cryptic message. He remembered the gaps in the story, gaps which roused in him a shapeless unease.

Remembering, Tarrant looked at the Right Honourable Roger Selby.

'You can rest assured that my report will be detailed and accurate, Minister,' he said.

It was nearly seven weeks after Dall's call from Istanbul when Tarrant came out of the reception lounge at Tangier airport. Willie Garvin was waiting with a Mercedes.

'Is Dall here, Willie?' Tarrant asked as the car moved quietly away.

'Flew in from the States this morning, Sir G. Modesty's 'oping you'll both be able to spend a few days 'ere at least. There's plenty of room.'

'What about Lucille?'

'Well . . .' Willie shrugged. 'The way it worked out, she didn't reckon me and Modesty much by the time it was all over. So I got Dall to take charge before we left Istanbul. The head-shrinkers 'ad a go at her, and the end of it was they decided we were incompatible.' Willie scratched his cheek ruefully. 'So Dall took 'er back to the States and found a nice American family that's adopted 'er properly.'

'You don't object?'

'No. It's best all round. The Princess and me . . . we're a dead loss for the kid now. Maybe we always were.'

Tarrant nodded. 'And . . . Modesty?'

'Fine. Looking like a million dollars.'

'I understand she had a rough time.'

'It was tatty caper. A shambles.' Willie spoke without

278

complaint, a professional giving an objective assessment. 'Any caper can get rough, but this was like trying to juggle with your eyes shut and no 'ands. We couldn't get any initiative until we found they'd got Lucille there.'

'But you got a message out before then, Willie.'

'Ah, yes. . . .' Willie's voice was casual. 'We managed to fiddle that bit.'

Tarrant said quietly: 'We interrogated a man called Carter a little while ago. He was among the men who were lifted out and deported after you'd wrecked the whole operation. So I know how you fiddled the bit about getting the message out. I know how Modesty fought The Twins. And I know what happened to her afterwards.'

Willie Garvin slowed the car to a halt by the roadside. He put on the handbrake and switched off, turning in his seat to face Tarrant.

'So what?' he said, lifting an eyebrow slightly.

'So I feel horribly responsible.' Tarrant's face was a little drawn. 'Surely you can understand that?'

'I dunno. You must've sent a lot of people out in your time. I reckon quite a few never came back—or came back with the springs broke. You can't afford to be the worrying kind.'

'I'm not,' Tarrant said tiredly. 'I've grown a hard shell and I can cross off names with a steady hand now. But Modesty isn't one of my people. To me she's something very rare. I value her friendship highly.' His voice was oddly stilted and he was staring straight ahead, his cheeks a little flushed now. 'I value *her* highly. No doubt I'm somewhat old-fashioned, but in view of what's happened I'm going to find it very hard to face her.'

'No you won't,' Willie said simply, and lit a cigarette. 'She'll see to that. It was a bastard of a caper, but you're not responsible. Neither am I. Modesty called the play all the way through, the only play that could win. What Carter told you doesn't matter. If she can forget it, you can do the same.'

'Can she, Willie? And can you?'

Willie inhaled thoughtfully. 'We'll remember it like we

279

remember other things. Some bad, some not so bad. But they've got no meaning any more. Bullet-wounds, knife-wounds, anything—we've 'ad the lot over the years.' He lifted the hand with a twisting scar on the back. 'That was where a bloke carved 'is initial with a red-'ot knife. But it didn't 'appen to me. It 'appened to the Willie Garvin who was there at the time. And whatever punishment the Princess took on this caper, it's over with now. And she's just the same.'

'You take the whole thing damn lightly,' Tarrant said with sudden irritation. 'God Almighty, I only wish I were twenty-five years younger and could get my hands on the men who . . .' His voice trailed away and he made a small helpless gesture, unwilling to put his thoughts into words.

'You needn't worry.' Willie smiled a cold smile. 'I got mine on 'em.' He started the engine again and the car moved on its way.

'Does Dall know all about it?' Tarrant asked after a while.

'I wouldn't be surprised. He's probably found out by now, the same way you did. Or maybe Modesty's told 'im. But it's none of our business.'

Tarrant looked at Willie's big hands on the steering wheel with bleak satisfaction. Those hands would have made no mistake. The thought gave him comfort, but his stomach was still tense with uneasiness at the prospect ahead, the prospect of facing Modesty Blaise.

'All right, Willie,' he said, and looked out of the window. 'It's none of our business.'

It was nearing dusk by the time they reached the house on The Mountain. At sea, a long row of lights shone from the ports of a liner moving towards the straits.

Dall was sitting in the big room with the casement windows opening on to the patio and the garden beyond. The lights in the room had not been switched on yet. Dall wore dark slacks with a fine white-and-red check shirt. He looked very brown and hard and handsome. Tarrant felt a twinge of envy.

'Good to see you,' Dall said, shaking hands. 'Modesty's been in the pool and gone up to change. She said to tell you we'll have dinner in half-an-hour if that suits you.'

'Could I just have a quick shower and change,' Tarrant said, looking at Willie. 'Casual wear?'

'Sure.' Willie picked up Tarrant's case. 'I'll show you your room. There's a shower off it.'

When Tarrant returned to the big living-room some twenty minutes later the twilight had deepened. Dall and Willie were sitting by the open windows with drinks.

'What'll it be, Sir G?'

'A cinzano bianca with ice, please.'

'Coming up.' As Willie moved to the little bar, Modesty's voice sounded from somewhere above.

'Do put the lights on, Willie love. It looks like a crypt down there.'

Tarrant stood very still, watching the dimly seen figure in white moving down the broad stairs which led up from one side of the living-room. He heard a series of clicks, and wall-lights sprang up in different part of the room. She was just turning at the angle of the staircase, moving quickly and lightly down the last few steps into the room.

She wore a very simple sleeveless dress in white nylon. It was short, with the hem just above the knees. Her brown legs were bare and she wore open pale-blue sandals with small heels. Her hair was loose and gathered back at the nape of her neck by a jet clip.

She was smiling at him, moving towards him with both hands extended.

'Sir Gerald.' Her eyes were warm with welcome.

Tarrant took her hands in silence. He could not have said what it was he had expected to see, but this held him spell-bound. She looked exactly the same as when he had last seen her in England, except that with her hair down and the simple white dress and the serenity in her eyes she looked a year or two younger. Her face showed no trace of damage and the broken tooth had been perfectly restored. There was only a thin fading pink line across her left arm near the

281

shoulder to show where a plastic surgeon had done his work.

Tarrant lifted her hands in turn to touch them with his lips. 'My dear,' he said, 'you look splendid.'

She laughed. 'I've been busy for the last half-hour trying to make sure you'd say that.'

He was still holding her hands. 'I've been very worried about you. This was a bad job, I'm afraid.'

She looked at him, surprised. 'Did Willie say that? Oh, you can't believe anything he tells you. Willie's an artist, and he likes every job to have the right shape and form and all that nonsense. The truth is we were very lucky.'

'Lucky?'

Dall laughed shortly and said: 'The quaint thing is, she means it, Tarrant.'

'Of course I mean it. The thing was a complete shambles. We could have gone under three or four times, but each time things just tilted our way when it was a hundred to one against.' She smiled, her eyes tranquil and completely honest. 'That's lucky.'

Tarrant nodded. 'I suppose,' he said slowly, 'it's all in the way you look at it.' He released her hands, feeling the tight knot in his stomach dissolve at last.

'Some people are born lucky,' Willie Garvin said reminiscently, putting a glass into Tarrant's hand. 'I knew a girl in Bangkok once, and her father was in the fertiliser business. He drove a sewage cart. Well, one day——'

'We'll have that later, Willie love.' Modesty slipped an arm through Tarrant's. 'Bring your drink with you, Sir Gerald. I hope you like paella. It's Moulay's speciality, and if we don't go into dinner now he'll burst into tears.'

Two hours later, in the warm night air, Dall walked with her beside the swimming pool, smoking one of Tarrant's cigars.

Light from the room flooded the patio, making a bright picture of Willie and Tarrant as they sat there at ease. Tarrant's cigar had gone out but he was seemingly unaware of it.

Willie was talking quietly, his hands moving in little descriptive gestures from time to time.

'I wouldn't have thought Tarrant could get that interested in the girl whose father drove a sewage cart,' Dall said, amused.

Modesty watched for a moment. She saw Willie's hands move out, hooked at the wrists, his feet rise a little from the ground.

'He's not on about the girl in Bangkok,' she said. 'He's talking about something that happened in the valley.'

Dall had been watching, too. 'When you were set up for execution by The Twins?' he asked.

She looked at him. 'You know about that?'

'Willie gave me a blow-by-blow account.' Dall's face twitched abruptly. 'Jesus,' he said roughly, 'I got scared listening, even though I knew how it came out.'

'Willie doesn't usually talk about me.'

'I've learned that.' Dall drew on his cigar. 'But he had to tell me one or two things, and I guess he reckoned this might keep me from asking about other things that happened to you.'

She was silent for a while, and when she spoke there was no attempt to pretend she had not understood. 'I see. You know about that, too?'

'Yes. One or two of the Americans in Karz's army are back home now. I saw the reports of their interrogation.'

They walked slowly to the far end of the pool.

'Will you take up my offer?' Dall said. 'There's the ranch in Texas, near Amarillo. There's the house on Long Island, at East Hampton. And there's a pretty lush kind of cabin on a lake in Sun Valley, Idaho. Make your own choice.' He took her arm gently as they walked. 'You're in fine shape again I know, but I guess a change of scene and a long rest wouldn't do any harm.'

She did not answer.

He said: 'I know you're independent. You can go where you want and do what you want, anyway. I'm only asking you to be my guest. As a favour to me.'

283

She stopped and looked down at the moonlight glinting from the pool. 'I want to belong just to myself for a while. Can you understand?'

'Easily. That's why I'm including myself out of the deal. I want you to be my guest wherever you like. But I'll be some place else.'

She laughed quietly. Her face was lit by a smile that came from deep within her, and she patted the hand holding her arm. 'That won't do either. Leave it till the spring. I'll come and be your guest then, and you won't have to be some place else.'

'Call me when you're ready.' There was warm pleasure in his voice. He spun the butt of the cigar away into the darkness. Together they began to walk back towards the patio.

Dall had no illusions. If she gave, she would give in full measure, yet no matter how much she gave to him she would never belong to anybody but herself.

This he knew. But with an excitement he had not felt for many a year he looked forward to the spring.

Modesty Blaise 3/6

PETER O'DONNELL

Latest creation in exotic high-speed
crime fiction.

'Comparisons of Modesty with James Bond
are irresistible. The similarities are marked —
the restless changing scenes, the ingenuity
of both sides, the violence, the surging
confidence in telling.'
EVENING STANDARD

Monica Vitti, Terence Stamp, and Dirk
Bogarde star in an inspired screen version
for 20th Century-Fox release.

John Michael Brett

First two of a new power-packing series
featuring the dynamic Man-about-Danger
HUGO BARON . . . ex-barrister, lover of
danger, Bond-style agent operating on
both sides of the law . . .

DIECAST 3/6

Hugo Baron enters the employ of a
megalomaniac Press tycoon, tangles
with Russian blackmail and joins an
international anti-spy organisation.

'Exciting and fast-moving'
DAILY EXPRESS

A PLAGUE OF DRAGONS 3/6

What are the Chinese doing with cages
full of fat, contented, piebald rats?
Hugo Baron investigates the terrible
doings of Dr Kwang and a plot to conquer
the world by race contamination.

'Fast-moving, to be read at
one sitting' SUNDAY TELEGRAPH

HUGO BARON . . .
'latest to join the Bond-wagon of
action and spice' YORKSHIRE POST